texas gothic

ROSEMARY CLEMENT-MOORE

texas gothic

delacorte press

Text copyright © 2011 by Rosemary Clement-Moore
Jacket photograph of girl copyright © 2011 by Elif Sanem Karakoo

All rights reserved. Published in the United States by Delacorte Press, an imprint of Random House Children's Books, a division of Random House, Inc., New York.

Delacorte Press is a registered trademark and the colophon is a trademark of Random House, Inc.

Visit us on the Web! www.randomhouse.com/teens

Educators and librarians, for a variety of teaching tools, visit us at www.randomhouse.com/teachers

Library of Congress Cataloging-in-Publication Data
Clement-Moore, Rosemary.
Texas gothic / Rosemary Clement-Moore. – 1st ed.
p. cm.
Summary: Seventeen-year-old Amy Goodnight has long been the one who makes her family of witches seem somewhat normal to others, but while spending a summer with her sister caring for their aunt's farm, Amy becomes the center of weirdness when she becomes tied to a powerful ghost.
ISBN 978-0-385-73693-0 (hc) – ISBN 978-0-385-90636-4 (glb) – ISBN 978-0-375-89810-5 (ebook) [1. Ghosts–Fiction. 2. Witchcraft–Fiction. 3. Farm life–Texas–Fiction. 4. Sisters–Fiction. 5. Texas–Fiction.] I. Title.
PZ7.C59117Tex 2011
[Fic]–dc22
2010047923

The text of this book is set in 11.5-point Berthold Baskerville.

Book design by Angela Carlino

Printed in the United States of America

10 9 8 7 6 5 4 3 2 1

First Edition

This book would not have been possible without Starbucks and St. Jude, patron saint of lost causes. (Me, not this book.)

1

the goat was in the tree again.

I hadn't even known goats *could* climb trees. I had been livestock-sitting for three days before I'd figured out how the darned things kept getting out of their pen. Then one day I'd glanced out an upstairs window and seen Taco and Gordita, the ringleaders of the herd, trip-trip-tripping onto one of the low branches extending over the fence that separated their enclosure from the yard around Aunt Hyacinth's century-old farmhouse.

"Don't even think about it," I told Gordita now, facing

her across that same fence. I'd just bathed four dogs and then shoveled out the barn. I stank like dirty wet fur and donkey crap, and I was *not* in the mood to be trifled with.

She stared back at me with a placid, long-lashed eye and bleated, "Mba-a-a-a." Which must translate as "You're not the boss of me," because she certainly didn't trouble herself to get out of the tree.

"Suit yourself," I said. As long as she was still technically in—or above—her pen, I didn't have much of an argument. When dealing with nanny goats, you pick your battles.

I suppose Aunt Hyacinth could be forgiven for trusting me to figure out the finer points of goat management for myself. And "for myself" was no exaggeration. Except when my sister, Phin, and I had run into town to get groceries, we hadn't seen a soul all week. Well, besides Uncle Burt. But you didn't so much see Aunt Hyacinth's late husband as sense his presence now and then.

This was Aunt Hyacinth's first vacation in ten years. The herb farm and the line of organic bath products she produced here had finally reached a point where she could take time off. And she was going to be gone for a month, halfway around the world on a cruise through the Orient, so she'd had a lot of instructions to cover. Even after she'd given Phin and me an exhaustive briefing on the care and feeding of the flora and fauna, even while my mom had waited in the luggage-stuffed van to take her to the airport in San Antonio, Aunt Hy had stood on the porch, hands on her hips, lips pursed in concentration.

"I'm sure I'm forgetting something," she'd said, scanning

2

the yard for some reminder. Then she laughed and patted my cheek. "Oh, why am I worried? You're a Goodnight. And if any of us can handle a crisis, Amy, it's you."

That was too true. I was the designated grown-up in a family that operated in a different reality than the rest of the world. But if the worst I had to deal with was a herd of goat Houdinis, I'd call myself lucky.

I gathered my dog-washing supplies and trudged toward the limestone ranch house that was the heart of Aunt Hyacinth's Hill Country homestead. It was a respectable size for an herb farm, though small by ranching standards. Small enough, in fact, to be dwarfed by the surrounding land. To reach the place, you had to take a gravel road through someone else's pasture to the Goodnight Farm gate, where a second fence of barbed wire and cedar posts surrounded Aunt Hyacinth's acreage. We often saw our neighbors' cows grazing through it. I guess the grass really was always greener. A packed dirt road led finally to the sturdy board fence that enclosed the house and yard with its adjoining livestock pens. Sometimes it felt like living inside a giant nesting doll. Ranching life was pretty much all about fences and gates.

The dogs had kept a respectful distance from the goats' enclosure, but they bounded to join me on my way to the house. Sadie nipped at the heels of my rubber boots while Lila wove figure eights between my legs. Bear, no fool, had already headed for the shade to escape the afternoon sun.

"Get off!" I pushed the girls away from my filthy jeans. "I just washed you, you stupid mutts."

They dashed to join Bear on the side porch. I clomped

up the steps, my arms full of dirty towels, and hooked the screen door with a finger. The dogs tumbled into the mudroom after me, then tried to worm into the house while I toed off my boots.

"Not until you're dry. Stay!" I managed to block them all except Pumpkin, a very appropriately named Pomeranian, who had asthma and got to come inside whenever he wanted. Which was pretty much all the time.

I closed the door and sighed—a mistake, because the deep breath told me just how much I stank.

Hot shower in T minus five, four, three . . .

The light over the sink in the kitchen went out. Not a crisis, since it was four in the afternoon. However, the soft hum of the air conditioner cut out at the same instant, which *would* be a problem very shortly. A *big* problem, because the only reason I'd agreed to spend my summer on Goodnight Farm—the last carefree summer of my life, before I started college and things that Really Count in Life—was that I knew it had civilized conveniences like climate control, wireless Internet, and satellite TV.

"Phin!" I shouted. I'd lived with my sister for seventeen years, not counting the last one, which she'd spent in the freshman dorm at the University of Texas. I knew exactly who was to blame for the power outage.

No answer, but that didn't mean anything. Once Phin was immersed in one of her experiments, Godzilla could stroll over from the Gulf of Mexico and she wouldn't notice unless his radioactive breath threw off her data.

Phin's experiments were the reason I was currently covered in dog hair, straw dust, and donkey dung. She had eagerly agreed to house-sit because she wanted to do some kind of botanical research for her summer independent study, and, well . . . where better to do that than an herb farm? But while the Goodnight family might be eccentric by other people's standards, no one was crazy enough to leave Phin solely in charge of Aunt Hyacinth's livelihood. She couldn't always be trusted to feed *herself* while she was working on a project, let alone the menagerie outside.

I peeled off my filthy socks and headed through the kitchen and living room to the back of the house, where Phin had commandeered Aunt Hyacinth's workroom as her own. The door was closed, and I gave a cursory knock before I went in, only to stumble on the threshold between the bright afternoon and the startling darkness of the usually sunny space.

Without thinking, I flipped the light switch, but of course nothing happened. All I could see was a glow from Phin's laptop and, strangely, from under the slate-topped table in the center of the room.

"Hey!" Phin's voice was muffled, and a moment later her head popped up from behind the Rube Goldberg–type contraption on the table. Her strawberry-blond hair was coming loose from her ponytail, possibly because she was wearing what appeared to be a miner's headlamp. "I'm doing an experiment."

"I know." I shaded my eyes from the light. "The fuse just blew."

"Did it?" She checked some wires, punched something up on her laptop, then flipped a few switches on the power strip in front of her. "Oh. Good thing I'm at a stopping spot."

"Well, thank heaven for that," I said, but my tone was wasted on her. Sarcasm was *always* wasted on Phin.

Aunt Hyacinth's workroom was normally a bright, airy space, part sunroom, part apothecary. Just then, however, it was dark and stuffy, with heavy curtains covering the wall of windows and the glass door that led to the attached greenhouse.

On the huge worktable, Phin had set up her laptop and a bewildering rig that included a camera with some kind of complicated lens apparatus, a light box (which I suppose explained why the room was blacked out as if she were expecting the Luftwaffe), and enough electrical wiring to make me very nervous.

It wasn't that Phin wasn't brilliant. The only thing that might keep her from getting a Nobel Prize someday was her field of study. Switzerland didn't really recognize paranormal research. Neither did most of the world, but that never stopped a Goodnight. Except me, I suppose.

In the dim light, I could see something like electrode leads connected to the leaves of an unidentifiable potted plant. It said a lot about my sister that this was not the strangest thing I'd ever seen her do.

"I don't think shock treatment was what Aunt Hyacinth meant when she gave you free rein over her plant life."

"It's a very low current," she said. "Just enough to get a baseline."

Part of me was tempted to ask "A baseline of what?" But the larger part knew that it would result in a half-hour lecture, at least, and I really wanted a shower more than I wanted to know the esoteric principles of horticultural electrocution.

"Did you turn off whatever blew the fuse so I can go flip the breaker?" This was not, after all, my first time at the Goodnight Rodeo.

"Yes," she said, removing the headlamp and shutting her laptop. "Since I'm stopped anyway, I'm going into town to pick up some supplies." The list she recited didn't mean anything to me until she got to "Vanilla Coke," at which point I perked up.

"From Sonic? Will you get me a cherry limeade?"

"Sure." She bent to rub Pumpkin's belly. He'd followed me in and now lay panting on the cool stone floor, already missing the air-conditioning.

I did a cursory check to make sure Phin was appropriately outfitted for the bustling metropolis of Barnett, Texas. She was, in flip-flops, a UT Longhorns tank top, and a pair of baggy cargo shorts that somehow looked cute on her. Her damp, wavy ponytail said she'd already taken a shower.

"How did you have time to get clean *and* blow the fuse?" I asked, more envious than outraged. We both had, theoretically, an equal amount of work. She took the flora—overseeing the herb farm, tending the greenhouse, plus watering plants around the house—and I took the fauna. But plants were generally pretty obedient, while the livestock seemed to enjoy making my job difficult.

She picked up her wallet and sunglasses from the counter near the door. "You do everything the hard way."

"Trust me," I said, with a bit of an edge, "if I could use magic to shovel out the donkey pen, I would."

"If you could do *that*," she countered evenly, "you'd be Mary Poppins. I just meant you didn't have to bathe the dogs."

I wrinkled my nose. "Yes, I did."

Opening one of the cabinets, she got down a canister and put it in my hands. In the light from the door, I read *Dry Dog Shampoo. For a mess-free mutt.* Under that was the Goodnight Farm logo and the motto *So good you'll think it's magic.*

Aunt Hyacinth had a sense of humor–and a healthy respect for what she could get away with saying on a product label. "This would have been nice to know about two hours ago," I said, pretty calmly, considering how dirty and wet I was.

Phin shrugged. "Two hours ago I didn't know you were going to do a Martha Stewart on the barn."

Point for my sister. Besides, telling me might not have made a difference. I couldn't get past the fact that things just didn't *feel* clean without water. That was just me, though. If the label said something worked like magic, it did. Which was why Goodnight Farm products were so popular, even if people didn't know *why* they worked so well.

Aunt Hyacinth had put together a binder of instructions, covering everything from what to do if the well stopped working to how to maintain the digestion spell on the septic system. I grabbed it and followed Phin out the front door.

The dogs, except Pumpkin, who hadn't budged from the workroom floor, trailed us down the path to the wooden gate. Stepping out of the yard, I felt a subtle change in the atmosphere—almost like a shift in air pressure, but not quite. Over the past twenty-five years, Aunt Hyacinth had woven strong protections around the house and yard, a sort of arcane security system. It wouldn't physically stop anyone, but it did have a subconscious effect on ill-intentioned trespassers.

A lifetime of living with witches and psychics had made spells a routine part of my life. I knew they worked, but I still preferred to put my trust in a locked door. My relationship with magic was like a president's kid's relationship with politics: I didn't participate, but I couldn't quite escape it. Especially not here, in the White House of the sovereign nation of Goodnight.

Stella, my not-quite-new Mini Cooper, and Aunt Hyacinth's antique SUV were parked just outside the board fence. "Do you have your driver's license?" I called after Phin. "Don't forget to close the outer gate."

She gave a typically distracted wave of acknowledgment and climbed behind the wheel of the Trooper, looking out of place in the big, battered vehicle. Along with her fair hair and pale skin, Phin had an elfin delicacy, in the Tolkien sense. It was hard to picture Galadriel driving an SUV.

I might have worried more about her if the sun-heated flagstones weren't scalding my bare soles. Instead, I hotfooted it over to the main breaker box to reset the fuse. Phin might have seemed otherworldly and half elvish sometimes, but I had an earthy and one-hundred-percent-human appreciation for things like electricity, satellite TV, and long, hot showers—all of which were in my immediate, blissful future.

2

Phin had used the very last towel in the bathroom.

Unfortunately, I didn't realize this until I was stripped down to my underwear, staring into the empty linen cupboard. Even more annoying, I'd done laundry yesterday, and downstairs was a dryer full of clean towels that I hadn't yet put away. The fact that this was equally my own fault did not help the situation a bit.

Dammit.

I closed the cupboard and took inventory. Fifteen different kinds of Goodnight Farm soap? Check. Running water, right out of an ancient well and smelling slightly of sulfur? Check. But not so much as a washcloth.

My clothes lay in a filthy heap at my feet. I *really* didn't want to put them back on, and I *couldn't* put on clean ones until I had washed off the dirt and dog slobber. Opening the bathroom door, I started to holler for Phin to bring me a towel . . . then remembered she'd taken the Trooper into Barnett.

I drummed my fingers on the doorframe. My only choice was to walk downstairs to the laundry room in my undies. Okay, so every curtain in the house was open. But my underwear, covered in cheerful red cherries with bright green leaves, was more modest than many bathing suits. Plus, there was no one within miles of the house.

There was Uncle Burt, though he generally hung out— when I sensed him at all—downstairs, away from the guest room. Even as a ghost, he was quite polite.

Too bad he couldn't bring me a towel. When I was a kid, I'd made a game of testing the limits of his ability to move things. He was pretty good at turning lights on and off, but I'd never seen a physical object move more than a few inches, and only out of the corner of my eye. I didn't know if it was a universal rule or just Uncle Burt's, but my eight-year-old self had figured out that ghosts operate best at the edges of your sight and in the space between blinks.

That was before I realized that most of the world didn't see magic or ghosts at all. At least, not that they admitted, if they wanted people to take them seriously. I'd learned *that* lesson the hard way.

In the upstairs hall, the pine floorboards were smooth under my feet. Then down the stairs, through the living room, with its oak beams and limestone fireplace. By chance I glanced out the window to where Stella was parked just outside the wooden yard gate.

And then I stopped, because there was something next to my Mini Cooper, and it was not Aunt Hyacinth's beat-up SUV.

It was a *cow*.

A half-grown calf, really. My aunt didn't have cows, so this guy was trespassing, which was inconsequential next to the fact that it was also *scratching itself* on Stella's bright blue fender. Scratching its *ass* on my graduation/early birthday present to myself, bought with years of savings from after-school jobs.

I leapt to the window and banged on the glass, scaring Pumpkin the Pomeranian, who was snoozing on the couch, half to death.

"Hey!" Bang bang bang. "Get away from my car!"

The calf didn't move, except to keep scratching.

"Son of a—" I whirled and sprinted through the kitchen to the mudroom. Nudging dogs out of the way, I shoved my feet into the oversized Wellies and straight-armed the screen door, sending it crashing against the wall.

I clattered down the steps. The goats watched me, chewing leaves unfazed as I went flying by their pen. If the cherries on my underwear tempted them, I was too furious to notice.

Varsity soccer had made me fast on my feet, even though the too-big boots slowed me down. When I banged open the wooden gate, the calf looked unconcerned, until it realized I was still coming.

It took off, and I took off after it, running across the pasture like William Wallace in *Braveheart*. Except in panties and a bra, which sounded like a Monty Python sketch but had become my life, thanks to my sister, who had obviously left the second gate open so the neighbors' bovine could mosey onto Goodnight land, and don't think I wasn't going to let her hear about it.

Stupid cow. Waving my arms, I chased the animal almost to our barbed-wire fence, where I realized the calf wasn't half grown at all. It was more like one-*quarter* grown, and its mother was big. Big, and also on our side of the fence, and *pissed* that I was yelling at her baby.

She lowered her head and mooed at me, a long, foghorn sound punctuated by the aggressive swish of her tail. The filed stumps of her horns were blunt but would definitely break a rib, at least, if she charged me. Or she might decide to knock me down to trample at her leisure. We're talking a creature the size of Stella.

And I totally didn't care.

"Don't yell at me, you stupid cow!" I jabbed a hand toward the calf, who taunted me from behind its mother. "Keep your juvenile delinquent away from my car!"

She stamped her hoof and let out another throaty bellow.

"No. *You* shut up. This is my side of the fence." I waved vaguely gateward. "Get your fat ass and your miscreant offspring back on your side of the barbed wire."

"Hey! You!"

I froze, with a screech of mental tires and the bug-eyed equivalent of a cartoon spit-take. What the hell?

"You! Crazy girl over there!"

The "over there" jump-started my stalled brain and ground my gears back into motion. It wasn't the cow talking, then. What a relief.

Slowly, I turned to see a horse, not far away from me, and a guy on the horse, sitting with one fist on the reins and one on his hip, looking down at me like I was insane.

"What the blue blazes are you doing to that cow?" he said.

"Me?" My voice went stratospheric with outrage. "That calf was *violating* my Mini Cooper."

The cowboy turned his horse in a leisurely circle, scanning the field. I really had run quite a ways from the house. He shaded his eyes to peer in that direction. "You mean that blue toy parked in front of Ms. Goodnight's place?"

I swatted a fly and sort of glare-squinted up at him. "Goodnight Farm. Yes."

"I heard Ms. Hyacinth was going on a trip this summer," he said, eyeing me and keeping his distance the way people did from lunatics. Even his horse was looking at me like I was nuts.

This was not a good time to realize that I was standing in the pasture in a state of highly questionable decency. Maybe if I pretended I *meant* to be out there half naked, he would think it was a bathing suit.

Placing a casual hand on my hip—then dropping it because the pose was ridiculous—I answered, "I'm house-sitting for her."

Then I called myself an idiot. Like axe murderers couldn't ride horses. Forget that he was tanned and rugged and had a sexy-young-cowboy thing going on, which I didn't need to be invoking in my head, because he was a stranger and I was in my underwear.

"Um, not just *me,* of course." I cleared my throat and folded my arms. Nice defensive body language. I was a National Merit Scholar, for God's sake. Soldiering on, I said, "Me and my sister. And our pack of big, ferocious dogs."

The guy was just close enough that I could see his brows arch, one sardonically higher than the other. "And you're out here sunning yourself in your skivvies because . . . ?"

So much for that bluff. God, this bravado thing was tough. "I told you. That cow was scratching its butt on my car. I saw it from the window and ran out—"

He'd raised his chin to look past me, toward the house. "Did you by any chance leave the gate open?"

"No! That was my sister, who— Oh *hell*!" I could hear the dogs barking. Worse, I could hear bleating. Joyful goat chuckles of freedom.

"The goats!" I clutched my head, an absurdly melodramatic reaction suited to this farce. "The goats were in the tree!"

"The . . . Wait, what?"

I didn't stay to enlighten him. For all my cursing Phin for leaving the outer gate ajar, I'd left the yard gate standing wide open. Running toward the house, I could see the dogs weaving mad circles around the field. Behind them were the goats, chasing them just for the hell of it, as far as I could tell.

The horse came up alongside me at a trot. Something

15

dropped onto my head and I screamed and batted it to the ground, then found myself staring stupidly at the cowboy's worn denim shirt. When I looked up, he called over his shoulder, now covered by just a sweat-blotched white undershirt, "Put that on. You're getting a sunburn."

Then he kicked his pinto into a slow lope and directed his efforts at rounding up the goats.

Focus, Amy. Just because he looked great in the saddle did not mean he wasn't an axe murderer.

I shrugged on the shirt, which was dusty and smelled like leather and horse, but I wasn't particular at the moment. Buttoning it up just enough for it to stay closed, I started running again.

The cowboy brought his horse neatly around to head off Gordita and Taco. "Go right!" he yelled, in case I was an idiot who couldn't figure out I needed to go the opposite way. "Get your dogs to help!"

The dogs were headed straight for me. I could see the whites of their eyes. Bear, the big, dumb coward, was moving as fast as I'd ever seen him.

I pointed to the house. "Go inside, guys! Go inside and I'll give you a cookie!"

They knew "cookie," and they knew that "inside" did not contain livestock. Lila, the smartest of the pack, gave an emphatic bark, and they made for the yard like greyhounds after a rabbit.

Most of the goats skipped after them, except Taco and Gordita. They seemed to consider the horse an awesome addition to their game of who-wants-to-be-barbecue-when-Amy-catches-us.

The pinto appeared to be enjoying the game, too, leaping and turning in the air to round up the stragglers, then working close to the ground, never letting them get around him. The cowboy seemed part of the horse, the way the pair worked together. I was a Texan, sure, but I was a city girl. This was new to me. I stood transfixed by the flex of the young man's legs, the effortless shift of his weight as he controlled the horse, until the dust became too thick for me to appreciate details, only the overall aesthetic.

Taco and Gordita ran for the gate and I shook myself into action. Waving my arms—and looking, I'm sure, a hell of a lot less graceful than the rodeo ballet—I chased the goats into the yard and slammed the gate closed behind us. At the clang of the latch, the cowboy gave his horse some silent command and the pinto relaxed, blowing a deep breath of satisfaction.

No rest for me yet, not while the herd was chasing the dogs and eating Aunt Hyacinth's zinnias. I ran to the pen and opened the feed bucket, banging the metal lid like a dinner gong. The goats trotted right in, as if they'd merely been for a stroll in the park. It was almost anticlimactic, in a way.

The cowboy had dismounted and followed me into the yard. He swung the gate of the goat pen closed, allowing me to slip out first. I latched it firmly, then leaned against the board fence, not knowing if I should laugh or cry, or just have hysterics and do both.

The dogs came running, their fear of the goats insufficient to outweigh their need for reassurance. Sadie spun in circles, and Bear, against all reason, wanted me to pick him up. Lila avoided the crowd and tried to get the cowboy to pet her.

Awkward didn't begin to cover it. Wrestling with goats and dogs, wearing nothing but a stranger's shirt over my underwear? If my mother had a crystal ball, she would be on her broom (figuratively speaking) and on her way over in a heartbeat.

Unable to look at him, I busied myself getting Bear and Lila to behave. "Sorry about the dogs. They weren't much help."

"They're completely worthless," he said, in an exasperated tone to which I could totally relate. "It's a *shepherd* and a *collie* and a—" He floundered when he got to Bear. "I don't even know what that one is."

"None of us do." I staggered as the hairy lummox bumped the back of my knee. "And they're not worthless. Lila here, she's a search-and-rescue dog." He looked at the border collie trying to climb into my arms like a toddler and appeared unconvinced. I assured him, "Really. They, uh, just happen to be afraid of the goats."

"Of course they are," he said, with a long exhale of annoyance. I caught a whiff of spearmint under the stronger smells of leather and dog and dust. "Leave it to crazy Ms. Goodnight to have a bunch of chickenshit dogs on a *ranch,* for God's sake."

"Excuse me?" I'd been fixing to say something else. Another apology, another inanity, I didn't know—the spearmint had distracted me. His tone, however, brought me up short, and my eyes narrowed to reevaluate him in the harsh sunlight.

He had just been pretty decent—gentlemanly, really, giving me his shirt and all. Up close I could see that he wasn't soft enough to be cute. He was too young to be rugged. (Which was a relief considering the underwear thing.) His eyes were very blue against his tan, and his teeth very white. But his brows were drawn down in a scowl that, even though it was aimed at the dogs, seemed to cover a lot more.

"It's just typical," he said, his tone a razor slice of derision, "Ms. Goodnight owning herding dogs that are afraid of goats."

"You mean as in typically kind of her to give these useless dogs a home?" The overly sweet question should have been a warning, if he'd been paying attention, but he seemed to take it at face value.

"Doubtless." His softly mocking snort ruined this admission. "She's a soft touch. I'm sure these dogs had a sob story to tell her. Ms. Goodnight is notorious around here. Everybody's kooky old aunt."

"Oh *really*." My voice painted a layer of ice on the Texas afternoon. Finally it sank in; his eyes flew to my red hair—a family trait—and I saw the flash of "Oh crap" on his face, even before I finished. "I just thought she was *my* kooky old aunt."

He could have saved himself—apologized, said that he meant it in the nicest possible way. I mean, no one knew better than me how kooky the Goodnights were by any normal person's standards.

But what he said, with an up-and-down glance that encompassed my bare legs, rubber boots, cherry-covered underwear, the dogs, the goats, and even the cow, was: "Well, that explains a lot."

This day kept getting better and better.

Fury erased the rapier reply I *wanted* to make. Even sarcasm failed me, and all I had left was indignation. "You have a lot of nerve," I heard myself saying, like some vapid Victorian heroine, "insulting my aunt like that."

The accusation seemed to score a hit. His cheeks darkened under his tan, but he didn't back down.

"Do you know what she tells people about this place?" He gestured toward the house and barn and Aunt Hyacinth's acres of herbs and plants, and even *that* managed to express contempt. "Why she won't sell it and move to somewhere she can have a bigger farm and decent staff to help her?" He paused, and familiar dread curdled in my stomach in the beat before he made his point. "Her dead husband doesn't want her to."

I knew where this was going, had to keep my head and try to steer away from the shoals. "So she's sentimental about his wishes," I said. "Just because some people have a *heart*—"

His snort ratcheted up my blood pressure, nearly drowning out the cautioning voice in my head. "She says his *ghost* won't let her sell. She talks about him like he's still living here."

"*So?*" I forced a careless shrug, as if this were the worst of our idiosyncrasies. "Lots of people believe in ghosts."

"I know." Sarcasm gave way to real anger, like we were getting to the root of his personality malfunction. "A lot of people now believe there's a ghost on *our* property, thanks to your aunt. As if we didn't have enough problems."

"Everyone's got problems." That didn't excuse his calling my aunt a nutcase. "I fail to see how your ghost is Aunt Hyacinth's fault."

"It's *totally* her fault!" He ticked off the reasons on his fingers, a pompous move that infuriated me even more. "She fed the flames of these idiotic ghost rumors, which only started because we had to build a bridge, which we had to do because she won't sell her land, and she won't give us an easement across her back acreage to cross the river there because it messes with the feng shui of her herb farm or something."

"That's ridiculous." I shook my head, my ponytail swinging. Something had short-circuited my normal instinct of self-preservation. Maybe because we were here, on Goodnight property. Maybe because he'd made me so *mad,* I wanted to return the favor, and channeled Phin at her most aggravating. "Aunt Hyacinth would never say that. She doesn't practice feng shui. She's a kitchen witch."

He opened his mouth, closed it, then scrubbed his hands up and down his face. When he dropped them, his gaze had turned scathing.

"I should have known." He looked me over, and I felt myself flush from head to toe. "From the moment I saw you standing out in the field in your underwear and gum boots, screaming at my cow, I should have known the whole family was crazier than a sack of weasels."

This was something I'd said more than once. Not the underwear thing, the crazy part. And they *were* crazy, not because they were psychics and potion makers and ghost whisperers, but because they couldn't pretend to be normal. They drove *me* crazy, too. But they were *my* family. Only I was allowed to call them nuts, not this stranger who didn't even *know* me. *Us,* I mean.

"Look, you." Anger burned off my facade of calm, and I poked my finger at his chest, near but not quite touching, because he was bigger than me and I was new at this. I didn't yell at people. I was snide, sometimes bitchy, but I'd never gone rubber toe to cowboy boot with a guy and glared right into his steely blue eyes, so close I could see the darker blue flecks in the irises and feel the heat of his—wow, really nicely muscled—chest through his thin undershirt. Not just in my jabbing finger but my whole body, the parts of me that were covered and the parts of me that weren't.

Damn.

Focus, Amy. He might not be an axe murderer, but he was definitely an asshole.

"I don't care who you are," I said, pushing aside all those distractions. "If Aunt Hyacinth won't sell to you, it's for a good reason. Maybe it's because this 'us' you speak of are all as nasty as you."

"Is that so?" He hooked his thumbs in his belt and shifted his weight so that somehow, without really moving, he was suddenly *looming* over me, as if he could tell how much that bothered me. I didn't budge, just set my teeth against the urge to either step back or kick him in the shin. "Since I'm so *nasty,*" he drawled, "next time I'll just leave you to round up your goats alone."

"There won't be a next time," I snapped, "because I'm going to chop down that blasted tree."

"Tree?" His brows shot down in confusion. "What the *hell* are you going on about now?"

"The goats!" I said, like he was an idiot.

If possible, he scowled even more deeply. "What does the tree have to do with it?"

"The fence!" I flapped a hand toward the pen, losing the battle for simple coherence. "They climb the tree and go over the fence."

He eased his weight back and peered down his nose at me. "You have some very strange ideas about livestock."

"Oh my *God*." I dug my dirty fingers into my hair. "Why are we talking about my stupid goats at all?"

"I don't know," he said, more infuriatingly calm the angrier I got. "I just thought maybe you wanted to say thank you for helping you round them up."

Despite the frustration burning my ears, I *still* felt a rush of shamed heat. Gritting my teeth, I forced a chill into my tone to hide that last degree of mortification. "Thank you," I choked, "for rounding up my goats . . ."

I trailed off where I would have coldly put his name, if I'd known it. Downright smug at my forced gratitude, he supplied the belated introduction. "Ben." He neglected to offer a handshake. "Ben McCulloch."

"Great, now round up your cows and get off the Goodnight property, Ben McCulloch."

His fingers tightened on his belt, self-satisfaction vanishing. "Fine. And you just keep away from *McCulloch* property, Underwear Girl."

"Can't think why I'd want to go there," I said, lifting my chin and arching my brows.

Hand on the gate, he said with matching disdain, "I don't know. To return my shirt, maybe? I'd ask for it back, but I'm a gentleman."

Past embarrassment, I shucked off the garment in question with reckless fury and threw it at him. Of course, *he* caught it easily. "Thank you for the loan," I said. "See you on the other side of never."

"Here's hoping that's true." Shirt balled in his fist, he slammed the gate, so hard the whole fence wobbled. The horse had been placidly cropping grass, and looked resigned when Mr. Personality swung onto his back and kicked him into a canter. It was a matinee western move that would have impressed me if I hadn't completely, irrationally, irrevocably hated the guy's guts.

3

In the shower, I soaped my hair with a minty green shampoo from the collection on the shelf, letting the hot water carry away my anger so I could figure out at what point I had totally lost my mind.

Sure, Ben McCulloch had been a jerk (other than lending me his shirt and helping me round up the goats, I mean). But you don't have a family like mine without developing some defenses. So why had my umbrella of sarcasm so utterly failed me just now? I really didn't want to think it had anything to do with the blue eyes and the biceps.

Austin, where I'd grown up, was a pretty big city, but

it could also be a bit of a small town if you lived there long enough. Everyone at my school knew about the Goodnights—possibly due to Phin's blowing up the chemistry lab during her junior year, when trying to enchant the football team's jerseys for indomitability. Something about batch lots and logarithmic synergism, she'd explained while Mom trimmed off the singed ends of her hair. As if I cared about anything other than having to pass the class now that my last name was mud.

Let's get this straight. Magic is a fact. When other kids were chanting "Rain, rain, go away," Phin and I were in the kitchen with Mom, cooking up spells to keep the tomatoes in the backyard from getting root rot. My cousin Daisy's invisible friends were the children of a pioneer family who died of a cholera epidemic in 1849, and Violet's crystal collection could cure a headache and pick up Mexican radio if she arranged them just right.

Maybe if these things were more flashy, or overt, the Goodnight reality would be everyone's reality. But magic was more about tendencies and probabilities, and, like Uncle Burt, worked best where you couldn't quite see it.

Being in on the secret might be a lot of fun when you're a kid, but not so much once you realize how often life hinges on everyone agreeing—at least outwardly—on the same reality.

Especially if you're the only one in a very eccentric family to realize that.

So now I was walking a tightrope between worlds, pretending I didn't believe in ghosts and magic. And my family? Oh, they were just having fun. The Bell, Book and

Candle was just a gift shop with eccentric merchandise. The Iris Teapot sold herbal teas that cheered you up only because they were so delicious. No, of course magic had nothing to do with my sister blowing up the chemistry lab.

I'd become very good at deflecting comments about my family without actually denying anything. Aunt Iris, the most sympathetic of my aunts, said I was too concerned with what other people thought. But it wasn't that I wanted my family to be normal. I just wanted them to be *safe*. Magic might be as real as Copernican revolution, but I was sure Galileo had kin who didn't want him excommunicated over that, either.

God, that made me sound like a coward. A coward and a hypocrite. No wonder my defenses failed me out in the yard. There was no sarcasm shield against the inner saboteur of my guilty conscience.

Oh *hell.* I froze midlather. That little piece of self-awareness was *way* too insightful to be random.

I rinsed my hair, squinting through the sluice of soap and water to aim a suspicious glare at the bottle on the shelf. *Goodnight Farm's Clear Your Head Shampoo.*

Crap. I picked up the bottle, rubbed my eyes, and read, *We can't say this will sort out your troubles or unknot thorny questions, but it will smooth your hair and untangle your tresses. Instructions: Lather, rinse, repeat with an open mind. Vegan, not tested on animals.*

That was the thing about the Goodnight world. No matter what the label said, you could never assume anything only worked *like* magic.

• • •

Once dressed, I turned my clear head to the next question: What the hell had Cowboy McCrankypants's denim knickers in a twist? And why hadn't Aunt Hyacinth warned me about it?

I chewed it over as I took my filthy clothes to the washer and carried a basket of clean towels to the living room. Even in the Goodnight world, laundry didn't fold itself. Though I wouldn't have minded a crystal ball to tell me what had Phin taking so long, and whether or not I should worry.

Dad once said that Phin didn't have the sense God gave a duck, but this was not true. She had a remarkable homing instinct. I'd never known her to get lost. Not geographically, anyway. But when she got distracted by a project, or a stroke of genius, or a random thought . . . For all I knew, she might be building a DNA model out of bendy straws in the Sonic parking lot.

All the same, I called her cell, let it ring until it went to voice mail, then hung up without leaving a message. Phin was notorious for not answering her phone. But right at that moment, I felt convinced she was doing it to annoy me.

I drummed my fingers on the counter, eyeing the door to Aunt Hyacinth's workroom. My laptop was upstairs, but to go up and get it was so . . . deliberate. Whereas if I just wandered into the next room to surf a little on my aunt's computer, and just *happened* to Google a name or two . . .

And, I figured, I should at least send my aunt a note to let her know I'd antagonized her neighbor.

It was as good an excuse as any.

The dogs seemed happy with my new sense of purpose

and trailed after me to the back of the house, their nails ticking on the tile floor, my own Bremen Town Musicians.

I headed for the desk where Aunt Hyacinth ran the business of Goodnight Farm. With the lights on and the ceiling fans turning, the workroom didn't look much like a sorceress's inner sanctum, though Phin's equipment gave it more of an alchemist's-lab vibe than usual, and I was pretty sure Aunt Hyacinth would have hated the blackout curtains. The room had once been the back porch, but Uncle Burt had enclosed it years ago. Potted plants crowded the space, and shelves of jars and bottles—green and brown and clear glass, all hand labeled—lined the walls, along with books of every vintage. Bundles of drying herbs and flowers dangled from the ceiling, and copper and iron pots hung near a large fireplace, their bottoms blackened by flame. At home, Mom cooked plenty of potions over the gas stove in our kitchen. I'd even seen her use the Crock-Pot. But Aunt Hyacinth was a traditionalist.

The dogs flopped onto the cool stone floor, sighing deeply. Not even I was immune to the peaceful energy that permeated the house and grounds. It was the same at my mom's shop, and my aunt Iris's, too. Positive magic—the only kind that Goodnights do—has that effect. Even people who don't recognize it as supernatural feel it.

This was why I'd been reluctant to come to the farm. It was part of the figurative bubble where my family lived, where magic was reasonable and *tangible*. It messed with my thinking and blurred the lines I'd carefully drawn between my private, family world and my determined public normalcy. It made me do stupid things like get into an argument about ghosts—*ghosts,* of all things—with a jackass cowboy.

After the computer booted up, I dashed off a note to Aunt Hyacinth, feeling virtuous. And *then* I opened a browser window and typed "McCulloch Texas ranch."

There wasn't much. No homepage, just a business listing. Primary Location: Llano County. Production: Cattle and calves. Owner: Dan McCulloch.

The second link led to a *Texas Monthly* article: "The Disappearing Independent Rancher."

I had a rudimentary understanding of the industry. Cattle were raised on pastureland, like the acreage surrounding Goodnight Farm. There were many small independent ranchers, but a large spread took a lot of money and resources. The article was basically about how drought, the cost of transportation, and the economy made things hard for the ma-and-pa operation. Cattle barons had given way to corporations. The author cited the McCullochs as one of the largest ranches in the state to remain a family-owned business. No shareholders, just Ma and Pa McCulloch.

Impressive, especially after I saw a map of the ranch. It was big. Really big, sprawling on both sides of the Llano River. Except for one small white spot in the middle— Goodnight Farm.

A book fell off a shelf with a heavy thump that made me jump. I spun the chair toward the sound, but everything was still. The dogs had barely roused from their snooze, and the rest of the books were lined up neatly, nowhere near the edge. It seemed Uncle Burt had decided to be helpful.

I retrieved the hardcover volume from the floor. *Texas Ranches, Circa 1920*. The pages had fallen open to an older map of the area, which showed that a hundred years ago the McCulloch spread hadn't reached nearly so far. It had been the biggest of about ten ranches in this bend of the river. The family must have bought up all the other land over the last century, because now there was only the one blue blob, wrapped around Goodnight Farm like a fat corpuscle trying to devour a stubborn cell.

Aha.

I sank back and the chair sighed beneath me, echoing my disappointment. Was that what Ben McCulloch's antagonism was about? The fact that Aunt Hyacinth wouldn't sell? Ninety percent of the world's conflicts were about property, what someone had and what someone else wanted.

"This is a bit of a letdown, Uncle Burt." I talked to him out of old habit. "I just think if you're going to be a jackass, you should be original about it."

But what was all that ranting about ghosts on McCulloch property, then? I tried to sort through my anger-muddled memory of what Ben had said. Something about a ghost, an easement, a bridge–

I heard a car out front, but the dogs didn't bark, or even stir in their slumber. That meant Phin had arrived home. Just as I'd been thinking of ghosts. Logic said it was coincidence, but the Goodnight part of me said not to be so sure about that.

Phin bounded into the workroom, a forty-four-ounce soft drink in one hand and a reusable shopping bag in the other. She started talking without any greeting, which was normal, but her words tumbled over each other in excitement, which made me very nervous.

"Hey, Amy! Guess what."

With most people, "Guess what" was a rhetorical opening statement, but Phin clearly expected me to take a stab at clairvoyance. I raised my eyes to the ceiling and sighed loudly. "You're late and you don't bother to answer your cell phone."

She waved off my tacit rebuke. "That's not a guess, that's self-evident."

Subtlety really was wasted on her. I eyed the Route 44 in her hand and the straw clamped in her teeth. "It is also evident you have forgotten my cherry limeade."

"Oh." Guilt flashed on her face. "Sorry." She held out the cup. "Vanilla Coke? There's still a lot left."

"No thanks." I'd written the drink off as a loss an hour ago. "So what kept you? Extraterrestrials landing at the supermarket?"

"Don't be ridiculous." She plunked her shopping bag beside the rest of her mess and announced, "There's a ghost on the neighbors' ranch."

I sat up so fast the dogs jerked out of their snooze. "What?"

"They have a *ghost* on their prop-er-ty." The last word was broken like she was spelling it out for a moron.

I ignored that—it was my fault for not saying what I meant, which was, *Really? Ben McCulloch wasn't just making up things to be mad about?*—and concentrated on the part that had my heart tap-dancing against my ribs. "You didn't go *over* there, did you?"

"Where?" Phin asked. " 'Over there' is a relative adverb phrase, Amy, and not much use without—"

"Onto the McCulloch prop-er-ty," I interrupted. Jeez Louise, sometimes I was sure she could only be that obtuse on purpose.

"Why would I go there?" she asked.

"To look for the ghost."

"Without any equipment?" Her tone implied that I'd

33

suggested she go snow skiing in a bikini. "Of course not. Besides, it's still daylight."

At just past midsummer, dusk lasted until almost nine o'clock, which let me breathe again. I still had time to make sure Phin didn't do anything stupid. "How did you find out about this ghost?"

"In town." She stabbed the straw into the ice at the bottom of her cup. "Everyone is talking about it."

That was what Ben McCulloch had said. Everyone was talking about the ghost, and it was making his life difficult. My brain spun, trying to fit this information into a very fragmented picture. "Then why didn't we hear about it before this? And why didn't Aunt Hyacinth say anything?"

"We haven't been off the farm in days." Phin dismissed the question with a shrug. "And Aunt Hy had a lot on her mind before she left."

The memory of my aunt on the porch, Mom waiting in the van, rushed back again. I guess there *had* been something she forgot to tell me. As for not going into town, that was true, too. And even if I'd watched the local news— which wasn't local at all, but out of Austin—that wasn't the type of thing most channels would carry except at Halloween.

"Do you think it's an actual ghost," I asked, "or just a legend?"

"It could be either," said Phin. "Or both—a minor paranormal event that gossip has blown up into a full-fledged haunting." She shook the ice in her drink and went on conversationally, "There is a sad lack of firsthand accounts. Mostly hearsay and anecdotal evidence. Nothing even to say what *kind* of apparition, if it's a will-o'-the-wisp, or a woman in white, or what. Since it's by the river, it could even be a variation of La Llorona."

The name yanked tight the coiled knot in my gut, making it suddenly hard to breathe. I tried to keep my reaction from showing, and the old emotions pushed into the corner where they belonged. "La Llorona is south of here, on a completely different river. On the San Antonio River, at Goliad."

Phin shook her head, mouth full of soda, and swallowed before she answered. "La Llorona—the weeping woman—is just a *type* of apparition. They fall into categories. Don't you remember any of this stuff? You read every book on the subject when we were kids."

"I've had other things to think about lately." Things like being devoted to reality. "Spectral taxonomy isn't something they cover on college entrance exams."

Her snort said that she found this a serious lack on the part of admissions boards everywhere. I was contractually obligated to *love* Phin, but she was idiosyncratic, to say the least, and sometimes outright infuriating. Other times, in spite of everything, she made me laugh.

Which I almost did—until she said, "In any case, I'm keeping an open mind that there's an actual haunting of some sort. After all, it *could* have to do with the body by the river."

"The *what*?" This was not a rhetorical question. I mean, it wouldn't be the strangest thing to come out of my sister's mouth, but the ultracasual way she'd said it made me doubt my own ears. "As in *dead* body?"

"Of course dead body." She raised her brows. "If it were a live body, I would have said 'man' or 'woman' or 'person.' Semantics are important."

I ignored that. "By *our* river?"

She nodded and sipped her soda. "A mile or two upstream, judging by where I saw the sheriff's cruiser when I drove by."

"Sheriff's cruiser?" I echoed. Again.

Phin's brows knit in concern. "Have you had some sort of sudden-onset hearing loss?" She bent to speak rather loudly a few inches from my face. "Are you having any dizziness? Ringing in your ears?"

I brushed her off and pushed out of my chair. "Of course not. I mean, *why* the sheriff?"

"To keep people away, of course. Until the forensic team gets in there and decides if it's a crime scene or not." She waved away such trivial concerns as homicide. "But that's really not important."

My mouth worked up and down, a soundless guppy face of . . . There were no words for my emotion. Finally I managed, "Not *important*? You didn't think you should *lead* with the fact that someone has been killed mere miles from where we're staying?"

"Well, not *recently*," she said, as if I were the one incapable of conducting a linear conversation. "That's why they had to wait on the physical anthropology team to come from the university."

I thought after "dead body" I could be excused for being a little slow to catch up. "Physical anthropology" meant that what they'd found were mostly bones. But it was summer in

Texas. Hot, but dry. How long would it take for a body to become a skeleton?

"When did this happen?" I asked, trailing her as she went to her laptop.

"No one knows yet." Phin ducked under the table to mess with some wires running down to the outlet in the floor. "They just started investigating today."

I addressed her rear end. "No, I mean, when was the body, skeleton, whatever, discovered?"

"A few days ago." She emerged, straightened, and pushed a few wisps of hair out of her face. "Somebody's building a bridge, and they'd barely begun when the crew uncovered a skull and some bones, and tomorrow the UT physical anthropology department will excavate the rest. Which is why the sheriff's cruiser is extremely irritating, because this would be the perfect chance to test my coronal aura visual media transfer device. . . ."

She started talking gadgets and I stopped listening. I was trying to sort through what Ben McCulloch had said in his litany of Goodnight offenses. Something about a bridge, one that they were building because Aunt Hyacinth wouldn't let them cross the river on her land. Which didn't sound like her, but I put that part aside. Maybe she'd explain if she emailed me back–

And that was as far as I got, because Phin's words had tripped my pay-attention-this-is-trouble switch.

So this is the perfect *opportunity to expand my research on the measurable paraphysical effects of supernatural phenomenon.*

"Hang on," I said when she paused to take a breath, and I pointed to the contraption on the table. "You mean this is some kind of ghost detector you're planning to use over on the McCulloch property?"

"Of course not!" she said in a huff. "It's a spectral energy visualizer. Weren't you listening?"

I placed my hands flat on the slate table, hoping to channel some of that cool into my demeanor. "Listen, Phin. You can't go around spouting off about supernatural phenomena. I mean, Austin is pretty open-minded, but we're not *in* Austin. This is a small town. And you definitely can't go ghost hunting or energy visualizing or whatever on the McCullochs' place. We need to keep well clear– What are you doing?"

She continued to open and close the workroom cabinets and drawers. "I'm trying to find an EMF meter in Aunt Hy's things. I blew mine out in an experiment for my physics final."

"You don't need an EMF meter. You need to pay attention. This is important." I followed her around the room, talking to the back of her head. Maybe if I threw enough words at her, some of them would penetrate her skull. "The McCullochs are already peeved at Aunt Hyacinth. If they're trying to build this bridge, and then this body turns up, and if the ghost talk is making it even harder to get business done, their tolerance for quirky girl ghost detectives is going to be really low right now."

"Aha!" Triumphant, she extracted something that looked like a ray gun from one of the drawers.

"What *is* that?" I asked in spite of myself.

"Infrared thermometer, of course. I knew she'd have one. Culinary equipment has made it so much easier to be precise in cooking up spells." She continued searching. "She's got to have an EMF meter, too. It's important to know where the electromagnetic fields are when you're working."

I tried a more logical approach. "The ranch is about a bazillion acres huge. How are you going to know where to look for spectral auras or whatever?"

She gave me a don't-be-ridiculous look. "At the shallow grave, of course."

"Oh, that's brilliant. Because the only thing worse than trespassing would be trespassing on a *crime scene*." I slapped a hand on the cabinet door she was about to open. "Are you listening, Phin?"

Finally she turned and faced me. "We wouldn't be trespassing," she said, as if stating something obvious. "We've been invited."

"By whom?" The only thing obvious to me was how much we would *not* be welcome.

"By Mark."

"And who is Mark?"

"One of the anthropology people. I met him in the hardware store. He's the one who told me they'd be digging tomorrow, and he invited us to come and see." She pulled at the cabinet door.

I leaned against it. "Right. The dig. Tomorrow. Not ghost hunting tonight."

"It needs to be dark to image the Kirlian aura!" *Pull.* "Plus if we go tonight, I can get data before and after excavation."

Push. "I'm not going."

She stopped and gaped at me like I'd told her I wanted fried kitten for breakfast. "But you *have* to go! Investigations have to be done in pairs to corroborate subjective experiences."

I dropped my hand from the cabinet and drew myself up to my full height, which was respectable but only nose high to my sister, Galadriel. I made the best of it, though. "I have *one* purpose in this family, and that's to convince people we're normal. I haven't done a bang-up job of it so far today, but I'm not going to make it worse by aiding and abetting your trespassing."

"But how else am I going to test my coronal aura visualizer?"

"Test it on Uncle Burt."

Snap. The lights went out and the air conditioner stopped humming. Again.

"Dammit, Phin!" With the blackout curtains still up, the room was pitch dark.

"It wasn't me!" she cried. "You see—Uncle Burt doesn't want me to test it on him."

"We're in the country. The power goes out all the time, even without your, or Uncle Burt's, help." It went out so often that there were flashlights stashed in all the rooms. I stumbled to a drawer by the door and rooted around for one.

There was the scratch of a match and then a flickering glow as Phin lit one of the many candles around the room. Aunt Hy made those, too, but I rarely lit any, since I didn't know what was for decoration and what held some arcane purpose.

"Maybe it's the McCullochs' ghost," said Phin, the dancing flame casting eerie shadows on her face, the stone walls and black drapes turning the cozy room into something from a macabre fairy tale.

"That's not funny." And then, because I wasn't sure she was joking, I asked, "A ghost couldn't get through the security system, right?"

"Of course not," Phin assured me. "Aunt Hyacinth knows what she's doing. Plus twenty-five years of positive energy use here has strengthened it until the spectral equivalent of an F-five tornado couldn't get through."

While I was picturing that with some dismay—did that mean there *was* a spectral equivalent to a house-leveling tornado?—something cold and clammy pressed against the back of my leg. I jumped with a startled squeal. In the dim light, Sadie's eyes shone back reproachfully, while the other dogs pressed close to me for comfort.

"For crying out loud." Spurred back to sense, I found two flashlights and gave one to Phin. "I'm going out to the fuse box. Keep the dogs inside so they don't give me another heart attack."

"Here," said Phin, running to her equipment and returning with the headlamp she'd worn earlier. "So you can keep both hands free."

I took it, even though I knew I would feel too ridiculous to put it on. "Thanks."

I went out through the mudroom, relieved to see that it wasn't as dark outside as it seemed in the house. The sun had set behind the big granite bluff to the southwest, casting everything into an eerie twilight of silvery blue and indigo shadows. Sunset had also brought a breeze to blow away some of the heat of the day, and dark shapes rode the currents overhead.

Bats. I shivered. They lived in the limestone caves that riddled the hills, and dusk brought them out to hunt bugs. I was generally pro-bat, except when I was trekking through the dark trying not to think about the inevitably dire fate of every horror movie character stupid enough to go into the dark with a flashlight and check the fuses.

The breaker box was outside the physical and metaphysical barrier of the board fence. A ridiculous arrangement. I slipped out of the gate, feeling the change like a pop in my ears, a tingle of warning. Maybe because I was still thinking of dead bodies. Aunt Hyacinth's protections around the house would stop a spirit. They wouldn't do anything against an axe murderer except make him queasy, which didn't seem like it would be much of a deterrent. I mean, a strong stomach probably came with the job.

The thought made me hurry as I tried to outrace my nerves. Unease had knotted tight under my ribs when Phin had mentioned F5 arcane tornados, and it hadn't loosened.

Phin's talk of ghosts shouldn't have bothered me so much. I'd grown up around Uncle Burt, and my cousin Daisy had been dealing with the dead as long as any of us could remember. But tonight I could not push away images of cold, silty water and slimy rocks, and thin, pale hands reaching–

The breeze lifted my damp hair and carried the rosemary scent of the shampoo, clearing my thoughts and bringing memory into sharp focus. I knew exactly what had my stomach in knots, why carefully latched mental doors were rattling their hinges. It was partly the argument with Ben McCulloch, but mostly Phin bringing up La Llorona.

The weeping woman. Another spook, another river. A camping trip to Goliad, a flashlight, two preteens with a really bad idea. Phin was twelve and I was eleven and we had snuck out of our rented travel trailer and gone looking for the veiled woman who, legend said, wept by the river for her drowned babies. The stories of her luring living children to their deaths didn't frighten us enough to make us waste the opportunity to investigate. Jeez, we were stupid.

I remembered nightmare snatches. The shadowed veil, the ashen skin of her clawed hands. Water closing over my head. But I didn't remember exactly what had happened at the river, or how Phin and I had gotten away.

I recalled vividly what happened after, though. Dad had flipped his lid when he found his wet, bedraggled daughters after a frantic midnight search. He'd driven home growling things like "your crazy mother" and "encouraging this BS." And scarier things like "court" and "judge" and "custody." Much scarier to me than La Llorona.

It had shaken even Mom. Since they had never married, I wasn't sure what his chances would be of getting custody. But even at eleven years old, I didn't need psychic powers to see the way things would go if Phin started telling a judge about magic and spells in the Goodnight household. Not after La Llorona had almost made us victims of our own idiocy.

I didn't ever want to see that look of fear and loss on Mom's face again. Trying to get anyone else to change was pointless, especially Phin. I could only change myself. So that night in Goliad was the last time I'd ever spoken of ghosts or magic to anyone outside the family.

Until today.

I didn't know what that meant, except that La Llorona was, in a weird sort of way, on my mind even before Phin brought her up. I had broken my rule when I'd talked ghosts with Ben McCulloch, right when I most needed to put up a good front.

A sound dropped me back into the present. I froze, one hand on the breaker box, and listened intently to the cricket-filled night. Had it come from the McCulloch place? The noise was otherworldly, the pitch so low I'd almost felt it rather than heard it. It was a visceral sort of *whump,* like the subwoofer on a stereo, overscored by a high, thin thread–

No, that was the bats. The dark shapes that had been swooping in a bug-hunting ballet now wheeled in unnatural and panicked chaos, as if someone had put a magnet on their internal compass. As I watched, two of them collided and plummeted to the ground. They hit with muted thumps and the leathery flop of wings, and then silence.

My throat clenched around my held breath. Just feet from me, their small black bodies lay unmoving in the circle of my flashlight. Had they knocked themselves out?

I edged closer, and when neither moved, I touched one with the toe of my boot.

Not stunned. Dead.

The practical part of me said I would need to get a shovel and bury them deep so the dogs wouldn't dig them up. Or maybe I needed to call Animal Control so they could be tested for rabies. Wasn't erratic behavior a sign of that?

The other side, the Goodnight side, knew that rabies didn't make two bats' radar go so haywire they'd collide hard enough to kill each other. But what would?

Leave it alone, Amy.

As omens went, it was pretty clear. Curiosity and ghosts didn't mix. I knew that, even if the memories were slippery as river silt and cold bony hands.

The ringing of the phone worked its way into my dream and became a burglar alarm, which was enough to scare me awake, given that my dreams—once I'd finally managed to drift off—involved skeletons riding goats chasing me in my underwear as Ben McCulloch and his horse herded me away from the safety of the house, all while Phin sat on the porch drinking a Vanilla Coke.

Well, it scared me half awake, anyway. I was so clumsy with sleep that I answered my cell phone, my iPod, and my paperback book before I finally found the house phone. Three large dogs sacked out on my bed didn't help. They made maneuvering difficult even when I was completely conscious.

"Unff," I said, brilliantly.

"Amaryllis, darling," said someone who sounded very like my aunt Hyacinth. "I have to tell you something."

"But you're in China." Maybe that was why she sounded like she was speaking through a cave. The phone was carrying her voice through the center of the earth.

"Yes, I am. But your email reminded me."

Oh yeah. My note threatening to chop down the goats' tree and her neighbor's son. I didn't expect to hear back from her for days. I certainly didn't expect a Jules Verne phone call.

"What is it?" I asked.

"I need for you to take care of the goats."

"What?" I struggled up to a thinner layer of sleep. "I *am* taking care of them. Phin got plants, I got animals."

"Dear, that doesn't make sense. Just promise me you'll take care of it."

"I will, Aunt Hyacinth. I can't believe you called just because of that."

"It's very important to me. I'm sorry to put the responsibility on you, but I know you're the one to handle this."

"Don't worry about it," I said, wondering if, just possibly, my aunt's *eccentricities* extended to a completely nonmagical area. "I've got it covered."

"You promise?"

"I do, no problem." Jeez, how many times was she going to ask me?

"I have to be sure, or I'll worry about it for the rest of my trip."

"I promise, Aunt Hyac—"

Just as I finished the third assurance, there was a pop in my ears and a strong tug in my belly, as if a knot had been yanked tight. It pulled me out of the fog of interrupted sleep and jerked me upright in the bed with a force that left me gasping.

The dogs didn't bark. They'd gone stiff, their heavy bodies pressed against my legs, trembling, their barrel chests heaving with fearful pants.

Bear gave a soft, terrified whine. I might have made a similar sound as I stared at the growing column of light at the foot of my bed. I was trapped by the weight of the dogs on the blanket, and by my own dread, as the glow began to take human shape.

5

the column burned blue as a gas flame, and in the incandescent center was a hazy outline of a man, washed-out and blinding. But cold. Cold as a gravestone iced by a winter moon.

The awful paralysis of nightmare gripped me. I couldn't move—not to shout, or speak, or run. Maybe I *was* dreaming. I could half convince myself of it except for the dogs' breath wreathing their quivering muzzles, and the stinging chill on my bare arms and neck.

New features molded out of shadow—a hint of a nose, a

jawline, a mouth. A caricature of a face, gaunt and stripped of definition. Then, movement. A half-formed arm lifted slowly, as if pulling against the weight of death to reach for me, and the shade of a mouth worked in horrific, soundless desperation, like a fish gasping at thin air, as the hollow eyes fixed on my face.

As it stared at me, icy bands tightened around my chest so that all I could take were shallow, insufficient breaths. The edges of my vision sparked a warning as my head seemed to float and spin away from the rest of me. It was a horrible helpless feeling, like passing out in slow motion. My fingers went slack, and the phone tumbled from my grip. If Aunt Hyacinth was still there, I couldn't hear her over the buzzing in my ears. But even if I could call out to her, how could she help me from China?

The door slammed open, crashing against the wall and rattling the picture frames to the floor. Through the empty doorway, a torrent of wind poured into the room, raging like an invisible animal. It pulled at my hair and flung papers and books from the desk and whipped the drapes like Fourth of July streamers in a sudden summer storm.

Lila jumped up with a woof of recognition. The ropes of ice around my chest thawed, and warm air rushed into my aching lungs—warm and scented with sage and mesquite, dusty denim, and a whiff of violet. The spectral blue light and the shape within it vanished, blown out like a candle in a gale.

The cyclone whisked out the way it had come, slamming the door behind it, an emphatic period on the ghostly tirade.

For a long moment, I sat staring numbly into the dark. The awful paralysis had drained away, but shock and bewilderment held me still. Then the rest of the dogs scrambled to their feet, letting loose a cacophony of barking sufficient to . . .

Well, to raise the dead.

The clamor bounced around my skull, knocking my tumbling thoughts into even more of a mess. *Telephone,* I remembered first. *Aunt Hyacinth.*

I searched through the tangle of blankets and twelve dog paws, fumbling the receiver to my ear when I found it. "Aunt Hyacinth? Are you still there?"

Nothing but a dial tone.

The door banged open again, and I gave a shriek that might have, under other circumstances, been overreaction but wasn't because there'd just been a freaking *ghost* in my room.

At *least* one ghost, plus whatever that was that had swept through and driven it away—Uncle Burt?—which had seemed almost benign next to the deathly cold *thing* at the foot of my bed.

The foot of my bed, ohmigod. My racing brain revved that single thought through my head, pushing out everything else.

"Amy! What's going on?"

Phin stared at me from the doorway, her pajamas rumpled, her hair sticking out in all directions. The hall light fell across the bed, and I caught a glimpse of myself in the bureau mirror: huddled in the safety of my dogs and blankets, the snarl of my dark red hair stark against the bloodless pallor of my skin, my freckles standing out like raisins in oatmeal. And my eyes—huge and wild and world-tilted-on-its-axis terrified.

No wonder Phin stared like she'd never seen me before. She flipped on the overhead light and goggled at the mess. "Holy moly! This looks like *my* room. What happened?"

"There was a ghost. Right there!" I pointed. The dogs jumped off the bed and circled the room, whining at the tension.

Phin frowned in confusion. "A ghost? You mean Uncle Burt?"

"Not Uncle Burt," I said. "I'm not scared of Uncle Burt." I kicked off the covers and went to the spot where the light and cold had coalesced. But not too close. "It was right there. Like a column of blue-white light, and a figure in the center."

It seemed like there should be a burn or a mark or something, the way the image was singed into my retinas. When I blinked, I could still see the glow, and I shuddered.

Phin hung back in the doorway, as if she were afraid of contaminating a crime scene. "A ghost shouldn't have been able to get in here."

"I know." I rubbed at the gooseflesh on my arms. My tank top and boxer shorts were meant for sleeping under a hundred and fifty pounds of dog, not for dealing with ghosts. "But it did."

"But it *shouldn't* have," she insisted.

"I know!" Though I didn't really, not until I *looked* at her—her features set and tense, her skin drawn tight into an anxious mask. She was genuinely shaken, and clinging to what she knew, because throwing that out was too frightening.

51

I sank onto the antique trunk next to the wall. "Oh." I forced myself to voice what I thought she was thinking. "For something to get in here, it would have to be stronger than Aunt Hyacinth."

She nodded, dispelling the hope I'd been wrong. "Aunt Hy and all the aunts who help renew the spells every year."

I felt sick. That was a lot of Goodnights, all combined. Thanksgiving filled the farmhouse to bursting. Hot queasiness warred with the chill of fear on my skin, and I shivered, wrapping my arms tight around myself. "Do you see my jacket?"

Phin took the inane question in stride, scanning the room, where my belongings had been flung to kingdom come by the supernatural tornado. "Did the ghost do all this?"

"No." I shook my head and ordered my thoughts. "That is, not the first one. First was the figure I told you about–"

"An actual apparition?" she asked. "Not just an orb or a column?"

"Yes." This inquisition was more like normal, unconquerable Phin, and it shored up my nerves, made me think I might be normal, unconquerable Amy again soon. "Sort of light and shadow, but definitely a human shape."

"Full body or torso?"

"Full body. Or, at least, I think so. The footboard was in the way, so I really didn't see." I shivered again, the phantom of memory prickling my skin and tightening my chest. "It was so cold. I couldn't breathe."

Phin walked to the end of the bed and extended a hand as if testing a breeze. "There's not much of a chill left."

"The wind blew it away." Watching her pace like Sher-

52

lock Holmes in mismatched pajamas had a perversely settling effect on me, too, and I considered the differences between the two events—the specter and the gale. "That's why
I think there were two ghosts. The second was invisible, just
this *force* that slammed open the door and drove back the
horrible cold."

And there was Lila, who had barked as if she recognized
something in it. Or someone. "I think that might have been
Uncle Burt," I said. "Or maybe a combination of the pro-
tection magic plus him. I don't know."

I spotted my jacket hanging from a light fixture and
stood to get it, relieved my knees held me up. Then, unable
to look at the mess anymore, I reached to straighten a potted
plant that had toppled, its soil spilled out onto the floor. "I
should probably try to call Aunt Hyacinth—"

"Don't touch that!"

The piano wire of my nerves sent me nearly to the ceiling. I snatched back my hand and whirled toward Phin, but
she'd already dashed from the room. Two of the dogs went
with her.

Should I follow? Was something going to blow up? The
dogs seemed calm. That should have been a good sign, but
alone again in the room, I felt my dread come crawling back
up from the place where I'd pushed it.

The problem was, in all my acquaintance with Uncle
Burt, I'd only seen him nudge things, turn lights on and off,
and rock in his favorite chair. The scale of destruction in my
room forced me to wonder, if it had been him, what awful
thing had motivated such violence.

I took the Goodnight oddities—herbs, crystals, potions,

ghosts, even Phin's paranormal chemistry set—for granted. Magical hair products and Uncle Burt hanging around his beloved wife, those were familiar and *natural* in a way even I could sense. This cold, desperate thing was an unknown, and when it reached for me, what I felt—the terrifying, visceral pull that robbed my breath and my body heat—was . . . *un*natural. It was out of joint, distorting the order of both worlds, normal and paranormal.

Phin returned, heralded by the slap of her bare feet on the pine floor. She was breathing hard, like she'd run to the workroom and back. My sister was no athlete. The only things that ran a mile a minute were her brain and occasionally her mouth.

She'd gone to get one of her gadgets—a camera with some kind of complex arrangement of wires and extra lenses on the front. Before I could decide if it was a Steampunk thing or an alien-invasion thing, she flipped off the light and started snapping pictures.

At least, that was what it looked like she was doing.

"Did you rig up some kind of night vision?" I asked, just to make conversation and avoid dwelling on how the moonlight-filled curtains echoed the glow of the apparition.

"No." *Click.* "This is the coronal aura visualizer."

She had a *tone,* one that I interpreted to mean *You wouldn't understand.* Irritation chased away the lingering chill of unease. "I'm not an idiot, Phin. I'm capable of grasping the principle, at least."

In the dark I heard her sigh. Loudly. "I *told* you the principle downstairs."

Awkward pause and . . . *Click.*

"Well," I said finally, reluctantly admitting I hadn't been listening. "I now have a pressing reason to pay attention."

Click and *sigh*. "It takes an image of the aura discharged by living objects which have been subjected to metaphysical or psychic energy." She gave a very detailed lecture as she worked, but I gathered the basics: Whatever a spirit had touched lit up with a sort of invisible halo that showed in the images she took through her camera gadget. The touch of a person might show a slight glow, but supernatural events or psychic episodes would get a brighter corona, as Phin called it.

Since I couldn't see what she was photographing, I wasn't expecting much as I peered over her shoulder at the camera's viewscreen. But the image made me inhale sharply. "Oh my gosh, Phin! That's so cool."

Against a dark background, the leaves of the plants that had been knocked over by the ghostly gale were lit around the edges, like a harsh halo of washed-out neon—blues and pinks blending to purple, cut through with angry spikes of yellow.

She shrugged off the compliment, but there was a hint of pride warming her voice. "It would be more functional if it worked in daylight. I haven't figured out why it only works in the dark. Since it's not a visual energy, ambient light shouldn't make a difference."

I studied the images as she thumbed through them on the screen. They changed shape and brightness, but they were all in the same color scheme. One of our cousins saw auras around people, and the halos looked like what she described. "Would two separate ghosts show up differently?"

"That is a good question. You mean the apparition and the unseen force that you say chased it away?"

"Yes." I decided not to remark on her unflattering surprise at my inquiry.

Phin thought about it. "In my experiments, different moods affected the corona's spectrum, so possibly different spirit entities would change the colors as well. Did the apparition move or touch anything in the room?"

I shook my head. "No. It was very . . . contained." If anything, the figure had pulled energy toward it. Eleven-year-old Amy—the one who went foolishly running after specters by the river after dark—knew that the theory behind cold spots at hauntings was that a ghost needed energy to manifest, and heat was a type of energy, so—

Eleven-year-old Amy needed to shut up. I was *not* getting sucked in. I'd made my decision to live as ghost- and magic-free as possible. Even if "as possible" was sometimes "not at all."

And yet I *still* found myself asking the very question that I *knew* would lead to trouble. "Do you think the apparition was the McCulloch ghost? The one people are talking about?"

Phin considered it but sounded doubtful. "I don't know. Most ghosts are closely tied to a location, and they take territory pretty seriously."

I knew what she meant. You wouldn't think barbed wire would slow down something without a body, but fences that merely marked a border for a human could be literal boundaries for a spirit. Like Aunt Hyacinth's security system was supposed to be.

Phin voiced the conclusion before I could. "If it *is* the

ghost from the neighbor's place, it wouldn't just wander over here."

Not without a reason. That was what she was getting at, the possibility I didn't want to face. Not without a fight.

"Maybe the McCulloch ghost is just a local legend," I said. "You told me the reports were mostly secondhand. Maybe that ghost story is based on one already on the Goodnight side of the fence."

"The geography still doesn't hold up." Phin might have been rattled earlier, but she sounded calm and logical now. "And even if that's true, it still means that the ghost came through all the wards around Aunt Hyacinth's house."

"Exactly!" I'd thought I wanted unflappable Phin back, but I didn't. I wanted someone as freaked out as I was, so she would know that I didn't want logic right now. I wanted reassurance. "It came in the house."

"I realize that's a little unnerving–" she said.

"Unnerving?" I swept an angry arm at the carnage around us. "Look at my room, Phin! There was a supernatural event *in my bedroom.* A spectral apparition nearly froze me to death, and a ghostly wind *touched all my stuff.*"

She lifted her brows in disapproval, whether at my tone or my priorities. "I don't see how arguing over whether it crossed one fence or two is going to help. *Something* came into Goodnight Farm, past our wards, and the only way we're going to figure this out is by applying reason and logic, not taking refuge in denial."

"Phin, the only thing more unnerving than realizing there's something that *can* get past Aunt Hyacinth's defenses is wondering why it *would.*"

"Why do ghosts haunt at all?" she said. "Because they want something."

The words hung in the air like an unfinished musical chord. There was the question I didn't want to ask: What did it *want*?

A knock downstairs shattered the moment. Someone was at the front door.

The dogs exploded into barking and took off in a thunder of paws and scrabble of claws, sounding like a pack of hellhounds on the stairs.

"Oh my God," I blurted, grabbing onto Phin as we faced the open bedroom door. "It's the axe murderer."

"I doubt he would knock," she said, but she was whispering, too, and didn't move away from me.

Another rap, imperative and authoritative enough to be heard over the dogs. That didn't seem like a nefarious thing.

"Maybe we should look out the window," Phin suggested.

Feeling stupid that she'd thought of it first, I hurried across the hall to Aunt Hyacinth's room. Even through the sheer curtains, I could see the front of the house and yard were lit like a shopping mall parking lot on the twenty-third of December. A normal person would have assumed the floodlights were motion activated, but Aunt Hy hadn't bothered with sensors when she had Uncle Burt to turn on the lights.

Which made it easy to see the police car parked next to Stella and Aunt Hyacinth's Trooper. The shield on the door said "Sheriff," and every instinct inside me screamed "Trouble."

there was never a good reason for the police to be at the door at one in the morning. My imagination was supplying all sorts of horrible scenarios, making me wonder if something had happened to Mom. But surely one of the aunts would have called if that were the case. So it had to be some other sort of bad, and there was no lack of possibilities there, either.

"Maybe it's another body," said Phin as we hurried downstairs to the accompaniment of the dogs' continued barking.

I knew she was not as macabre as her enthusiasm

would imply. I was sure she meant "another long-dead skull for the anthropologists to dig up" and not "somebody's husband or kid."

What I couldn't explain was why the memory of the two dead bats weighted my feet as I quieted the dogs and answered the front door.

The officer on the porch reminded me of a wolverine. Not as in X-Men, but as in Animal Planet—very compact, kind of squat and solid, with a mean look about the face.

I opened the door a crack, with Phin right behind me, and he held out his badge just long enough for me to see that his last name was Kelly, which matched the name tag on his khaki shirt. "Miss Goodnight?"

His tone told me two things: no one in my family had died, and he meant to be intimidating.

"Yes, Deputy?" I said, in my politest voice. He narrowed his gaze, as if wondering if I was being a smart-ass.

I wasn't. When your family is twice as weird as normal, you have to be twice as polite to authority, because authority hates weird. Unfortunately, it's hard to sound naturally polite when someone's tone sets your back up. So maybe I was being a *little* bit of a smart-ass.

"What's going on?" I asked, more genuinely. Behind me, I heard Uncle Burt's rocking chair creak, as if he were getting up to join Phin and me. I shivered slightly, because it was eerie, but eerily reassuring, even after the night's adventures. "Is everything okay?"

Deputy Kelly didn't answer but peered over my shoulder and said, "Is that your sister in there with you?"

"Yes." I opened the door a smidge, obliging his implied request to see her, as if checking our alibis.

Phin waved. The deputy eyed her purple cow pj bottoms and yellow spaceship pj top dubiously, and I doubt he missed the corona camera still in one hand. "It took you a while to get to the door," he said, with an undertone of accusation.

"We were asleep," I answered, preferring not to explain about the ghost. And we *had* been asleep before the apparition invasion.

He made a deliberate show of looking at all the lights on outside. "All your lights are on."

"Motion sensors," I lied, before Phin could say anything about Uncle Burt turning them on. I knew that his refusing to say what was going on was a power play, but I was out of patience. "What's this about, sir?"

Despite the "sir," the question came out more sharply than I intended, because my insides were twisting into an anxious knot. The night was too full of omens.

"There was an accident out on the McCulloch place," Deputy Kelly said bluntly, as if watching for our reaction.

I heard Phin's quick inhale of concern, and my hand clenched on the doorframe as in my mind's eye I saw the two bats hitting the ground.

"Was anyone injured?" I asked. Ben? His family? Even if they were feuding with Aunt Hyacinth, I didn't want anyone hurt.

"Ranch hand was working late to clear the cattle out of

the pasture 'fore those university folks start digging, and he fell down a ravine." The deputy hooked his thumbs on his belt, broadening his already antagonistic stance. "When I went to the hospital to interview him for the incident report, well, he was saying some mighty odd things."

"Like what?" Phin asked. She'd been content to let me do the talking until now. I had a sinking feeling I knew what the deputy would say. I think Phin did, too, but just wanted to hear how the ghost had manifested itself, according to the ranch hand.

"Oh, you don't need to worry about that," said Deputy Aw-Shucks, laying the good-ol'-boy country cop thing on a little too thick. "I was just stopping by, though, to make sure you two kids were okay, especially as you're house-sitting for your aunt and all. I promised her I'd keep an eye out for you."

He was checking up on us, all right. Checking to see that Phin and I, kooky nieces of kooky ol' Ms. Goodnight, had been home all night, and not out hunting for ghosts or pretending to be one.

Did he think I was an idiot? Yes, he obviously did. His feelings about Phin and me, because we were city girls, or just girls, or just *Goodnight* girls, were written all over him. Maybe he'd switched tactics to put us off guard, but the hard edge of suspicion was still there.

"We're fine," I said, swallowing my anger. Anger at the condescending deputy, and because I suspected *someone* had told him we needed checking up on. "We've been here all night."

Deputy Kelly could have felt the car hoods and made sure the engines were cold, I guess. Or maybe he thought he'd be able to tell if we were lying, with his super-cop skills.

"All night?" he challenged, glancing from me to Phin, whose bed head was impressive, but nothing compared to mine. I looked like I'd been in a wind tunnel, and I could feel the sting of a furious flush in my cheeks. I was sure that didn't look guilty at all.

"Since Phin got back from the store." I forced myself to relax before my anger and my nerves got me in trouble for something I hadn't even done. "I was reading and she was working on her independent study for school."

"Which is?" the deputy asked, still with his thumbs in his gun belt.

Phin pointed at the thing in her hands and said, "Coronal aura visual medium transfer device," and then *stopped*, thank God.

The deputy, after a blank look, pretended he was smart enough to know what that was. "I see." Then he turned to me, since I was obviously the spokesperson. "Well, you know, there's some pretty wild stories going around these days, thanks to what they found out by the river. I just wanted to make sure you girls were tucked in tight over here."

My heart hammered, because he was so patronizing and so threatening at the same time. We'd done nothing wrong—yet—but all I could think of was the park ranger in Goliad standing witness to Dad as he ranted about our crazy mother letting us believe in ghosts.

Phin saved me in the most unlikely way. She cocked her head, as if studying some strange species of wildlife, and said, "Waking someone up to see if they're asleep is counter-intuitive. You wanted to see if we were home. We clearly are. If you want us to be tucked up tight, you'll have to leave."

The deputy stared at her, jaw slack. I shouldn't have been happy to see my sister call him on his bullshit. But I was.

"As you can see, sir," I said, starting to swing the door closed, my polite facade back in place, "we're fine. Thanks for your concern, and I hope the ranch hand gets better soon."

He recovered his dignity, with a stern nod of dismissal and an "All right, then. You girls take care." He turned to go, and the front yard lights went off just in time to make him stumble on the last porch step.

"That's not funny," I told Uncle Burt, addressing his rocker after I'd closed the door. "If he had twisted his ankle, we'd be stuck with him until help arrived." Now that the deputy was gone, outrage could blossom without the intimidation factor. "The *nerve* of him!"

Phin, caught midyawn, looked at me, puzzled. "Why?"

"He practically accused us of going over to the McCulloch place tonight and . . . I don't know what he thought we were doing. Ghost hunting and causing that accident or pretending to be a ghost, like some kind of Scooby-Doo cartoon."

"Why would we do that?" she asked, applying logic to an illogical situation. And I had to admit, I wasn't exactly being reasonable just then.

"I don't know. Because our aunt is the local nutcase, according to Ben McCulloch. I'll bet he told the deputy to come check on us."

Phin fiddled with the controls on her camera. "I'm very curious to meet a guy who makes you completely forsake the scientific method in favor of unfounded supposition and speculation."

"It's called *intuition*," I snapped, at my wits' end. She just snorted, so I took a deep breath and changed the subject. "Do you at least see why you can't go around talking about ghosts and ghost hunting?"

She sighed heavily. "I suppose this means you're still not going to investigate the McCulloch haunting with me. Even though this is an unprecedented opportunity."

I wanted to answer "Absolutely not," no, I would not climb fences and trespass and traipse around in the dark with her, and it had nothing to do with the deputy—or Ben McCranky—telling me not to. But when I opened my mouth, nothing came out. My mind went blank, and I couldn't even form the word "no."

And who would blame me for going brain-dead? I'd had a very rough night. I didn't want to start another argument at that hour, so I finally just said, "I still think it's a terrible idea. But I doubt that will stop you."

"So you don't want to go to the dig tomorrow, either?"

"Oh, I'm going." I *hadn't* meant to say *that*, but once the words were out, I realized how much I did want to know what the crew from the university were uncovering by the river. It was a mystery, and I'd have to be dead not to be curious. And at least that was something normal.

The fact that an uncovered skull was the most mundane

thing in my life right now didn't bear thinking about. I warned Phin, "I want to head out first thing in the morning." Before my resolve deserted me.

"*First* thing in the morning?" she echoed. Phin was not a morning person.

I sighed and started up the stairs. "Right after I take care of those blasted goats like I promised Aunt Hyacinth."

The phone call, in its way, was as surreal as the appearance of the ghost. Why was Aunt Hyacinth so worried about her livestock? Surely she didn't think I'd go through with my threat to barbecue them. I really should try and call her back.

But later. After I slept.

Which brought me to my most immediate problem. One look at my room and I knew I'd never get to sleep in there. Forget the ghostly afterimage on my eyelids; the place was a disaster area.

Instead, I grabbed my pillow and the quilt and went back down to the couch. The dogs came with me, Pumpkin worming under the covers and Sadie a welcome weight on my feet. Yet I still couldn't seem to get warm.

Phin was all about the gadgets, but some things just couldn't be measured. There was no way to quantify the difference between the comforting cool around Uncle Burt's rocker, like a fresh breeze on a hot day, and the hard, unforgiving cold that had come with the *other* thing.

I shivered and tried not to think about it. Maybe I should worry about Deputy Kelly's suspicions instead. Or I could dwell on whether everyone here viewed Aunt Hyacinth like the McCullochs did, and what had sparked the bad blood in the first place. Goodnights were quirky but usually likable. Or maybe I could just worry about the dead body by the river, and how long it had been that way.

No wonder I lay sleepless, even as Uncle Burt's chair rocked in a reassuring rhythm and the dogs melted into boneless piles of comfort. Fatigue made my eyelids too heavy to hold up. But inside . . . an icy thread wove through the knot still coiled around my insides, like a snare ready to close tight.

"Why does any ghost haunt?" Phin had said. "Because it wants something."

What could any ghost want from *me*?

7

right after breakfast—mine and the livestock's—I set out with the dogs into the kind of sweet, dew-spangled Texas morning that nearly made up for the blistering heat that would come later. The first of July, you could still hope for a few temperate hours if you got up early enough to enjoy them.

Phin was not there to see it. My knock on her door was met with an indecipherable complaint. I called that I was going without her and took the barely audible grunt as acknowledgment. I had no doubt she'd catch up, probably by car. The dogs weren't part of my plan, but once I'd laced up my hiking sneakers and slathered myself with sunscreen, they had worked themselves into such a frenzy of anticipation, I didn't have the heart to leave them behind.

Since I had neither instructions for how to reach the site nor Phin's uncanny sense of direction, my idea was to head along the river until I found the dig. And there my plan ended. I didn't like freewheeling it, but I had to keep up momentum or be hogtied by my own arguments.

On one hand, it would have been weird *not* to be curious about the discovery. Maybe a bit macabre, but I didn't think even Phin could wrangle an invitation if the professionals didn't think the dig was more history than homicide. I'd have felt no conflict about heading over the fence at all if it weren't for the ghost.

Given my family's reputation, even the *rumor* of a ghost complicated things. Deputy Kelly's visit had invoked my paranoia about judgmental authority. As long as the Goodnights were quirky but harmless, that was okay. But if someone got the idea we were *involved* somehow? Maybe it was far-fetched to worry, but there *had* been an officer of the law on the doorstep last night.

Only, it wasn't just a rumor. *Something* had appeared in my room. Maybe it was the same entity as the storied ghost of McCulloch Ranch or whatever had caused the ranch hand's fall the night before. But even if those were fiction, the ghost beside my bed had been fact.

A chill swept over me despite the warm air, and I congratulated myself for spoiling the morning.

I focused instead on the barn and the greenhouse and the dew-sequined foliage as the dogs and I walked along the rows of fragrant herbs and down the hill into the lavender fields–my favorite part of the farm. This had once been a vineyard, one of many in the area. But Uncle Burt had turned the land from grapes over to my aunt's ventures when they got married, and it had worked out pretty well for everyone.

When we reached the river, I turned northwest, upstream. The graveled path turned into two parallel wheel ruts cut into knee-high scrub grass. They led to a barbed-wire fence and a five-rail gate between Goodnight land and the McCulloch place. The grass had grown up around the bottom, so I didn't bother to pull the gate open. The dogs went easily through the rails, and I braced my hands on the top, my foot on the bottom, like they were the rungs of a ladder.

Curiosity welled up in me like the fizz in an ice-cold Coke. Excited curiosity, the kind that had made me take a flashlight to the haunted river in the middle of the night all those years ago. And *that* made me nervous. My carefully laid-out boundaries existed for a reason. I didn't like how fuzzy they got when I spent too much time in the Goodnight world.

Who was I fooling? Visiting the dig was like poking around a fire-ant mound. And whether it had a ghost that was real or rumor, I'd have to go carefully not to get stung.

While I was at it, why didn't I just admit that climbing the fence into McCulloch property–by (secondhand) invitation–was a sort of spit in the eye to McCranky for (maybe) setting the sheriff's department on me.

Oh, and by the way, I sure thought about him a lot for someone I never wanted to see again.

Whose fence you are about to climb.

Jeez Louise, that settled it. I had to do *something* just so I would stop talking to myself.

I hauled myself over and joined the waiting dogs.

Committing to an action seemed to ease the knot in my stomach and quiet the voices in my head. With a new spring in my step, I set off along the cattle trail beside the river embankment. The dogs snapped at dragonflies and explored the shrubs for rabbits, except for Lila—the part-time search-and-rescue dog (when she wasn't fleeing from goats)—who trotted ahead, nose in the air, then back to make sure I was following.

The land certainly didn't look like a likely spot for a haunting. The breeze carried the smell of dust and sage and juniper. Later in the day, the sunlight would bleach everything to austere brown and beige, but at the moment the colors were all contrast—puffy white clouds and seamless blue sky, pale limestone outcroppings and rich umber and deep green live oak and mesquite.

In the spring the rugged hills were carpeted with wildflowers, and in the summer it was stark and hot, but the rivers made green ribbons of respite from the heat. As I picked my way up the hill, avoiding cactus and cow patties, I could see why getting cattle to the other chunk of McCulloch land might be a problem. As the land went higher, the river ran faster and deeper, cutting into the rock and making a natural fording impossible, unless you were part mountain goat, part amphibian.

At the crest of the next hill, Lila gave a bark and started down the other side, leaving a puff of white dust in her wake.

Sadie took off after her, and even Bear looked tempted to desert me. It seemed I'd managed to find the dig.

And then I had a horrible thought. Dogs plus dirt plus bones equaled an excavation nothing like what the University of Texas had in mind.

"Oh *hell.*" This was not going to keep me under the McCulloch radar.

I sprinted up the hill; the first thing I saw on the other side was a big yellow bulldozer, parked in a cleared space by the river, looking abandoned in the middle of its work. I took it in with a glance, along with a van with the burnt-orange UT logo, a canopy pitched to shade folding work-tables, and a handful of people digging in the dirt like kids in a sandbox.

Lila and Sadie were still running full steam ahead. In desperation I gave a shrill two-fingered whistle—a useful thing I'd learned on a soccer field. It stopped all three dogs like I'd superglued their paws to the ground.

The dogs weren't the only ones startled into stillness. Heads turned, as they say. Baseball caps, wide-brimmed straw hats, and one Stetson I recognized—oh *effing* hell—all swiveled to stare up the hill.

I'm sure I made an unimposing picture in my T-shirt and cutoff shorts, my hair in pigtails. On the other hand, I was fully clothed, so this was a marked improvement over yesterday.

Nothing to do but brazen it out. "Lila, Sadie!" I didn't bother to yell at Bear, because he had only gone five steps and was looking very ashamed of himself. "Stay right there."

I made my way down the steep slope, which was full of

loose scree that made my descent anything but graceful. But I stayed on my feet, more or less, and caught up with the dogs at the bottom.

Ben McCulloch crossed the field on an intercept course. He did not look happy to see me. There was a shocker.

"What the hell are you doing here?" Mr. Personality stopped in front of me, his hands resting on his hips, which should have looked prissy but didn't. It made him seem imposing, which I was sure was his aim.

But I needled him anyway. "Were you *born* a cranky old man?"

The dogs swarmed around him, holding no grudges, beating his legs with their ecstatic tails. He ignored them and glared at me. "What happened to 'see you on the other side of never'?"

Slayed with my own words. "I didn't know you'd be here. And as it happens," I began with dignity, intending to tell him I was invited. But it occurred to me that "we" were invited might well be Phin's interpretation and not the mysterious Mark's intent. And that would have been humiliating. So I finished lamely, "I was just taking a walk."

He gave me a look of exaggerated suspicion, and feeling like a coward, I busied myself calling the dogs to heel. "Stop that. *Sit,* Lila."

To my shock, she did, and what Lila did, the others imitated. Ben raised his brows, but he looked more sarcastic than impressed. "They've learned some manners since yesterday. What did you do, cast a spell?"

If I *could* have cast a spell, it would have been to wipe that snide curl off his lip. I hadn't forgotten the deputy's visit.

But I *had* forgotten about the ranch hand until just then. "How is your guy?" I asked. "The man that went to the hospital."

He looked confused, but that might have just been from the rapid-fire change of expressions on my face: anger, realization, chagrin, worry. His made its own progression: bemusement, surprise, irritation, then finally grudging admission. "He's recovering. Cracked ribs, mild concussion. Lots of bruises." Then, even more reluctantly: "Thanks for asking."

And *then,* because he couldn't be nice for a millisecond, he asked, "How did you know? Did you see it in your crystal ball?"

"No," I snapped. "Don't you think I would have better things to spy on in my crystal ball than your ranch?"

He shrugged and adjusted his stance, hooking a thumb in his belt, oh-so-unconcerned. "Well, you don't have anything better to do than to trespass on it."

I drew my words out sweetly. "I just wanted to stretch my legs. We have such an itty-bitty two hundred acres, and y'all have such a big, fine place over here."

His eyes narrowed. "You're a lot sassier with your clothes on, Underwear Girl."

While I struggled for a riposte to that, a young man joined us—a tanned Latino god in jeans and a worn-thin T-shirt. For a startled moment, my brain had no room for anything but appreciation, until I saw his amusement and curiosity. He'd definitely heard what Ben had just said. And I definitely wanted to die, but not without taking McCulloch with me.

74

"Hi," said the newcomer, sounding very collegial for a deity. His razor-sharp cheekbones were sunburned and his straight blade of a nose was peeling. Human after all. "Are you Amaryllis?"

Ben's brows shot up, and I saw the first hint of a smile from him. At my expense. Of course. "Amaryllis?"

"Amy," I corrected, my arctic tone daring him to make something of it.

The other guy held out his dirty hand, then brushed it off on his equally dirty jeans before offering it again. "Mark Delgado. I'm an intern on this dig. I met your sister in the store yesterday. She isn't with you?"

I wondered if he didn't look a little disappointed. Phin was nuts, but she was pretty and delicate and strawberry-blond. And magic clings to her; it gives her a sort of charisma. People sense it, but they dismiss her eccentricity as genius. Or the blondness.

"So, your sister found out about the dig yesterday," Ben said, after watching our exchange, "and you just *happened* to be walking your dogs in this direction?"

"Oh, I invited them," said Mark, throwing me a rope and cutting me loose in my lie with the same unwitting sentence. "Since Phin seemed interested and they are your neighbors."

I thought about bluffing it out, but the sound of truck tires on gravel made it pointless. The dogs woofed in greeting as the Trooper rolled to a stop at the end of the current road, well above the river excavation and future bridge.

Ben lifted one brow, and said with pointed understatement. "This must be her now."

The door opened and slammed shut. "Hey, guys!" Phin paused to pet the dogs, then joined us, smiling when she saw me. "Oh, Amy, good. I knew you'd figure out where it was."

I ceded this round to Ben. And judging by his grin, Mark seemed to find us *all* very amusing. Behind them, I could see that work on the dig had dwindled to just a pretense with a lot more stares on us than on the ground.

"I'm glad you both found us," said Mark. "I realized this morning I hadn't told you how to get here."

"Oh, I always know where I'm going," said Phin, with a careless shrug.

"That's handy," said Mark, looking charmed.

"Extremely." She ran her curious gaze over Ben. I saw him echo the gesture, and something in my chest tightened in a way that I didn't like to analyze. Normally, I compare well to my sister and cousins. Phin might have been elfin and blond and *quirky,* but I could rock a soccer field and a C-cup. Okay, B and a half. And some guys, I'd been told, liked freckles. At the moment, however, *Phin* wasn't covered in dust and dog hair and sticky sunscreen.

"You must be Benjamin McCulloch." She inhaled to go on, and without a shred of psychic powers I just *knew* she was going to say something unfortunate. Like "Funny, you don't look like a humorless SOB." Or "My sister couldn't stop talking about you last night."

"So, Mark!" The words burst out in a way-too-loud way that made all three of them stare at me. I dialed back the volume and went on. "McCulloch is acting like we've crossed into Area 51. Is it an *alien* skeleton you've found?"

He grinned. I liked his ready smile and sunburned nose.

76

The impact of his good looks was fading, making him seem more approachable. Certainly more than Mr. Personality and his scowl of doom.

"Plain old human," said Mark. "That much we can tell in the field. Dr. Douglas is doing a few preliminary measurements before we take everything to the lab."

"Are you sure you should be discussing this?" Ben asked. "Shouldn't you check with your boss?"

Mark gave him a sharp glance, but I was so used to intervening for my family that I responded before he could.

"Phin and I are staying just a few miles away." I realized I'd mirrored Ben's belligerent stance, and hastily dropped my arms. "If someone was killed here, we should know about it."

"It's not a crime scene." Mark's friendly demeanor returned as he told me, "At least, not a recent one."

His tone, I think, was meant to be reassuring, but factoring in ghosts and all, I said, " 'Recent' is a relative thing."

"Our guy has been in the ground a very long time." He jerked his head toward the excavation. "Come and meet Dr. Douglas."

Phin fell in beside Mark, peppering him with eager questions as they started toward the dig. "You said 'guy.' Is that a nonspecific colloquialism, or have you actually determined it's a male skeleton? You get that from the pelvic bone, right?"

Mark's answer began with a "Yes, and . . ." But I lost the rest of it because I was distracted by the dogs, who were eyeing the excavated square of earth with an anticipatory glee that made me very nervous. I hated to miss anything, but

Lila and the others had been shockingly obedient, and I figured my luck would run out any moment.

"I'd better secure the dogs," I said, not to anyone in particular, except that Ben was still standing there. "I'll catch up."

"I'll wait," he said, probably because he knew it would annoy me.

"Suit yourself." I'd come prepared with a drawstring sports pack, and I dropped it from my shoulders as I called for Lila to follow me. The rest followed *her,* and somehow I wasn't surprised that the cowboy stalked after us, too.

"Where's your horse?" I asked. I'd seen the bulldozer and the UT van, and now I noted that, in addition to the people excavating the dig, there were several other tanned and work-hardened men hanging out by a cluster of pickup trucks. But no horses or horse trailer.

Ben paused, like he was searching for anything snide in the question. Which was fair, I supposed. Finally, when we'd reached a mesquite bush substantial and shady enough for me to tie up the dogs, he answered. "I was only riding yesterday because we were herding the cattle out of this area and into the next pasture. And rescuing strays from neighbor girls gone wild."

Funny how with all that had happened I was still able to blush about that. I pretended I was holding back a retort when really I just couldn't think of anything witty. At least, not while I struggled to extract a leash, any leash, from the nylon snarl I'd pulled out of my bag, which would have been a *lot* easier without the blushing.

I thrust the mess into Ben's hands. "Here. Make yourself useful."

He took them, too surprised to refuse. I got out a collapsible bowl—Aunt Hyacinth didn't stint when it came to her pets—and a bottle of water. Bear scootched his furry bulk into the shade and slurped up the water as soon as I'd put it down.

When I straightened, wiping my hands dry on my jeans, Ben held out the first leash, looking extremely grumpy about it, like I'd tricked him into helping me or something. "Are you going to tell me what you're really up to?"

I clipped the leash to Bear's collar, then knotted it around a thick, thorny branch. "Who says I'm up to anything?"

"Call it a hunch," he said, and handed me the other two leashes. "Don't scratch yourself," he added.

"I'm not an idiot," I said, reaching into the mesquite to tie up Lila and Sadie.

"If you say so."

I promptly impaled myself on a gargantuan thorn. I hissed at the sting, then pressed my lips together over a curse.

"Did you say something?" Ben asked, too blandly not to have heard me.

Gritting my teeth, I backed out of the bush, ignoring the pain in my arm, as well as the one in my backside. Or I would have if he hadn't been standing in a way that blocked my path, unless I wanted to push aside one of the mesquite branches and risk another scratch. As if I weren't irritated enough, the close quarters emphasized everything I didn't like that I liked about him. It wasn't just that he was muscular and tan, with broad shoulders and big, long-fingered hands. It was that I'd seen him ride that horse, and I knew his brawn wasn't just for show. There was something practical and *capable* about that strength that made my insides flutter in an extremely galling way.

Get a grip, Amy. You are not a fluttery *sort of girl.*

Maybe it was a question of contrasts. I'd only dated high school boys, though I did have an ongoing flirtation with the barista at my favorite coffeehouse, who was majoring in prelaw at UT and promised we'd go out after I'd graduated, only Phin had dragged me *here,* so *once again* it was all her fault that I was overwhelmed by the overwhelming not-in-high-school–ness of Ben McCulloch.

"You didn't answer my question," he said, looking down at me from quite close quarters. His eyes weren't bright blue at all but rather steely, which suited him better than something more cheerful. I sternly told myself that my prelaw friend with caffeine benefits was probably a lot smarter than him, and that smart was what I liked best.

"No, I didn't say anything," I answered, glaring up at him. He wasn't even that tall, really. He just seemed that way from so near. *Really* near.

He tightened his mouth like he might have wanted to smile at my evasion. "I mean, what are you doing here? Is your whole family made up of nosy busybodies?"

Actually, we were. My aunts and cousins were up in each other's business all the time. But I wasn't going to tell him that. "Who wouldn't be curious? You're acting like they're digging up the lost Ark of the Covenant in your back forty acres."

He gave me a sidelong squint. "Do you think that's a possibility?" I let my glare answer for me, and he raised his hands as if surrendering, though obviously he was not. "I'm just saying. You Goodnights have a track record as eccentric meddlers."

I folded my arms, calmly, like we were just shooting the breeze. "You know, Phin told me about the ghost rumors in town. That it's some old story that resurfaced because your construction crew found a skull in the ground. I don't see how that could *reasonably* be Aunt Hyacinth's fault."

His snort wasn't quite as rude as yesterday's. "Nothing about your family is reasonable."

"You don't even know us," I said, determined not to lose my temper today.

"I know there isn't any *reason* for you to be here other than morbid curiosity."

Despite everything, that made me laugh. "Jeez, McCulloch. Isn't that enough? I can't be the only one with an addiction to the Discovery Channel. It's like a forensic detective show in my backyard."

He seemed surprised by my laugh, and I had to admit, I hadn't exactly been Little Miss Sunshine up to that point. After a considering pause, as if searching for artifice, he said, almost with humor, "*My* backyard, actually."

"Fine. I'm trespassing." I dropped my arms and refilled the dogs' bowl before capping the water bottle. "If you're going to run us off, can I at least get a look at the cool stuff first?"

"You swear you're just here to satisfy your curiosity?" he asked, still skeptical.

I drew an X over my chest and raised my right hand, careful what I said, because oaths have consequences. "My motives are pure."

If I was lying to anyone, it was to myself. I wanted nothing to do with ghost hunting or rumors of haunting, but the apparition, its reaching hand and gasping mouth, was never far from my thoughts. It had only moved to the corner of my mind, where the morning sun couldn't reach.

Ben seemed satisfied, and he stepped back to let me pass. As I did—ignoring the tingle where my shoulder brushed his—I added, for the hell of it, "But I can't promise my sister won't get a wild hair and decide to experiment with raising the dead."

His brows shot back down; they were extremely expressive, really. "You aren't nearly as funny as you think you are."

"Who's joking?" I said as I headed toward the dig site and the uncovered grave by the river.

8

ben and I made our way toward the bottom of the hill, where I could see Phin and Mark talking. I was almost more worried about missing something interesting than anything Phin might be saying. After all, I'd just suggested she might raise the dead. Clearly the Goodnight way was rubbing off on me.

The site below consisted of a six-foot-square hole that had been partitioned off into smaller squares. A couple of people were on their hands and knees around the trench, combing through it with small trowels and brushes. Beside that, a handful of students sifted through a pile of dirt that the bulldozer had scraped up; literally sifted, each using a box frame with a wire screen across the bottom, like a sieve.

We had almost reached the cleared area when the sound of an engine made us both stop and turn. A pickup had pulled in behind the SUV my sister had left in the middle of the gravel road, and if I were a whimsical person, I would say the truck gave a throaty diesel grunt of irritation as it backed up and cut across the grass.

It parked near the other trucks, where the ranch hands sat on the tailgates, some of them smoking, some watching the dig, nobody working. A sandy-haired man got out; he was dressed in the cowboy uniform—jeans, twill shirt, sleeves rolled up, T-shirt visible at the neck. His skin was tanned and weathered, making it hard to guess his age, but he seemed old enough to be Ben's dad. So curiosity kept me where I was.

Truck Guy strode up to Ben, looking harried. "Got a call that the fence needs repair out in the north quarter. If the bone folks are going to be digging here the rest of the day, I'll take these guys"—he nodded to the idlers by their trucks—"and get to work on it. No sense in their standing around here doing nothing."

Ben nodded, all businesslike. "Go on. The professor said they'd be done today, but I don't know what time. Fence has got to be fixed, and it'll take you an hour to get over there anyway."

The man, arms akimbo, glared at the river like it personally offended him. "And God knows we'll never get anyone to work late after last night. Hang that Goodnight woman and her stories. Making life difficult even while she's on the other side of the planet."

Two things I noted, standing there being ignored: Ben McCulloch seemed to be in charge, at least nominally, despite the difference in their ages. And I liked Truck Guy even less than I liked Ben McCulloch, who at least had the grace or good sense to look mighty chagrined right then.

Ben cleared his throat. Truck Guy's gaze flicked my way, and I realized he'd either just seen me, or dismissed me as one of the dig crew. I knew when he became aware of his mistake—boy, there must have been some kind of foot-in-mouth disease in the water—because he pulled a pair of sunglasses out of his pocket and put them on, hiding his expression.

Ben seemed to weigh his options, then realized he only had one. "Steve," he said without inflection, "this is Amy Goodnight. She and her sister are staying at the farm while Ms. Goodnight is away. Amy, Steve Sparks is our ranch manager."

Mr. Sparks weighed *his* options and settled on a nod, one hat tip short of a movie western gesture, and a formal "Miss Goodnight."

I responded in kind, with a chilly "Pleased to meet you, Mr. Sparks."

"You girls doing okay there at the farm?" The question surprised me until he added, lengthening his drawl with a measure of sarcasm, "Not having any trouble with ghosts, I hope."

"Just the usual amount of trouble," I answered, adding

85

an overly sweet, screw-you sort of smile. I was only obliged to be polite to my elders to a point.

With less awkwardness than you'd have thought, Ben shot *me* a look, then hurried his manager on his way. "Thanks, Steve. Get the fence done today, and hopefully we'll be able to go back to work here tomorrow. I'll call you after the university folks clear out."

"Sure thing." Sparks gave a tight nod to Ben, then to me, before heading toward the trucks. He didn't seem too happy with the dismissal, but I couldn't tell if it was because it came from someone so much younger than him, or because he'd been caught out looking like a jerk. I suspected it was the first thing. And that I might have been unfair in thinking Ben was the only one likely to tell Deputy Kelly he should pay Phin and me a call.

In any case, Sparks gave a sharp whistle and a circular, round-'em-up wave of his hand, and the loitering men pushed off their perches to join him.

I turned to Ben. "My. What a charming lot y'all are over here."

"Don't start, Amaryllis."

He crammed a lot of editorial about my family into my dreadful name, and I decided to give him the point. Pots, kettles, etc. Except that my family *was* charming. Literally, in some cases.

Besides, I had more important questions. The *Texas Monthly* article had said this place was big. But I hadn't considered the practical reality of that until Ben's comment about travel time. "It'll take an hour to get to the fence in the north quarter?"

He pulled his Stetson down a bit, hiding his expression, his bland tone an accusation. "It does when you have to go *way* out of your way to get across the river."

In other words, another old problem he was laying at Aunt Hyacinth's door. "It seems to me that you've needed a bridge for a while," I said, "and it's just bad luck you decided to build one on top of some poor soul's unmarked grave."

My own words gave me a moment's chill, but Ben didn't notice. "We offered to build a bridge at the Goodnight bend," he said, not chilly at all. Just the opposite. "Construction would have been much easier there. We would have paid the entire cost in exchange for access. But your aunt refused."

I didn't point out that if she didn't *need* a bridge, the offer wasn't as generous as all that. On the other hand, it did seem odd of Aunt Hyacinth to be so unneighborly. "I'm sure she had her reasons."

His biting glance let me know what he thought of those. "So this was already taking longer than it could have," he continued, "and that was *before* it turned into an episode of *Bone Detectives.*"

"Gosh," I said, "it's really disobliging of someone to be dead right where you want to build your bridge. Maybe this ghost everyone's talking about just wants to apologize for ruining your summer."

"There is no ghost. It's the crazy neighbors who stir up rumors about him who are making my life difficult."

I jabbed back, because there was that *word* again. "Must be annoying, having one thing you're not the boss of. Don't you have parents?"

His hesitation lasted a fraction of a second, but it was weighted and taut, and there was no missing the quick clench of his jaw before he tried to play tension off as annoyance. "Of course I have parents. Man, you're nosy."

He must be telling the truth. The magazine article had named his parents. But there was something *stricken* in that pause. Something that made me blurt out, without knowing why, "I'm sorry."

He stopped walking and looked at me, his gaze somehow confused and closed and wary at the same time, and I knew I'd hit a nerve. Not a fair target, either, but something deep and out of bounds. And I *was* sorry.

I waited for him to tell me to butt out of his personal business, his ranch business, to just butt out in general. Only, when his glance finally dropped from mine, what he said was "You're bleeding."

"What?"

"Your arm."

I bent it to look. A string of crimson droplets had oozed from where I'd scratched myself on the mesquite tree. The blood collected into an unimpressive trickle, and a lonely drop fell from my elbow and onto the earth, making a tiny spot in the limestone dust.

The blood sank quickly into the soil, looking like a rusty raindrop, turning the pale dirt to umber. It was nothing. Just a drop from a scratch that barely hurt anymore. There was no reason that my vision should sort of go cloudy and dim around the edges.

Only for a moment. Just long enough for the last

person I wanted to detect any weakness, to, well, detect weakness.

"Are you okay?" There was concern in his voice, and that, irrationally, annoyed me.

"Fine," I said, and scuffed the drop between us with my shoe, erasing the spot and mixing my blood into the dirt. But the movement put me off balance, and the landscape seemed to tilt to the left.

Ben grabbed my elbow, too close to the scratch, and the hot sting steadied me as much as his support. "Maybe you should sit down."

"No! Jeez, I'm fine."

"Uh-huh." His disbelief was obvious. "I see. You're one of *those* girls."

His tone put my back up and righted my world. I yanked my arm from his grasp. "I am *not* one of those girls." I was not fluttery *or* queasy. I'd gotten plenty banged up on the soccer field, and I was the one the family came to for patching in that gap between a Band-Aid and an ER visit. I mean, I was pre-med, for heaven's sake.

"Whatever you say." He raised his hands, and I saw, mixed with the dust and dirt there, some of my blood, too.

"Hang on," I said, before he could move. "Someone's going to think we've been sparring with more than words." Rummaging in my bag, through the mostly empty water bottle, a tube of sunscreen, and lip balm, I found what I wanted. The small plastic bottle had a Goodnight Farm label on it, and when I popped the lid open with my thumb, Ben backed up a step.

"What is that?" he asked, with a mix of snark and genuine suspicion. "Some kind of potion?"

I held it so he could read the label for himself. "Antibacterial gel. Mostly alcohol, lavender, and tea tree oil."

"Mostly?"

"Stop being such a baby." I gestured for him to put out his hand so I could squirt the stuff onto it.

"Trust me," he said, "I work cows and ride horses. A little blood is not the most disgusting thing I get on my hands."

"But it's human." I suspected he was being stubborn on principle. "Do you want to get some kind of disease?"

His brow lifted. "Do you *have* some kind of disease?"

"No! Of course not." I grabbed his wrist and pulled him a step toward me, upending the bottle with a squeeze. A huge glob of gel squelched out and plopped onto his hand, complete with disgusting sound effects. Very classy.

His fingers were dirty, and the dirt mixed with the gel as I rubbed it on, since he just stood there, stiff and bemused. The extra—and there was plenty—covered my hands, and some of it dripped onto the ground, too. We were standing close, and the alcohol was cool in contrast to his skin, which seemed very hot under my fingers. Cool and bracing, the sharp smell mixed with the strong scent of lavender floating up and filling my head.

The smell slowed my brisk motion, and I stared at my fingers. At the dirt—*McCulloch* dirt—mixed with that drop of my blood and the herb that Aunt Hy included because it had antibacterial properties and smelled good, but had some other purpose, I was sure. More sure by the moment.

Because the fizz of curiosity I'd felt all morning had turned to funny, queasy bubbles in my stomach.

That couldn't be good. Even though it didn't feel very bad at all.

Ben cleared his throat, and I realized I was still holding his hand. I let go quickly, but caught his studying gaze as he shook his fingers dry. I wondered if he'd felt something, too, but then he asked, exaggerating his central Texas drawl, "How is it you got left in charge of the farm, again? Because picking you isn't exactly convincing me of your aunt's stability."

The languor of the moment snapped. "I'm actually the responsible one," I said, in something surprisingly like a normal voice.

"Yeah," he drew out the word, but I couldn't tell if he was being ironic or not. "I can see that."

I dropped the hand gel into my bag, jerked closed the drawstring, and slung it over my shoulder, pretending I hadn't been affected *at all* by holding his hand. Or whatever the hell had just happened. "Let's go."

Near the excavation was the canopy I'd seen from the hill, where Phin and Mark were already chatting with an academic-type woman. I glanced at my watch and hoped I hadn't missed too much. It felt like Ben and I had talked for an hour, but it had been a matter of minutes.

"Where have you been?" Phin asked when Ben and I stepped into the shade.

"I had to tie up the dogs," I said, hoping no one had

...uced the hand-holding in the middle of the field. I was grateful the men who'd been sitting around on their tailgates had piled into the cabs and followed Mr. Sparks off to the north quarter, or wherever they were going.

"And the ranch manager had to talk to me," Ben added.

The older woman standing by Mark gave Ben an arch look, somehow annoyed and amused at the same time. "I told him yesterday. We'll be done when we're done."

Ben kept his expression almost neutral, but I was getting a lot of experience with the varieties of his annoyance and the barometric pitch of his eyebrows. "Any idea when that would be, Doctor?"

She smiled slightly, relenting in her torture. Her face was austerely handsome, with sculpted bone structure and an olive complexion that had seen a lot of sun. Her hair, dark brown shot with gray, was braided back, and her clothes—cargo khakis, hiking boots, denim shirt—were worn and practical. "We should be out of your hair by the end of the day, and you can put your bulldozer back to work in the morning."

Ben's rueful smile acknowledged his impatience. "Thank you, Dr. Douglas. I realize you have to be systematic."

"Well, yes." She looked from Phin to me with slightly vexed humor. "Of course, when we actually finish will depend on how many more visitors Mark has invited to drop by."

I grimaced, aware that the students were barely working, distracted by Phin and me. Or possibly Ben, I amended as I caught the direction of one girl's gaze. She caught me catching her, and grinned—sort of conspiratorial, sort of sheepish—

before returning to her work. She was crouching in the pit that had everyone's attention, and the back view of Ben McCulloch's Wranglers was likely hard to resist from that vantage point.

Mark made good-natured excuses to the professor. "I just figured since Phin and Amy were UT students, and their place is spitting distance from here . . ."

"And Amy is a huge fan of the Discovery Channel," said Ben, in a taunting monotone.

Dr. Douglas took that at face value, missing my glare at Ben. "All right," she said. "Since they're friends of the McCullochs."

My glance turned wary, but Ben merely hooked his thumbs in the pockets of his jeans and hung back, letting the assumption stand. I supposed if he'd really wanted us gone, he would have sent us packing already.

"What's going on here?" I asked, gesturing to the work-tables, where a girl was numbering a glass jar that looked like it held—but I very much hoped didn't—some kind of huge black hairy spider.

Dr. Douglas gestured for Mark to explain. "Jennie is tagging and cataloging any artifacts we find among the bones."

Phin leaned in closer. "Is that fabric?"

The girl—Jennie—answered, "It is. We won't know exactly what kind until it gets back to the lab. But it's very old."

I could see it now, a tattered scrap, the thick threads hardened and fragile. Phin asked, "Old like your grandmother, or old like the Texas Revolution?"

"Well, there's a lot that affects that." Jennie seemed to take the interrogation in stride. She didn't look much older than us, with a round, amiable face, and light brown hair worn in two braids that didn't really flatter her. "Soil, climate, moisture. We'll test it back in Austin."

Phin gave one of her ambiguous "hmmm's," as if she was contemplating what tests she would do, given a chance. It occurred to me I'd better keep an eye on her hands and her pockets.

"Check this out," said Mark, picking up a labeled box and holding it so I could peer in.

"An arrowhead?" It came out as a question, even though the shape of the stone was unmistakable.

"Yep. This type was used by Native Americans in the area around two hundred years ago."

"Could it have killed our guy?" I asked.

"No way to be sure, but we might find something when we examine the bones—"

"In the lab." Phin parroted their usual response, and Mark chuckled. Dr. Douglas did not.

"What about the age of the skeleton?" I spoke a little too quickly, to divert attention from my sister. "Can you guesstimate if it's as old as the arrowhead?"

"I'm not one for guessing," said the professor. "I'm only sure it's been here for well over a hundred years. We can tell from the roots of the vegetation that has grown around the interment. Come and look."

She led us to the edge of the excavated plot. The bulldozer loomed over us; the two students shifting the soil there slowed their work to watch us approach.

Mark pointed to the students and their wire-bottomed wood trays. "That's Dwayne and Lucas. They're going through the soil that the dozer turned up, to find any other bone fragments or artifacts it may have uncovered. But Caitlin and Emery have been excavating the grave itself."

Caitlin was the girl I'd caught appreciating Ben's Wranglers. Her hair was pulled up and through the back of her dark red baseball cap, and a trickle of sweat ran down her neck as she worked. She and the skinny guy working with her had dug down maybe two feet; the clay topsoil was only about that deep before you hit stony ground. That was why the area was good for growing grapes and herbs and grazing cattle, and not much else.

Dr. Douglas pointed to a lantana shrub, half ripped out of the hole in the ground—by the bulldozer, I was guessing. "The roots were growing through the skeleton's ribs," said the professor. "The students have been working around them to extract the bones carefully."

Caitlin was uncovering a row of vertebrae from the soil with a stiff-bristled brush. They didn't gleam white and clean like the skeletons I'd seen in museums, and it was unsettling, seeing the unmistakable shape of the spine emerging from the dirt.

"How much of the skeleton have you found?" I asked.

Mark took over the explanation. "Shallow burials, a lot of times you don't get much. Animals and the elements can unearth and scatter the remains."

Phin was uninterested in delicate phrasing. "You mean scavengers drag off pieces to eat."

Dr. Douglas tutted. "We try and give the remains some dignity. It was once a person, after all."

I gazed at the vertebrae, tumbled like a stack of blocks,

and wondered if there was any remnant of human energy clinging to this spot, to these remains. Maybe it was some Jungian resonance, the aversion of the collective consciousness to reminders of death, that raised the hair on the back of my neck. Maybe it was something else.

I had been trying to avoid thinking about the apparition in my room, but the more I tried, the more the knot of dread, the one that hadn't quite untied itself since last night, kinked and twisted in my chest. "Do you have any idea who it might be, or how he died?" I asked.

"Unless there's damage to the bones," answered Dr. Douglas, "it's impossible to tell the cause of death. And after so long in the ground, it's very difficult to tell at what point the damage occurred."

"The poor guy had a bulldozer driven over him," said Mark.

Dr. Douglas shook her head in sad disapproval. "Such a shame."

Ben gave a suffering sigh, as if he'd heard this before. "It isn't as if we knew he was there."

"That's true," said the professor, though she still sounded like a disappointed parent. "It couldn't be helped, I suppose."

Mark, better at staying on the subject, told me, "Back at school we'll analyze those shreds of cloth we found, find out what kind of fabric it was. That might give us some clues."

"Can you tell from the skull if he was Anglo or Hispanic or Native American?" asked Phin, and I wondered what *she* was thinking.

"Yes," said Dr. Douglas. "Though we do those measurements back in the lab or the morgue."

Phin sighed pointedly at the now familiar response. Dr. Douglas's eyes narrowed, like Phin was topping her list of Students to Flunk If I Get the Chance. I had to admit, some things did look a little more exciting, or at least more timely, on TV.

The professor went on to say, as if offering a huge favor, "I did measure the femur that Mark found, and it indicated this man was rather small of stature. Five foot two or so. Which points to an older origin. Modern nutrition has raised the average height substantially in the last centuries."

The bones looked so lonely there in the hole. I wondered if, after they arranged all the pieces in the cold, sterile lab, that would be any better a resting place than the warm Texas earth. Who had this been? An immigrant, or a settler? A Native American? Centuries, plural, was a big time frame.

A familiar noise infiltrated my deep thoughts, bringing me back to the twenty-first century. I realized Bear was barking. And so was Sadie, raising a raucous canine alert.

"What on earth . . . ?" began Dr. Douglas.

"Sorry," I said, already moving around the excavated pit, intent on settling them down. But I bumped into Ben, then careened off of Mark. We pinballed like the Three Stooges, *all* intent on getting to the dogs. I froze in horror as we sorted ourselves out and I saw why.

Lila wasn't barking with the others. She was too busy making her own canine excavation, dirt flying around her as she dug, while Bear and Sadie encouraged her.

Oh hell.

I untangled myself from Ben and Mark and started running, too fast to sort out the sensations in my gut—anger at the dogs, worry they'd get us kicked off the property, and something else. Some tug at my vitals that I couldn't explain, except it spurred me on so that I had no trouble keeping up with the guys.

"Lila, stop!" I shouted, to no visible effect. "Leave it!" I tried again, in a less panicked, more alpha-dog voice. This time she obeyed, stepping back and sitting primly at the end of the leash, still tied to the mesquite tree. She grinned at us as we reached her, muzzle and paws covered with dirt, proud of her accomplishment.

The four of us—Ben, Mark, me, and the dog—stared at the hole while the others hurried up the hill.

"It's probably a rabbit," said Mark, but his tone implied he hoped for something more grisly.

It's not a rabbit.

It wasn't just the sprint making my heart pound. Adrenaline flagged, leaving something different, a kind of ringing excitement vibrating through me. I'd never been sensitive, let alone psychic, but just then I had a *hunch* like you would not believe.

Dropping to my knees, I examined the hole that Lila had made, maybe a foot deep in the crumbly gray-black earth. There was something smooth at the bottom. I could see a tantalizing silver-dollar-sized bit of it.

I thrust my fingers into the dirt and pulled out two handfuls of soil, dropping them to the side. Quickly I widened the conical hole, uncovering a curve of bone that became a dome, then became something unmistakable.

"Here." Mark handed me a brush like I'd seen Caitlin using on the bones in the excavation by the bulldozer. "Use this."

"Thanks." I took it and shifted to lie on my stomach. Mark took a mirror position, pulling the dirt away when it kept falling back into the hole, as if the earth didn't want to give up what we'd found.

Through a kind of buzzing drone, I was aware of the others around us. I could hear the dogs whining and see Phin's shoes next to several pairs I didn't recognize. They stayed back—the hole was only big enough for four hands.

A sweep of the brush revealed the forehead—the frontal bone, I amended with a tiny shiver, realizing what I was seeing. AP biology had come in handy sooner than I'd thought.

"Careful, now." Dr. Douglas's voice was patient and professorial, but there was an undercurrent of anticipation that told me—if I hadn't already guessed from the dome shape and slightly porous texture—that there was something *important* under my fingers. "Don't try and uncover the whole thing. Without the support of the surrounding earth, it may come apart."

I nodded, somehow unwilling to speak and break the spell of discovery. As she had instructed, I left the dirt supporting the back of the skull—the occipital bone—and concentrated on the front. The nasal bone, the brow ridges, the cheekbones and maxilla. The things that had made it a face. Even if I hadn't remembered the names of the bones, their shapes were iconic, the stuff of nightmare and mortality, and in the heat of the day, I felt a graveyard chill.

Gently I smoothed the dirt from the eye sockets with my thumbs and wondered what was the last thing this person had seen. The relentless drowning wave of a flood? The snake that had bit him? Did he stare his *own* mortality in the face before he died?

Another shiver gripped me, and I pressed my hands against the cold dirt to hide their trembling. There was no ignoring the similarity between the empty eyes of the skull and the hollow, dark gaze of my midnight visitor, the apparition I could still see when I blinked, like the afterimage of a flame.

9

I couldn't seem to get completely warm, which on a Texas afternoon in July was saying something.

Once I'd uncovered a good bit of the skull, Dr. Douglas had instructed us all to stand back while she called the sheriff. Apparently they liked you to do that when you found human remains, even old ones. As they waited for the authorities, Mark and the others swarmed over the ground like excited ants, measuring distances from the original find to the new one, diagramming, making notes.

The most useful thing I could do, according to Dr. Douglas, was keep out of the way. But I couldn't leave, either, in case the authorities wanted to talk to me. I was sure Deputy Kelly would be just as thrilled to see me as I was to see him again so soon.

So I sat at the top of the rise in the shade of a live oak tree, feeling as unnecessary as a pair of swim fins on a catfish. The dogs sprawled sleeping, and Phin was writing a to-do list on her arm—a habit that even our ultra-accepting mother hated. As I watched the others work, my mind spun in restless, uneasy circles. I envied them all—the dogs' peace and the students' uncomplicated excitement, and even my sister's ability to organize her thoughts and make a plan. Though I knew that last one would probably bite me in the ass later.

Her list was getting long. "I would love to take EMF measurements at that spot to see if there was some kind of subliminal stimulus that you and Lila sensed. It's too random that you tied her up right on top of a skeleton."

"Depends on the skeleton-to-square-foot ratio, I'd think."

My own words jarred me. I'd only meant to mock her scientific tone, but the image took hold and another chill seemed to come up from the ground, leeching my warmth. "If there are remains all over this field," I said more cautiously, "wouldn't it be much less coincidental that I'd left Lila where there was something to find?"

I could see Phin put my first and second comments together and total them up with growing excitement. "I hadn't considered a whole *field* of bones. We have *got* to come back here with the coronal aura visualizer."

Funny how she and I had completely opposite reactions to the idea of the ground being full of human remains.

"I hate to rain on your phantom parade," I said, "but I can't imagine that the McCulloch Ranch is going to give you permission to do that." Especially not if the rest of the family shared the ranch manager's opinions of the Goodnights.

Phin was undeterred. "Maybe you can talk your boyfriend into letting us."

"He's not my boyfriend," I snapped. And then regretted it, because I hadn't even asked whom she meant. God, I was transparent.

"Uh-huh," said Phin. "So, you *weren't* holding hands earlier?"

It figured. She never noticed interpersonal details except when it was inconvenient to me. "Not like that."

At least it was refreshing to squabble about someone who wasn't dead. I glanced across to where Ben McCulloch paced while talking on his cell phone. The slope of the hill, from the end of the gravel road down to the bulldozer and future bridge, was about the size of a baseball diamond. The two excavations—the first one near the river, and the second hole that Lila had started—made home and second base. Ben and I were roughly first and third, as far as possible from each other.

As if he felt me watching him, he turned my way. Even from that distance, I could see the furrows of his frown deepen, all the more intimidating with his eyes hidden by his sunglasses.

"Boy," said Phin. "If he was that guy in the X-Men, you'd be a scorch mark on the sand."

"Thanks," I drawled, but I didn't disagree.

"He must like you a lot to hate you so much right now."

I swiveled to stare at her. "For someone majoring in chemistry, you don't have much of a grasp on the metaphorical kind."

She clicked her pen and started another note on her arm. "There is no such thing as metaphorical chemistry, if you mean between two people. Pheromones are chemicals, too."

So was kitchen witchery, or so Phin had always insisted. I found myself rubbing my fingers, smelling lavender and dirt and thinking about warm skin and, well, chemistry. "Just out of curiosity . . . what would you use lavender for, magically speaking?"

Her pen didn't pause. "Attraction and love spells."

I wheezed like she'd punched me. "Are you serious, or are you jacking with me?" With Phin's deadpan delivery, I could never tell.

In this case she looked seriously affronted. "I never jack around about magic. What did you do?"

She listened as I quickly explained the incident with the dirt and my scratch and the hand gel. Right as I finished, Ben hung up his phone, scowled up at us for a long moment, then turned deliberately away. "Well," she said thoughtfully, "pheromones aside, I think we can safely rule out the possibility that you made him infatuated with you."

"Ha, ha," I said, hiding the fact that, against all reason, his angry dismissal still stung. "Obviously."

"Well, I *am* joking this time. Love spells are false advertising. You could heighten sexual tension or the euphoria of infatuation, but you can't make someone attracted to you against their will." She considered for a beat, then amended, "Well, maybe *I* could, but certainly not by accident."

I figured that piece of arrogance was better left unchallenged, in case she decided to prove it. "But the . . . whatever happened, if anything did . . . it wouldn't have had anything to do with finding that skull, right?"

Phin's long, speculative look worried me, like she might be concocting some kind of experiment. "Maybe it's not about him, but the dirt. Some people use lavender to attract prophetic dreams. Maybe you've given yourself some kind of visionary connection to the land."

Her casual tone conflicted with the uncurling anxiety inside of me. "But I tied up the dogs in that particular place *before* the hand-holding happened."

"Yes, but I saw your face when you looked into that hole. We all did. You knew something was there."

Despite the dappled shade of the tree, the river running in a soothing hush, the students chatting excitedly about their find—all that, and still a cool finger of apprehension slid down my spine.

"Or," said Phin cheerfully, in a jarring change of mood, "you may just be attracted to him. I understand that people *do* get light-headed under such circumstances."

The one thing I *didn't* need? My sister the mad scientist explaining human attraction to me.

A plume of dust from behind the hill heralded the arrival of the law. It was sad that I viewed that as a fortunate thing.

Dr. Douglas was under the work canopy, alternately talking on the phone, texting, and giving orders to the students through Mark and Caitlin. But as the Blazer pulled up next to the university van, the professor keyed off her Black-Berry and put it in the pocket of her cargo pants.

From our hillside lookout, Phin and I watched as she, Ben, and Deputy Kelly—his stocky frame was easily recognizable—met and walked together to the new hole. The dogs pricked their ears at the activity. So did I, wishing I could hear what the cabal was saying. I gathered from the way the students hung back it was grown-ups only—Ben's age notwithstanding.

I was so intent on the meeting that I jerked in surprise when a shadow fell across me. I looked up, squinting, and Phin did the same, shading her eyes with her hand.

Mark grinned down at us, the sun behind him. "What are you doing?" He nodded to the writing on Phin's arm. "Experimenting in tattoo art?"

"Hardly," she said, and stuck her pen into her ponytail. "Are you done measuring the field like a dressmaker?"

The analogy made him chuckle, and echo, "Hardly." He joined us on the ground with a little exhale of relief. "Feels good to sit for a minute."

"So, what happens now?" I asked. "Will you get to dig out the skull today?"

"Probably, so we can preserve it. Then the deputy has to file his report, and hopefully we'll get to excavate for the rest of the remains tomorrow. It's pretty obvious this isn't a recent burial."

I knew what he meant. Everything about the skull had seemed old and entrenched. "Is it the same age as the other one?"

"We'll have to get it back to the lab to make sure," he said. Phin snorted at the predictable answer, and Mark laughed in rueful acknowledgment. "But if they *are* related, it *could* be an exciting find. Seriously, we owe you a drink, Amy. You and Phin need to come out with us tonight to celebrate."

I'd missed the significance of the students' glee when Dr. Douglas had confirmed I'd uncovered a separate interment. But now, considering what I'd said to Phin about the skeleton-to-square-foot ratio, I thought I understood. "Do you mean there could be more bones and artifacts here?"

"There could be a *treasure trove* of artifacts here." He said it with such anticipation, some of my surprise must have shown, because he laughed. "Not literally. That only happens in the movies."

Phin had to show off a bit. "I heard that fossils and archaeological finds can go for millions of dollars."

"Yes," said Mark, "but we're not talking *Australopithecus.* This is a modern skull."

"But—" I started. That couldn't be right. The bone had *felt* old. Literally and in some way I couldn't quite define. "You said it wasn't recent. And Dr. Douglas said the site by the river had been here maybe a century or two."

He grinned. " 'Modern' on an evolutionary scale. As in 'less than half a million years old.' "

"Oh," I said, embarrassed because I should have known that. They *did* teach evolution in Texas public schools.

"It might still be prehistoric, though," said Mark. "If this turns out to be a mass burial of some kind, the value will be in information."

My gaze roamed over the sloped baseball diamond that Mark and his crew had staked out. It looked so normal. Dry, dusty soil. Crispy summer grass. "What do you mean by 'mass burial'? A graveyard?"

"Maybe," said Mark. "A Native American site or pioneer cemetery that was washed out at some point. But with the shallow interment, maybe a battle or massacre site."

Massacre. The word gave me a jolt, and horrible, history-textbook images flooded my mind. "Like some kind of killing field?"

He hurried to reassure me, as if the atrocity I imagined showed on my face. "Very unlikely. More likely an undocumented skirmish during the Texas Revolution, or something earlier, from the colonial days. The Apache and Comanche weren't entirely keen on being Christianized."

"You mean by the Spanish missionaries."

"Well, you know about San Sabá, right?" He nodded vaguely westward, as if we could see that far into the next county. "The mission was attacked by the Native Americans. Possibly egged on by the French, who wanted to expand from Louisiana. Anyway—they destroyed the mission. It was lost for hundreds of years, but a team from Texas Tech excavated the site in the nineties."

He sounded like a kid talking about Santa Claus, like he was envisioning something like the San Sabá find here. He was all but rubbing his hands together in anticipation.

"Where would you start with an excavation like that?" Phin asked.

Mark's eyes lit up with expository glee. Phin looked like that whenever she started talking gadgets. Though I was more interested in these details than I was in coronal aural whatsits, the talk of surveying the field, marking out a grid, digging test holes and trenches before a systematic, layer-by-layer dig . . . it sort of faded out as I warily watched my sister's face.

She wore an expression that too often preceded burnt fuses and chemistry lab evacuations. "That doesn't seem very efficient," she told Mark when he was done. "I wonder if my coronal aura visualizer might help."

"Phin!" I barked, because we had an agreement. All right, maybe less of an agreement and more of me haranguing her not to talk about these things in public and her placating me, at least when I was around to know about it.

"What?" she asked, seeming genuinely guileless. "It might pick up disturbances under the ground where there's vegetation. And *he* already has permission to be here."

Mark looked from one of us to the other. "What's a coronal aura visualizer?"

The crunch of boot heels on limestone interrupted Phin's answer. But my relief was short-lived. Ben McCulloch stopped on the hill so that he was level with us as we sat. He surveyed the three of us—six, counting the dogs—and ended with me. "Deputy Kelly wants to talk to you."

I sighed and pushed to my feet. "This should be fun."

Ben offered me a hand, but I pretended I didn't see it. After the last time we'd held hands, I wasn't risking any more weirdness. We walked down the hill to where the officer waited with Dr. Douglas.

In the daylight, without the distraction of a recent near-ghost experience, I could see that, allowing for years of sun through the patrol car window and squinting behind his mirrored sunglasses, Deputy Kelly was probably about my dad's age. And I'd called it right; he did *not* look happy to see me.

"Miss Goodnight. Fancy meeting you here."

"Good afternoon, Deputy," I said very politely, aware of Ben standing to one side and Dr. Douglas with her arms folded, drumming her fingers on her sleeve.

The deputy poised his pen over his notepad. "I just want to get your statement for my report. Your first name is Amy?"

I sighed. "My legal name is Amaryllis."

The deputy glanced up from the paper. "That's a new one on me. Could you spell that, please?" I did, used to the question. "And your sister's name?" he asked.

"Delphinium," I said tightly, ignoring the twitch of Ben McCulloch's smirk. *"D-e-l-p-h-i-n-i-u-m."*

Kelly wrote it down, along with my last name, my age, and my permanent address, while Dr. Douglas radiated impatience. I would have suspected the deputy of illiteracy, except I got the feeling he was taking his time in order to irritate the professor. Finally he finished writing and looked up at me; I was mirrored in his sunglasses, my hair dusty, my nose rather pink. "So . . . what were y'all doing here at the dig? Just out for a stroll?"

"As it happens," I said with some satisfaction, "the professor's assistant was nice enough to invite us, and Dr. Douglas was showing us around."

The deputy glanced at Mark and Phin, their heads bent together as Mark laughingly studied the to-do list on my sister's arm. "I see," said Kelly, setting my teeth on edge. He sounded professional on the surface, but contempt seeped out from beneath. "And how did you come to find the remains? Ouija board? Spirit guide, maybe?"

I couldn't seem to make myself answer. Maybe I was afraid of what I'd say if I let myself speak. Aunt Iris had often counseled me to imagine myself as a duck, to visualize scornful comments rolling off my back like rain. I felt more like a bristling hedgehog, all tight in my middle, wanting to roll up in a ball—not just to protect my soft parts, but to stick him with some pointy spines, too.

Deputy Wolverine reminded me of too many jackasses I'd had to deal with after Phin and her magic charm had left our high school. The "Do you want to play with my magic wand?" jokers. Worse, with his badge and his uniform, it wasn't just anger that tied my tongue in knots, but fear. Nameless, formless fear of what people in authority could do if you marched too conspicuously to a different drum.

"It was the dog," said Ben. I glanced at him, startled by his help, and found him staring at Deputy Kelly with ill-disguised dislike. Then Ben looked at me, met my eyes without much softening in his. "Didn't you tell me she was a search dog, Amy?"

Speak, Amy.

"Uh, yes." I shook off my surprise and turned back to the deputy. "Lila found them. I just cleared away the dirt."

Kelly narrowed his eyes. He wasn't stupid, and he probably hadn't missed any of that exchange. "I've worked with Ms. Hyacinth and Lila once or twice. I thought that dog was only trained for SAR, not HRD."

Dr. Douglas interrupted, outraged. "You brought a Human Remains Detection dog to my dig site?"

I raised my hands, frantically warding off her anger. "I didn't know!"

With an exasperated huff, she turned to the deputy. "Well," she snapped. "I think that settles it. Unless you'd like to interview the dog."

Deputy Kelly seemed satisfied that fate had decided to punish me for hopping the McCulloch fence after he'd tacitly warned me not to. He pocketed his pen and notepad and made a show of checking his watch. "I'll just head into the office to file this report. I imagine it'll take me the rest of the afternoon. We're kind of backed up."

Dr. Douglas visibly bit down on her impatience. If they couldn't dig on the new site until the paperwork was done, then Kelly's taking his own sweet time about it was seriously passive-aggressive. I wondered what the professor had done to piss him off. Or maybe he just hated academics on principle.

With a tight smile, Dr. Douglas said, "Of course. We'll be ready to excavate when you give the all clear. I know the sheriff won't want to waste time when it comes to human remains."

Point to the professor. Deputy Kelly pursed his lips and nodded to her, then to Ben. "I'll be in touch."

He headed toward the Blazer, his khaki uniform blending in with the terrain. As soon as he was gone, I turned to Dr. Douglas and groveled, "I'm *so* sorry about Lila. I only knew about the search and rescue, not the . . . um, other part."

The professor waved my apology away. Her demeanor

had unbent as soon as the deputy left. "It got Deputy Kelly on his way."

"Then you're not angry?"

Okay, maybe she hadn't softened entirely. "I would have been if the artifact had been destroyed."

Mark and Phin had joined us, leaving the dogs in the shade. Caitlin had jogged up from the riverside site, too. "No work on the new grave today?" she asked.

"Only the preservation of the remains already uncovered," Dr. Douglas told her, then addressed the rest of the crew gathering around. "Mark, you remove that skull. Take Emery, too. Do your best to keep it intact." She pulled her phone from her cargo pocket and started a text. I tried to imagine Indiana Jones with a BlackBerry and failed. "Caitlin, you're in charge at Site A. Get that excavation wrapped up, and you and Jennie pack up those artifacts for transport to Austin."

"On it, Dr. D," Caitlin said, with a jaunty swish of her ponytail. She chucked me on the shoulder before she left. "Nicely spotted on that skull. We may recruit you."

"Lila found it," I said, for the fifteenth time, but Caitlin was already gone. A fast mover, that one.

"You two," Dr. Douglas said to Phin and me, then paused, as if considering her words. I suspected they were between "Get lost," and "Take a hike." But she surprised me. "Mark seems to think you've earned some adjunct status, so you can hang around, as long as you don't touch anything unless he tells you it's okay. But the dogs have to go."

With that, she headed to the river. Ben watched her go,

then exhaled—half sigh, half exasperation—and tugged his hat down to shade his eyes. "I'd better update my folks. Let them know what the Goodnights have dug up this time."

"I didn't know about the dog!" I protested. Again.

He looked at me, more inscrutable than usual. "You have your own nose for trouble, Amaryllis. You don't need a dog."

Later, when it would do me no good, I would think of a response to that. But just then I was blank.

Still stewing over a killer comeback, I watched him walk toward his truck. He was parked near the UT van, and Caitlin, who hadn't quite gotten to work yet, stopped him to chat. They were too far for me to hear their conversation, and I wouldn't say she was flirting—she didn't seem like a flirter—but as they spoke Ben's scowl unknotted a little. Not as far as to become *relaxed,* but, well, he didn't look like he wanted *her* to go jump in the river.

I had a sudden thought. The bones I found meant an even longer delay in building the bridge. The McCullochs might have to find a new location entirely. Even if they had legal grounds to stop the excavation, that seemed extremely mean-spirited (so to speak). Ben couldn't get mad at dead people, and that left me and my family.

And the dog. Lila was trained to scent for people lost in the hills and in the caves. Even in rubble. I didn't think she was trained to pick out remains, though. Just the living. Did it mean anything that Lila had alerted to the skull? Ghosts, bones, *rumors* of ghosts . . . each kept rising to the surface of my mind, then slipping back under, like beans in a boiling pot of soup.

The revving of a truck engine shook me out of my thoughts, and I realized I was frowning at an empty spot of land, as Ben and Caitlin had gone their separate ways.

I needed to go, too, for completely practical reasons, and I interrupted Phin's conversation with Mark to tell her so. "We should get the dogs home. And I have to feed the goats."

She fished the truck key from her pocket and handed it over. "Take the Trooper. We're going to the roadhouse out on Highway 287 later. I'll text you when we head over there."

"Will you really?" I asked, because her anti-phone tendencies went both ways: incoming and outgoing.

"I'll remind her," Mark said. While he seemed an agreeable guy in general, I got the feeling his quick offer might have had more to do with Phin herself. She, of course, seemed oblivious, and I couldn't decide how I felt about that. Her cluelessness made me feel older and protective, but I liked Mark, and . . . well, what grounds did I have to say anything?

The sleepless night, the emotional excesses and tossing and turning, heaped on top of finding a body, or at least part of one, all settled on my shoulders as soon as I loaded the dogs into the Trooper. They were happy to be headed home, and I drove back to Goodnight Farm in a fog of thought and with a vague hope that I would get back to a goat- and ghost-free yard.

I arrived to find an old man sitting on the porch, boots up on the railing like he owned the place.

10

"**O**ld man" implies someone frail and elderly, but the guy sitting on one of the rockers under the lazily turning fan was not. Oh, his tanned skin was lined with age, and I could tell he was lean and rangy, but his back was unbent and his white hair was thick, though it had been creased by the Stetson resting on his knee.

It didn't occur to me to worry. For one thing, he looked utterly at ease within the boundaries of the Goodnight Security System. For another, the second chair rocked along in a companionable rhythm, like Uncle Burt was keeping him company. Just two old guys hanging out on the porch.

The man stood as I climbed out of the SUV. He moved like he had logged long hours in the saddle over his seventy or so years. Old-school cowboy.

"Hyacinth?" he called.

Maybe he didn't see very well. "I'm Amy," I yelled back as I let the dogs out of the Trooper. They ran to the gate; I had to wade through their wagging tails to get to the latch and let us all into the yard, where they rushed to greet the visitor with wags and wet noses.

"Aunt Hyacinth is in China," I said, walking up the path. "Well, the China Sea."

The stranger scratched the dogs' ears for a moment more, then said, "That's too bad. I came to talk to her about this damned ghost business and find out what the hell she's going to do about it."

Well, *that* was unexpected, when everyone I'd met seemed to vilify my aunt for "this damned ghost business." I wasn't sure it was a good change, since I was so determined to stay *out* of it.

I'd have to choose my words carefully. He could be the town kook (after Aunt Hy, of course) or he could be a respected founding father of Barnett. Either way, it wouldn't do to make him mad.

"Would you like a glass of water or something, Mr. . . ." He just looked at me and didn't supply his name. "You must have walked quite a ways."

"Oh, I rode my horse." He nodded toward the donkey pen. "I put him in there. Usually do when I come to visit Burt and his little lady."

"Uh . . ." I didn't know how to answer that. Goodnights

117

would talk to anyone about the paranormal, but I wasn't used to people talking about it back. Maybe in Mom's store, but aside from the regulars, most of her business was in pretty stationery and fairy figurines. So I just said, "Great. How about that drink. Water? Lemonade? Iced tea?"

"Some tea would be mighty fine." He eased back into the chair, and the dogs settled around him, careful to keep their tails away from the rocker. "Family won't let me have it at home. Caffeine." He tapped his chest. "Bad for the ticker. Like I care. When I go, I go."

"Uh-huh." Not on my porch if I could help it. I went inside and brewed a pot of herbal tea, caffeine free, and poured it over ice.

When I came back out and set the glass on the table beside him, I reintroduced myself. "I'm Amy. Hyacinth's niece."

"I heard you the first time," he snapped. "I'm not deaf."

"Yes," I said calmly, "but you didn't tell me who *you* are."

He looked at me as if I should know *exactly* who he was. And between the grumpy and the Stetson, I was beginning to get an idea. So I wasn't completely surprised when he said, "I'm Mac McCulloch. Now, what are you going to do about this Mad Monk character, missy?"

It was all a little much to take in standing up, so I sat down, hoping Uncle Burt had vacated the other rocker. "I'm sorry. Did you say *'Mad Monk'*?"

I did not want to invite this conversation. I did *not* want to get involved in a ghost hunt. But I *had* to ask. *Mad Monk,* for crying out loud.

"Don't look at me," crabbed Mac McCulloch. "I didn't make up that fool name. That was that woman. Came around asking questions, writing a book or some nonsense." He shook the ice in his glass at me. "Don't ever trust anyone who's writing a book. They make up lies for a living."

"Yes, sir." I agreed just so I could stay on the subject. "So the lady who came here, asking about ghost stories . . . she invented the Mad Monk?"

"Oh no. She only named it. 'The Mad Monk of McCulloch Ranch.' Pah! I should sue her."

"So should the ghost," I said. "Saddled with a name like that, no wonder he haunts."

"Ha!" He slapped a hand on his knee. "I like you, Hyacinth, even if you do talk like a city girl."

"It's Amy," I corrected, but still felt flattered to be liked by this odd, cranky man.

Ben's grandfather. Holy smokes. It had to be. Just when I'd thought my day couldn't get any weirder.

"That's what I said. Amy." Mr. McCulloch took a sip of the tea, let out an appreciative smack and a sigh, and set down the glass. "No, the ghost is real. Bastard pops up every now and again, makes everyone crazy for a while, bashes a few people on the head, settles back down."

"Bashes people on the head? Like your ranch hand last night?"

"Damned straight."

"That seems rather violent for a man of the cloth." But as I said it, I remembered how hard it was to breathe while I stared at the ghostly column, how the cold had seemed to constrict my chest.

"Some people say he's a soldier. Maybe one of those priest-soldier types who came up from Mexico back when it belonged to Spain."

I thought about the conversation with Mark at the excavation site. "You mean a conquistador? Or a missionary?"

He flapped a hand, batting away these inconsequentials. "It doesn't matter. He bashes people because he's protecting a treasure. Everyone around here knows this story. Hyacinth should have told you."

I sat back in my chair and breathed the hot afternoon air, letting it fill my lungs and chase away the remembered cold. "Yes, she really should have. She was more worried about her livestock, I think."

"Well, that doesn't sound like Hyacinth at all." He was right about that. "She'd agree that something has to be done before any more people get hurt."

"Who else has gotten hurt, other than your ranch hand?"

"Well, there were those idiot Kelly boys."

"As in Deputy Kelly?" That guy did keep popping up. I wouldn't have described him as a boy, but I wasn't seventy-odd years old, either.

"Him and his idiot brother," said Mr. McCulloch. "Or maybe it was his idiot brother and their idiot friend. Out horsing around like fools on their fool ATVs." He shook a finger at me. "Never trust a Kelly."

I definitely couldn't picture Deputy Kelly horsing around on an ATV, though it had a lot more to do with his demeanor than his position as an officer of the law. "When was this, Mr. McCulloch?" He squinted up at the planks in the porch's ceiling, like he might be trying to count the years backward, so I helped him out. "Who was president?"

"The father of the governor." I translated that to mean when Bush Senior was in the White House. An odd way of putting it, but for some Texans, politics outside the borders were just a nuisance.

So, this ATV business was a while ago. Phin did say this seemed to be a recurrent ghost, just going by the stories. I knew that some specters only turned up under certain conditions, or on a certain timetable. Or even just arbitrarily—

Eleven-year-old Amy needed to sit down and shut up. I firmly closed the door on her mental cupboard and turned to Mr. McCulloch. "I'm a little surprised you're here. I got the feeling your family didn't believe in ghosts. And, um, in fact, aren't too fond of the Goodnights right now."

"Well, that's just claptrap. I'm here, aren't I?" He drained his iced tea and set the glass down with a punctuating thump. "And not just for the iced tea. Don't tell Emily, but hers doesn't hold a candle to this."

"Who's Emily?" I asked, hopping out of my rocker as he pushed himself up from his. Just in case. He looked strong, but there was something . . . I don't know. Maybe it was another hunch, or maybe I was just worried because of his weak ticker.

"My wife," answered Mr. McCulloch. Once up, he moved more easily to the steps, barely leaning on the handrail. "Who will tan my hide if I'm not home for supper."

"Well . . ." I told myself I had enough to fret about without adding Mac McCulloch to the list. On the other hand, Ben might blame me for that, too, if anything happened to him. "Be careful on the ride home. Do you need me to, um . . ." I was going to say "help you up," but I sensed how that would go over. ". . . hold your stirrup or something?"

"No, dammit," he barked. "I'm not a debutante riding in a fool parade." He said it "deb-u-tant," as in, rhymes with "ant," and I bit back a smile. "You just tend to your business, missy. When you've got this Mad Monk malarkey sorted, then you tell me how to ride a horse. I've got saddles older than you are."

Which was sort of my point, but I knew better than to say it. I did weed out the pertinent part of that speech, though, as he headed down the stairs.

"Mr. McCulloch," I called, and he turned at the bottom. "I didn't say I was going to find the Mad Monk."

"But you will," he said, placing his worn and stained Stetson on his head. "You've got that look about you."

"What look is that?" I asked, tired of his family maligning mine. "A Goodnight look?"

"A responsible one." He adjusted his hat, in a motion I'd seen Ben make a dozen times that day, right before he drove home his point. "Like you're the girl who takes care of things. So take care of it, dammit."

I watched him head over to the donkey pen, and a few minutes later, Mac McCulloch went trotting by on a horse the color of strong coffee. He didn't look so old while he was riding, which made me worry a little less.

Take care of this Mad Monk malarkey. Did that mean I

had permission to ghost hunt on McCulloch land? Somehow I doubted Ben or Deputy Kelly would see it that way.

Not that I was even considering it.

I'd walked to the fence to see Mr. McCulloch off, and my foot crunched on something as I turned back to the house.

Fresh wood shavings littered a trail back to the gatepost. I approached it warily, my heart thudding as I saw the newly carved design in the wood. Then I compared it to the older glyph above it—familiar and weathered and barely visible. I traced the smooth one with my finger, and a pleasant, warm tingle spread up my arm. The new one would give me splinters, but I knew what it was.

"Darn it, Phin," I whispered fondly.

At some point that morning, my sister had reinforced the security system around the house and yard. I knew just enough to realize that this took some time and effort, especially by herself. She must have stayed up all night, because I didn't think it could have been done between when I left for the dig and when she arrived.

My heart grew two sizes, like the Grinch's. *This* was why I put up with her blowing fuses. I had my way of keeping the boundaries between the Goodnights and the world. And Phin had hers.

The question was, would either of them be enough?

i could not escape the Mad Monk of McCulloch Ranch.

"The *what*?" Mark asked, with an incredulous laugh. I was glad of the ambient volume in the bar, the loud music and raised voices of the crowd.

"A mad monk!" Phin sat forward in excitement, elbows on the scarred table of the booth where we sat with the student dig crew. "That's so old-world. Like a rampart guardian or a white lady."

I had not told them about the ghost. Certainly not by that melodramatic name, *let alone* in the middle of the roadhouse on the outskirts of town. The gang had already been discussing it when Mark, Phin, and I arrived.

The Hitchin' Post was a neon-lit, sticky-wooden-table, sawdust-and-peanut-shells-on-the-floor place that chain restaurants can only imitate. There were three entrées on the menu—burger, chicken fingers, hot dog—plus fries, nachos, or fries with nacho cheese. There was a bar at one end of the long, narrow building and a stage at the other, and there'd been a herd of motorcycles in the gravel parking lot when I'd parked Stella.

Mark and Phin had arrived in Mark's Jeep just ahead of me. The others were already inside, seated at a booth big enough for the eight of us, and discussing the guy at the bar who had waylaid Lucas and Dwayne when they went to get the bucket of ice, beer, and soda that sat in the middle of the table.

"That's what he said," Lucas reiterated. He was a graduate student in Latin American history volunteering on the excavation, but he looked more like a linebacker than an aspiring professor. "The Mad Monk of McCulloch Ranch. And apparently our digging has got him all riled up."

Dwayne (junior, business major, also pitching in as unskilled labor) backed up this story with an earnest nod. "Even hinted we were to blame for the guy who went to the hospital last night."

"How could we be?" asked Jennie. She was the freckle-faced girl who'd been cataloging artifacts under the awning at the dig, a senior forensic science major and future criminologist. "We only started digging this morning."

"You guys are taking this way too seriously," said Caitlin.

She came from Alabama, which explained her accent, and was an archaeology grad student picking up extra field hours. "A pottery-and-flint girl hanging with the bone guys," she had said as we went around the table making introductions. "Gotta go where the digs are." I wanted to find a reason to not like her—other than being jealous, which I was *not*—but so far she was personable, if a little snarky. And if snark were grounds to dislike someone, no one would be friends with me at all.

"So what's the theory?" asked Mark, grabbing a Shiner Bock and wiping off the ice. "Are we digging up the monk's grave?"

The last member of the team to weigh in was Emery Rhodes. He was a graduate student in physical anthropology, like Mark, but the resemblance ended there, given that Mark was Mark and Emery . . . well, he looked like a guy named Emery. He talked like one, too. "*Tell me* you're not *seriously* composing a theory based on the nutcase at the bar."

I watched the discussion silently, keeping Mac McCulloch's visit to myself for now, since I'd have to explain why he'd come to Goodnight Farm for ghost expertise. I didn't want to be lumped in with "that nutcase at the bar" any sooner than I had to. Or at all, if possible.

"*Apparently,*" said Dwayne, mimicking Emery very slightly, "there have been noises and lights in the pasture since construction on the bridge began, but worse since the bulldozer uncovered the first set of remains."

"That doesn't make sense," said Phin. "It's not like he

was resting in peace. Your professor said it was a shallow burial, not a proper one."

"It's a ghost story," said Caitlin with a laugh. "It doesn't have to make sense."

Oh boy. Phin drew herself up and was clearly about to spell out just how many ways Caitlin was *completely* wrong on that point. I headed her off, because that was my job: keep the crazy contained.

"Ghost stories are folklore," I explained, "and like every other kind of story, they have an internal logic."

Phin took my interruption in stride and I continued my point. "Even if the tales get twisted by rumor and inflated by superstition, they're usually based on something. I'm sure you know cases where folklore has led archaeologists to sites they would not have found, or even known to look for, without rumors and stories."

Caitlin blinked at her, then picked up her beer with a grimace and took a bracing swig. "Oh my God. I've just been schooled by a freshman. How embarrassing."

"Well," said Phin, in a don't-feel-bad tone that made Mark laugh even harder, "I *am* a sophomore."

I picked up my Dr Pepper and smothered a groan. At least my sister was an *amusing* know-it-all.

Mark sobered to tease Caitlin. "It's not her fault that she's right." Elbows on the table, he leaned in and took a teaching sort of tone. "That's how the San Sabá Mission was found. The one I told you about today, Amy. An archaeologist came across an old pamphlet in an archive. Something printed up for tourists, by a family who was always finding artifacts when they plowed their fields. Academics had dismissed these stories for decades, but it turned out to be the clue that led to discovering the site."

"Speaking of finds," I said, eager for any subject that wasn't the Mad Monk, "what happened after I left the river? Did you get the skull out in one piece?"

Mark was happy to describe the excavation, giving Lucas time to get another round, and me time to regroup my strategy for keeping my balance on the tightrope between *Goodnight* and *normal.*

All afternoon, ever since Mac McCulloch had ridden off, I'd been lecturing myself: *Treat the story like a story, not like a ghost.* I'd expected that the ranch's haunting would be a major topic of discussion in town, even in the crowded, noisy bar. *Especially* in the crowded bar. Where else were folks going to gather to gossip about it? I just hadn't expected to get hit with "Mad Monk" quite so soon out of the gate.

"Oh, I'll bet you'll be interested in this, Amy," said Mark, reeling back my attention to the discussion at the table. "Dr. Douglas made a preliminary estimate and thinks your skull may be as old as the first one. So tomorrow we'll excavate around that spot, looking for more remains, and probably dig some test holes between the two finds."

"So this could really be a big deal," I said, a little tentatively. "Like you were talking about this afternoon."

Everyone else was too excited to hear the conflict in my voice. They chattered about historical significance and writing papers and getting to name the site. But for a moment, the din of the bar retreated, and I was back in the field, back to hot sun and cool earth, and I was thinking about bones and ghosts and wondering how I would be able to sleep tonight without seeing the hollow gaze of the skull in my dreams.

Caitlin had shaken off her pique and joined the speculation. "My money is on a lost settlement."

"It could date back to the Spanish colonization," said Lucas. "There were a number of failed colonies in the area."

"Missions, you mean." Phin's train of thought wasn't hard to follow. It might as well have been as neon as the beer signs over the bar.

"You're thinking about the Mad Monk?" asked Jennie.

Emery gave a dismissive snort. "Even for a ghost, that sounds ridiculous, like something out of a gothic novel. *The Mysteries of Adolpho* or something."

"*U*dolpho." I took some pleasure in correcting him. His scorn made me reckless. Even without ghosts in my room and an eleven-year-old ghost hunter in the back of my head, it was hard to resist piecing the story together. Like I'd told Caitlin, there had to be some logic to it. "And it's not so ridiculous. Texas had plenty of monks in its Spanish colonial days."

Lucas nodded, in the spirit of the mystery. "Explorers looking for gold for the Mother Church. Missionaries here to civilize the natives."

"Like Coronado," said Phin. "Still searching for his lost city of gold."

"Except that Coronado died in Mexico," Lucas pointed out. "Though I suppose he could have come back in the afterlife. Do ghosts have to worry about transportation?"

"But Coronado wasn't a monk," said Jennie, mirroring

Phin's posture and enthusiasm. Mark, Lucas, and Dwayne leaned in, too. Caitlin looked reluctantly interested, though Emery was trying to appear above it all.

"Were there missions this far north?" Mark asked.

Lucas made a "so-so" gesture. "The largest and most successful ones were farther south, along the Guadalupe, and east, up near the Neches. The soil here wasn't really good for sustaining agriculture, so most of the missions in this area failed. Or met a more violent end. You mentioned San Sabá. That's not far from here."

"Wasn't there a mine or something associated with San Sabá?" asked Phin. "Ghosts are often guarding a treasure."

The word struck a chord of excitement around the table, everyone caught up in the possibility for the space of a held breath.

Then Emery broke the spell. "Oh my God," he said, equal parts exasperated and disgusted. "You all watch too many movies."

The gang laughed, breaking the runaway-train tension.

Phin's suggestion had startled me, too, but for different reasons. Mac McCulloch had mentioned treasure but I hadn't had a chance to tell Phin about that. Although, like she said, folklore was full of ghosts unwilling to leave their riches unprotected.

"This elective turned out to be way more interesting than I thought," said Dwayne. "It's like an episode of that *Bones* show or something."

"Good grief," said Emery, in the same disgusted voice. "Thanks to television, our classes are full of dilettantes who think the field is all sexy anthropologists solving crimes and flirting with FBI agents."

"I take exception to your point," said my sister, in a debate-club sort of tone that, intentional or not, amused the hell out of me. "Mark is clearly sexy, and clearly an anthropologist."

When he recovered from choking on his beer, Mark said, "Thanks, *chica,* but I don't know any FBI agents."

"I'm applying to the FBI," Jennie assured him, "and I'd flirt with you."

"And Caitlin's no dog, either," said Dwayne, and Lucas raised his bottle in agreement. Caitlin rolled her eyes, but I caught her laughing as she sipped her beer.

"Very funny," said Emery, with *no* jealousy, I'm sure. "But you've completely missed my point."

I wasn't ready to let him off the hook, because for one thing, it was steering the conversation away from ghosts. For another, what kind of snob uses "dilettante" in a sentence without irony?

"I get your point," I said, "but I read somewhere that the number of female students in the hard sciences has gone up across the board, and a lot of people credit the geek chic on TV."

"Let me guess," said Emery, looking down the table—and his nose—at me. "You're a science major?"

"Pre-med," I confirmed, with a bit of a challenge in my voice. "And Phin is majoring in chemistry and physics."

I realized, as their heads turned to my sister, that I might have opened a can of worms, talking about Phin's studies.

But I *was* proud of her, even if she chose to express her genius in an unconventional way, and Emery's attitude pissed me off.

"Chemistry *and* physics?" echoed Mark, clearly impressed.

"Well," Phin said modestly, "they're not entirely unrelated."

"Were you inspired by *CSI*?" Emery's sneer earned him a glare from Jennie and Caitlin.

Phin answered him literally, of course. "It was *Ghost Hunters,* actually."

They laughed, as if she were joking, which she wasn't. I groaned—silently. *This is why I can't take her anywhere.*

"Then why not parapsychology or something?" asked Emery, who probably would have mocked her no matter what she said.

Phin looked at him as if she couldn't believe he would ask such a stupid question. "Because I'm not interested in the psychospiritual nature of the paranormal. I'm interested in the physical and measurable aspects."

Jennie seemed delighted to have Emery put in his place. "I get it. Like how on those shows, they use gadgets to measure things like cold spots, electromagnetic energy, that kind of thing."

"Exactly." Phin nodded. "Though my concern is not only hauntings but all paranormal phenomena: ESP, mediums, spellcraft of various traditions. Only, no accredited university offers a degree in preternatural science. So—" She shrugged. "Chemistry and physics."

"All the double majors *I* know," said Emery, again with that *tone,* "are taking summer school."

She answered a lot more calmly than I would have. "I'm doing two online classes and an independent study project. It's based on the work of Semyon Kirlian in the 1930s, capturing the image of the corona electrical discharges of an object when laid on a photostatic plate subjected to a certain voltage."

When Emery's only response was a baffled blink, Jennie laughed. Dwayne, searching for the joke, asked, "Care to translate that for the business major?"

Mark gave him a wry look. "I didn't get half of that, either, dude."

Phin waved off their confusion. "It's not important. I'm merely basing my work on that principle. The coronal aura visualizer measures the energy aura of objects in response to metaphysical energy rather than electricity."

"This is the thing you mentioned this afternoon?" asked Mark.

"Yes. I'm curious whether anomalies underground might appear as coronas in the surface vegetation."

That actually didn't sound too crazy, especially for something from Phin. Smoking chemistry labs and blown fuses aside, her gadgets did usually work, once she got the bugs out. And considering she was doing things that no one—that I knew of, anyway—had ever done before, some bugs were to be expected.

I began to hope we'd get through the Gadget Girl Show without mentioning anything *too* out-of-bounds. But then Caitlin asked, "What do you mean, metaphysical energy?"

Don't do it, Phin. I tried to send her psychic messages—as if I had suddenly developed a previously nonexistent skill in that area. *Don't say it.*

But of course she did. "Oh," she said, in a no-big-deal voice, "everything from ordinary high emotion to psychic events—ghosts, spells, things like that. I'm particularly interested in the herbomancy potential." At their blank looks, and before I could do anything to stop her, she clarified, "Plant magic."

Oh hell. My insides in knots, I gripped the table and contemplated whether I could fake a medical emergency to save us from laughter and ridicule. They'd probably ignore what she'd just said if I could manage a convincing heart attack.

But this was Phin. In the months she'd been away at school, I'd forgotten how she could make the most out-there statements seem no worse than eccentric.

Mark scratched his chin. "You think this might be able to image disturbances underground?"

She nodded. "It's possible, if there's some kind of stimulus."

"Oh for crying out loud," said Emery, and flopped into the booth corner to sulk.

Dwayne gave me a bit of a wink, unaware of my incipient mostly fake heart attack. "Is that how you found the skull, Amy?"

"Lila found it," I said automatically.

"*I* think she did a spell by accident," said Phin, because she always had to go there.

His grin turned teasing. "Do you do a lot of magic spells?"

"No," I answered emphatically.

"That's true," said Phin. "Amy prefers to operate in a more mundane world than the rest of our family."

Jennie asked, "So is your family . . . what do you call it? Wiccan?"

"Good grief, no," said Phin. "We're all Lutherans."

They laughed, and I slumped back on the hard wooden bench, letting the raucous country music wash over me along with my relief. I should have been furious with Phin for saying these things. Whatever immunity she had, whether it was personality or some kind of inherent magic, the safety net around her words didn't extend forever. Outside her sphere of influence, who knew what this would set off? I only knew I'd be the one dealing with it.

But today I couldn't throw stones. I was seriously losing my objectivity. My job was to keep the Goodnight eccentricities inside and the scary real-world judgments outside. How could I do that when I kept losing my footing on the fence?

"You know what we should do?" said Dwayne. "Go look for the ghost."

I sat up so quickly, I kicked someone under the table. "Hang on," I said.

"That's a great idea!" said Jennie. Was she naturally that enthusiastic, or was it happy hour talking? Either way, the bad ideas kept on coming. "We can use the corona vision thing. It will be awesome."

"Coronal aura visualizer," Phin corrected her.

"You guys aren't serious," said Caitlin, then to Mark and Lucas, "Tell me you're not buying into this idea."

Lucas took a swig of his beer. "Not until after some food, at any rate."

Why wasn't Phin saying anything? I expected her to grab her oar and start paddling us up this creek of crazy.

And even more important, why wasn't *I* saying anything? I needed to put the brakes on this, but I couldn't seem to form the words.

Mark said, "I wouldn't mind seeing if Phin's invention does show any disturbances underground. I mean, anything that would make digging easier."

"Come on," said Dwayne, flashing a game-for-anything grin. "We can video it and maybe get on a TV show."

"I don't think so," said Phin repressively. "I don't intend to prostitute my scientific integrity on YouTube."

Mark laughed, and Emery said, "I'm glad *someone* is holding on to their scientific integrity."

"It's just an experiment," Mark said, then drained his beer. "But Lucas is right. Not on an empty stomach."

They kept talking, but I'd stopped listening. My knuckles ached from grasping the table like the safety bar on a roller coaster. My stomach felt like it was on the same ride. Sweat dampened the back of my neck and prickled along my ribs.

This is a terrible idea. I fixed the sentence in my mind but couldn't make myself say it. It was like someone had turned up the dial on my cognitive dissonance to eleven, until I was paralyzed between one option and another, right brain and left brain.

Only that wasn't it, either. I *knew* what I wanted. I wanted my family to stay safe and under the radar. I didn't want the McCullochs to sue Aunt Hyacinth for delaying the building of their bridge. I didn't want them to make life so miserable for Aunt Hy that she couldn't stay in the stone farmhouse with Uncle Burt. So where was this conflict in my brain coming from? Amy the eleven-year-old ghost hunter? Or Amaryllis the unmagical daughter of a magical family, suddenly unable to break Goodnight tradition?

Dammit, I was stronger than both of them. I took a breath, and a figurative leap, and blurted, "I think that's a *terrible* idea."

Everyone at the table looked at me. Hell, it felt like the whole *bar* looked at me, though a quick peek assured me the music and drinking and flirting continued without interruption.

So had the conversation in our scarred wooden booth. They'd been talking about something else entirely, and now they all stared at me like I'd lost my mind.

Way to stay under the radar, Amy.

Mark cleared his throat and leaned across the table, lowering his voice. "So, it's *not* okay with you if Ben joins us? Because if it's not, you'd better say so fast."

I glanced around, found various expressions of amusement and disapproval from the gang, and Phin *studying* me, and Caitlin staring at me like some kind of insect. *Freshmanicus tactlessicus.*

When my gaze returned to Mark, he bit back a smile—a sympathetic one, but still—and pointed behind me.

12

i could not catch a break from Ben McCulloch.

Even when he wasn't *personally* giving me grief, the timing of his arrival made my awkward word-vomit even worse than it was.

Ben had spotted our table from across the bar and headed our way. He'd cleaned up, and it looked great on him. Not too neat, though. His dark blond—or light brown, I hadn't decided—hair was mussed, his collared shirt untucked from his unpretentious jeans. Somewhere behind me, sounding far away, I heard Caitlin explaining that she'd invited him to join us, though she probably meant join *her,* and I didn't think she'd be wrong, because when Ben McCulloch saw *me* his steps stuttered just a little before he continued through the jostling crowd.

Or maybe someone had stepped on his foot, I didn't know.

I only knew that it was one thing too many. The roadhouse had filled up, and the buzz of voices joined the blare of music from the speakers pounding in my ears and splitting my head. The roller coaster hadn't stopped, it had just taken a bone-jarring turn.

"I'm going to the restroom," I said, and zipped out of the booth without meeting anyone's eye, not caring—much—that Phin, crazy gadget and all, was looking like the picture of sanity compared to me.

The restrooms were on the other side of the bar. I should have skirted the edges of the room instead of going straight through the crowd in the middle, where the drinking and flirting was a little rowdy and the music was loud enough to drum out conscious thought. I ducked between two big guys who were both intent on a single girl, right as *another* guy turned, his hands full with two brimming plastic cups of beer.

I ran right into him. Or he ran into me. I was a little unclear on the details, except that we both tried to occupy the same space at the same time and I was suddenly drenched in beer.

A *lot* of beer. And the sign over the bar did not lie. That was some *ice-cold* draft.

The shock of it stilled the ping-ponging of my thoughts, at least. I think Beer Guy cursed, but nothing registered past the chill and the smell of hops and the drip of foam from my hair. A spot cleared in the crowd as people edged away from the swearing and the mess, staring at him, at me, and—oh hell—my soaked white T-shirt. Was I going to get through one day without showing the whole county my bra?

"Are you okay?"

The question did not come from Beer Guy. It was a familiar voice, deep and close to my ear so he didn't have to yell. All things considered, Ben McCulloch's appearance, as if out of thin air, didn't surprise me at all.

"Your friend needs to watch where she's going," said Beer Guy.

Ben had taken a protective hold of my upper arm. I drew a breath, ready to fight my own battle, but by his cutting stare, it was pretty clear he had his own beef with the guy.

"Accidents happen, Joe," Ben said coldly. "And I don't see *you* covered in Budweiser."

Joe certainly seemed dry, as far as I could tell in the neon light. The two cups in his hands were mostly empty, and what beer I wasn't wearing had already soaked into the rough wood floor.

"I'm out two beers," he said.

Ben reached into his pocket, pulled out a bill without looking at it, and dropped it into one of the plastic cups. "Have a pitcher on me."

I didn't think it was possible for the guy to look any angrier, but at the sight of the twenty soaking in that inch of beer, his eyes narrowed to slits of cold loathing. "Good luck with your bridge, McCulloch. Must be tough with the Mad Monk sending people to the hospital. Hope you have some ranch hands left by the time you're done."

The only sign of Ben's anger was the tension in the hand on my arm. His expression was coolly composed, which I realized, because I'd seen it a *lot,* meant he was *really* angry. "Thanks for the concern, Joe. If I'm still hiring before you've found a job, I'll let you know."

Joe looked like he was going to explode, so I didn't resist as Ben steered me away. The crowd murmured their disappointment that there wasn't going to be a fight. So did Joe's friends, who'd shouldered up beside him. But if Ben was half as accurate with his fists as with his words, someone might end up in the hospital. And not from the Mad Monk.

"Friend of yours?" I asked when I'd recovered my powers of speech.

Ben kept me close as we wove through the crowd. I didn't really like to be steered, but didn't think I had much of an argument where driving myself was concerned. Not while my bangs still dripped beer onto my nose, anyway.

He gave a rueful sigh, as if to make light of the ugly incident, but his underlying tension remained. "Somebody's great-grandfather hangs someone else's for cattle rustling, and they never get over it."

"Cattle rustling!" I started to look back, but Ben's grip tightened, keeping me from a very obvious goggle.

"Don't stare," he said. Then, once we'd gained a little breathing room, he asked, "Are you okay?"

"Well, I'm wearing enough beer to get arrested, but I'm not such a delicate flower that I'm going to crumple when a big meanie yells at me. I mean, you should know that."

His brows lowered, and he seemed to contemplate a

number of answers, but before he could pick one a cute His-panic girl in a Hitchin' Post T-shirt intercepted us.

"Oh my gosh," she said, handing me a clean bar towel, which I took gratefully, blotting my dripping bangs. "I saw what happened. Are you okay? Joe Kelly has been a jerk since grade school."

"Joe Kelly?" I echoed. "As in *Deputy* Kelly?"

"His son," said Ben, eloquent in his brevity. But I heard his grandfather in his tone. *Never trust a Kelly.*

I mopped at my T-shirt, but quickly realized the towel wasn't going to cut it. "I can't go back to the table like this," I said. "I'm not decent."

Ben glanced down, then quickly back up, clearing his throat. "Does your family know about this exhibitionist ten-dency of yours?"

My face flamed, but before I could work up a retort, the waitress hit his arm. "Be nice. I've known *you* since grade school, too." Then she turned me toward the restrooms with a little shove. "Come on. Let's get you cleaned up. I'm Jessica, by the way."

"Amy," I said automatically, looking over my shoulder at Ben, who seemed amused to see me herded like a nanny goat. "I think I'm a lost cause. I should just go home."

Jessica kept propelling me to the hallway in the back of the bar, and a door that said Cowgirls. "Then let's get you dry enough to not set off a Breathalyzer if you get pulled over."

Deputy Kelly would love that, I bet, so I stopped fighting.

In the bathroom, where I tried to touch as few things as possible, Jessica had me strip off my T-shirt so she could rinse it in the sink—it couldn't get any wetter—and dry it under the hand dryer. I stood in my bra and toweled off my hair and debated whether it was "nosy" to seize the opportunity that fate had given me.

Jessica looked barely old enough to work in a bar, and she was obviously a local, since she knew Ben and Joe both. Maybe it wasn't playing fair, but I figured, what the heck. The roar of the hand dryer would cover our voices.

"So," I began, in what I hoped was a subtle sort of way, "it sounds like you know all the families around here."

She grinned. "You mean like the McCullochs?" At my expression—clearly I hadn't been subtle at all—she laughed. "It's kind of a logical guess, you being neighbors and all."

I sighed and leaned against the counter, then thought better of it and stood up. "Okay. So, what's his deal? Was he always such a crankypants?"

"Not really." She thought about it while she waved my shirt under the hot air of the dryer. "He and Joe were a year behind me in high school, but it's a small campus. Ben made good grades, went to parties, had lots of girlfriends. *Lots* of girlfriends."

Her gaze slid sort of speculatively my way, and I sucked in my stomach a little bit. I mean, I wasn't vain, but I was human, and also standing in my underwear under fluorescent lights.

Jessica went on. "But he wasn't *popular* popular, if you know what I mean. Even with his being a McCulloch, which you can imagine is a pretty big deal here. He was too laid-back to be really A-list."

"Laid-back?" I couldn't picture it.

143

Jessica nodded. "I don't think he got so serious until he came home from college."

She could have meant when he graduated, but something in her tone, in the knit of her brow, said not. "When was that?" I asked.

"Sometime last year." She glanced at me in the mirror. "You know about his dad, right?"

"Uh, no." Just that I'd made an idiotic statement about him *having* parents, and that he'd stuttered over his answer in a way that now gave me a sinking dread in the pit of my stomach.

"His dad died not long ago." She said it solemnly, but without the hush of a very recent death. "And Ben's granddad isn't doing so well. The ranch is kind of a lot for his mom to handle on her own, even with the help of Mr. Sparks, so Ben came home to help out for a while."

"How long is a while?" I asked.

She thought about it. "Well, it's been since last year sometime. So . . ."

Someone came into the restroom and went into a stall without looking at me twice. Jessica hit the blower again, and I retreated to my thoughts.

The idea of Ben putting school on hold for his family gave my heart an odd and painful twist. As much as I complained about my own family, I'd do anything for them. I mean, I was *here,* dealing with Phin and her inventions for a month. But my whole world was wrapped up in going to college—I'd picked all my high school classes and extracurricular activities based on what would look good on an application. If I had to stay home and run the shop for Mom for an indefinite amount of time . . . ? I'd be *twice* as cranky as he was.

The girl from the stall came out, washed her hands (thank God), and left, drying them on her jeans. When the door had swung closed behind her, Jessica turned to me in a decisive sort of way. "Can I ask *you* a question?"

"Uh, sure." I hoped it wasn't "Why do you give a fig about Ben McCulloch?" because I didn't have an answer to that.

"Are you going to catch the Mad Monk?"

The knot in my chest, the one that had sent me fleeing the booth in the first place, the one that had slackened in my distraction, wrenched tight. So tight and so hard that I let out an involuntary wheeze. I grabbed the counter by the sink to steady myself, and deliberately rolled my eyes, hoping the sound came off as exasperation and not *Holy-smokes-what-is-wrong-with-me?*

I stalled, because I couldn't come up with an answer to my question *or* hers. "Why does everyone keep asking me that?"

She stated the obvious. "Because you're a Goodnight. Everyone knows about Ms. Hyacinth." She spoke so matter-of-factly, as if *I* were the weird one for not realizing this about my family. "How her potions have a little something . . . extra."

I stared at her. "You *know* about that?"

"Oh, honey, everyone knows about that." Her nose made a rueful little wrinkle, and she amended, "Not everyone *believes,* but I do. And . . ."

The dryer had run down again. She cast a look at the

door, then hit the button once more with her elbow. "My boyfriend works for the McCullochs. They're good people, and don't make the guys stay late if they don't want. Vincent's not scared . . . but I am."

I could see that. I could also see, from the level way she met my eye, that she trusted me, my family, to make it right. I wanted to tell her she was putting her faith in the wrong person. She should be talking to Phin—not that Phin exactly inspired confidence—or any of my aunts or cousins. Anyone but me.

"What all has happened?" I asked, without quite meaning to. "Besides the guy who was hurt last night."

"There have been these strange lights and noises in the pasture after dark. Rumbles and moans that echo around the hills. Sounds like chains rattling." My face must have shown what I thought about that, because she rushed to tell me, "I know it sounds silly. But Vincent and I were, um, well, we were out parking one night, up on the lookout near the bluff? And I heard it myself. It's eerie. Comes from everywhere and nowhere, and you kind of hear it in your bones as much as your ears."

What she described was exactly what I'd heard outside the night before, right before the bats had gone on their erratic and fatal flight. I pictured the ominous fall of the twin winged bodies, and could understand why she looked so frightened.

"Could it have been some kind of digging or construction?" I asked, looking for a mundane explanation.

"At midnight?" She hit the dryer again, to cover our voices. "The thing is, stuff only started happening since they began clearing the ground for the new bridge. The sounds and lights. Steve Sparks got thrown when his horse got spooked, and something keeps knocking down the fence in the west pasture. Then Joe Kelly reminded everyone of the time his dad and uncle saw the Mad Monk—it was when they were sinking a new well."

"Were they out on an ATV?" I asked, remembering my chat with Mac McCulloch. As I weighed truth against legend, it occurred to me that if you were joyriding where you shouldn't have been and got in an accident, a Mad Monk might deflect the blame and make people forget you were misbehaving.

"Yeah. Joe's uncle Mike had a broken arm and fifteen stitches in his forehead. And folks have been saying that the last time it was this bad, back when they were working on the highway? A guy was killed."

"Killed?" She had my full attention. It was still a lurid sort of story, but her face was pale and earnest.

She nodded. "They found him at the bottom of one of the ravines with his head smashed in. No one could figure out how, though the coroner supposed he must have hit a rock when he fell."

"Was it the same ravine as the guy who fell last night?"

Another serious nod. "That's what they say."

"*Who* says?" I asked, maybe too strongly. Because Aunt Hyacinth had been gone for almost a week, and I knew *that* gossip couldn't be laid at her door.

"Everyone," Jessica answered, then paused, chewing her bottom lip. "So . . . *are* you going to look for the Mad Monk?"

My quick denial caught in my throat. I wanted to help

147

her, but I knew I couldn't, and I needed to tell her that, to say something. But my throat had seized on the words like a miser's fist on a nickel and wouldn't let go.

The harder I tried, the worse it got. Much worse than at the table—the knot in my chest seemed to wrap around my lungs, making it painful to breathe, and a clammy sweat broke over my bare skin.

The horrible pregnant pause went on and on, until Jessica dropped her gaze, trying to hide her disappointment, to gloss over how she'd silently pleaded for my help and I had ripped her heart out and stomped on it. "This shirt is a loss," she said. "Let me go see if we have any Hitchin' Post ones in the office."

She dashed out, and I sagged against the counter, the tightness easing. I filled my lungs, pushing away the panic, only to have new fears rush in.

What *was* wrong with me? This wasn't my normal struggle to balance my worlds. I didn't hunt ghosts. So why couldn't I just say that?

And why did I have such a hard time looking myself in the mirror? When I did, all I could see was Jessica asking for my help, and Mac McCulloch demanding it. Because I was the one who took care of things.

Apparently, I wore it like a sign.

13

You could fit two of me inside the Hitchin' Post T-shirt that Jessica brought me. I hoped to make a stealthy exit and call Phin from the car, but Ben was waiting in the dimly lit hall outside the bathrooms, leaning against the wall next to a pay phone with an age-yellowed Out of Order sign.

When I came out, he straightened and peered at me critically. "You okay?"

"I'm not going to melt, if that's your worry." And then I bit my tongue, because I remembered about his dad, and why he was so tightly wound, and that not five minutes ago

I'd been thinking I should be nicer to him. "Sorry," I said, the weight of the day dragging down my shoulders. "I just want to go home. Can you tell the others bye for me?"

Ben studied me a moment longer, and I wondered if there was an actual reason he'd asked if I was okay. Like maybe whatever was going on in my head showed on my face. "I'll walk you out," he said, in a don't-bother-arguing sort of way.

Fortunately I didn't really feel like arguing. As we made our way through the main room, he didn't take my arm again, but when the crowd jostled us, his hand touched my back, not quite encircling me, but keeping me close so we didn't get separated.

There was something so . . . *stalwart* about Ben. I'd only known him two days and he'd managed to infuriate me most of that time. But there I was, protected by the curve of his arm, and grateful for it. And not just because it felt nice, though it did.

We finally broke through the rabble and out into the warm summer night lit by a few paltry streetlamps and occasional headlights going by on the highway. I hadn't realized how late it had gotten, and now I was doubly glad for Ben's company, even when he dropped his hand from my side.

"My car is over here." I nodded to Stella in the gravel lot.

"It's not hard to spot," he said, and he had a point. The Mini Cooper did stand out from the cluster of Harleys and the rank and file of pickup trucks.

"So, about Joe Kelly," I began as we walked toward my car. Ben glanced over warily, but waited for me to go on, which I did. The episode with the deputy's son was fairly near the top of my overflowing mental in-box, so the topic wasn't as arbitrary as it sounded. "He's *actually* still pissed about what your granddad did to his?"

"Great-granddad," Ben corrected. He gestured for me to precede him between two trucks, then said, "Grudges last a long time here. Doesn't help that my dad bought up the Kelly land during the oil bust in the nineties."

I noted that the McCulloch manifest destiny didn't sit too well with everyone. "Wasn't that rubbing salt in the wound a little?"

"Just business." We'd reached Stella's back bumper. Ben slouched with his hands in his pockets, watching me fish my keys out of my pocket. "And he paid better than market value. I think he felt bad about the granddad thing."

"I guess that explains why Deputy Kelly is a ray of sunshine whenever he pops over to your land. But not why the Goodnights put such a burr under his saddle."

"Oh, *I* can imagine."

The comment lacked bite. In fact, he seemed almost *at ease.* Ironic, when my brain was so overloaded that I couldn't even seem to get my keys into the car door. I fumbled them and they hit the gravel with a *thunk.*

Ben reached for them at the same time I did, and we narrowly avoided knocking our heads together. I gave up and leaned against Stella's fender with a slightly hysterical laugh. "I'll be glad when Run-into-Things Day is over."

He retrieved the keys from the ground—after making sure I wasn't going for them again—and dropped them into my hand. "Any day that includes multiple dead bodies, you should get a pass on running into things."

He was part of the problem, too. When he was being *nice,* I couldn't help wondering whether I owed him an apology over the "Don't you have parents?" thing or a thank-you for extracting me from the Situation in the bar. Not to mention my inappropriate curiosity about his opinion of my addiction to Victoria's Secret.

Rather than voice any of those things, or do something sensible like get into my car, I said, "We were talking about the irony of Deputy Kelly being the scion of cattle thieves. And why Joe hates you."

He gazed at me a moment and I took the opportunity to study him in the dim yellow haze of the flyspecked streetlamp, without a hat or sunglasses. His nose was a little crooked, with a scar across the bridge, and his jaw a little too square. Maybe. "Is that what we were talking about?" he asked. "And not why the Goodnights are a saddle burr?"

"You don't think we've exhausted that subject?" I asked. "Besides, I have a reason for asking." It seemed odd that the Kelly name kept popping up whenever the Mad Monk did. And even if I didn't want to go hopping the fence in the middle of the night with Phin's PKE meter, I was still curious about the ninety-nine other mysteries of McCulloch Ranch.

After a moment Ben shrugged and said, "Joe Kelly and I graduated together. Started at the University of Texas together. Pledged rival fraternities. Destined to be antagonists, I guess."

"Maybe it's genetic," I said. "Your family, his family."

His mouth relaxed into something like a very small smile. "A good old-fashioned feud?"

"Never trust a Kelly," I echoed.

152

Wham. The shutters slammed back down. "Where did you hear that?"

Oh hell. *Now* what? Until I knew where I'd gone wrong, I could only answer with the truth. "From your grandfather. He rode over to the farmhouse this afternoon."

"Grandpa Mac?" Ben echoed. "Rode over to your house?"

I scratched the side of my nose and chose my words carefully, because I knew better than to tell him *why*. "I guess he forgot about Aunt Hyacinth being gone." He continued to stare at me, until I couldn't stand it. "All right. What did I do *now*?"

"He road his horse over to your house, and you just let him ride back?"

I should have clued in *right then* that there was more going on in his head than what was coming out of his mouth. I had known him long enough that the flat tone and expressionless gaze should have been dead giveaways.

"What was I supposed to do? He's a grown-up! He knew the way to Goodnight Farm; I figured he, or the horse, would know the way back. *And,*" I went for the big, I'm-so-logical finish, "he said your grandmother was expecting him back, so I knew someone would be watching out for him on your end—"

That was the moment the pieces clicked: What Jessica said about the ranch getting to be too much for Mac McCulloch, and his confusing me and Aunt Hyacinth and talking about Uncle Burt like he was still living. And most of all, why any talk of talking to dead people sent Ben straight up and sideways.

"Oh." I breathed all that revelation into the sound. All my feelings about Ben churned together inside of me—the hard, bitter feelings and the squishy, tentative feelings—and I don't know what showed on my face, but I could see that Ben knew that I knew, and he was not happy about it.

"Don't say it," he said, at the same time I said, "I'm sorry."

I don't know what he'd expected me to say, but that wasn't it. "For what?" he asked, bluffing it out, I guess.

"About your grandfather," I said, refusing to play the let's-not-talk-about-it game. "And about your dad."

His exhale was more complaint than sigh. "You've been busy."

"Jessica told me."

"Uh-huh." His hands clenched briefly in his pockets, and I wondered if he was picturing them around my neck. "And my family just happened to come up in conversation?"

"Actually," I shot back, because this is where my sympathy got me—arguing in a bar parking lot like trashy reality-TV stars—"I came right out and asked her if you were always such a jackass, or if it was only for my benefit."

"What is wrong with you?" he demanded, sort of making my point. "Can you not let anything lie? All I want is to get this damned bridge built. And you're digging up ghosts and skeletons . . ."

"Look. It's not like your dad passing away isn't public record. And you just let me stick my foot in it this afternoon and didn't correct me."

He clamped his teeth on a retort, then grudgingly admitted, "All right, that's true." Then he was back on the

154

warhorse. "But my granddad is not a subject open for discussion. And I sure as hell don't want people gossiping about him in bars."

"It was the *bathroom.* And it wasn't gossip. It was a sensitive relay of information." I poked him in the chest, though not, I admit, quite hard enough to make him back up a step. "And for the record, it was making me feel very kindly toward you until—"

"Was it?" He folded his arms. "Because it's a little hard to tell with you."

I glared and refused to be sidetracked. "I was *going to say,* that for a *nanosecond,* I could actually understand why you've been such a jerk."

"Maybe you should just quit apologizing. It doesn't seem to be doing any good."

"Obviously not."

I hadn't noticed the bikers coming out of the bar until one of them, leaning on his handlebars like he was watching a movie, shouted, "Aw, just kiss her already, dude."

Oh. My. God. Incendiary mortification seemed a real possibility, especially when Ben, just to infuriate me, I was sure, waved back and said, "Thanks for the advice, man. I've got this."

"If you do," I warned him, my finger raised between us. But then I stopped, because he lifted a challenging brow, like he wanted to know what *I* planned to do if he did. And I didn't have a clue.

But here's what I did know: he was standing very close, so we wouldn't have to shout across the parking lot. Which had seemed practical until that moment, when I realized how much I didn't mind him looming over me, when I should have minded a lot. Instead, I was picturing him putting a hand on either side of me on the roof of the Mini Cooper and leaning in and locking his lips on mine.

Dammit! I had much more important things to worry about than how it would feel if Ben McCulloch kissed me.

Ben stepped back so quickly, I knew I wore that question all over my face. He certainly wasn't wondering the same thing I was. Because I smelled like I'd taken a bath in a brewery. And also, he pretty much hated my guts. And vice versa. Sometimes.

"Should you call your sister or something?" he asked.

"I'm right here."

We both jumped. Phin stood by Stella's front bumper, giving Ben one of her dissecting stares, and I could tell it unnerved him. Good.

Mark had walked out with her, and he gave me a sympathetic wave. "Heard about your adventure from the waitress. If it makes you feel better, my mom always said beer makes your hair shiny."

Ben looked, for a moment, as if he would ask how Phin knew to come outside, then thought better of it and answered Mark instead. "Some guys I knew in college would disprove that."

"It's the protein and B vitamins," said Phin, like this was an actual conversation about grooming and not two guys trying to dispel some serious awkward. "But you have to rinse with it, not drink it."

"Right." I opened my car door. "If I get arrested for

drunk driving based on the fumes coming from my hair, at least I'll look great when they arraign me tomorrow."

"Drive carefully," said Ben, as if he couldn't help himself, "and you'll be fine."

"Thanks, *Dad*," I snapped, then cursed. Jeez Louise, what was wrong with my mouth? "I'm—"

Ben put his hand on the top of my door, essentially trapping me in the space between him and Stella, almost like I'd imagined, but with a *completely* different expression.

"Just stop apologizing," he said. "It's better that way."

"How about this?" I said, because now it was the principle of the thing. "I'm sorry, *jackass*."

I got in, slammed the door—not very hard, because Stella was delicate—and started the engine. It didn't cover his laugh.

"Hell's bells," I growled as Phin got in beside me. I gripped the steering wheel, watching Ben and Mark walk back to the bar. "Why does he make me so *mad*?"

"Is that a rhetorical question?" asked Phin. "Because I'm pretty sure you don't want to hear what I think."

Finally. Something with which I could unequivocally agree.

14

midnight found me sitting on a rock in the McCullochs' pasture, watching my sister pace between one excavation and the other, talking to herself. Or possibly to her equipment. I couldn't be sure.

My feelings on ghost hunting had not changed. My feelings on *trespassing* had not changed. I'd laid out all the pitfalls of this plan in the car on the way back to the site.

"What about not prostituting your scientific integrity?" I'd asked Phin.

"I just said that because I don't want a bunch of well-intentioned amateurs getting in the way."

I'd taken my eyes from the road just long enough to make sure she wasn't being ironic. "You know, when it comes to the dig, *we* are well-intentioned amateurs."

"It's not the same thing at all. Paranormal events are difficult enough to document in a meaningful, repeatable way without adding *more* variables. I don't want anything to interfere with my test of the Kirlianometer."

"You're really going to call it that?"

"You're the one who said I need a better name for it. And you are very good at thinking like normal people."

This lavish praise wasn't what convinced me to go with her. Neither was it the worry that she would justify going without me, or worse, invite Mark along, even if he was an amateur. It wasn't even to spite Ben McCulloch.

It was that I was more afraid of what would happen if I said no than what would happen if I said yes. The awful mental paralysis was still too fresh in my memory to even try—especially while I was driving.

I rationalized my participation by the fact that Phin was measuring metaphysical stimuli in order to look for remains and not for ghosts. And someone had to make sure she didn't trip in a gopher hole or get carried off by coyotes. Or bitten by a rabid bat, or fall in the river. Or even, you know, get hit on the head or pushed down a ravine by a Mad Monk.

How I would prevent any of those things was a mystery.

I rubbed at a fire ant bite on my hand, concentrating on the burning sting to keep alert. When we'd first reached the excavation site, you could have bounced a quarter off my tautly strung nerves. I flinched at the cool, damp breeze that ruffled my hair. The moon made eerie patterns on the rough ground, and the places where the topsoil had worn down to the limestone clay glowed with reflected light.

But after an hour and a half of jumping at shadows, I was more worried about mosquito bites than spectral manifestations.

"Holy smokes," said Phin. "What a bust."

I shook myself out of my thoughts, and my boredom, and looked at her. There was a good bit of moonlight to see by. "Isn't it working?"

"Too well." She thumbed through the images she'd taken, the glow of the screen on her frustrated face.

Curiosity nudged me off my rocky seat. I leaned around Phin's shoulder and peered at the image of a faint neon footprint. It was eerie to see something on the camera that I couldn't with my eyes, but since Phin wasn't excited about it, I figured it was normal. Relatively speaking.

"Is this your footstep on the grass?" I asked.

She sighed. Loudly. "Yes. That's all I'm getting. I don't know if the stronger stimulus is masking weaker, older ones, or if there's nothing else to read."

"Are you ready to call it quits?" I didn't bother to keep the hopeful note from my voice.

"For tonight." She sounded distracted, like she was already working out the problem in her head. "This is so frustrating. I should have tested it in a controlled environment first, but I didn't want to miss the opportunity. Who knows when I'll get another chance to image an unconsecrated grave pre- and post-disinterment?"

I'd been doing fine until she said "unconsecrated grave." The words conjured images of restless spirits with unfinished business, and disquiet skittered up my spine, making me shiver despite the warm night.

Phin took her sweet time putting away her stuff and zipping her backpack. We'd walked from the river gate, the way I'd come that morning, which seemed eons ago. "And you saw no fluctuations on the EMF meter?"

I glanced down at the electromagnetic field meter in my hand. Paranormal events often made the EM fields spike or dip. But so did a lot of other things—microwaves, uninsulated appliances, and electrical cords, for example. The interaction of natural and supernatural fields could make a mess of one's spells, which was why a lot of kitchen witches like Aunt Hyacinth wouldn't do spells in the *actual* kitchen. Or they'd unplug everything first, which was a bit of a nuisance.

The thing was, naturally occurring EMFs could make you feel unsettled and uneasy, mess with your sleep, or even make your pacemaker do wonky things. All of which could make your house feel haunted, when it was really just too close to a high-voltage power line.

I'd run the EMF meter over both dig sites and gotten no fluctuations. Whatever Lila had sensed that made her dig up the second skull, EMFs weren't it.

"What about the voice recorder?" Phin said. "Did you keep it running for EVPs?"

She was asking me about the MP3 recorder I had going to catch electronic voice phenomena. That was when a voice you didn't hear during an investigation turned up when you were listening later. There were a *lot* of gadgets to juggle when Phin was involved.

"It's been running the whole time," I told her.

"Did you ask questions while I was taking Kirliano-graphs?" Phin's impatient voice said she knew the answer. The area wasn't so big she wouldn't have heard me talking to myself. But I answered her anyway.

"No."

"Amy! Why didn't you ask questions?"

"Because I hate EVPs. They creep me out."

They always had. EMFs and EVPs might seem mystifying if you were new to investigating, but this was like getting back on a bike I hadn't ridden in years. Other kids go through dinosaur phases. When I was eight, I could name every kind of spirit from revenants to poltergeists. That was how I knew that apparitions were so rare.

I was thinking that maybe I should have Mom send me the books and videos I'd boxed up after the La Llorona incident. That was how far I'd slipped out of my entrenched position. Except calling might get her hopes up that I was changing my mind, which was *another* reason I didn't want to be in the pasture doing what I swore I would never do again.

Phin exhaled in exasperation. "If we're going to do this, we have to do it right."

"I said I would come and test your Kirlianometer to see if it could visualize any anomalies with the ground. And I went along with measuring EMFs. But I'm not here to look for—"

I bit my tongue. Literally. After cursing in pain for a while, as Phin waited impatiently for me to make my point, I rephrased.

"I don't want to invite the ghost to talk to me. I just want it to go away. From me and everyone else."

My sister looked at me like I was an idiot, which was not uncommon, and then said something that made me *feel* like an idiot, which was much more rare:

"How can you know how to make it go away if you won't even ask it?"

This was remarkably sensible. Maybe if I didn't have so many hot buttons about ghosts, I would have thought of it myself. I started to tell her as much, but she was looking at the display screen of the camera with an expression of . . . well, it could have been either concentration or consternation.

"What?" I said, because that look often preceded blown fuses and blown tempers.

"Nothing."

And then she turned off the gadget. Sure, we were wrapping up, but the *way* she did it set my alarms to pinging. Phin had no subtlety, and if there was something she didn't want me to see, it could *not* be good.

"Delphinium, what is in that picture—"

I broke off as another noise caught my attention. Phin went still, and nodded to show she heard it, too. I didn't want to stir the air with even a whisper.

The indistinct ripple of sound continued, a hushed rise and fall. The rocky hills threw voices like a ventriloquist. The noise could have been coming from over the ridge or over the river.

I scanned the night in a slow circle and nearly strangled myself on a swallowed shriek when I saw a pair of glowing eyes staring at me from the dark. But at my half-audible gurgle, the eyes disappeared, and the deer they belonged to bounded away with a flick of her white tail and a clatter of hooves on the rock.

The murmuring broke off, and its abrupt absence was somehow easier to locate. Phin pointed east, where a hill obscured any long-range view. I gestured that we should go the other way. She shook her head and turned on her Kirlianometer and jabbed an emphatic finger at the EMF meter and voice recorder that I held.

She started up the hill, crouching low to keep her silhouette hidden. I went after her, worried she would fall and break her neck, worried about what would come over the rise to meet us. Worried about things that bump in the dark and grab with cold hands . . .

Memory and imagination wound me in knots, and just when I thought I would snap, three figures appeared over the hill.

In between "Holy crap!" and "What the hell?" I recognized Mark's close-cropped hair and chiseled profile. Ditto Jennie's Pocahontas braids and Dwayne's linebacker shoulders.

Phin straightened like a shot. "What are you doing here?" she demanded, like we had any more right to be at the site than they did.

"Aw, man!" said Dwayne, lowering his video recorder.

Jennie laughed, but Mark gave more of a crow. "I knew it! You ditched us to play Ghostbusters all on your own. Unfair!"

His word choice had Phin vibrating with outrage. "We're

trying to conduct serious paranormal research. If you want to *play,* go do it somewhere else."

"Where?" asked Mark. "This is where the graves are. *Our* graves, I might add."

"Don't tempt me," she snapped. I had to cover my mouth to hold back a laugh, because I'd never seen my sister like this. "I'm *trying* to control the variables in this experiment."

Mark raised his hands. "Dial it down, *chica.* You could have controlled these variables much better if you hadn't ditched us to come here on your own."

"I didn't think you'd follow us."

"We didn't follow you. You're not the only one who can look up ghost hunting on Wikipedia."

"Wikipedia!" If Phin got any more indignant, she was going to be in orbit. It didn't help when Mark laughed.

Dwayne, Jennie, and I watched them like a tennis match. When I was reasonably sure Mark was safe from my sister, I asked Jennie, "Where's everyone else?"

Jennie answered, "Lucas was enjoying himself at the bar, and we ditched Emery because he'd tell on us. Caitlin was trying to ditch him, too, so she could talk to Ben."

Nice. Now I was *doubly* embarrassed that I'd been thinking about inappropriate Mini Cooper kissing when Ben really was at the bar to meet Caitlin.

Focus, Amy. He's just a guy.

"Did you try your corona thing on the dig site?" Mark asked, which might have gotten him back into Phin's good graces if the unsuccessful experiment weren't a sore point with her.

"I'm still working the bugs out."

Before she could go on, something stopped her. The same thing that made us all freeze, at exactly the same moment. So I knew I wasn't imagining it, the sound that, just like before, was more of a sensation in my middle, as if the noise were too low for my auditory sense to register.

Then came a soft grumble, like a cranky complaint from an ancient man.

The taut air of a collective held breath kept the five of us still until the last rumbling echo. Only then did we turn toward the sound.

"Look!" said Dwayne. There was the faintest flickering glow against the starless silhouette of the big granite bluff to the south.

Mark punched Dwayne's arm in excitement. "Let's go see."

"You are *not* blowing this test for me," said Phin, and she and Jennie ran after them.

I would have, too, but I knocked the voice recorder out of my pocket, and it hit the ground with a clatter.

"Crap." I crouched to feel around for it, and then I had to find the batteries that had fallen out. In the dark, I re-assembled the recorder, then made sure it still worked. Which it did. Phin might be the death of me, but she wouldn't be killing me for losing evidence.

Then I stood, looked around, and found myself utterly alone.

Logic said the others weren't far, maybe just over the hill. But for all I could see of them, they might have vanished to another dimension. I was pretty sure this was against the buddy-system rule.

Something brushed the back of my head, like a hand catching on the strands of my hair. My heart banged against my ribs and I spun to see—

Nothing. A tarp lay like a dark pool over the now-empty grave by the river. The stakes and cord that Mark had measured out looked like faint, shadowy facets on the diamond-shaped field.

The caliche road ran down the hill like a silver-gray snake. The calcium carbonate makes the dirt roads pack down hard; it's very white and very dusty, and it gets all over your car and your clothes. It rises up in clouds when you drive on it, catching the moonlight like a spectral fog.

Like it was doing now.

An eerie paleness hung like smoke over the field, as if swept up by the breeze that swirled around me. It lifted the hair on the nape of my neck and crept up the cuffs of my jeans and the gap under my shirt, and my skin prickled at the chill.

Fear took a white-knuckled grip on my vocal cords. This wasn't comfortable hearth magic or cozy Uncle Burt in his rocker. There was a *wrongness* about the sickly mist coiling into a column in front of me, a fierce foreignness that arrowed straight into my self-preservation instinct.

An intangible hand sculpted moonlit fog into the translucent form of a man. Not tall, but straight and slender, somehow youthful, though the details of hair and clothes were obscured by the unearthly glow.

The eyes were shadowed but no longer hollow. They bound my gaze, and I couldn't tear myself free.

There was something in my hand. The voice recorder.

My joints ached and cracked as if frosted over, but I managed to move my thumb, fumbling for the on switch.

Drawing a breath was like breathing ice. I had never been so cold in my life. My teeth wouldn't stop chattering, but I made my numb lips form a question.

"Wh-wh-what d-d-do you want?"

With slow, forced effort, he raised his arm. His hand grasped at the air between us, and his mouth worked in futile desperation to speak, but only shaped soundless syllables.

Only my choked gasps broke the eerie silence. I couldn't breathe. Frigid fingers reached into me, squeezing my lungs. My insides felt brittle with ghostly cold, as if I might shatter. The dark night was growing darker, and sparks danced on the spreading blackness.

I was going to pass out. If I was lucky.

Through the ringing in my ears, I heard the others running back. I felt them through the ground.

"Amy!" Phin called.

And then another voice I didn't know. "Miss! Miss, come back here."

I spent the last of my strength in the effort to call out, then hit the ground and curled into a ball, and wondered how anyone would explain my death by hypothermia on a July night.

My vision went black, like someone had flipped a switch. For a moment I thought I was dead, or unconscious, but my skin still hurt and I could smell the beer in my hair.

The apparition had . . . disapparated.

I heard a scrabble of feet on dry ground, and then Phin's

voice, and the others. Then a flashlight was shining right in my eyes.

"Amy! Are you okay?" asked Phin, owner of the flashlight. "Say something!"

"Ugh. Light. Eyes." That was all I could manage through my chattering teeth, and I sounded like a three-pack-a-day smoker, but I could talk. Yay. I took a quick inventory. A deep breath filled my lungs with wonderful, warm air. I still thought I might pee ice cubes, but I could feel my fingers and toes.

Jennie put her very warm hands on my face. "Good grief. She's freezing."

"I'll b-b-be ok-k-kay." That would have sounded more convincing if my teeth weren't rattling my brain.

All their flashlights were on. I guess we weren't worried about ghosts or preserving night vision anymore. Mark turned to—oh hell—a uniformed man and said, "Aren't you supposed to have a Thermos of hot coffee or something? Isn't that a stakeout requirement?"

The young officer—who was not, thank God, Deputy Kelly—said, "Wait right here. Do *not* move." And took off at a jog.

"Who was that?" I asked, more or less, through the chattering, and tried to sit up. My joints mostly cooperated.

"Apparently, they're keeping an eye on this area because of the recent activity," said Dwayne. "*Are* you okay?"

"A warm drink will help get her core temperature back up," said Jennie. She felt my face and hands again. "But she's warming very quickly."

"I'll be f-f-fine." The shivering was letting up a little, too.

"Holy moly," said Phin, sinking to a seat as if weakened by her reaction. "You scared the life out of me. I had *no* idea how I was going to explain this to Mom."

I was so touched by her concern that I told her, "You should take a Kirl—a corona—a picture of that spot right there." I pointed.

"The apparition?" she said, excitement restoring her strength. *"Again?"*

"Quick!" I said. "Before the deputy comes back."

She jumped to it while Dwayne and Mark and Jennie stared. "An apparition?" Jennie asked. "As in, you *saw* the Mad Monk?"

"Again?" echoed Dwayne.

"Shhhh." I was much more worried about the deputy than what the three of them thought just then. I heard the officer coming and gestured Mark closer so I could whisper, "Tell him you came out to check something on the site, and we tagged along. Just don't tell him we were ghost hunting."

Mark gave me a doubtful look. "I'm good, *chica,* but I'm not sure I'm that good. Everyone here thinks you're a—"

"—Goodnight. I know."

"I was going to say *bruja.* But tomato, tomahto."

He'd just called me a witch in Spanish. I watched him walk to meet the officer, and penciled Mark Delgado onto the things-to-sort-out-later list.

"Look!" said Phin, holding her camera out to me. In the dark, the images on the display screen were very vivid. Not footprints, like ours, but bright, hot swirls, like a slow exposure of a neon-lit sky.

"That's so cool!" said Jennie, and she and Dwayne oohed over the pictures for a moment. "That's the after-image of the ghost on the grass?"

"Close enough," said Phin. I couldn't believe she'd fore-gone the lecture, until she turned to me and said, "I don't suppose you took any EMF readings."

I wasn't quite up to rolling my eyes. "Before I passed out from hypothermia, you mean?"

She sighed. "That's what I thought. I suppose it's forgiv-able under the circumstances."

Jennie and Dwayne were like a pair of excited puppies with a new toy. "Can you describe it? Did it say anything?"

"It was a pale figure, there—" I pointed. "Where Phin's standing." A chill prickled my neck, but it was only a memory, a ghost of a ghost. "It pointed at me, and was mouthing . . ."

"What?" Jennie breathed, on the edge of her figurative seat.

I really didn't want to say it, but I was too frazzled to come up with anything but the truth.

" 'Boo,' " I admitted with a cringe. "It was saying 'boo.' "

15

deputy Martinez was a very nice young man. I didn't know
what magic Mark worked on him, but he read us the riot act
and sent us on our way without making any kind of official
report. What *unofficial* reports would be circulating, I didn't
want to know. But Martinez seemed like a skeptic—which
was probably why he'd been chosen for the duty—so I was
hopeful that tomorrow's headline on the *Barnett Herald*
would not read "Goodnight Girl Caught in Scandalous
Hookup with Mad Monk."

Mark had driven us to Goodnight Farm in his Jeep, and
Phin made strong, hot tea, since the Goodnights weren't big

on coffee. Not when one of our major family businesses was a tea shop. And Aunt Iris's Study Session Tea ("For when you absolutely, positively have to be up all night") was as effective as any espresso.

I huddled under a quilt on the couch in the living room while Phin loaded her pictures onto her laptop. Dwayne and Jennie sat with her on the floor around the coffee table, talking excitedly about the ghost hunt.

Mark sat on the couch with me, looking askance at his teammates. They were a bit annoying in their enthusiasm, and it was kind of weird how only Mark and Phin seemed to remember finding me in a shivering heap on the ground.

I found myself assuring him, "The excitement will wear off when you head back to your motel." The Phin Goodnight Effect was making tonight seem like a game, nothing weird. Outside of her bubble of influence, they would wonder what they were thinking and have a good laugh. "Everything will seem normal in the morning."

"Will it?" he asked, sounding unconvinced.

"Yes," I said, because *my* job was to appeal to reason, make the abnormal seem sane even after the Phin Effect had faded. "Think how easy it is to turn a random light or the flare of a camera lens into something unearthly. Or someone falls, and imagination gets the better of everyone."

Mark studied me for a long moment, a skeptical smile touching the corner of his mouth. Then he said, as if letting me off the hook, "Okay, *chica*. We'll pretend we both believe that."

I blinked. He'd called my bluff. The spin-doctoring wasn't a total lie. It *was* easy to turn a spooky setting and a little adrenaline into a ghost. But I was fooling myself if I thought tomorrow I would feel any less abnormal.

Mark was more insightful than his amiable grin and laid-back good looks implied. "Why did you call me a *bruja* before?" I asked. "In the field."

He shrugged, with a little more warmth. "I call it as I see it."

The thing about the supernatural was, if you believed in it, you saw it, and if you didn't, you didn't. For the true skeptic, no amount of proof could convince them the world wasn't black and white, real and unreal. And for the true believer . . . well, they sometimes saw unicorns when there was nothing but horses.

But most people fell somewhere in the middle, accepting the paranormal in their lives in selective ways: lucky charms, superstition, ghost stories, aromatherapy, chakra energy, transitional meditation . . . *brujería.*

Mark had clearly picked his side. But I did set him straight. "Phin is the witch. I'm just . . ." I trailed off, because I couldn't seem to think of a word for *what* I was.

"A ghost whisperer?" Mark asked, with a touch of his usual grin.

Oh no. Not that.

"I've never shown any kind of supernatural ability," I evaded.

"But the rest of your family . . . ?"

Glancing at Phin, and the Kirlianographs on her laptop, a lie seemed silly. With a sigh, I admitted, "The Goodnights aren't exactly average."

"I knew that as soon as I met your sister." He was taking

this completely in his stride. Really, and not because of Phin's influence. "So you really are all witches?"

"And psychics," I confirmed. Might as well. He'd made up his mind about us already. "Some are talented one way, some the other. It's sort of like the arts versus sciences." I paused, then warned him, "Don't get Phin started on the differences between them unless you want an earful."

"I'll keep that in mind."

Phin insisted that what she did was all chemistry and smarts, but the lines were more fluid than simply magic versus ESP. The Goodnights were supernaturally talented, like some families were gifted musically. Most of us had at least a tiny psychic sensitivity—even *I* got hunches—and most of us could follow a recipe for a spell. (Yes, me too.) But each had some specialty. For the psychics it was an ability they developed.

For the magical ones, they gravitated to some *type* of spell, like an artist chose paint or clay or marble. Mom called it an affinity. Phin was a little odd, even for our family. Kitchen witchery—a combination of cooking and chemistry experiments—was her closest fit. But she was really all about the science and the gadgets. Like some kids take stuff apart to see how it works, I think Phin wanted to take magic apart and put it back together again. Better, stronger, faster.

Maybe being the gatekeeper was my affinity. The paranormal touched people's lives, even if they didn't realize it. Sometimes it was good, sometimes it was bad, and mostly the Goodnights tried to make sure it was good. I needed to run interference for them so they could do that.

At least, that was what I told myself. But I never got as

175

excited about anything as Phin did about her gadgets . . . or Mark did about old bones. Considering how long I would have to be in school to be a doctor, maybe that was an important realization.

"You okay?" asked Mark. "You look like you've just seen a . . . well, you know."

I laughed, reluctantly, and pulled the quilt up closer to my chin. "Just thinking." I changed the subject so he wouldn't ask about what. "Did you see anything when you ran off after the sound? Any explanation?"

He shook his head. "Nothing but dark. Then the deputy found us—he'd heard the noise, too—and that was that. Until Phin suddenly dashed back to you, without any reason we could see." He slid a glance her way. "Is that a Goodnight superpower?"

"When it works, which it doesn't always." He'd done it again, gotten me to admit more than I would have with anyone else. "We, uh, call it the heebie-jeebies. Doesn't every family have that?"

"My mother sure did," he said. "Mostly when I was misbehaving. She just called it motherhood."

"Hey, Amy." Phin got my attention from the floor by the laptop. "What did you do with the voice recorder?"

Good question. A quick search revealed I'd stuck it in my pocket at some point. I handed it over, and she immediately noticed the scratches on the case.

"You dropped it," she accused.

"See if it still works," said Jennie eagerly.

Dwayne grinned at me. "See if the ghost really said 'boo.'"

Oh, he was a laugh riot. As if I hadn't had enough disbelief and teasing when I'd confessed that.

Phin fast-forwarded the sound file all the way to the clatter of the recorder hitting the ground, when it went dead for a bit. When it came back on, for a few seconds you could hear my breathing, with labored rasps. Then finally, my voice, quaking with cold, "Wh-wh-what d-d-do you want?"

Then silence. No one spoke in the room, either. The terror in my voice was clear, even through the chattering, full of visceral fear that twisted my vitals in memory.

The dogs, who'd been sleeping around the room, started barking. I was relieved to have something to do, to calm my nerves as I calmed theirs.

Phin ran the recording back to listen again. But there was nothing after my question but more harsh breathing, until it stopped entirely.

Finally Jennie spoke. "I guess it didn't get any voice."

"EVPs aren't always audible until you amplify and filter the recording." Phin plugged the recorder into her computer and loaded the file.

"What's an EVP, anyway?" asked Dwayne while we waited. "All these initials are hard to follow."

"An electronic voice phenomenon," said Phin, in a lecturing tone, "or EVP, is when a voice can be heard on an audio playback that wasn't audible during the live event."

Jennie giggled. "'Live.' Heh. That's funny."

It was so silly, even I laughed. Phin gave her an I-don't-get-it frown, and when Jennie explained, "Because it's ghosts," she raised an eyebrow, Mr. Spock style which made Jennie—and me—laugh harder.

I felt punch-drunk. It was almost two in the morning, and the night had passed "surreal" a long time ago. I'd talked to Mark about my family. I was laughing at ghost jokes. I'd fallen so far off the fence, I wasn't sure I'd ever get back up.

Jennie and I composed ourselves as Phin turned the computer so we could see the sound-mixing program. She turned up the volume as a vertical bar moved across the time line, leaving spikes where my ragged breath lurched through the white noise of the maxed-out speakers.

And then a new sound stabbed through the silence, leaving a buzz of white on the screen. The others jerked when they heard it, then got intently still.

"Well, I'll be damned," said Dwayne. "It *did* say 'boo.'" On the computer playback it was clear.

Mark frowned in concentration. "Play it again, Phin." His shoulders were stiff, his elbows braced on his knees as he leaned forward. His tone took the levity out of the air.

Phin obliged. I held my breath as the five-second clip played again, and again the ghostly word hissed through the silence. But this time I heard what Mark had before.

"There's more," I said, the fingers of unease crawling up my spine. "After the 'boo.'"

Phin pointed to the sound wave on the screen. The "B" made a big spike followed by two trailing points. "Three syllables. They fall off, but they're distinct."

"Shhh," said Mark. He slid off the sofa to sit next to Phin, shoulder to shoulder by the laptop speaker. "Play it again."

Three syllables, emerging from nothing, an auditory specter taking shape in the air between us.

"Búscame." Mark spoke the word aloud, bringing it out of Neverland into the room with us. "It's Spanish."

"Búscame," I repeated. I'd taken Spanish in school, and even remembered some of it. "As in *buscar?*"

My brain supplied the word, but meaning lagged behind, and implication trailed even further.

" 'Look for me.' " Mark's warm and human voice hung over the electronic whisper like a curtain over smoke. "It's saying 'Look for me.' "

16

at least I knew what it wanted. I hadn't decided if that improved things, though.

Despite the hour, Jennie and Dwayne wanted to go over every millisecond of the recording, until Mark pointed out that Emery would put out an APB on them, just for spite, if they didn't get to the hotel soon.

That got the excited pair headed for the door, but Mark hung back and helped Phin gather her laptop and equipment. "We'll see you two tomorrow, right?"

"Definitely," she said. Her enthusiasm made Mark smile,

even when she explained, "I have another experiment I want to try."

"Dr. Douglas is okay with that?" I asked. "I mean, our coming back to the dig, not Phin's experiments."

"I told her you two are good luck." He grinned at me. "And she liked the way you took direction with that skull today. Er, yesterday," he amended, glancing at his watch.

He turned to say goodbye to Phin, but she'd already disappeared into her workroom. With a rueful smile, he told me instead, "See you tomorrow, *chica*. Don't forget to lock up."

I followed him, said goodbye to Jennie and Dwayne, too, then closed the door and leaned against it. We never locked up Goodnight Farm. I wasn't going to start for a ghost. Not that it would do any good if the shored-up security system failed.

As I headed for the workroom to look for Phin, I ran my hand over the back of Uncle Burt's rocker. I didn't pretend to understand how much of the real Uncle Burt remained, whether it was a shadow of his soul or just a wisp of residual personality, but I'd always tried to stay on good terms with whatever it was. I believed souls had someplace better to be, but who knows? If I loved someone like Burt loved Aunt Hyacinth, maybe I'd hang around, too.

But Uncle Burt fit here like a puzzle piece. The *other* did not. There was nothing peaceful or contented about whatever shred of a man had stood gasping and grasping in front of me. What remained of him was wretched desperation.

Look for me.

The cold in my chest expanded. I took a deep breath—a whiff of denim and violets pushed it back.

The ghost could have been talking to anyone. His image might play like a recording when someone stumbled over that spot at any particular time. So why did it feel like he had been talking to, waiting for, *me*?

"You're going to have to do it, you know."

I jumped, shaking myself back to the present. "Jeez, Phin! That was freaky even for you." She stood in the door of her workroom, and I glared at her for scaring me, and speaking directly to my thoughts. "You haven't suddenly added mind reading to your talents, have you?"

"Pfft. *My* talents are actually useful and reliable. Are you going to get with the program?"

Casting a longing look toward the stairs and my bedroom at the top of them, I asked, "Does the program involve going to bed and thinking about it in the morning?"

She ignored the question. "This is the second time the ghost has singled you out."

I sighed. "Thanks for that, Phin. It will really help me get to sleep."

"Why are you being so obtuse?" She folded her arms when I didn't answer. "I know the implication has occurred to you. You're not normally an idiot."

"No," I said, "but I'm very tired, so why don't you explain it to me?"

"We already talked about this," she said with a huff. "Hauntings are usually very localized. Cold spots, apparitions, orbs, knocks and noises . . . they all tend to happen in the same place, often around the same time under the same conditions."

"I remember all that," I said, because I wanted her to get to the point. A point I dreaded, because she was right. Since the ghost had appeared in my room, I hadn't faced the full meaning. I'd sat on the knowledge, beaten it down, drowned it out by arguing with cranky cowboys and tinkering with Phin's gadgets. I'd smiled right at Mark and told him not to worry. But I knew what she was about to say. "So just say it."

"The ranch may be haunted, Amy. But it's obvious that you are, too."

17

at way-too-early o'clock, I stumbled down the stairs, trying to figure out why the dogs weren't barking at the racket from the front of the house. I finally realized the thumping came from the door and threw it open to find my cousin Daisy on the porch, nearly hidden by the big cardboard box in her arms.

"You look awful," she said, hardly glancing at me as she breezed in. With my rumpled pajamas and bleary eyes, I didn't exactly make her a liar. "Clearly I've arrived just in time."

I closed the door and followed her into the living room,

where she set the box on the coffee table. Daisy was a lot to take, even on a good day. She was a high school senior, but she'd skipped a grade, so she wasn't quite seventeen yet. With her *very* red hair, black tee, short plaid skirt, and platform Mary Jane shoes with knee socks, not to mention all the spikes, she looked like the Goth love child of a Catholic schoolgirl and Lucille Ball.

"I didn't sleep at all last night," I said. "Also, Phin's furious with me."

"Are you sure you didn't have a sleepless night *because* Phin is furious with you?"

I considered the question. Was Phin capable of doing some hoodoo to make me toss and turn like the princess and the pea all night, my brain spinning like a corrupted hard drive?

Absolutely. *Would* she?

When I did doze, the luminous specter waited, then turned into La Llorona, dragging me underwater, where I froze and couldn't breathe, until I jolted awake, huddled in the middle of my bed, bones aching, teeth chattering.

If not for the physical misery, I might not put it past her. But Phin was never petty.

"What are you doing here?" I asked, following Daisy again, this time into the kitchen.

"Delivery service," she said, rooting around in the refrigerator. "Your mom said you needed those books. Also, you should call her, because she's getting some intermittent heebs and jeebs, and it's rocking the vibe in the store. That's *my* message, because I'm working there this summer and I need the commission."

185

She emerged with a Dr Pepper and a handful of baby carrots. "Why's Phin mad at you?"

"Because I wouldn't let her do experiments on me last night."

"Hmm." Daisy contemplated my face as she cracked the top on the bottle of DP. "That's either rather wise or extremely foolish."

"Why?" I asked, because I knew perfectly well that she hadn't driven an hour and a half out here, leaving before the sun was up, just to bring me books and tell me to call my mother.

Phin picked that moment to appear from the workroom. She already looked thunderous, but at the sight of Daisy, she clouded even darker. "Great. That's all we need. A psychic."

"Hey, Phin. How are things in the la*bor*atory?" She said it like Boris Karloff, with an emphasis on the *bore*.

"Have you been up all night?" I asked my sister.

"Of course not." She went to the cabinet and got down a pottery mug with a black cat on it, then put the kettle on to boil. "I got my usual four hours."

Daisy munched on a carrot. "Don't people who don't get enough sleep eventually snap? I'd lock up the axes and knives if I were you, Amy."

"I'm pretty sure I'll snap first," I said dryly. In fact, I was pretty sure what would make it happen, too.

"So, why does Phinster want to do experiments on you?" Daisy asked.

Phin folded her arms and raised her brows. "You mean you don't know already? What kind of clairvoyant are you?"

"One who works best with dead people," said Daisy, popping another carrot into her mouth.

Another sardonic look from Phin. "Which is, I assume, why you're here. Because of Amy's ghost."

I didn't need a road map to see where this was going, so I took a shortcut. "How can I be haunted?" This was the argument we'd had the night before. "The ghost was around before I got here. Hell, the ghost was here before I was even *born.*"

"If you don't believe me," Phin said, "ask Daisy. You don't really think she drove all the way out here on whatever flimsy excuse she gave, do you?"

I looked up at Daisy. She wrinkled her nose in apology. "Sorry, Am. It wasn't just your mom with the heebie-jeebies. And now that I'm here, I'm definitely getting a vibe. The dead are sort of my thing, so as much as I hate to say it, Phin is right."

Phin snorted but didn't gloat. I looked from one implacable face to the other and felt the sand shift under my arguments. Which, to be honest, weren't built on certainty so much as hope.

"I think it's extremely unfair of the two of you to gang up on me this way."

Daisy took my shoulders and bent to look me in the eye. "We're doing it because we love you, Amaryllis. The first step to solving your problem is admitting you have a problem."

"Very funny."

She grinned and dropped her hands. But I noticed she shook them at her side, like shaking the feeling back into cold fingers. A small movement, tactfully hidden, but in its way, the most convincing argument of all.

"What about the people who say they've seen the Mad Monk?" I said. "That would mean it's not just me who's haunted."

"Unless they haven't really," said Phin. "You said it yourself, the McCulloch Ranch ghost might be legend based on another ghost, shored up by accidents and imagination." She paused. "Actually, you didn't say that last bit, but you know it's true."

"Or," said Daisy, "it's appeared to other people before. Or it's a separate entity to worry about. The important thing is, you have to deal with the one attached to you, whether it's the Mad Monk of legend or something else."

I went to the kitchen table and sat down before my knees could give out. "You're saying that this thing is tied to me and . . . what? It's not going to go away? *Ever?*"

They exchanged looks of rare agreement. It figured they would finally see eye to eye when it meant that I was screwed.

"So, what do I do?"

"Well," said Phin, "you told me last night that all these people—Mac McCulloch and the girl at the bar—want you to find out about the Mad Monk. *So* . . . maybe you should listen."

Commit to the ghost hunt. My heart started pounding and a cold sweat prickled my skin. Defy Deputy Kelly and Steve Sparks and Ben. Go look for the freezing specter in the middle of the night—

Daisy interrupted my spiraling panic as if she could read it on my face. "Start small. What were you going to do today?"

"Go to the dig. Excavate some bones that might be related to the ghost." The skull was found near where it had appeared, after all.

"That's a start." She downed the last of her Dr Pepper. "I can't tell you how much I wish I could stay. I'll come back as soon as I can. But right now I've got to get to San Antonio or the police are going to come after me."

Daisy consulted for various police departments, something everyone kept on the QT. For some reason the local and federal law enforcement didn't like it getting around that they occasionally called in a sixteen-year-old psychic for help solving crimes.

"Wait," I said, following her to the living room. "You're coming back?"

"Don't bother on our account," Phin called from the kitchen.

Daisy paused in the doorway. "Oh, from the look of things out on the highway, it's about to get really interesting. I wouldn't want to miss it."

Then she was gone, scratching the dogs' heads on the way to her Prius, parked just outside the gate.

I turned to Phin, who had come into the room when Daisy left. "What did she mean, the look of things on the highway?"

"How should I know? I'm not the clairvoyant."

Phin liked things measurable and predictable—or as

predictable as anything supernatural ever was. Spells and potions were chemistry and physics to her. And even though it wasn't as simple as she liked to think, her way of doing things was less influenced by factors like emotions, bias, expectations . . . things that make us *human.*

I went to the box on the coffee table and pulled open the flaps. Inside were all the books and videos that I'd boxed up after the incident in Goliad. On the top was a trade paperback I didn't recognize. *Haunts of the Hill Country,* by Dorothea Daggerspoint.

Fourth in the table of contents was "The Mad Monk of McCulloch Ranch." This must be the book Mac had mentioned, the source of the nickname. The author did love alliteration. And purple prose—the chapter wouldn't be quick to scan.

"You see?" said Phin, reading over my shoulder. I hadn't heard her come over. "Even Mom thinks you ought to be investigating this ghost."

I fanned the pages and dropped the book into the box to look at later. "Do you think Daisy could be right about its being two different events?"

She snorted. "Psychics." Then, more helpfully, she told me, "The monk story and the bones in the pasture are what you have to go on. So that's the best place to—"

The dogs interrupted her from out in the yard, barking to scare off the devil.

"Now what?" I groaned. With leaden feet I went to see who was at the gate. I really hoped it wasn't Deputy Kelly. Or any Kelly at all, really.

But it was worse. It was the press.

I stood on the porch in my boxer short pajamas and bare feet, staring into a television camera. Long-distance, fortunately, since the crew didn't want to come into the yard with the dogs going crazy and all. A woman with a big fat microphone yelled at me over their noise, "Miss Goodnight! Care to comment on your exciting find yesterday?"

"No!" Oh my God, Ben was going to kill me. And so was Dr. Douglas.

"Would you call off your dogs so we can talk to you?"

"No!"

"Would you care to tell us about finding the severed head?"

"For crying out loud," I snapped. "It was a skull, not a severed head."

Aw, hell. I'd gone and *confirmed* something. The reporter looked amazingly smug, even from far away.

"What about the rumor going around that you've found an Indian burial ground?" she asked.

"I don't know anything about a Native American burial ground. But I *do* know this is private property!"

I stepped back and slammed the door, breathless with indignation. I wished I had the nerve to sic Uncle Burt on them, but a paranormal event on the evening news was exactly the kind of thing I lived to prevent.

Phin watched me from beside the door. I told her, "We'd better get to the dig site and warn Mark."

"Oh," she said, with remarkable calm, "chances are, he already knows."

18

Outside the gate leading to the excavation was not, thank goodness, the circus I feared. Just a small sideshow: a handful of protesters with signs against digging up a sacred site, one news van from an Austin TV station, plus the one that had been at the farm. And the sheriff himself, keeping the peace and providing a sound bite.

But when I saw Deputy Kelly, my hands flexed tightly on the wheel. I recognized his stocky khaki form while we were still a ways down the road. "Do you think the deputy knows we were here last night?" I asked Phin.

She knew exactly who I meant. "Well, the officer at the

site told Mark he wasn't going to write it up. But he might have mentioned it over donuts."

I guess it was unrealistic to think we could keep our nocturnal adventures a secret. Not once the gang from the dig got involved. "I hope Dwayne and Jennie don't say anything about the ghost."

"Oh, they won't," Phin said, unconcerned. "They promised three times."

That rang a distant bell. "I thought that was only in Scotland for getting married. You call someone your spouse three times and you're hitched."

"Where do you think it came from? Three promises equals a vow." She stared tactlessly at the protesters as I slowed to turn into the gate. They stared right back. When we passed the reporter with the big microphone, Phin waved. "Anyway, it's not unbreakable, but close enough that it'll prevent accidental slips."

It occurred to me, as I braked in front of the closed gate, that I might not give Phin enough credit. I'd always thought the Phin Effect was accidental. But if she knew about it and used it on purpose, that made her leaving me to deal with the consequences even more infuriating.

A rap on the window startled a squeal out of me. I bet that just made Deputy Kelly's day.

I rolled down the window. I was driving Aunt Hyacinth's Trooper, so I had to *manually* roll it down, which gave me time to compose my we-haven't-been-running-around-where-we-shouldn't demeanor.

"We're volunteers today," I told him. "Mark Delgado okayed it."

The deputy took his time about looking for our names on the list on his clipboard. Then he gave me, Phin, and the Trooper a long inspection. "Have you girls been staying out of trouble?"

"Absolutely." I sounded fake, but he probably wouldn't believe me regardless. Whatever he suspected, if he knew we'd been trespassing, he wouldn't bother fishing.

The deputy set his jaw like he very much wished he *could* tear into us about something, but finally he opened the gate. "You two are on the professor's list to go in. But you're on *my* list, too, so keep your noses clean."

I drove through, hands at two and ten on the wheel and going about zero-point-eight miles an hour. Unfortunately, Phin didn't quite wait until the window was up before asking, "Why are you so nice to him? He gives me a pain."

"I make it a policy not to antagonize the law." I glanced at her as we headed down the packed dirt road. "What are you complaining about? Ninety percent of his interactions are with me."

"You're our self-appointed envoy. When he talks to you, he means us."

I was pretty sure she was right about that. I glanced in the rearview mirror and saw that the dark-haired reporter from the farm had left off interviewing protesters and gone to talk to Deputy Kelly. The way they both turned to glance at the Trooper . . . that couldn't be good.

It was a long drive from the highway to the excavation site, and we passed it mostly in silence, punctuated by the occasional grunt as I hit a pothole. At the end of the road, I parked next to Mark's Jeep. The university van was there, too, next to the work canopy, where I saw Jennie busy cataloging and packing. She waved but kept on working.

Mark stood on the side of the field, holding one end of a measuring tape. Emery held the other, checking distances for Dwayne and Lucas, who were resetting the stakes and surveyor's twine that marked the field off in squares.

"What happened?" I asked, because I knew perfectly well that the grid had been in place the night before.

"Some cows came through, pulled up half the stakes." He looked past me toward the Trooper. "Where's Phin?"

"She moves slow in the morning." I got back to the important question. "I thought they'd cleared all the cattle from this area." That was why Ben had been rounding up that stray on the day we'd met. "Are you sure that's what happened?"

He pointed to the ground, where there was fresh evidence of cattle trespass. "They think a fence must be down. Ben's got some of his guys taking care of it."

In the bathroom of the Hitchin' Post, Jessica had blamed falling fences on the Mad Monk. That kind of prank seemed mischievous compared to the specter I'd seen. Was that a clue that the monk was separate from my apparition? Though today it *had* succeeded in delaying the dig.

And speaking of delays. "How is Dr. Douglas taking the media circus outside the gate?"

Mark glanced toward the tent, where the professor was talking to Jennie. "She's seen worse. As long as the paparazzi and protesters stay outside the gate, there isn't much she can do."

Phin joined us just as the guys finished restoring the grid.

While Mark reeled in the tape measure, Lucas got straight to business. "Did you tell them about the note?"

"Not yet," said Mark.

"What note?" Phin and I spoke at the same time.

Lucas explained, "Dr. D found a note on the windshield of the van this morning, telling her not to disturb the dead. It was written in red marker."

Phin chewed that over. "Red is a powerful color. And of course, the suggestion of blood implies a threat."

"Very melodramatic," said Mark, not quite successful at laughing it off.

"I don't know, dude." Lucas shook his head. "It should have been cheesy, but . . . it gave me the creeps."

Anonymous warnings *were* creepy. The red ink was unsettling because it was *meant* to be scary. A malicious thing to contemplate on a summer morning.

Emery could be relied upon to break the mood. "You guys are getting worked up about a stupid prank."

"You know," I ventured, following the thread of an earlier thought, "if the stakes were ripped up by a person, could the note writer have done it? Thinking he'd delay things or scare you off?"

"Why would someone want to keep us from digging?" Emery asked. "Those remains are well over a hundred years old."

"Maybe it's an old family scandal," Lucas suggested.

Dwayne, who'd been listening with enthusiasm, seized on that idea. "A hundred-year-old murder! Or a new body, buried with the old."

"Television!" said Emery. "This is exactly what I was

talking about. Without dental records, without a cause of death, what could we prove? Nothing. Just that John Doe met his end next to the river."

I entered the argument, because this was how I planned to find the identity of the ghost, and I had to give myself hope. "What if the circumstances match up with a mysterious disappearance in the right time frame?"

"It's still just circumstantial evidence," said Emery. "And the murderer would be long gone, too."

"This is a small community," I said. "Even circumstance is enough to condemn someone in public opinion, and even if they're dead, it's a black mark on the family honor."

Mark nodded. " 'The sins of the father' and all that."

I thought about Joe Kelly, carrying a grudge for three generations. "Exactly."

"Do you still have the note?" Phin asked.

Mark seemed surprised at the question. "I suppose Dr. D might have kept it. Why?"

"You could examine it for trace evidence." She nodded toward the tent. "Jennie's a criminology major. She could check for fingerprints or whatever. And I'd definitely like to see–"

Emery cut in impatiently, "For crying out loud. Who do you think you are? Nancy Drew?"

"Hey," I snapped, because no one sniped at my sister but me, and Mark echoed with a stern "Chill, dude."

Phin was unperturbed. "Those books were highly unrealistic. Do you have any idea how much brain damage a person would have if she were hit on the head and drugged with chloroform that often?"

"Brain damage?" Dr. Douglas's question made us jump. The guys looked at her with shamed-puppy-dog faces as she continued, "That's the only reason I can think that you'd be standing here flapping your jaws when there's a skeleton to be excavated. It's not going to dig itself up."

Emery, Lucas, and Dwayne hurried off, and Dr. Douglas turned her disapproving gaze on Phin and me. "If I let you two work on this dig, are you going to be helpful? No more keeping my students from their work?"

I shook my head emphatically. Phin, standing slightly behind me, must have made some kind of satisfactory response, because after a long, steely-eyed stare, Dr. Douglas gave a curt nod and said to Mark, "Show them what to do and get them set up."

I didn't let my breath out until she turned and walked downhill, pulling her BlackBerry from her pocket as she went.

"She doesn't like me," said Phin.

"Trust me," said Mark, "if she didn't like you, you wouldn't be here." He shepherded us uphill, near the uncovered hole that Lila had dug yesterday, where a six-by-six-foot square had been staked off, just like the first excavation closer to the river. "Pick your spot. Any square in this marked-off grid. We want to try and find more of this skeleton to make a case for excavating the whole area."

Phin pointed to his clipboard. "Is that a diagram of this section?"

"Yeah. I'll keep track of who digs where, and in which square we find any artifacts." At her gesture, he handed it

198

over, looking confused as to why she wanted it. "It's just an empty grid right now."

"It's all I need," she assured him, and pulled a pendant of pale stone from her jeans pocket. Mark watched her with indulgent curiosity. *I* wanted to crawl in the excavation hole and pull the tarp over my head.

Hell, Phin. Could you possibly be more conspicuous?

Okay, to be fair, she probably could. With no fuss, hand waving, or incantation, she let the pendant hang freely over the hand-drawn map. As it swung, she judged its changes in pattern, moving her hand until the stone made a tight circle over a small area.

"What is she doing?" Mark asked in a fascinated whisper, as if he didn't want to break her concentration.

"Picking a spot." I shrugged, as if this weren't weird, as if I weren't seething at Phin for flying her freak flag at every opportunity.

The simple divination took seconds, and I hoped it would pass as a theatrical equivalent of eeny-meeny-miny-mo. Mark was the only one nearby, and he had already made up his mind about us, but I was very aware of the other students peering over curiously.

"G-three," said Phin, and handed the clipboard back to Mark. "Bingo."

Mark chuckled, and when I said, "Please don't encourage her," he laughed again, and motioned for us to follow him.

"Come on. I'll show you what to do. After yesterday, I'm not going to question how you two decide where to dig."

He set us up with a screen box, trowels, and brushes. The idea was to dig shallow layers of dirt out of our squares, and put it through the sieve to catch any small objects. If we came across anything that looked like it might be a bone, we could clear off the dirt with the brushes, being careful to avoid scraping the artifacts with the hard edge of the tools.

As soon as he left us to our work, I sat back on my heels and glared at Phin. I'd taken the square next to her, and we weren't terribly far from the others, so I kept my voice down. "That was your experiment? The one you mentioned last night?"

"Yes, but 'experiment' was a bit of a lie." She made the first divot in her section with her trowel. "It was a basic locating spell. Though I am curious about what it turns up."

"What did you use?" She tossed the pendant to me, and I caught it automatically. It was white and weighed less than I expected. "Is this bone?"

"Not human, of course." She held out her hand and I tossed it back. "But it should still work. Alchemy 101. Like attracts like."

"Jeez Louise, Phin." The others' heads popped up like prairie dogs, and I lowered my voice again. "We've already got reporters at our door and half the town thinking I'm the ghost whisperer."

"Then what does it matter?" she asked. "Do you want to find something helpful or not?"

I did. My hands seemed to tingle with the memory of yesterday's dig, the thrill of dirt and discovery. I didn't trust how much of that was my own reaction, and how much was this . . . whatever was happening to me.

But Phin was right. I had to find out what was haunting me, or nothing else would matter.

19

"It looks a lot more exciting on television, doesn't it?"

Emery was officially starting to piss me off. I hated I-told-you-so's. Especially when they were true.

My back ached from hunching over the shallow trough with the trowel and a soft-bristle brush. I had so much dirt under my nails I could start another Goodnight Farm. Digging for human remains in limestone earth, hard-packed by time, elements, and a whole lot of cow hooves, was grueling work.

We'd been at it all morning, with Mark and Dr. Douglas periodically checking our progress and technique. I was beginning to wonder if the skull might have been separated from its body, since I hadn't found anything but a rock that I'd thought was a patella but was just a rock.

Then Dwayne uncovered a real kneecap, as well as a tibia and a jumble of bones that had once been a foot.

"Come here and look at this, gang," said Dr. Douglas. When we'd gathered around, she pointed out the tarsals, metatarsals, and a few tiny phalanges. "Since the bones are in accurate positions, merely collapsed and distorted by the weight of the soil, this body was likely buried before it decomposed, preserving the remains in place."

"Is this the foot that belongs to the skull Amy found yesterday?" Dwayne asked.

"The position and proximity do seem consistent with that." Lecturing as she worked, she scooped some dirt into a vial, then labeled it with a Sharpie. "When we find remains that haven't been moved, we want to get as much information from the soil around the body as possible. Lab analysis will help us to determine the answer to Dwayne's question, as well as to piece together how the bones came to be here."

"Look at this," said Mark. We were all crouched shoulder to shoulder around Dwayne's trench, and Mark lightly touched a piece of tattered and blackened leather sticking out of the dirt beside the bones. "That could be the bottom of a shoe or boot."

"Don't remove anything until Jennie takes pictures," said Dr. Douglas. "I'll send Caitlin, too. She'll be thrilled to have something to catalog that isn't a bone." The professor was way too stoic to rub her hands together with excitement, but she definitely had a *vibe* going on, as Daisy would say. "And call me if you find anything else."

As she left, I stared at the ragged leather, my mind filling in the gaps, until I saw the sole of a boot, tattered by wear and innumerable miles. A soldier's boot? A conquistador's?

Or maybe it was the sole of a monk's leather sandal.

"Imagine the ground that shoe traveled on the way here, the places it may have been." I didn't realize I'd spoken aloud until I saw the others looking at me. I cleared my throat, a little embarrassed at my whimsy. "It's just . . . here's this utilitarian thing, like what we're all wearing now. Whoever wore it walked on this same dirt, had the same mud on his heels, but centuries ago."

Emery had his own commentary. "Very poetic. Except we try not to do much *imagining* in science."

I gave him a narrow-eyed stare. "I can see why you picked a field where you mostly work with dead people."

"And *I* imagine things all the time," said Phin, backing me up. "It's called 'invention.' Or sometimes, 'making a hypothesis.'"

"Don't provoke him," chided Mark, not quite hiding his laugh. "We have to work with him all year. So let's get back to it."

Emery set his jaw, which emphasized his prominent chin. "Those of us who are actually working, and not just amusing themselves."

A hand smacked him in the back of the head, and it wasn't mine. Caitlin had arrived, digging tools in her (non-smiting) hand. "Don't knock the volunteer labor," she said.

"Of which I'm one. Now show me this thing that might be a shoe so I can earn my unpaid-predoctoral-candidate-archaeologist's keep."

Phin tugged at my shirt. "Come on, Amy. If that troglodyte finds something significant before I do, you are going to *owe* me big-time."

I suspected the debt might involve being her test subject in a school project, so I got back to work as ordered. My whole life felt like an experiment since the ghost had appeared.

Over the rest of the morning, Lucas and Dwayne worked together and uncovered a femur, then the iliac crest of a pelvis. That caused another flurry of excitement as they dug down to expose the rest of it so Dr. D could identify its gender as male. I realized I'd been already thinking of the remains as male. Was that a hunch or just bad science? Emery found the other tibia and another piece of rotted leather, and at Phin's dark look, I bent my head to my work and didn't look up again.

The only problem was, digging and sifting didn't take much brain power, so my mind was free to wander and worry.

What would happen if finding the whole skeleton didn't satisfy the specter?

Maybe these remains had nothing to do with the ghost. It seemed like if I was wedded to this thing somehow, I would *sense* something when I touched the bones. I'd felt the age and mortality of the skull yesterday, but nothing that really tied it to the apparition.

I was pinning my hopes that digging here would lead

me to some clue, but if this didn't work, what did I do then?

My work was much more orderly than my thoughts. Back and forth across my three-by-two rectangle of ground, on each pass I dug down another layer. Six inches deep didn't sound very impressive, but I had to put every shovelful of dirt through a sieve, to make sure I didn't miss any tiny bones or artifacts.

A pair of very worn boots stepped into my line of sight. They crumbled the edge of my nice, neat trench. You could have measured the sides with a ruler, until then.

"Hey." When I didn't respond right away—digging was sort of hypnotic—he gave a whistle. "Earth to Underwear Girl."

I didn't need the boots or the horrible nickname to tell me who it was. Because it figured.

"You're collapsing the side of my trench. I worked very hard on that."

Ben stepped back, sending clods of dirt skittering down the sides of my excavation. I tried to look up at his face instead of his feet, but my neck was knotted tighter than a toddler's first shoelaces.

I could only turn my head enough to see that Phin and the others were gone. "Where is everybody?"

"Ordinary mortals have to stop and eat." His feet shifted, and I could picture him hooking his thumb in his belt the way he did. "My mother brought lunch."

"Your mother?" Surprise made me move too fast, and I bit off a gasp as the muscles between my neck and shoulder seized into one big, searing spasm.

"Don't sound so shocked," he said. "I told you I had one."

"Cramp," I choked, dropping my trowel and grabbing my shoulder.

"Oh for Pete's sake." He slid a hand under my arm and pulled me smoothly to my feet—a move I wouldn't have been able to do on my own, since my leg muscles were kinked and knotted, too.

"Careful—" I flinched as he touched my neck, but despite the manhandling, his fingers were gently firm. Not enticing or soothing, but effective. He kneaded the tightly wound muscle that ran from behind my ear down to my shoulder, and the blinding pain of the cramp began to ease.

"Relax," he said.

Was he kidding? All the voluntary tension was running out of me, leaving only the knots. My insides were melting, too, at the steady, capable strength of his hands.

"You do this a lot?" I asked, not nearly as snarky as I wanted to be.

"Sure," he said, oblivious—I hoped—to the breathless catch in my voice. "I do this to my horse all the time."

"Lucky horse." No lie. I was willing to bet he treated his horse better than some guys treated their girlfriends. His thumbs worked the cords in my neck, and I bit my lip to hold back an embarrassing sigh. "You have a funny way of showing how much you don't like me."

"I don't like gophers, either, but I wouldn't leave one to suffer. I'd shoot it to put it out of its misery."

"Nice." I started to slide out from his hold, but his fingers tightened just enough to stop me.

"Almost got it," he said, working out the very last of the

cramp. He also answered my unasked question. "Phin sent me. She said no one else annoyed you enough to break your concentration. Not even Emery. I think she likes me."

I gave my head an experimental turn. "If your skin hasn't turned green and bumpy, then she likes you."

"If she didn't, she'd turn me into a frog?"

"Why mess around with transformation when an embarrassing rash will do?"

He exhaled on a chuckle, a half laugh that stirred the hair at my nape. I fought a shiver, despite the hot sun. The cramp was gone, but he continued to work on the kinks, thumbs on either side of my neck. "Have you looked up at all in the last hour?"

No. I hadn't. I'd been working with a mindless intensity, my thoughts on the ghost, trying to make this dig count. Some clue to the mystery *had* to be here.

"I guess I lost track of time."

"Thinking about your ghost?"

I spoke before I could chicken out. "About yours, actually. The Mad Monk."

His hands fell away. "Seriously? That ridiculous story?"

"Yes, the *story*." I emphasized the word and turned to face him. "Just hear me out—"

Then I stopped, because he looked like five miles of bad road. His eyes were shadowed, and he hadn't shaved, and though it kind of worked on him, in a work-hard-play-hard sort of way, I didn't think it was a styling choice. "How late were you out last night?"

He gave me a pointed once-over. "No offense, Amaryllis, but you look a little haggard yourself."

"I had horrible nightmares and couldn't sleep. You?"

A rueful grimace, and he admitted, "Got a call about cows on the road in the wee hours. We've got fences down all over the ranch. I was up all night repairing the ones by the highway. Steve's got a crew out working on the rest."

"You were? By yourself?"

He scowled and slipped into the exaggerated accent he used when he was mocking me about the ghost. "Well, I couldn't rightly ask any of the men to do it, what with the Mad Monk bashing people on the head." Then honesty made him relent. "I had some volunteers, though."

I wondered if Jessica's boyfriend was one of them. "Isn't that sort of weird? So many fences going down at once?"

His eyes narrowed. "Odd, but not out of the question. This place is full of limestone caves, and sinkholes open up. . . ."

"*Did* sinkholes open up?" I asked.

"Well," he admitted, "not that we've found yet. But they could have."

"All over the place?"

"Of course not all over the place," he snapped.

"That's what you said!"

"Maybe it wasn't sinkholes," he said, "but it sure as hell wasn't the Mad Monk!"

"Why not?" I asked.

"Because why the blue blazes would a *ghost* tear down a bunch of fences?"

"I don't know! But I need to find out."

That stopped us both. Him because I'd come right out and said it, and me because . . . well, because I guess I'd found my next step. Just like local folklore helped archaeologists find actual buried sites, following the legend of the Mad Monk could be the thing that led me to the real ghost. But I needed to ask questions, piece together the internal logic of the story.

"Why?" Ben finally said. "Why can't you just leave it alone?"

Because it wouldn't leave *me* alone, and I didn't want to be saddled with a spectral shadow my whole life. But I couldn't tell him that. I had to find another way to convince him I was doing a crazy-sounding thing for noncrazy reasons.

"Look, Ben," I said. "Whether the Mad Monk is real or not, people are scared. If I get to the bottom of this legend, find out how it started and what's stirring it up, maybe it will help."

It was a good argument, though I felt a little guilty because I'd implied I was going to disprove the Mad Monk story. But maybe I would, if my specter and the monk were two different things.

He narrowed his eyes, still doubting. "So, you want to do a ghost stakeout, like on television?"

I didn't see a reason to tell him I already had. "More like detective work. Ask questions, talk to people who've heard the stories before they've been warped by time and rumor."

"Like who?" he asked, as if he was chewing it over.

"Well, I could start with you." He snorted, but I was undeterred, even though he wasn't going to like my next suggestion. "Your mother . . ."

"No."

"Your granddad."

"*Hell* no!"

He turned at that and stalked up the hill toward the copse of trees where Phin and I had sat the day before. Today there was a huge SUV there, its tailgate open to serve as a makeshift buffet table. The students sat on the ground and on a few camp seats from the work areas. Dr. Douglas lounged in one of the chairs, chatting with a woman I couldn't see behind her enormous sunglasses.

None of them, fortunately, was paying attention as I trotted after Ben. I'd totally mishandled him—again—and trying to repair my case was like trying to bail a leaky rowboat.

"I would only talk to him if he was having a good day," I bargained. "Alzheimer's patients sometimes remember the past more clearly than the present—"

He stopped. Turned. Leaned down so he was right in my face. "No. Do *not* talk to Grandpa Mac about ghosts. He sees enough of them already."

My mind snagged on that for a moment, wondering if he saw them in the present or the past. Was his Emily like Uncle Burt, or was she only in his mind?

The question wouldn't matter if I didn't fix things with Ben.

"Look," I said, "the only stories I have are via the Kellys. What the Kellys said they saw or heard, or what their cattle-rustling grandfather said." In fact, it seemed like the Kellys had done a lot more talking about the ghost than Aunt Hyacinth could have, given that she'd been on a slow boat to China for a while now. But I didn't point that out, since Ben was mad enough already.

"Fine," he said, proving how angry he was. "Why don't you take Joe Kelly out to dinner and ask *him* about the Mad Monk."

"Maybe I will," I said, because apparently I was five.

"Wear a raincoat for the beer and your rubber boots for the bull—"

A woman's voice, syrup thick and laced with maternal disapproval, rolled heavily down the hill. "Benjamin Francis McCulloch! I told you to bring that young lady up here for some lunch, not to yell at her like a hooligan."

Francis? I was never going to let him tease me about Amaryllis again.

The triple-name whammy had an astounding effect on Ben. He colored to the tips of his ears and, after one last acid glance, wiped his face of anything but pleasant solicitude and gestured me onward to the picnic. With the same exaggerated courtesy, I swept by him . . . and knew I was just as red-faced as he.

Most of the gang were too busy eating and talking to pay much attention, but Mark looked vastly amused. Caitlin's expression implied she was updating her taxonomy to include *Freshmanicus buttheadius.* And as I passed Phin, she murmured, "What was that you said about not antagonizing the law?"

I ignored her and focused on the blond woman who literally greeted me with open arms. "Amy! I've just been chatting with Phin. It's so delightful to meet you both."

Mrs. McCulloch had a big Texas drawl to go with the big Texas hair, and she seemed utterly genuine. Her warmth threw me off balance. If there was any bad blood between

211

her and Aunt Hyacinth, it didn't affect her greeting at all, and she clearly didn't hold my public argument with Ben against me.

Either that, or she was the best actress in the world. I glanced at Phin, who shrugged—her mouth full of sandwich—which I interpreted to mean she'd taken the woman at face value and so should I.

Holding me at arm's length, she gave me a rather matriarchal inspection. "Aren't you adorable! Look at those dimples. I expected you to be taller."

"Understandable," I said, still a little bewildered by the reception. Phin and I bookended average height, but Aunt Hyacinth was something approaching Amazonian. "My aunt Iris always said Hyacinth married Uncle Burt because he was the first man she met who didn't insist she wear flats on their dates."

She laughed. "I can't imagine anyone insisting your aunt do anything. As we well know."

"Mom," Ben chided her in a long-suffering sort of tone.

Mrs. McCulloch breezed along. "Come have a sandwich. Ben, get Amy a drink."

He shot me a warning glance behind his mother's back, as if I was going to ask her about the Mad Monk right then. Which I might have, but not while he was within earshot. Or while I was so hungry.

Mrs. McCulloch chatted while I cleaned my hands and made a cheese sandwich. "Can you believe all the excitement down by the gate? Who knew one bridge would lead to all this?"

Mark ambled over for some more potato chips. "You

never know what's going to turn up in construction, Mrs. McCulloch. When the highway department expanded the road through the town where I grew up, they uncovered a graveyard. That's how I got interested in anthropology. A team came from the university, identified the graves, and relocated them so the highway could go through."

I wondered about Ben's sharp look. I got that the bridge would make their lives easier, but they'd done without it this long. What difference did a few months make?

"Good heavens," said Mrs. McCulloch. "That must have taken forever."

"Years," answered Mark. I coughed in surprise, and he realized the tactless hole he'd dug for himself. "That was an extreme case, of course. Property rights and legal issues, as well as identifying the remains from very old church records . . ." Ben usually played things close to the vest, but all the color drained from his face as the scenario kept getting worse. Mrs. McCulloch looked rather stricken herself.

From his seat on the ground, Lucas offered tentative reassurance. "Those shoe remnants we found should rule out a Native American burial ground, at least. The construction technique is more sophisticated than the foot coverings of the local tribes."

Dr. Douglas sighed in displeasure. "Let's please, if at all possible, keep anything *else* from leaking to the press. It would be nice not to make this any harder on the McCullochs–and me–than it has to be."

"I appreciate that, Serena," said Mrs. McCulloch, and it took me a second to realize who she meant, because Dr. Douglas did *not* look like a Serena. "Now, I hope this question doesn't seem rude, but how much longer do you think you'll be here at this stage of things?"

The professor surveyed the field, as if picturing what might be below the surface. "We'll finish excavating the B site today, then tomorrow we'll dig some test trenches between the two."

"What about all this?" I pointed to the big grid the guys had relaid this morning. The baseball diamond.

"That's much too big a project to tackle without a grant and a dedicated team. I only have these guys for one more day. Well, I have Caitlin for the summer, and I'm stuck with Mark and Emery full-time. But Dwayne, Jennie, and Lucas are almost finished with the mini-term."

She rose from her seat and stretched. "What we'll do is dig some holes at regular intervals and see if we turn up anything worth investigating. Then we can come back with funding and a few willing bodies."

An awkward pause weighted the hot, dusty air. I think we were all thinking about Mark's story. I wondered if the McCullochs had a Plan B for their bridge.

"Well," said Mrs. McCulloch with determined cheer, "whatever you find tomorrow, at the end of your day you should come to our Fourth of July party. That includes you girls, too," she added to me and Phin. "Your aunt never misses it. Your uncle, either, when he was alive."

Uncle Burt had been gone for fifteen years. My surprise must have shown, and Mrs. McCulloch laughed. "Yes, it's a hundred-year-old tradition. No one misses it."

"Not even the Kellys," said Ben, who'd been quietly sitting on the tailgate of the SUV.

I smiled at him very sweetly. "Then I won't, either."

Ben's mom either missed or ignored the exchange. "And in the meantime, girls, if you need *anything,* you just give us a call. There's no cause for you to ever feel spooked or anything in that house all alone. You have Ben's phone number?"

"Um . . . I, uh . . . No," I stammered. Ben, with a careful absence of expression, dutifully took out his cell for the ritual exchange of digits. Not at *all* awkward with an audience. I gave him my number and he called me to send me his. Fortunately, my ringtone was the UT fight song, and it would have been unpatriotic to smirk during "Texas Fight."

Dr. Douglas marshaled her troops. "Break's over. Let's see if we can get the rest of our John Doe out of the ground before dinnertime."

20

mrs. McCulloch—to my surprise—held me back with a question, waiting until the others had cleaned up their lunch trash and moved downhill. Even Ben left, carrying the camp chairs back to ops for Caitlin, but I was pretty sure he hadn't noticed he'd left me alone with his mother.

She busied herself putting away deli meat and cheese into a big cooler. "I hope that Ben hasn't made things too difficult for you, Amy."

How was I supposed to answer that? Of course he had. But I couldn't tell his *mother* that.

"He's obviously under a lot of pressure," I said carefully,

then added, to be fair, "And he's been a gentleman when it counts."

That pleased her, which was my aim. Because I had questions. I just had to figure out how to phrase them tactfully. "I'm relieved to know that there isn't as much antagonism between Aunt Hyacinth and your family as I thought."

There. That sounded much better than *What the hell is your son's problem?*

Mrs. McCulloch closed the ice chest and pushed it into the SUV. "We've always gotten along with your aunt, but Ben and Steve—Steve Sparks, our manager—they've had a lot of frustrations lately. Hyacinth never had a problem with us fording the river on her property, but Steve wants us to lease the bluff to a cell phone company to put a tower on, and Hyacinth . . . well, she's adamantly against it. She says—" Ben's mom broke off with an embarrassed laugh. "Well, she has her reasons, even if we don't understand them."

I looked at the bluff she meant, a big, beautiful hunk of granite that dominated the vista like the prow of a red-rock ocean liner in a rolling sea of hills. "It would be a shame to ruin that view."

That was grounds enough for me, but Aunt Hyacinth was undoubtedly worried about electromagnetic fields, which was probably the part Mrs. McCulloch didn't understand.

"It would," Mrs. McCulloch admitted, following my gaze. "But Steve says it would also be a lot of money. And it would be nice in case Mac . . . Well, just in case."

In case Grandpa Mac someday needed long-term residential care. That was how folks tactfully phrased it.

Mrs. McCulloch didn't have to finish the sentence for me to hear the looming nightmare in her voice. Ben's mom, I'd noticed, tended to say a little more than she meant to.

Like how she seemed to say Steve Sparks's name a lot, which, on one hand, was natural if they worked closely together on ranch business. But she was also a widow with a lot on her shoulders.

Maybe I felt protective of her because I'd grown up with a single mother whose "I march to the beat of my own new age synthesizer" was sometimes mistaken for "I need a big strong man to tell me what to do." Or maybe it was just that Steve Sparks was a condescending jerk, without Ben's mitigating qualities.

Such as the charm with which he compared me to vermin. Or to his horse, which I supposed might be construed as a compliment.

I was working my conscience around to asking his mother about the Mad Monk, but I was too slow. Ben returned, sliding his phone into his pocket and looking, if possible, even more tired than before.

"Fencing accident, Mom. I've got to go."

"Oh dear," said his mother.

"Fencing accident?" I assumed another one had fallen down, but I didn't tease him about sinkholes or any other cause. He looked too grim.

He answered me tersely. "Barbed wire. High tension. It snapped with a man in the way."

My imagination filled in the gaps, and I felt an odd stab of responsibility. My palms were sweating, and I shoved them in my pockets, shaken by the strength of my reaction. "Can I help? I'm certified in first aid."

Ben looked surprised by my offer, and said genuinely, "Thanks. But Steve took Clint to the ER, where he'll be okay with some stitches." He ran a hand over his face. "If this gets blamed on that ghost . . ."

He didn't look at me, but he didn't really have to.

"Don't be silly, Benjamin," said Mrs. McCulloch. "Why would anyone think it's the ghost? It's the middle of the day, and no one got hit on the head."

If someone weren't injured, maybe seriously, I would have laughed at Ben's exasperated reaction to his mother's logic. I pressed my luck with a question. "Why would a ghost—a hypothetical ghost," I corrected at Ben's dark look, "want to injure someone repairing a fence?"

"Why does the f—" He caught himself and looked at his mom. "—ictional thing do anything?" said Ben scornfully. "Just ask anyone: to protect his 'treasure.'"

His air quotes were *aggressively* ironic, and Mrs. McCulloch reassured me with a hand on my shoulder, "He's not angry with you, honey. Just at the situation."

"Amy knows how I feel, Mom," said Ben, shepherding her toward the SUV's passenger seat.

"Right back atcha, Francis," I called, then felt awful because some poor guy was cut up by barbed wire and though it couldn't possibly be my fault, I *felt* like it was. Which meant I'd better get back to searching, and planning what to do if digging continued to make things worse instead of better.

• • •

I was running out of time, at least for that day. Phin and I both had chores back at the ranch. Spectral obligation or not, the goats had to be fed and the plants had to be watered. And we still hadn't found anything.

Phin's square and mine were a knight's move down from Lucas and Emery on the chessboard of the Site B section. "Maybe we picked the wrong place," I said. "We seem to be well below the feet, going by where they found the tibiae and leather fragments."

"You're welcome to move if you want," said Phin, digging into her next layer. "What does your gut tell you to do?"

My gut—and her tone—told me not to imply a lack of faith in her methods. I knelt back down, groaning just a little, and returned to work.

21

my faith was rewarded in less than an hour. Phin and I had both moved to lie on our stomachs, and I saw her hands still before she reached to trade her spade for her brush.

"Hey, Mark!" I called. "I think Phin found something."

He stepped carefully over the grid of twine to look, then called for Dr. Douglas. The other students crowded around, too, as the professor arrived and instructed with subdued excitement, "This hand is obviously undisturbed. See how all those small bones are in place? Use the brush carefully, Phin. Where's Jennie? We need pictures."

What emerged from the dirt was a delicate mosaic of

earth-stained bone. Jennie snapped photographs as Phin worked to expose as much as possible without shifting anything.

"It's a right hand," said Mark. "Do we have one of those yet?"

Caitlin had joined us on the B site after lunch, and she checked the notes before answering, "We have metacarpals and carpals in two different locations. This is a third hand."

Phin had found a third set of remains. The crew didn't quite cheer—surely there was some etiquette about cheering over dead bodies. But I was focused on the tiny spheres barely visible *beside* the bones under her brush.

Stretching out, I fanned my own brush across the shapes, worried they might disintegrate. The next pass of my brush lifted the veil of dirt from a spill of beads and a small cross, lying as if the fingers had opened in death and let them fall.

"A necklace?" suggested Caitlin.

Mark shook his head. "A rosary."

Jennie lowered her camera and exchanged a look with Dwayne. "The Mad Monk!"

"I'm going to pretend I didn't hear that," said Dr. Douglas.

"There's something else." Lucas pointed to something flat, dark, and leathery emerging as Phin worked her brush outward from the hand.

Emery speculated, "Another sandal?"

I bent over the trench. "It looks like a satchel. Some kind of bag?" I pointed to what appeared to be a rough, fist-sized rock. "Phin, brush that off."

She did. The sweep of the brush burnished it in the sunlight.

The stillness of a held breath hovered over the trench. My own felt lodged in my chest as, for an unscientific moment, I wondered if this confirmed the rumors of the Mad Monk. First the rosary and then this? Could it be so simple?

"Is that . . . ?" Dwayne started, speaking for all of us.

Dr. Douglas, refreshingly pragmatic, pulled the rock out of the dirt, crumbling off the soil that clung to the underside. "If you mean 'Is that a chunk of gold ore?' then yes. It is."

She started the rock around the circle so everyone could examine it. Jennie turned it over in her hands. "That doesn't look like something Yosemite Sam would dig up with his pickax."

"It's unrefined," said Mark, taking it from her and pointing to the metallic yellow sheen. "It has to be processed before it looks like a gold nugget."

Jennie took it back, laughing. "Do you think you could get a ring out of that? Maybe there's a diamond to go with it."

"Maybe if you had about nine more of them, as long as you have a tiny finger," he said.

Dwayne looked at the nugget in disappointment. "Not much of a treasure, then."

"The treasure," said Dr. Douglas, in a drolly academic tone, "is in the discovery and the search for knowledge."

The ore made it around to Lucas, who held it like Hamlet holding Yorick's skull. "Search for knowledge. Like, why did our guy have this?"

"Obviously," said Caitlin, "he never made it to the refinery."

"But why just one?" Mark asked.

"He wouldn't be carrying a fortune in gold ore in a satchel," said Lucas. "Maybe this was just a sample."

"Maybe there's more somewhere else," said Dwayne, always eager for excitement.

"Maybe," said Dr. Douglas, "you should all get over your gold bug and get back to work."

Chastised—at least a little bit—they did. The professor pushed herself to her feet, brushed off her hands, and gave Phin a long, evaluating look. "You are a strange but rather useful girl."

That was Phin to a tee. But were we any closer to the truth behind the Mad Monk legend? Did the gold or the cross or any of these three sets of bones have anything to do with the real ghost—the one that haunted *me*?

When I came in from tending the goats, the house smelled worse than I did. Hell, it smelled worse than *before* I took my boots off. I traced the stench back to the workroom, where Phin was cooking something over the Bunsen burner.

"Holy compost heap, Delphinium. *What* is that smell?"

"Hex-breaking potion," she said, as if that explained everything.

The blackout curtains were still up, but the lights were on. On the slate worktable a glass beaker bubbled vigorously over the gas flame. It looked like pond scum and smelled like Christmas potpourri, sauerkraut, and turnip greens. *Old* turnip greens.

I saw where this was headed. "You don't seriously expect me to drink that, do you?"

Phin gave it a stir. The clumps only made it more nauseating. "Well, if you're tied to the ghost by some kind of spell, this should break it."

I sank onto one of the high stools beside the counter. "So, you don't think we found the Mad Monk today, either."

She glanced at me as if I'd confirmed her suspicions. "I figured you would have said something on the way home if you'd sensed a change."

Spreading my fingers on the slate, I braced myself literally and figuratively. I hadn't talked to Phin about supernatural stuff in years, and I felt like I was blowing dust from parts of my brain. "It doesn't really matter, does it? Even if I weren't bound to the specter, I still have to keep looking for whatever is haunting here. If I stopped now, and people got hurt . . ."

I didn't finish the sentence. Phin knew me and my sense of responsibility well enough. "It *does* matter. What if we find the Mad Monk, or whatever it is, and the ghost is still tied to you? Do you want to be trailing that thing along to the sorority house or dorm? Your roommates won't thank you for it."

This was a very good point. I eyed the brew again. "Are you *sure* this is going to work? Because I don't want to drink that for nothing."

She thumped her fist onto the counter; the glass stirring rod stuck up like an antenna vibrating in a stiff breeze. "The parameters are somewhat unknown at the moment, Amy. It might be a spell, it might be something else. It might be that the ghost likes the smell of your shampoo. But all we can do is try."

I raised my hands in surrender. "All right. I trust you." Phin might have blown a few fuses and chemistry labs when inventing stuff, but she'd never poisoned anyone. That I knew of.

She dipped out a spoonful into a ladybug teacup and set it in front of me. My stomach turned over, and I almost lost my nerve.

"Are you sure you're not just making me do this so you can test your Kirlianometer?" I asked.

"Of course not!" Though she already had the gadget in her hand. "But would you mind drinking the potion in the dark?"

A god-awful eternity of seconds later, when I had a half a cup of the vile concoction down my gullet—in the dark—I changed my mind about trusting her.

"Oh God," I said, not at all sure the potion was going to stay down. "Will it still work if I hurl?"

"Don't be so dramatic," she said, clicking away with her Kirlianometer. "It just tastes bad, that's all."

"That's *all*? Did *you* taste it?" The only answer was another click. "Get ready, because you're about to get a picture of it coming back up again."

"You're talking too much to be really sick." She flipped the lights on and dug around in her backpack until she found some stale Goldfish crackers in a Baggie. "Here." She tossed them over. "Stop whining."

She let me eat enough to get the taste of the potion out of my mouth before she asked, "Do you still feel hexed?"

"I didn't feel hexed before." I was starting to feel less like I was going to barf, though.

"That's the spirit," she said. "Now, what's your plan?"

I considered the question, and my conversation with Ben earlier. "Could you make a spell that would help me run into a Kelly who can tell me about the ghost? Joe's the most obvious choice."

She nodded and started gathering supplies. "I approve of this plan, though you may want to rephrase 'run into.' Sometimes these things can be very literal, and you've done that once."

"Point taken."

She had me write my name on one small piece of paper, "Joe Kelly" on another, fold each lengthwise, and then make an X with the slips. Before she dripped wax onto the X, I asked, "This isn't going to make us suddenly fall in love or lust or something, is it?"

"Why do you always question me?" She dribbled a generous bit of wax where the slips of paper crossed. "Now, keep that in your pocket. And after you've met up, just break the seal, or you'll keep on bumping into each other."

"It's that simple?" I picked up the paper X gingerly, careful not to touch the still-soft yellow wax.

"Well, if you want it to work faster, you should go somewhere he'd likely be. I suggest the roadhouse, where I'm meeting Mark at eight."

"And you need a ride." Then I realized she'd said "Mark" and not "the gang." "Wait . . . is this a *date*?"

"Pfft. A date." She scoffed and put the candle back in the

cabinet. "I think he wants to ask me about the divination I did today."

I rolled my eyes, wondering how she could be so smart *and* so clueless. "I don't think so."

She frowned slightly. "The Kirlianometer, then?"

"Yeah," I said, wasting some sarcasm on her. "That must be it."

I got up with a groan. Between hunching over a trench all day and barnyard duty, I was stiff and sore. "While you're doling out potions, what have you got for aches and pains?"

"Aspirin." Her hands were full transferring the dregs of the pond scum into a jar. "You really are nuts about those goats. The schedule Aunt Hy left in the binder is much more relaxed."

"I know. But she was worried enough to call me from China, for Pete's sake. I must have promised and prom—"

Crap. How could I be so *stupid*?

I looked at Phin. She was standing frozen, potion dripping onto the floor, struck by the same lightning bolt of realization as me.

"Great Caesar's goats. I mean *ghost.*" I clutched my head to stop my spinning thoughts. "I'm such an idiot."

"You promised three times?" confirmed Phin.

"I was half asleep." That was my excuse for not making the connection sooner. "She kept saying, 'Promise you'll take care of the goats'—or that's what I thought—and I just said, 'Yes, I promise.' Three times, then poof. Specter in my bedroom."

"Of course!" Phin still held the beaker and stirrer as she

did a quick pace back and forth by the counter. The dogs sniffed the drips and ran for the other room. "That's why the ghost got past Aunt Hyacinth's protections. You opened a door when you took responsibility for it with the triple promise."

I staggered to the desk and plopped into the chair. "Can't I just renounce it three times?"

She looked doubtful. "I don't know. There could be repercussions. You vowed to take care of it."

"What does that even mean?" Frustration spiked the question.

"That's the problem with ambiguity in spells and arcane bargains," said Phin. "Wording can mess you up. I always say—"

"Semantics are important," I finished with her. I'd just thought she was being pedantic. She was, of course, but for a *reason.*

I looked at the beaker and the dripping stir rod she held, and groaned again, sinking my head into my hands. "Oh my God, do you know the worst part?"

"What?"

I couldn't think about full implications yet. I could only think as far as, "This means I drank that sludge for nothing."

22

"to the Goodnight girls." Mark lifted his beer, the toast almost drowned out by the band and the holiday weekend crowd at the Hitchin' Post. "Fortune favors the floral."

"That's not how it goes," corrected Phin. *"Fortes fortuna adiuvat."*

I reached over and clinked her bottle of soda with mine. "Pretend to be normal, Phin, and drink your drink."

The Dr Pepper tasted so much better than the pond scum.

But as vile as it had been, I would've drunk the potion again if it could have told me how to solve this problem. The only thing I knew to do was stick with my plan. Look for the ghost. Do what it had told me. Which was why I was in the Hitchin' Post with the crew, paper spell in my pocket, on the hunt for info on the Mad Monk.

If Mark had wanted to meet with just Phin, he should've picked somewhere other than the roadhouse. The rest of the crew were there, too, celebrating the find, and dissecting what it could mean. Since this was what I needed to know, too, I was happy when, after his toast, Mark set down his beer, rubbed his hands together, and said, "Okay, let's brainstorm. Rosary and gold nugget. Where did they come from?"

"Did you find anything else after we left?" Phin asked.

"More bones that appear to be from the third skeleton," said Mark. "Tomorrow we dig test holes around the field to see what else turns up. Then home so Dr. Douglas can write a grant proposal."

"Well, some of us are staying for the party," said Lucas, his eyes following a pair of women who walked by, checking him out in return. He lifted his beer to them, and they laughed and hurried on.

"Is it just me," said Jennie, amused by the exchange, "or are we getting even more stares than usual?"

"Everyone's talking about the dig," said Lucas. "I'm not fooling myself that it's because of my stunning good looks."

"Don't sell yourself short," she said.

Emery hunched over his bottle. "They're a lot more interested today than yesterday."

Dwayne elbowed him. "Stop sulking because Phin found some buried treasure and trumped your bones."

Jennie giggled. "Trumped your bones. That's funny."

I was going to miss Jennie when she headed back to Austin. Emery, not so much.

"That's the lamest treasure I ever saw," he said. "A fist-size hunk of gold ore. Even at today's prices, that would hardly be worth the cost of refining."

"Well, I'll ask the question no one has yet," said Dwayne. "Where did it come from?"

Lucas tore his attention away from another passing woman and answered. "There are records of several Spanish expeditions to look for gold in central Texas."

"Like Coronado?" Phin asked.

Mark turned to her with a laugh. "What is it with you and Coronado?"

She shrugged. "He's the only conquistador I remember."

I cleared my throat, hesitant to tell them their business. "While I was home this afternoon, I looked up that San Sabá mission that Mark talked about. There's supposedly a lost San Sabá gold mine, too, that no one has ever found." The Google hit had startled me, since buried treasure kept coming up in conversation. Ben had even reminded me today: the Mad Monk was supposedly guarding his treasure.

Lucas straightened with interest. "The San Sabá mine is just a legend, but there *are* actual records of a mine in this area. Los Almagres." He stared at a neon beer sign for a moment, checking his mental files. "Or maybe that was silver. No surprise it was lost, because this was Apache country, and they weren't keen on prospectors."

"Maybe what we've found was a prospecting expedition," said Jennie.

"But what about the cross?" asked Dwayne, tag-teaming

the speculation. "Doesn't that mean they were monks or missionaries or something?"

"Maybe it was both," said Mark. "Missionaries wanted to convert the heathens; conquistadors wanted their land; everyone wanted their gold. It's not like Spain had separation of church and state."

Emery wrapped it all up with a sneer. "So we're all agreed. The Mad Monk is a totally plausible theory based on historical record."

Phin turned a considering gaze his way. "You would be sort of funny if you weren't so obnoxious."

Lucas laughed, and nudged me to let him out of the booth. "Well, you guys are great, but I've been with you all day. I'm going to do some socializing. Who's with me?"

"I need something to nosh," said Jennie, "and I cannot eat one more Hitchin' Post burger or hot dog."

"You forgot nachos," Dwayne said.

"And nacho cheese fries," added Mark.

"So who's for trying that Mexican food place on Main Street?" Jennie looked at Phin, then me. "Wanna join us?"

I realized we were down one. "Where's Caitlin?"

"She's, um, on a date," she confessed, so apologetic I would have guessed whom the other girl was with even if I hadn't seen them talking at the dig today.

Which was fine. No, it was *good*, because it meant Ben was busy, leaving me free and clear to (hopefully) run into Joe Kelly. Which I realized I was less likely to do if I was in the middle of a crowd.

"You know," I said, "I'm beat. I think I'm going to grab something from a drive-through window and head home."

Mark volunteered, as I'd expected, "Phin, I can drive you home later if you want to hang out."

"Sure," she said, and one by one they slid out of the booth until only Emery was left. I thought they might just leave him, but Jennie relented and said, "Come on if you want, Emery."

"I figured I was too *obnoxious.*"

"So's rap music," said Mark, "but some people like it."

Emery didn't give them a chance to reconsider.

As the rest headed for the exit, I caught Phin's arm, holding her back. "How's this spell supposed to work? Should I do something?"

"Just go about your business," she said. "It's not instantaneous, just sooner rather than later. These kinds of spells merely affect probability. But you can't manipulate the human factor. Influencing free will is a *much* bigger deal."

"Okay," I said, squaring my shoulders. "Tell the others I'm going to the restroom, then heading home."

Phin frowned. "I don't think the ladies' room will up your chances of meeting Joe Kelly."

"It's not a tactical stop. It's too many Dr Peppers."

In the "Cowgirls" room, I washed my hands and hit the dryer with my elbow and just a little bit of déjà vu. I was taking Phin's advice and going about my business, which unfortunately meant wondering whether Ben had asked Caitlin out (or accepted her invite) before or after the backrub, and why it mattered.

The door opened and a woman in the Hitchin' Post uniform (jeans, T-shirt, apron) came in. She was older than

Jessica by a long shot, and might have been a natural blonde at some point in her life, but not now. She watched me as the dryer ran out, but I thought maybe she was just waiting for the sink.

I had no hint of anything odd until she asked, "Are you the witch that's digging up the bones in the pasture?"

Warily I dried my damp hands on my jeans, meeting her eyes in the mirror. "I'm one of the volunteers working with the crew from the university."

"I know who you are." Whoever *she* was, her eyes were hard as flint, her voice a bitter pill. "Jessica told me you're not just digging up bones. You're digging up the ghost."

"I'm not—"

The words stuck in my throat like a tongue on a frozen flagpole.

No, no, no! Not now!

Think, Amy. This is what you do.

But I couldn't. I reached for my store of clever evasions and found nothing but cold, empty space. Panic spiked, my mind raced, but I couldn't find a single word.

"You are," said the woman. I silently begged her not to be a small-town, small-minded cliché. "You're poking your nose where it shouldn't be. No wonder the Mad Monk is stirring. A witch like you digging up his bones."

"Trust me," I managed. Hope flared, and I tried again, "I'm not—"

But my tongue knotted on that, too, and *holy crap* what was wrong with me? I wasn't a witch. Why couldn't I say that?

Maybe because there was a spell in my pocket and a

ghost paying calls at my house. But it wasn't honor or nerves or guilt that stopped me. I *physically* could not speak. This was *not* natural.

"You are." She spit words like daggers. "All of you Goodnights, passing yourself off as hippie, new age types, thinking you can charm this town with your money. But what you're doing is unnatural. And so are you."

She poured out her venom on me, thinking I was young and defenseless. And, horribly, I *was*. I couldn't control this conversation and couldn't even walk away. I was paralyzed by my inability to deny what she said and my unwillingness to just *own* it.

No one was that bitter without some cause. I seized on that and used it to say *something*. "I'm sorry for whatever's happened to you."

"You should be." Her voice hitched, but her fever of anger didn't break. "My husband is in the hospital right now because of you. Hit on the head because you city types can't leave things alone."

"I'm so sorry," I said again. I didn't try to explain that I hadn't even heard of the ghost until two days ago. Excuses wouldn't make any difference.

"You tell those college folks to stop violating those graves. And you—" Her voice quaked. "Just get out to your farm and stay there, before you hurt any more decent people than you already have."

She straight-armed the door and left. In her wake, I sagged against the counter, the strength washing out of me. My eyes burned with tears I'd held back while she was flaying me.

My hands shook too hard to turn the knob on the faucet. It took me three tries before I could splash cold water on my face and begin to sort through my tumbling thoughts.

Why couldn't I lie?

What was wrong with me? How had I lost the ability to steer my own voice?

I heard Phin's words in my head. *Influencing free will is a much,* much *bigger deal.*

Was my bond with the ghost enough to do that?

Panic rose up to choke me. Maybe I could live being haunted, but how could I exist without the ability to spin-doctor my crazy dual life? My glib explanations, my denials and dodges . . . those were my lifeline. They were how I kept my balance between my worlds, and how I protected my family from the skeptic authorities and the crazy believers.

Even if the Goodnight Effect would keep them safe without my help, I didn't even have that. Could I handle a life-time of living in a magical world with no magic, and no defenses, dealing with situations just like this? Because the only other option would be to disown my family and become a totally different person.

It was too much to hold in, and I did *not* want to cry in the bathroom in front of the condom machine. I fled the cowgirls' room and in the hall turned away from the throng in the bar, toward the back door with the half-dark exit sign.

I burst out into the night air. Or more specifically, into a haze of marijuana smoke. And in the middle of it, sitting on an upended milk carton, two minions lounging with him, was Joe Kelly.

This was why I didn't mess with magic.

23

mom always knows the right time to call, even when it seems like the wrong time.

When I rushed out of the bar, Joe Kelly shot to his feet. Impressive, considering what he was smoking. He stared at me, and I stared at him, and finally he thought about holding his joint somewhere less obvious than right in front of him.

I didn't care. I had reached my limit and couldn't possibly construct a sensible sentence just then. Ironic, when searching him out had put me in this situation in the first place.

So I turned and ran to Stella in the parking lot. I flung myself into her, closed the door, and sat soaking up the toasty warmth of the car.

When I'd collected myself, I headed home. *Screw you, Mad Monk. I'm taking the night off.*

Usually I love to drive, because it gave me time to think. No teachers, no TV, no Internet. But tonight, the best part of the Hill Country was that you *couldn't* think and drive. The twilight shadows and the curving stretch of highway took all my attention, like meditation. By the time the phone rang where I'd tossed it in the passenger seat, I thought I'd re-covered at least a surface calm.

But there was no fooling Mom.

"Sweetie, what's wrong?"

I put the call on speaker rather than pull over. "I'm fine, Mom."

"You don't sound fine."

I didn't want to talk to her. I didn't want to cry, I didn't want I-told-you-so's, and I *didn't* want to admit how fear had turned to fury.

Stupid ghost.

"I'm sure Daisy told you what's going on," I said.

"No one likes to hear secondhand that her daughter is under a geas to a spirit."

Geas. The word was heavy and old-fashioned, which was about right.

I scowled at the windshield, because she wasn't there in person. "Well, I didn't really like finding it out firsthand, either."

"Are you taking a *tone* with me, Amaryllis?"

I took a deep breath and eased my foot off the gas pedal as the road dipped. It was tempting to put Stella through her paces, but there were other drivers out. And also, my mother was on the phone.

"Sorry, Mom."

"Tell me what happened, sweetie."

"Aunt Hyacinth has cursed me, that's what happened."

"Oh, honey. She would never do that."

"Not literally. But I have this ghost tied to me, and I can't say it's not real, or that I'm not looking for it, or even that there's no magic involved. My mind just goes blank and my mouth will not work."

She paused, and I felt the point even over the phone. "So, you can't lie?"

"It's not lying, Mom. It's smoke screen." Except that it was *totally* lying, with one exception: "I couldn't even speak to say I'm not a witch."

"Sweetie, saying you're not a witch is like saying you're not a carnivore if you get your meat from the supermarket instead of hunting it yourself."

The road took a steep curve, a little too on the nose, metaphorically, to what just happened in my head.

"I hadn't thought of that," I said when things leveled out.

"You must have, or you would have been able to say it. Triple promises work on your own conscience, even if it's *sub*consciously."

It was true. I didn't practice magic, but I used it like some people use the Internet. No, not the Internet, because I couldn't function without that, but something life enhancing yet nonessential, like text messaging. Not spells, usually–teas and bath potions and the occasional crystal jewelry.

"How did you know it was a triple promise?" I asked, even though I could guess.

"I talked to Phin, of course. I'm so proud of you, honey, for taking on this task. I always knew you had an affinity of your own, but I'd almost given up–" She corrected herself with a laugh. "No, that's not true. I'd never give up on one of my babies."

I flexed my hands on the wheel, my knuckles stiff from gripping so hard through twists and turns, literal and figurative. I wished I had pulled over while I had the chance. This was taking much more concentration than the venting/bitching session I'd anticipated.

"What are you talking about, Mom? I didn't volunteer for this."

Her voice cut in and out, and when she came through clearly again, she was speaking as if she hadn't heard me.

"Funny, I suspected your talent might be spirit related, because of–"

She cut out again.

"Because of what, Mom?" I yelled at the phone on the console, as if that would make a difference in reception. "If I'd volunteered for this, I could get rid of this ghost, right? Mom?"

"Yes, dear?" And she was back.

"Did you hear what I said? I'm losing the connection in the hills."

"Are you on the road?"

"Yes. I must be going through a dead spot." Wow. There was a poor choice of words. "I'd better go."

"Amaryllis Goodnight! You're not talking while you're driving, are you?"

"I'm on speaker—" A hiss of static cut off the conversation. I glanced at the phone, saw the call had dropped, and when I looked up, there was a man in the middle of the road.

I slammed on the brakes. Stella struggled to grip the pavement and I clutched the wheel, bracing myself for something horrible, every muscle tensed as if I could *will* the car to stop in time.

Please, God, stop in time.

A squeal of tires and an explosion of static from the radio. Then everything went quiet, and dark, and I was stopped in the middle of the two-lane highway, surrounded by mountains and fences, with nothing ahead of me but more road, a long strip of winding yellow line, and no one in sight.

"What. The. Hell."

I stared at the spot where I would swear—where I would bet my *life* if I hadn't managed to control Stella's swerve—someone had been standing just an instant before.

Nothing.

Fear crept up my spine with sharp, cold feet. When I say nothing, I mean *nothing*. There was no man, there were no other cars, not even a distant house or barn light. I was completely alone.

What, exactly, *had* I seen? A flash. A figure in the headlights, man-shaped, standing straight, arms to his sides. I had no memory of what he looked like. It was just an impression, a pillar of a person. A shade.

I pried my fingers from the wheel and flicked on the hazard lights. The thought of leaving my car, my bubble of safety, even if it was just an illusion, spurred my racing heart. It hammered in my ears as I climbed out and searched either side of the highway. The contrast from the headlights to the dark was too great for me to see much, but if someone had run off to one of the shoulders, I would know it.

Nothing.

Sagging, weak-kneed, against Stella's hood, I rubbed my trembling hands on my pants to get the feeling back into them. I was being foolish to react now to something that hadn't happened. But I had a good imagination and could hear the thud in my head, of a body hitting the hood, the crack of bone against windshield.

I felt like I'd been pranked. This ghost was starting to really piss me off.

With a surge of anger, I jumped to my feet and I shouted at the empty road, "What do you want?" Then I spun and called to the limestone hills, "I'm *busca*-ing for you, you stupid ghost. What more do you want?"

Only silence answered.

The ghost wanted me to stop. I was stopped. I remembered the EVP, and though I'm sure Phin would be ready with a digital voice recorder, all I had was my phone. Maybe the voice-note app would work.

Before I could get it from the car, I heard a strange, deep *whump*.

I knew that subwoofer sound. It was soft and distant, but not as distant as when I heard it at the farm, or at the dig site.

I caught a flicker of light in the darkness past the fence that ran along the highway. There was a gate about a hundred feet from me, and the sign told me I was in the middle of McCulloch land, but the twists of the road made it hard to know *exactly* where. Which probably made what I was about to do even more stupid.

There was something out in that pasture, and I was going to follow it, and I was going to *find* it. Ghost, mystery, Mad Monk . . . I was hell-bent on putting them all to rest.

Before I could talk myself out of it, I got in the car and drove closer to the gate, pulling off the road and into the weeds on the shoulder. Then I grabbed my phone and my flashlight and clambered over the gate.

I was doing exactly what I'd sworn never to do again. I was chasing ghosts into the darkness. But my determination was stronger than my fear.

The deep sound didn't repeat, but I could hear a throaty rumbling. The hills made it impossible to localize. I left my flashlight off and picked my way down the white caliche road until my eyes adjusted to the moonlight. Something *big* moved in the shadows to my right, scaring my heart into my throat—until I heard rhythmic chewing. A cow.

The cows had been cleared from around the dig site, so I was in a different section of the ranch. I thought the looming bluff in front of me might be the big granite outcropping that Mrs. McCulloch had pointed to at lunch, which helped me get my bearings.

The light I'd seen from the road winked out. I fixed the

point where it had disappeared in my mind and, trusting my night vision, set off at a slow jog across the pasture. At first I kept to the packed-down cattle trails, but when it became too difficult to keep on target, I abandoned the path for the more uneven ground.

The hill was a black shadow against the charcoal of the sky, and as I neared it, I heard an intermittent rumble. It took me a moment to identify the sound as a diesel truck engine, coming toward me.

Coming *right* toward me, I realized with a start. The bounce of its shocks, the crunch of rock and dirt under big tires, but no headlights. Who drove over this terrain in the dark with no headlights? There were ravines and ditches and cows and girls with more determination than sense out in these hills.

In those heartbeats of frozen confusion, I couldn't think of a single person who wouldn't be extremely annoyed to see me. But I also couldn't think of any good reason for someone to be driving without lights. I mean, no reason that wasn't sneaky and dangerous. I didn't want to be caught there by anyone, but especially someone who didn't want to be caught there, either.

For another second I danced indecisively from foot to foot, then spotted a rocky outcropping like a gift from heaven. I ran for it and rolled into the concealment of shadow beneath it.

Only it wasn't a shadow. It was a hole.

And I was falling.

I slid down an almost vertical slope, sharp rocks tearing my shirt and scraping my back, but slowing my descent.

Before I had time to let out more than a startled screech and pained yelp, I landed on something soft and yielding and *really* foul.

My flashlight clattered down beside me and hit with a squish.

The blackness was so profound it hurt my eyes. From overhead I heard the faint rustle of leathery wings in the keen, cutting silence that followed my landing.

I took stock of the mess I'd gotten myself into. On one hand, I was bumped and bruised and scraped, but when I tested arms and elbows and knees, they all still worked.

On the other, I was trapped at the bottom of a sinkhole, and my neck had just been saved by a ginormous pile of bat guano.

I was well and truly in the shit.

24

i felt around for my flashlight, promising myself that when I got out of this—*however* I got out of this—I would indulge in an almighty freak-out about the fact that I was covered in bat crap. But for now I'd be thankful it had broken my fall.

Turning on the light helped. Knowing your situation, even when it sucked, was better than not. I was in a cave of reasonable size. One section seemed to go deeper into the ground, though I couldn't tell how far because stalactites— or stalagmites, I could never remember which—blocked my view. I was not at all inclined to investigate, because that would mean crawling on my belly into places where neurotic control freaks were never meant to go.

In central Texas, school field trips to the big tourist caves are a requisite. Inner Space, Natural Bridge, Longhorn Caverns . . . limestone caves riddle the hills—big, little; dry, active; open, closed—and I knew from helpful docents—not just from Ben McCulloch—that sinkholes *do* open up now and then.

This one, judging by the pile of guano, had been there for a while. It only *felt* as though I'd been swallowed by the earth. Really I had just, literally, leapt before I looked.

The slope I'd slid down was way too steep to climb. The mouth of the cave was a flat oval with an overhang, ten feet or so above my reaching fingers. A few fluttering black shapes clung to it; it was probably solid with bats during the daytime.

I had nothing against bats. They ate bugs and were good for the ecology. I just didn't want to be there when they got back.

Get a grip, Amy. You're going to get out of here. It's a bat cave, not the Grand Canyon.

And this wasn't the Dark Ages, either. The solution, once I'd calmed down, was simple. I wiped my hands on a tiny clean spot on my shirt and fished my phone from my pocket with two fingers. There was not enough Purell in the world to make me happy just then.

Phin did not answer her phone.

"Dammit, Phin!" My shout scared the last of the bats away.

Habitually not answering her phone was annoying. Ignoring it while we were in the middle of a mystery was infuriating. Shouldn't she be getting the heebie-jeebies about now?

I thumbed through my recent connections, hoping I'd phoned Mark or vice versa. But there was only one recent call that didn't have a name attached to it, and I knew exactly who it was.

Would I rather die a slow, lingering death and be found by archaeologists someday, buried in petrified bat crap? Was that seriously worse than calling Ben McCulloch for help?

I swallowed my pride and hit "dial." He answered on the second ring.

"Hello?"

That pride stuck in my craw when I remembered he was on a date with Caitlin. My night just kept getting worse.

"Hello?" he repeated. "Amy, is that you?"

"Yes." Where to begin? "I don't suppose you have a rope in your truck."

"A rope? What kind of rope?"

"About fifteen feet long? Strong enough to hold, um–" I rounded up generously for safety. "–a hundred and twenty-five pounds?"

Over the phone, I heard a car door opening and closing with a slam. "Stop being coy. Where are you?"

I leaned my head against the stone wall. "Other than down a very deep hole, I don't really know."

After a pause–I didn't even try to interpret it, because I was miserable enough–he said, "Does that phone have GPS on it?"

"Yeah. I think so. It finds the nearest Starbucks for me, so it must, right?"

Another pause, and this one I *could* interpret. "I can't believe your aunt said you were her smartest niece."

"She must have been talking about Phin."

"God help your family, then." I heard the gruff growl of his truck starting up. "Hang up, then find your position with your phone. You should be able to send it to me in a text, and I'll put the coordinates into the GPS in my pickup."

"I can do that."

"Of course you can. It's not rocket science."

I decided to forgive him for being a jackass, because the spark of annoyance warmed my insides, which had gone cold with worry. "I'm in town," he said, "but I'll be there soon. You're not hurt, are you?"

"Only my delicate sensibilities."

I must not have sounded as resilient as I intended, because his reply was firmly reassuring. "Just sit tight, Amy. It'll be all right."

I accepted his word for it and tried not to think about snakes. Or rabies. Or suffocating from the methane fumes from the guano.

After sending him my location, I turned off the flashlight to save the battery. It was very, very dark, with the overhang blocking out any stars or moonlight. The damp crept into my skin and made my tired joints ache.

I closed my eyes to pretend I wasn't down a deep, black hole. It was a horrible feeling to just . . . sit there. Waiting on help. Maybe this control-freak thing wasn't working out for me as well as I thought. Especially since I had lost so much control over my life.

Time stretched interminably, then snapped back as the

sound of tires on rocky ground and the rumbling chug of a diesel pickup truck shook me out of self-pity. Ben must not have been very far away. He may not have liked me, but I never doubted he would come for me.

I opened my eyes and reached for my flashlight to signal him, but something jolted my hand. The unseen force knocked the light from my fingers, and it clanged against the rock.

Heart slamming against my ribs, I swung around, putting my back to the wall so nothing could sneak up on me in the pitch dark.

Only it wasn't pitch dark anymore. The inky blackness lightened until I could see the shadow of my hand in front of me. Then the shape of my fingers, then the lines of my palm, bathed in a cold glow that was the color of moonlight where moonlight couldn't reach.

A faint breeze, like a frigid breath on the back of my neck, stirred my hair. I could smell leather and metal and damp stone as the cave floor pooled with icy fog, cold creeping up from the earth.

The air, as always, stung my throat and lungs, and I took shallow breaths, even though fear said to grab deep gasps so I could fight, or run.

Where could I run? The specter gathered in front of me, mist and light pulled together. I wanted to change what happened next, but I couldn't look away from its dark eyes and gasping mouth. He raised his arm, grasping, and the cold rooted at my heart spread through me like a vine of ice choking off my air.

One thing was different. Nonsense sounds wove through

251

the blood rushing in my ears. They grew louder and louder in my skull, ricocheting around like bell peals in a church tower. I stumbled, fell back against the cave wall with a grunt, pushing out the last of my breath.

The panicked gallop of my pulse had become a lurching stumble. I was going to die in this hole, and no one was ever going to find me. I knew it with a certainty.

Tears blurred the pale figure of the ghost; it ran like a chalk painting in the rain. The tears were for my mother, who wouldn't know what happened to me.

The sob of fear and fury was for me. I was so scared and so *pissed.*

Only the wall kept me on my feet. My vision was nothing but pinpricks as I raised a trembling hand, fingers outspread, warding off the cold that the specter had brought with him from beyond the veil of death.

And the ghost vanished, leaving the cave so black and silent, I thought for a moment I *had* died. That this was now my grave.

But I could feel my aching lungs taking gasping breaths, and hear my heart, pounding but steady. The air was warming slowly to a normal cavelike chill.

Where had the specter gone? And why?

In the restored quiet, the nonsense syllables that had rattled my brain settled into a pattern in my mind. Not nonsense at all, but a foreign word.

Cuidado. Cuidado.

Be careful.

Was it a warning or a threat?

25

Cuidado. The ghost had frozen me and choked me and nearly wrecked my car. A threat seemed redundant.

But why warn me? Was there something *else* going on, other than skeletons and neighbor feuds and haunted pastures and Mad Monks bashing people on the head?

The last thing jolted my runaway thoughts to a halt. *My* specter hardly ever moved. I wasn't sure it could. How could it hit people on the head when it seemed barely able to lift an arm?

I jumped as the UT fight song echoed through the cave.

My cell phone. My hands were still shaking so badly, I could barely get it out of my pocket.

I had never been so happy to hear a human voice as I was to hear Ben's. "According to the GPS, I should be right near you. Can you yell or something?"

"Hang on." I used the glow of the phone to locate the flashlight. "Watch for a light. There's a ledge over the cave opening, so you might not see it from the wrong way. I'll flash you."

"That's not necessary. Just blink the light."

He'd already hung up before I realized he'd made a joke. The world was clearly coming to an end.

The phone rang again, and I didn't need to look at the caller ID. Especially when she started speaking before I could get a word out.

"Amy! What's going on?"

"I'm okay, Phin. But we're going to have a talk about this letting calls go to voice mail–" Call waiting buzzed in, and I glanced at the screen. "I'll talk to you back at the house. Mom's calling. The heebie-jeebies are going around."

I hung up before Phin could ask more questions, then reassured Mom. I didn't have time to do more than tell her I was okay before the crunch of footsteps on rock drew my gaze up to the mouth of the cave. Ben's face appeared. He flinched at the flashlight in his eyes and put up a hand to shield them.

"Boy," he said, "I'm going to *love* hearing this story."

Ben took a good look at me—whiff, rather—after I'd climbed up the rope he'd tied to the bumper of his truck and lowered down the hole. My options, he said, were to ride in the bed of the pickup or strip down and wrap up in a horse blanket to sit inside. It wasn't much of a choice for the risk-adverse.

I sat on the tailgate and toed off my sneakers. "What would your mother say?"

He returned from the cab of the truck with a thick felted-wool blanket. "That I'm being practical."

"Is that an *actual* horse blanket?" I asked as he held it up like a curtain, closed his eyes, and turned his head.

"Don't worry. Rusty won't mind if you borrow it."

I took my phone out of my pocket, set it on the tailgate, then shucked off my cargo pants and shirt and threw both in the bed of the truck. That got most of the actual gunk off me. Except–

I must have made a little whimper, because Ben started to look, then quickly averted his eyes again. "Are you hurt?"

"It's in my hair." I held the strands miserably between my fingers and tried not to cry. It would be stupid to cry at this point. I was safe, just really stinky.

He made a sound halfway between laughter and sympathy. "It's probably in worse places than that." He shook the blanket. "Wrap up and I'll drive you home so you can shower."

I wrapped the blanket around me like a big, ugly, scratchy towel. My bra straps still showed, but considering how much he'd seen of me in the past, I was positively prudish.

Wherever *he'd* been, it had been casual. He wore jeans and a vintage-looking T-shirt. But he smelled really nice. Spicy and woodsy with a hint of horse. Well, that last part was probably the blanket. But it wasn't an unpleasant smell. Certainly not in contrast to me.

"You seem very calm, under the circumstances," I said warily.

Shoving his hands in his pockets, he raised his brows in sedate inquiry. "Will it make any difference if I yell? Or tell you what an idiot you were, or how badly you could have been hurt? Or how this is *precisely* why you shouldn't be out here 'ghost hunting' or whatever the hell you were doing?"

By the end of that speech, he wasn't so sedate, and I self-consciously tucked the ends of the blanket more securely. "Will it make any difference if I explain?"

He sighed. "I doubt it. Get in. Let's get you home."

I followed him to the cab of the truck and climbed in, smoothing the blanket primly around my legs. It wasn't much help; it only came to the middle of my thighs. But at least it covered that much. "I have to get Stella," I told him, once he'd climbed behind the wheel.

"Who's Stella?" he asked, starting the engine.

"My car. I left her on the road where I saw the–"

I bit off my words, but didn't fool him. "Saw the what?" he demanded. "The ghost? Is that what you were following across the pasture?"

"Actually, no." The word came out freely, because it was true, even though it hadn't been a completely ghost-free adventure. Not by a long shot. "I did see something strange, but it turns out it was a truck." I frowned, focusing on the difference between the chug of Ben's pickup and the throatier rumble of what I'd heard. "A diesel engine. Twice, once while I was in the cave."

He thought that over. "Steve Sparks drives a diesel. Maybe he was out here checking on something. It's been known to happen. Fence down, cow in trouble, birthing gone wrong . . ." He slid a glance my way. "Crazy girl in her underwear, running around, falling down sinkholes."

Before I could do more than glare, the truck hit a bump and I had to grab for the door handle and the blanket at the same time. When things leveled out, so did I. "If someone was out here on ranch business, wouldn't they have their headlights on?"

He was slow to answer, and glanced at me again, as if judging my veracity or my sanity. "Probably."

I subsided with a thoughtful "Hmmm." I would say I was playing my cards close to the vest, but I didn't really know what kind of hand I held. Lots of people drove diesel pickups, so that wasn't much of a clue. And what *non*-legit reason could someone have to be out here? Tearing down fences, maybe? Pulling up survey stakes? I couldn't imagine *why*, but it was clear the ghost—the real ghost—was only one piece of the McCulloch Ranch puzzle.

We'd reached the dirt road and I could see the gate ahead, and Stella on the other side. I only had a minute to say thank you, and you wouldn't think gratitude would be so hard to put into words. For answering the phone, for coming to get me out of the hole I'd gotten into, and for not being nearly as awful about it as he could have been.

"I appreciate the help," I said, and should have stopped there. "Sorry if I interrupted your date."

He didn't look away from the road, and the barometer of his brows was hard to read in the dashboard light. He seemed to contemplate a couple of responses, then settle on "It wasn't a date like that. Caitlin and I know some of the same people at UT."

"Oh." What was the appropriate response here? My silly, girly self was doing a joyful dance, and the rest of me was telling her to sit down and shut up because this changed nothing.

We'd reached the gate, freeing him to stop the truck and give me a look I couldn't read. "What about you? Where are your ghost-hunting buddies? For that matter, where's your sister? What kind of idiot let you run around in the dark all by yourself?"

"Just this one." I pointed to myself. "I was headed home to feed the goats, and stopped when I saw . . ."

"A ghost." He caught my second verbal fumble.

I lifted my chin primly and pretended I was above responding, when really I couldn't. Stupid triple-promise spell. My subconscious knew it had been the ghost that stopped me on the road, even if the deep sound and distant light had more mundane explanations.

I skipped ahead to the part I *could* talk about. "I saw a light out in the pasture, and heard a noise, and just . . . rushed in." I didn't have to fake chagrin. It had been stupid, but I hadn't quite been myself.

Ben watched me, reading the emotions that flitted over my face. Finally he sighed—a weary, heavy sound. "Amy, you could have been killed tonight. Or at least seriously injured. You can't keep doing this. If those had been poachers out there, you could have been shot, mistaken for an animal in the dark. I'm not just saying this to be a jackass."

I hadn't even considered poachers. I heard the ghost again in my head. *Cuidado.* Had he purposefully kept me from signaling whoever was in that other truck?

Taking my silence as assent, Ben got out to open the gate to the highway. The one I'd jumped over earlier. I hadn't told him where Stella was; she just happened to be at the closest entrance to the pasture.

He got back in and pulled through, and I jumped down from the truck while he was closing the gate again behind us. I'd reluctantly put my shoes back on, because there would be rocks and glass on the side of the road. I did scuff them as I walked, however, to get as much bat crap off as I could.

The pickup's headlights lit our path as Ben insisted on walking me over to the car. But as we neared it, my steps slowed, because Stella was listing slightly, and I hadn't parked on a slope.

Ben noticed, too, and went around the driver's side, putting out a hand as if warning me to stay back. *That* was not going to happen. Rounding the car after him, I saw that her rear tire was flat and somehow . . . lifeless. I'd had a flat tire before, but tonight there was something chilling about the way the black rubber seemed to pool ominously in the gravel.

"Could that have happened when I slammed on the brakes?" I asked, too tense to even curse. "Or maybe I ran over something when I pulled off the road."

"I don't think so." Crouching by the wheel, Ben sank his finger into the two-inch hole in the sidewall of the tire. There was no way that had been made by anything other than a knife.

Stella had been stabbed.

I stepped back, as if I could distance myself from this sickening fact. As I did, a flutter of white on the windshield caught my eye. With trembling fingers, I pulled a folded slip of paper from under the wiper.

Leave the dead in peace.

26

"**G**et in the truck."

Ben's voice left little room for argument, but I tried to squeeze one in anyway. "I don't think–"

"Amy, I am not messing around." His face was grim, and he held out his hand. "Give me your key so I can get your purse and whatever else you want. I'll drive you home."

"I am not leaving her here on the side of the road."

"You did before, to hare off across the pasture."

"That was different. I didn't think I'd be gone long. I wasn't expecting your land to be booby-trapped."

He took my arm, turned me toward the truck. "I'll call Triple A from your house."

"*I* can call them from right here," I said, pulling out of his grip and turning toward Stella.

He turned me right back. "At least call from in the pickup. In case whoever did this is still around."

I could have pulled away again—he was persistent, but not rough—only his words distracted me. "What? You think someone is waiting in a tree to snipe me?"

We reached the truck and he backed me up against its side before I could react, taking my shoulders in his hands— my bare shoulders in his hands, and oh my God, the places that made me shiver. He seemed blessedly ignorant of that, unobservant of the blush spreading up from the blanket or the hitch in my breath as he gazed intently into my wide eyes and said, "What kind of idiot are you?"

That snapped me, mostly, out of my haze. Before I could form words, however, he went on. "Someone slashed your tire. With a *knife*. Not a ghost, a person."

"I know that." I met his stare, willing him to see the *reasonable* Amy beneath the flake I knew I must seem.

He studied me for another moment, his thoughts visibly shifting in patterns I couldn't read. His hands, though—I didn't think he realized his hold on my shoulders had softened, and that as he was thinking his thoughts, his right thumb was sliding back and forth over my skin in an unconscious motion that, if we had been any other people in any other situation, would have been a caress. The traitorous flutters in my pulse didn't know the difference.

Or maybe he did realize it, an instant before he dropped

me like I was hot, and not in a good way. His gaze zipped away from mine as he stepped back and cleared his throat. "So. Your key?"

"I'm not leaving Stella here," I said, putting iron in my voice. "I bought it with my own money when my dad didn't want me to and my mother said she'd pay for it for my graduation present. It was almost new, and it's not a Goodnight car, it's *mine*."

I broke off—hell, I nearly slapped a hand over my own mouth—because some insight clicked behind Ben McCulloch's eyes and I realized I'd given too much away somehow.

He confirmed it when he said, after a long, digestive pause, "Okay. I'll change the tire and you can drive home on the spare."

An automatic objection jumped to my lips—I could and had changed a tire before. My family called *me* to do it for them. But it might be hard to do naked, wrapped in a horse blanket, and I couldn't bring myself to put my guanofied clothes back on when there was another option.

Sadly, I was more fastidious than feminist, and I dropped the key into Ben's waiting hand.

I didn't even consider protesting when Ben said he'd follow me to Goodnight Farm. It was only sensible, given that I was driving on one of those donut spare tires on a very lonely road.

I'd been joking, but alone in the car on the way to the farm, the possibility of someone hiding and watching us—*me*, if I'd been alone—loomed large and unpleasant. Someone had taken a *knife* to something I owned. The note on the windshield only underscored the maliciousness of the act.

So I was darn glad to have Ben McCulloch following me home, opening the gates for me, and parking his truck beside Stella in front of the house.

I was *not* happy to see the goats cavorting through the yard.

The security lights were on, but the house was dark. I heard a muffled bark and saw the dogs hiding under the porch. With a sigh, I climbed out of my car. Phin must not be home yet.

Ben met me at the front gate, opened it for me, and handed me the clothes I'd left in the back of his truck. "Go inside and get in the shower. I'll feed the escape artists."

"You have to bang the lid of the feed—"

"I remember," he said. Of course, he'd seen me do it the day we'd met. Which seemed like an awfully long time ago.

I let him handle it, which felt like a major breakthrough somehow. The dogs emerged from hiding and waited impatiently for me to let them into the safety of the house. I kicked off my filthy shoes and left them, and my clothes, outside. As I opened the door, the lights came on, and I allowed myself a little sigh of relief at being inside the security system, and inside the house.

"Thanks, Uncle Burt." I started for the stairs, then paused with my hand on the rail and addressed his immobile rocking chair. "Don't mess with Ben, okay? He helped me out of a jam tonight."

The chair gave no sign of agreement, but I was too tired and stinky to argue.

Upstairs in the shower, I scrubbed under water as hot as I could bear it, even though the soap stung the scrapes on my back and my palms—especially my palms—as I lathered my hair about five times. I avoided Clear Your Head shampoo and went for Mellow Mood ("Breathe deep and let your tension go down the drain"). Mom was so right. Saying I had nothing to do with the supernatural was like saying I was a vegetarian just because I only ate chicken and fish once in a while.

By the time I'd dried off and combed out my hair, I'd stopped feeling like I was going to hit the ceiling at the faintest noise. I put on flannel pj pants because I wasn't sure I'd ever be too warm again, and searched for a baggy old T-shirt because the scrapes on my back were bleeding.

I winced at them in the mirror. Aunt Hyacinth would have something useful in her workroom, so I headed downstairs.

And stopped when I saw Ben sitting on the couch, thumbing through a copy of *Texas Gardener* without really looking at it.

I'd expected him to leave after feeding the goats. Or maybe I hadn't, because I didn't say goodbye. So maybe I'd unconsciously invited him in. He'd certainly made himself at home, his legs up on the couch, but not his feet. I'll bet that was his mother's doing. His hair, under the lamplight, was the burnished gold-brown of the rock we'd unearthed that afternoon.

He looked up, and I pretended I hadn't been staring. "Better?" he asked.

"Almost. You didn't have to stay."

"Where's your sister?"

I came down the rest of the stairs, oddly a lot more self-conscious in my pj's than I'd been in the horse blanket. "Still out with the gang, I guess."

"Did you call her?"

I gave an exaggerated roll of my eyes. "Wow. What a great idea. I'll have to try that next time I'm stuck in a cave."

He held up his hands in surrender. "Fine."

Since he didn't look like he was about to leave, I went into the workroom and opened the cabinet closest to the door. First-aid supplies for every need, including mine. I grabbed a jar of ointment and, after a moment of indecision, headed back to the den.

I handed Ben the jar. "Since you're here, and you've seen most of this already, you might as well be useful." Turning around, I reached over my shoulder to gather the back of my shirt, while I held the front down securely. Because modesty is my middle name.

"Jeez, Amy."

That didn't sound like admiration of my alabaster skin, so I figured it must look as bad as it felt. "I'm sorry," I said, embarrassed, and let go of the fabric, wincing as it slithered down. "I'll wait for Phin."

"You'd better not." He hooked the ottoman with his foot and pulled it over, then sat in Uncle Burt's chair before I could stop him. "Sit down," he said, indicating the ottoman in front of him.

I did, gingerly, then reached over my shoulder again to hold my shirt out of the way. Lavender and tea tree oil and bergamot wafted pleasantly as Ben unscrewed the lid, adding to my mellow mood. At least until the cool ointment touched my abraded skin.

I flinched with a hiss and a whimper.

"Don't be such a baby," he said.

"Distract me," I ordered. He was a bit of a distraction just being there, and his touch was gentle as he smoothed on Aunt Hyacinth's potion. The lavender scent was clean and crisp, and the bergamot smelled like Earl Grey tea. "Tell me about the Mad Monk of McCulloch Ranch."

"No. I am not enabling you. Especially not if you use that ridiculous name."

"So . . . what do *you* call it?"

"I call it bullshit."

I twisted to glare at him then regretted it–vocally–because the places he hadn't reached yet still hurt when I moved.

"That's what you get," he said, and dabbed another raw spot.

I wanted to tell him I was asking about the story so I could sort it out from the reality of the specter that haunted me. I had ample, painful evidence of my ghost, but there was only hearsay and questionable accounts for the head basher they called the Mad Monk. The theory that they were separate things had solidified in my mind, but I still didn't know what the Mad Monk was. Rumor or real?

Did the fact that Ben didn't believe in the Mad Monk count *for* its existence, or *against* it?

He got to another deep scratch, and I hissed at the sting.

He made an apologetic sound, but coated the spot thoroughly. "I ought to make you go to the doctor. God knows what got into these scratches."

"Unfortunately, I know exactly what got into them." A horrible thought made me stiffen. "Oh my God. I wonder if I need a rabies shot."

"You can't get rabies from guano."

I twisted, despite the twinges, to look him in the eye. "Are you sure?"

He smiled sheepishly. "I looked it up on my phone while you were in the shower."

Ben McCulloch had a devastating smile. It was sad that he didn't use it very much. But probably safer. I seemed to always end up in my underwear around him. I didn't want to think what would happen if he was actually *nice*.

The dogs had been sleeping on the floor in front of the fireplace, and their sudden explosion of barking made me jump. Ben did, too, since one minute they were zonked and the next on their feet and running to the door.

A sweep of headlights lit the front windows, and I heard an engine rumble, then cut off. "It's probably Phin," I said.

Ben pulled his phone from his pocket with his un-greasy hand and looked at the time. "I should hope so."

I pulled down my shirt carefully. The scrapes barely stung at all anymore. Good old Aunt Hyacinth.

There were two sets of footsteps on the porch, and then Phin and Mark came in. Before I had time to remember I'd been angry with her for not answering her phone, she rushed over to me and said, "I swear, I didn't hear my cell. I got a five-alarm heebie and called you as soon as I could."

"It's okay," I assured her. "You called when it mattered." Appearance of the specter put simply falling down a hole in perspective. Or maybe that was my mellow mood.

Ben stood, his returning tension making me realize how much I hadn't missed it since I'd come downstairs. Mark gave him a bit of a look, surprised and curious, maybe a little doubtful, then asked, "Everything okay?"

"No," said Ben. "Someone slashed Amy's tire. And left a note on her windshield."

I was wondering if he'd forgotten about that. Obviously not. Mark looked at me again, with more alarm. "Are *you* okay?"

"Fine." I realized I was holding the jar of first-aid ointment. "It's been an interesting night."

"Do you still have it?" Phin asked. When I looked at her blankly, she clarified, "The note."

Ben pulled it from his pocket. I hadn't seen him put it there. Phin turned it over, front and back. "Looks like it was torn off of something else. And it's not in red ink like the other one. He or she must have written it with whatever was on hand." Holding it up to her nose, she sniffed delicately. "Smells like cannabis."

I hadn't noticed, but Phin handed it to Mark, who smelled it, then looked at Ben, who raised his hands, protesting innocence.

"It's not because of my truck. Right now it mostly smells like bat crap."

Phin took the paper back and headed for the workroom. "I'm going to do some *CSI* magic. Don't tell Emery."

Ben watched her go, then glanced at me. "She's just joking about the magic part, right?"

"It's a fifty-fifty chance with Phin," I said. Not a lie.

He put on his let's-get-serious face and turned to Mark and me. "Here's what bothers me about this. There's an implied threat in that note, especially with the tire. What if she'd been alone out on the road?"

Mark got to business, too. "You think someone specifically meant to threaten Amy?"

"I think everyone in town knows that the Goodnight sisters are turning over rocks and literally digging up skeletons."

The woman in the bar bathroom came to mind, but I didn't think she could have gotten out to put the note on my car since she was working, so I didn't mention her. "It's not just me, though. The dig crew got a note on their van. And there are plenty of people of the sentiment that we should let sleeping monks lie."

I also didn't mention that Ben was one of them. But he seemed to take my point.

"Ever since we started this bridge, it's been chaos. Weird noises in the pasture, men not wanting to come to work, fences down, cows going where they're not supposed to be." He ran a frustrated hand through his hair, then looked at me, grim and determined. "Amy, you asked me about the Mad Monk, and I'll tell you, I don't believe in him for a minute. But something is going on. And someone doesn't want you poking around. Who knows what they'd do to stop you."

I sat down in Uncle Burt's chair. The note, the tire, the woman at the bar–they were fairly dwarfed by everything that happened in the cave. But hearing Ben put it that way was a fresh, new slice of disturbing.

Mark leaned against the wall to the kitchen, arms folded, thinking over what Ben had said. "Maybe I should stay here tonight. I mean, not to be sexist or anything–" he added, in response to my indignant noise.

"The dogs–" I began, but Ben cut me off with "Are the world's biggest chickens."

Which was true, though I didn't like *him* saying it. "But they bark loud enough to scare off the devil." There was also Uncle Burt, and Aunt Hyacinth's less-traditional security system. The one place I did feel safe was at the farmhouse.

Mark said rationally, "It's already one o'clock. I have to be at the dig early if we're going to get done before the Fourth of July party. I might as well catch five hours of sleep on your couch."

"Fine," I said, because I was tired of discussing it.

Ben nodded, as if he had any say in the matter, then went to the door. "I have to go. The party preparations start at oh-dark-thirty, and I also have actual work to do."

I walked with him, as if this were a normal social call and I were a normal hostess. Ben had been plenty chatty with Mark, but when we stood at the door, he seemed suddenly at a loss for words. He finally settled on "Be careful, Amy," and let himself out.

When the door closed, I cut my eyes to Mark, daring him to comment. He raised his hands, protesting his innocence.

271

"I didn't say anything. But . . . why are you in your pajamas?"

"It's a long story. Where were *you* that Phin couldn't answer her phone?"

"Trying out the other bar in town." He flashed a devilish grin, but I didn't *quite* buy misbehavior from him.

"Whatever." I went to the couch and started taking off the extra cushions. "You'd better not have volunteered to stay here in order to make time with my sister."

"I would never take advantage of the situation." Then he glanced again at the door where she'd disappeared. "Do you think it would work?"

I couldn't give him an answer. "Phin is predictable in some ways and completely random in others. She's got great powers of observation, but she's a little obtuse about the things—the non-science things—closest to her." I smiled brightly. "And if you break her heart, I will put a hex on you myself."

He laughed as if I were joking. I was getting to be more of a Goodnight by the minute.

I couldn't give an answer on what I thought about that, either.

27

i would truly know I had laid this ghost to rest when I got to wake up on my own time, and not to the dogs performing the Howllelujah Chorus every morning.

At dawn, to the cacophony of their barking, interspersed with a cell-phone ring, I stumbled down the stairs clutching the fireplace poker I'd taken to bed with me, just in case. There was enough light to see Mark struggling out of the cocoon of his blanket, trying to get to the cell phone on the coffee table while the dogs went nuts. They must have forgotten he was there.

"Hello?" he finally said into the phone, his dark hair standing straight up. He gave a start when he noticed me standing there, brandishing the fireplace poker. I lowered it and watched his expression change from comical alarm to sober concern.

A loud yawn at the top of the stairs said the dogs had even managed to wake up Phin. She was just in time to hear Mark tell whoever was on the phone, "I'll be right there."

He hung up and looked at us. "Something's happened at the dig."

Even Phin got a move on. Mark drove us over in his Jeep, and we arrived just ahead of Dr. Douglas in the university van. Ben, Steve Sparks, and Deputy Kelly were already there.

Dr. Douglas parked the van and jumped out, ignoring them all as she ran down to the big, ragged hole where a neat excavation used to be.

"Son of a bitch!" Her reaction killed any doubt of the seriousness of the situation. "Those cretinous bastards!"

It was unnerving to see the stoic professor come unglued. Phin, Mark, and I stood back and watched her rant and curse. There wasn't really anything else we could do.

The tidy, organized square where we'd worked was now a ragged-edged crater. Worse, bones that had still been buried deep were now scattered obscenely across the field. It was a desecration.

"These are human remains," ranted Dr. Douglas. "What kind of morally bankrupt monster does this kind of thing?"

The list of suspects would fill a roadside honky-tonk.

Anyone in the Hitchin' Post could have heard about the gold. Hell, anyone in *town* could have known about it.

"What happens now?" I asked Mark softly, after Dr. Douglas had wound down and Deputy Kelly had judged it safe to talk to her.

"I don't know." He looked grim. "We need to collect the scattered remains. Anthropological findings aside, like Dr. Douglas said, they used to be people."

The thought hurt my heart. Whether these bones had belonged to *my* ghost or not, they once had been human beings, travelers who had never made it to their destinations. It was deeply *wrong* that someone motivated by greed had interrupted their journey again, this time on their way to permanent graves.

Across the field, Ben stood with Steve Sparks, the ranch manager. Mark told me that it had been Mr. Sparks who'd discovered the vandalism while he'd been making rounds through the pasture, checking fences. He looked across and, finding me staring at him, said something to Ben, who shook his head as if making an excuse. For my being there, maybe?

When Deputy Kelly finished with Dr. Douglas, Mark excused himself and went to talk to her. The deputy traded places, heading toward Phin and me. A coil of worry twisted tight in my stomach, and, eyes still on the approaching man, I grabbed Phin's hand to get her attention.

"I can't lie about the ghost," I told her. "Or about being in the pasture last night. You're going to have to cover for us."

"But we didn't do anything wrong," said Phin.

"I know. But he already doesn't like us, remember?" And with more than just a ghost prowling the fields at night, I thought it was better to keep as few people distrusting us—or fearing us—as possible. "Just . . . no ghosts, no magic, okay?"

Deputy Kelly reached us before she could reply. Flipping to a new page in his notebook, he looked us up and down and asked, "You girls hear or see anything weird last night?"

Well, there was a loaded question. I could have filled his notebook. Phin said, "Like what? 'Weird' is a very relative term."

He gave a snide sort of chuckle. "Especially for your family, huh?"

I stared at him coldly. Like his cattle-thieving relatives had room to talk. "I didn't see or hear anything here at the dig site," I said truthfully.

My phrasing didn't get past him. "What about anywhere else?" he asked meaningfully. "Were you out and about last night?"

Phin, prompted by my squeeze of her hand, said, "I was out with Mark in town until around one. And at home after that."

But the deputy was looking at me. "How 'bout you, Miss Amaryllis? Did you go anywhere on the McCulloch property?"

Crap.

I blinked innocently. "Like where, Deputy?"

He lowered his notebook and looked me in the eye. "What about the rumor I heard that your car was parked out by the three-six gate?"

"The what?"

"That's the mile marker. How we identify which gate

276

we're talking about when someone has to run up here for the latest emergency."

"Oh."

"Well?" he asked impatiently. "Were you parked outside the three-six gate?"

Phin stepped in for me. "Flat tire, didn't you say, Amy?"

Deputy Kelly looked at me. *Waiting.* On one hand, he was the law and maybe someone should tell him that my tire had been slashed. On the other, I noticed that Ben, who had been so worried about it, hadn't told the officer when he'd had the chance, either.

I picked my words carefully, and it seemed I didn't have a lot of conscience when it came to Deputy Kelly. "Yes. Flat as a pancake."

He closed his notebook and put his pen in his pocket. "Listen, girls. I'm hearing all kinds of rumors about you two. Looking for ghosts in the middle of the night. Doing some kind of hoodoo voodoo to find these bones in the ground. But I got to tell you, I'm not going to put up with any hinky goings-on. Trespassing. Roaming around at all hours. Digging up people's graves on your own."

I stared at him, *almost* too shocked to be outraged. "You think *we* did this?"

"That's ridiculous," said Phin, dismissing the accusation entirely. "That would destroy valuable scientific evidence."

"And besides," I added, "we've been here helping the dig for two days. What reason would we have to come back at night and do something like this?"

"I don't know," he said, hostility curdling his voice.

"Maybe you've got the gold bug. Maybe you're trying to exorcise the Mad Monk. Maybe—"

"Is there a problem, Deputy Kelly?" Ben stood behind the lawman, Mark at his shoulder to back him up. Steve Sparks completed the group, though he stayed to the side, distancing himself.

"He thinks we did this," said Phin, calmly pointing out that there was, indeed, a problem.

"They couldn't have," Ben told the deputy. "I was with Amy until late, and Mark was with Phin. And then Mark was with them the rest of the night."

The deputy's brows shot up. "With both of them? All night?"

"I crashed on the couch at Goodnight Farm," said Mark. I hadn't thought it possible for a warm-natured guy to be so icy.

Robbed of a target, the deputy pocketed his report book and faced Ben, but I noticed he addressed Mr. Sparks just a little bit more, as if they were the adults and Ben was just a kid college student. "I don't see what else I can do here. I'll file a report, of course. And Dr. Douglas says she'll be responsible for gathering the, er, remains. But I doubt we'll figure out who did this."

Mr. Sparks said, "I could put a man out here at night to watch over the place."

"Oh, I don't know," the deputy said casually. "If they didn't find anything, they won't be back. If they did, they won't, either."

Ben looked annoyed at the way the officer seemed to have wrapped everything up in his mind. "Thank you,

Deputy Kelly," he said, implying dismissal with the formal address.

The deputy colored slightly but took his leave–slowly, wasting our time in his passive-aggressive way–and walked to his Blazer.

As soon as he was out of earshot, I exploded. "The nerve of him! What kind of person accuses someone of grave robbing?"

Mr. Sparks raised his brows. "A lawman who knows, but can't prove, that you've been jumping fences?"

It was such a casual yet accurate accusation that I floundered for an answer. To my surprise, Ben came to my defense. "You can hardly compare a bit of nosing around to this," he said. "The Goodnights are odd, but they're decent folks."

Sparks looked *pointedly* doubtful about that. "Whatever you say, boss," he drawled as he turned to follow the deputy down the hill.

Ben frowned after him. I wondered if he had noticed how often Steve Sparks came up in his mother's conversation, and how *he* felt about leasing the beautiful bluff for cell towers the way the ranch manager wanted. Whatever was going through his mind as he watched Sparks walk away, he didn't share it. Not even in his expression.

"When are you headed back to Austin?" Ben asked Mark when he'd turned back to us.

"We were supposed to dig some test holes today, but we'll probably spend our time cleaning all this up and packing things to take back to UT. Some of us are staying through the party, since your mother was nice enough to invite us."

He glanced at Phin and me. "I thought I might hang around longer. Keep an eye on things."

He could have meant the dig site, but I was pretty sure he meant our mystery. And from Ben's nod, that was why he'd asked.

"You can stay at the farmhouse," said Phin. "Might as well, since the deputy now thinks we're hooking up anyway."

"Well then," said Mark, managing his first smile of the morning. "That's a gracious offer."

She frowned, confused by his roguish tone. "It's just a couch."

Mark put his hand on his heart like she'd wounded him, flashed a short-lived grin, then excused himself to go back to Dr. Douglas.

"Just FYI," I told Phin, "he was flirting with you."

She looked at me, then at Mark's departing form. "Oh. That explains a lot. I'm good at a lot of things, but flirting isn't one of them. Especially with someone I find extremely attractive."

I was very aware of Ben standing there, watching our exchange with confusion. "Here's a tip," I said to Phin. "Don't overthink it. It's more of an instinct than an intellect thing."

"Right," she said. "Pheromones."

With a sage nod, she followed Mark, leaving me with Ben, who shook his head in gentle disbelief. "You really are the weirdest family."

"Thanks." I fidgeted awkwardly for a moment, thinking of the irony of me telling Phin anything about flirting. "How are you?"

"Fine. Though I'd like one morning without a crisis." That made me smile, and he asked, "What?"

"I was thinking the same thing when the dogs woke me up."

He smiled slightly, too; then it slipped away. "Listen, Amy. I meant what I said last night. You need to be careful. No more jumping fences. Not to ghost hunt, and not to play girl detective."

My amusement evaporated, and I raised a challenging brow. *"Play?"*

"You know what I mean." It wasn't quite an apology. "Someone doesn't want you nosing around. Maybe the same someone who doesn't stop at desecrating graves."

I didn't want to admit he had a point, and I couldn't lie and say I wouldn't poke around or ask questions. Especially at the party that afternoon, with all the county concentrated in one spot.

"I'll be careful," I said.

He wasn't fooled, and gave me a long stare. I stared back until he rolled his eyes in exasperation.

"Fine. I'll see you at the party later." As invitations went, it wasn't the most gracious. Even when he added, "You don't have to climb over the fence; you can use the front gate."

Phin and I walked home. The early-morning air was cool and damp, especially so close to the river. The plants in their beds soaked in the dew, row upon row of them in orderly, irrigated ranks. All that organization wasn't very Goodnight, until you breathed in the jumble of fresh, green

281

scents, which tumbled together in my head and pushed out, just for a moment, all of the noise and worry.

It was a shame to spoil it, but I had to tell Phin about the ghost in the cave. I hadn't had a chance the night before.

"So," she clarified when I finished, "it told you to be careful at the same time it was choking you?"

I'd realized that Phin's questions weren't out of disbelief, but a sign that something didn't square with her logic. And in this case, I agreed.

"I know. I can't figure it out, either." I stopped on the path through the lavender fields, glad for the sun and the smells. "Unless it *was* a threat."

"But you're doing what it said." She sounded outraged on my behalf. "You're looking for it in the ground and you're looking into the stories."

"You're not telling me anything I don't already know, Phin." For once I was calmer than she was.

"I just wish I knew how to help you." She set her hands on her hips, her ponytail swinging indignantly. "All I can think is that this ghost is an *ungrateful bastard.*"

At the sight of her looking like a tall, irate pixie in pink cargo shorts and cussing out a ghost, I had to laugh. It was slightly hysterical but utterly uncontrollable. Maybe frustration and anxiety had sent me over the edge. I laughed until I was wiping tears from my cheeks; then Phin's offended expression set me off again.

I finally pulled myself together and started walking back toward the house. The goats awaited their breakfast, and I had a lot of detective work ahead of me.

And then I stopped again. "I just remembered something Mom said."

"That Daisy is coming today? I hadn't forgotten. Trust me."

"No." I waited until Phin had stopped, too, and turned to look at me. "She said my conscience controlled the triple promise. The, um . . ." I tried to remember the word she used.

"Geas," Phin supplied. It sounded like "gesh" when she said it. "Mom's right. That's why the vow isn't unbreakable. Enough willpower can override the subconscious, um, conscience. Except for people who are *all* conscience."

"I am not." I faced her, mirroring her earlier posture, hands on my hips. "But here's the deal. If *my* conscience is in charge, why did the vow take, when I thought she was saying 'goats'? I should be obsessively cleaning their stalls and putting out their feed and . . ." I trailed off at her expression. "Oh. I guess I am."

"Yes. You are," she said. "But the other part, the ghost vow, that's simple. Your *subconscious* realized what needed to happen. You *knew* the ghost needed dealing with."

"That doesn't make any sense," I said, but some truth of it wouldn't shake loose.

Phin sighed and started walking again. "I know it doesn't. That's why I hate psychology."

Dogging her footsteps, I spoke with a desperation that came from trying to convince myself. "For me to do that would be the most illogical, counterintuitive, self-destructive . . . Phin, ghosts are the whole reason I stay out of the supernatural."

She stopped abruptly and stared at me. "Ghosts are your *thing*, Amy. Your affinity. Don't you remember? Have you *seen* the size of that box of books and videos that Mom sent? Grown-up books that you read when you were ten."

"I beg to differ," I said, because that was crazy. "First La Llorona tries to drown me, now this thing is freezing me to death at the same time it wants me to look for it—"

This time when Phin put her hands on her hips, it wasn't funny. "Do you even remember what happened with La Llorona?" she asked, chiding me like a kid.

"I remembered they found us soaking wet from the river." Pulled there by cold, slimy hands, water over our heads . . .

"Amy," said Phin, yanking me out of the past. "You *saved* me."

I gaped at her, uncomprehending. "I did what?"

"The ghost was exactly what they said in legend. A woman with a veil. She grabbed me, threw me into the river, and the veil wrapped around me, dragging me down. And *you* made her go away."

Her words percolated through my memory but didn't meet any answering images. "How is it possible I don't remember that? Maybe Dad and the park rangers scared it away."

She gave me an irritated look. "I think I remember who saved me. I couldn't see or hear what you did, but it was you. *You* made her let me go."

That settled it for Phin. She headed for the house and didn't look back.

My sister had never been delusional. Eccentric, absent-minded about some things and infuriatingly single-minded about others, yes. But I'd never known her to imagine something, or even misremember it.

Except this. Because it could simply not be true.

28

i'd been a little worried about how we'd be received at the McCullochs' barbecue. Hate mail will do that to you. But when I saw the size of the party, I relaxed a bit, hoping we'd be anonymous in the crowd.

Well, some of us would be. We'd see how long that lasted once Daisy arrived.

Mark parked in the makeshift lot behind the horse pens. I gawked at the view—we were in the highest part of the region, overlooking nothing but hills and river and cattle pasture for miles.

An enormous live oak tree—easily hundreds of years

old–shaded a courtyard made by a long building with well-tended wood walls and a huge stable with training pens for the horses. The party, though, centered around a marquee tent, pitched for the day. Crowds ate at long folding tables, and a band played on a stage, raised in front of a dance floor.

There was also a large, fenced swimming pool, a sand volleyball court, and a horseshoe pit. And food. From the parking area, I could see the smokers and grills and the full-to-groaning buffet tables and beer kegs.

Mark glanced at me in the rearview mirror. "I guess when you have a hundred years of practice . . ."

"No kidding." I climbed out into the afternoon heat and the smell of dust, roasting meat, and a bit of chlorine from the pool. "Okay, here's what we have to accomplish today," I said as the others joined me. "Try and find out about the Mad Monk's previous appearances. See if there's any correlation of location, timing, and what's going on nearby. I'm on the lookout for owners of diesel trucks–"

"Can we eat first, Nancy?" Mark interrupted, sounding amused. "Amateur detective work is hard on an empty stomach."

"If you must." I looked at my sister, who was eyeing the people with trepidation. Crowds were one of the few things that rattled her. "Remember, Phin," I said, "don't talk about magic or real ghosts if you can help it. At least, not with anyone you don't know."

She sighed. "All right. I'll try."

"Come on, then." Pushing my sunglasses firmly onto my nose, I prodded her toward Mark, who took the hint–or the chance—to put an arm around her waist and keep her moving.

"Amy! Phin!" Jennie waved from the sand around the volleyball net, where she, Caitlin, and the guys were playing. Lucas waved, too, and I winced as Emery spiked a ball that hit him in the side of the head.

We waited while the dig team dusted off their sand. "Oh my gosh," said Jennie when she reached us. "Mark told us about your car. I'm glad you're all right."

I made a no-big-deal noise. The only way I could not give in to my anxieties was to keep focused on my goal. I figured that was why Nancy Drew took being conked on the head and tied up in attics in stride. There wasn't room for hysterics *and* clue hunting.

"Did you collect everything at the dig site?" I asked. That had been the plan, but Mark hadn't said whether they'd finished. He'd been distracted teasing Phin for looking like Gidget, with her strawberry-blond ponytail, cuffed shorts, and puff-sleeved top. The reference was lost on Phin, who didn't watch a lot of movies at all, let alone ones from the fifties. But I thought it was funny.

"We did," Caitlin answered. "Those bastards . . ." The band covered up the rest of her comment, though I probably would have agreed with it. I was feeling free to like her since Ben said their "date" wasn't "like that."

"Do you think they got anything valuable?" I asked her.

"To quote Dr. D, 'The real treasure lies in historical significance.'" She scowled. "But if they did find anything, I really hope they don't profit from it."

Lucas walked up with—what else?—a beer. "Helluva party, huh?"

"Where's Dwayne?" I asked, realizing we were missing one.

"We set up a schedule for keeping an eye on the site, just in case the grave robbers come back."

I looked at Mark. "You made him miss the party?"

"We'll trade off," he said. "I made a schedule."

"Did you put us on it?" Phin asked. "We can keep an eye on paranormal occurrences, too."

Some of the warmth went out of the day. I knew we'd have to go back, and possibly face the ghost again. But Phin's words brought the distant duty into the moment, so I could dread it sooner rather than later.

"Done." Mark's agreement was chipper.

He seemed to believe in the ghost, but as far as I knew, Phin hadn't explained that for me it was a lifetime commitment if I didn't get this mystery sorted out. Somehow.

"You don't really think the 'Mad Monk' could have been responsible for the vandalism, do you?" asked Emery. He really did put air quotes around the name.

"There's absolutely no reason to think it was," said Phin, without rising to the bait.

"Then who?" asked Jennie.

Lucas leaned forward to talk under the music. "It could be anyone. The whole town probably knows about the gold ore. We weren't exactly discreet talking about it in the bar."

An awkward silence dropped over our circle as we realized we were talking about it—again—in public. Then Mark laughed, breaking the tension. "We'd make lousy covert operatives."

"And you know," said Lucas, taking a drink of his beer, "we could sit down for the same amount of money."

While Mark muttered something about food, I looked for a table, not too close to the stage. The music was good, sort of college-indie-country-crossover. Ray's Garage, according to the front of the kick drum. The musicians were all male, all the same age as the guys on the dig crew, and all in need of haircuts, according to my dad's voice in my head.

Except for the guy playing rhythm guitar.

Holy moly. I knew that guy. Or I thought I did. He was dressed in jeans and a T-shirt, his non-work clothes, and the sunlight caught the gold in his light brown hair.

"Is that *Ben McCulloch* up there?"

"Hey," said Mark. "I didn't know Ben was in a band."

"He started this band with Ray," said Caitlin, and I wondered if that was their mutual friend. "But he had to drop it when they began to get more gigs than he could make with his family situation."

I watched him play, his fingers working over the frets, his other hand keeping the steady, driving beat. He hardly looked at his hands at all, but his eyelids were lowered as if he was concentrating, or maybe just enjoying the rhythm and the music and the synergy of joining his sound with the others to make something more than the sum of its parts.

This was the Ben I glimpsed sometimes, the one who kept me from just blowing him off. I liked the other Ben, too, if I let myself admit it. Uptight and cranky, yet responsible and trustworthy. But knowing that *this* was inside the other? I loved that.

And I was so *pissed* at him for keeping it hidden. Caitlin got to know about the band, his friends, his nice side. *I* wasn't even allowed to ask about his "family situation."

A situation that wasn't going to get any better with ghosts–real and maybe not-so-real–lurking where he needed to build the bridge. Ben McCulloch might not want my help, but he was going to get it.

I realized I was wasting a perfect opportunity. Nancy Drew wouldn't sit here obsessing over Ned Nickerson (who was at least good for kicking in doors sometimes). She would take advantage of the fact that her main obstacle was busy onstage and there was a field full of pickup trucks out there, and some of them *had* to be diesel.

I headed to the parking area, a little too pleased with my own brilliance. The people attending the party would know their way around the McCulloch property. Ranch hands, locals, contractors, neighbors, family friends. I pretended I was texting, and clicked pictures of the diesel trucks I came across. I wasn't sure exactly how I'd put a name with a truck. Probably through the magic of the Internet.

The problem with feeling clever is that it usually makes you stupid. I heard a door open down the row of cars and trucks, and then I smelled pot, and then the screen of my camera phone was filled with T-shirt.

Joe Kelly, spiller of beer, scion of cattle thieves, relative of the county law enforcement, and, oh yeah, pothead.

"Hey," he said.

"Uh, hey," I answered. Yesterday's spell had completely slipped my mind. The paper and wax X was in the pocket of my guano-covered clothes. I had never broken the seal over our names.

"Listen, about last night," he began. I raised my brows, waiting for him to explain how he had glaucoma or something. He seemed to realize the less said about that the better, and switched tacks. "You took off before I realized who you were. I wanted to apologize. I shouldn't have yelled at you for spilling my beer the other night. I'd really had too much already."

His face reminded me of a boxer—a dog, not a pugilist—and his wheedling don't-tell-my-dad-on-me grin intensified the resemblance. *I* had not spilled his beer, but thanks to his good friend Mary Jane, I suspected he was connected to the note on my window and possibly the knife in my tire, so I decided not to antagonize him.

The knife in my tire. My stomach dropped, and suddenly the crowd at the barbecue seemed terribly far away.

Don't panic. Maybe it had just been his notepaper, not his vandalism. And he was not the only one in the world who loved weed.

I shrugged and said oh-so-casually, "It's no big deal."

Still wheedling, he said, "I know McCulloch probably gave you an earful about me. We don't really get along."

"Oh?" I feigned more ignorance than was strictly true. As long as I was courting trouble, I might as well try and get some information.

"I'm a Kelly. He's a McCulloch." On the surface, he seemed to shrug off the old feud. But there was an underlying venom that sent prickles of warning down the back of my neck. Then his tone lightened as he abruptly changed the subject. "And you're a Goodnight. You're the one, aren't you? Who found the Mad Monk's skeleton and the treasure?"

With an opening like that, I didn't bother being subtle. "What do you know about the Mad Monk?"

He didn't seem surprised by the question. "My uncle saw that ghost. He's here today. You should ask him about it. He saw his friend Russell Sparks get all busted up. Waited for the ambulance, scared on his life that the sumbitch was going to come back and finish them off."

"Russell Sparks?" I asked, surprised at the name. "Related to Steve Sparks?"

"His brother." Joe hooked his thumbs in his belt, looking just like his dad. "Ask Uncle Mike about it. Then you wouldn't be so quick to go digging around out there."

This was a pretty low-key threat, but I didn't mistake it for anything else. I had just decided to listen to the knot of unease in my belly when his friends joined us.

I recognized the pair from outside the bar. Standard-issue country boys, despite their college T-shirts. Nothing about them looked intimidating, except there were three of them and one of me.

"Hey!" The one in the Longhorns shirt brightened when he saw me, like I was a celebrity or something. "Aren't you the girl that found the treasure?"

"I . . ." Well, crap. How to word this? "My sister and I helped dig up several artifacts. It wasn't really much of a treasure."

"It was gold, though." His friend in the burnt-orange cap studied me like an alien creature. "I heard you Goodnights are witches. Did you use magic to find it?"

Longhorns Shirt tagged that question with his own. "Could you use it to find more?"

"Dude," said Orange Cap. "Let her answer."

They stopped talking and stared at me with slightly red-rimmed eyes. This is your brain on drugs.

"Do *you* believe in magic?" I asked, feeling like I was on a tightrope made of words, over a dizzying cliff, and trying to look like I was strolling through the park.

Shirt jabbed Cap with a snicker, and Joe Kelly gave a snort. *"No,"* Cap said, in a five-year-old voice.

"Then doesn't that answer your question?"

Dumb and Dumber stared at me until Joe slapped them on the back of the heads, one after the other. "She means no, morons."

"Okay," said Shirt. "But if there *was* such a thing, could you find the lost mine—"

"Guys!"

A new voice from behind me made me jump. I turned and found a man about my dad's age scowling at the three stooges. He was compact and kind of bulldoggy under his ball cap. I'd bet money this was another Kelly.

"Are you bugging this young lady?"

"Just shooting the breeze, Uncle Mike." Joe gave me a look like I'd better not contradict him. I thought about poor Stella's tire and agreed.

"Well, go shoot it somewhere else," said Mike Kelly. "She looks like she'd like to get back to the party."

Joe hit Cap on the shoulder, who did the same to Shirt. "Let's go," Joe said, and they sauntered off, talking about something completely different.

I turned to the bulldog. Running into Joe Kelly had been worthwhile after all. It had brought me exactly the guy I needed to talk to.

"Thanks," I said, indicating Larry, Joe, and Curly as they walked away.

"No prob." He moved aside, clearing the path between cars, hinting I should go back to the barbecue. "Boys are just doing a little partying. But maybe you shouldn't be wandering around."

I took my time walking, hoping he would fall in beside me, and he did. "If you're Joe's uncle Mike," I said, "then we were just talking about you."

"Don't believe everything you hear." His manner was hard to read, not unfriendly but far from warm. I needed info, though, so I forged ahead.

"People have been telling me a lot. With all this talk about the Mad Monk . . ." I trailed off, leading him to finish.

"Oh, that is true. Most horrible night of my life. Fifteen stitches. And poor Russell with a concussion, lying out there in the dark. No one had a cell phone back then, you know."

"And this happened where they found the bones?"

"Somewhere around there." He shrugged. "I always tell people, best to stay away."

"So you were on McCulloch land?" I tactfully kept "joyriding" out of the question.

That got more of a reaction. "McCulloch land?" After a moment of surprise, he gave a humorless laugh. "I forgot.

You're not from here. That land, where the bridge is going, and north of there to the highway, used to be Kelly land. It was our place to ride ATVs on. Dan McCulloch used to hang out with me and my brothers. We were pals, not that Mac McCulloch liked it. Then they went and bought our land out from under my dad. And now it turns out there's treasure on it. Convenient, huh?"

The undisguised venom in his voice made me very glad it wasn't directed at me. I edged back, and, as if realizing his slip, he dialed it down a notch. "I just want you to know who you're dealing with. The McCullochs act all neighborly, but they're just like big corporations, buying up all the little guys. They'd buy up Goodnight Farm if they could. So . . . just know who your friends are."

Mike Kelly left me cold in a way that had nothing to do with any ghost. It must have shown in my face, because he laughed and said, "I can see they've already gotten to you. 'Never trust a Kelly,' right?"

"Um . . ." I might as well admit it. "I might have heard something like that."

"Well, don't be so quick to trust a McCulloch, either." He looked beyond me and said, "This must be your sister. Y'all run back to the party now, and make sure you eat and drink a whole lot. It's on the McCulloch dime."

He nodded to Phin as he left, and she frowned watching him go. "Who was that?"

The encounter had left a bad taste in my mouth. A clear case of be careful what you wish for. "Long story."

"Save it, then. Mrs. McCulloch is looking for you. If you're done sleuthing, Grandpa Mac wants to say hi."

296

29

Mrs. McCulloch was in full-on hostess mode as she greeted me near the corner of the marquee tent. "Amy, you look so cute! That little sundress is so Audrey Hepburn. And I swear, you have the prettiest hair." She fluffed one of the locks hanging over my shoulder in a fondly maternal way. "I'm so glad you and Phin came to the party. Did you hear Ben play with the band?"

"Yes. I had no idea he could play the guitar." That was a very understated synopsis of my infatuated, infuriated feelings when I saw him onstage.

"His dad taught him." She gestured for Phin and me to

walk with her. "We're excited for Ray that the band is taking off. And Ben is enjoying playing with them for the afternoon."

The set had been going for a while. It would probably wrap soon, and Mrs. McCulloch wasn't moving in a hurry. I knew Ben wouldn't be nuts to see me talking to his grandpa. But on the other hand, Mac had asked to see me.

"How is Mr. McCulloch today?" I asked.

"Call him Grandpa Mac," she said. "Everyone does. He's feeling pretty well, though he does better away from the crowds." She'd led us past the buffet and the swimming pool, toward the tree-shaded courtyard between the buildings. "Did Hyacinth tell you girls anything about the last year? About Ben's dad?"

Jessica had told me only a little, and I hadn't shared with Phin. "I just know he passed away not long ago. I'm so sorry."

She nodded, accepting my sympathy, but moving on with a determined sort of cheer. "Dan was in an accident and Ben came home from school to help out. Then Dan passed away about a month later and I'm afraid—well, it was a bit of a blessing. He was hurt real bad."

There was an eloquence of understatement in that, more evocative than any pitiful details. I could only imagine how it would feel if something happened to my dad. And we weren't even close.

I spotted Grandpa Mac under the giant live oak tree. Its trunk must have been ten feet in diameter, and some of its branches were propped up on posts so they wouldn't touch the ground.

"Hey!" he called when he saw me. "Goodnight girl, right?"

I waved, and Mrs. McCulloch looked surprised. Grandpa Mac had asked for me, but maybe she didn't expect him to recognize my face.

"Hey, Mac," she said, in that too-chipper way people do with the aged and infirm. "Are you having a good time?"

Mac McCulloch flashed her an annoyed glance and said, "Jim-dandy. I'd enjoy it better if knitting Nelly over here would let me have a beer."

He'd jerked a thumb toward a middle-aged Hispanic lady sitting across the table, who didn't interrupt the rhythm of her flying knitting needles as she replied, "It interferes with your medicine, Grandpa Mac."

Mrs. McCulloch gestured to the woman. "This is Mrs. Alvarez. She helps look after Grandpa Mac."

Grandpa Mac snorted. "Keeps me on a leash."

Not a very tight one, apparently, since he'd been able to visit me. On a horse.

His hand, as gnarled and weathered as the oak tree, tapped along with the band. "Are you enjoying the party? The music is decent. My boy Dan plays a mean guitar."

Ben's mom stiffened slightly and corrected him. "That's not Dan, Mac. Those are Ben's friends."

Confusion passed over his face, quickly replaced by annoyance and embarrassment. "I know that."

Phin, who'd been oddly quiet until then, smoothly redirected the conversation away from his slip. "We're Ben's friends, too. You know Amy, and I'm Phin Goodnight."

He chuckled, his mood changing quickly. "Always liked

that name. Easy to remember." He started to hum, and then sing in a pleasant baritone, weathered like old leather. *"On the Goodnight Trail, on the Loving Trail . . ."*

Mac sang the verse and the chorus of an old song about the cattle trail with my family's name. A coincidence, but the serenade was nice. Mrs. McCulloch looked like she would interrupt, but Phin pulled up a chair and sat down to listen, so I did, too.

He finished on a poignant note that drifted off to be absorbed by the band. He sat for a moment, with a smile that slowly slipped away. "Why the hell can I remember all the words to that song, and not what I had for breakfast this morning?"

I glanced over at Phin, who didn't have an answer, either. For an unguarded moment, I saw fear and compassion mingle on her face. We all had our own personal nightmares.

Grandpa Mac changed direction again. "So! How is your aunt?" he asked Phin gleefully. "Is she still giving old Burt fits? Did he ever get her to marry him?"

Phin answered the question smoothly. "Yes, he did. They've been happy for thirty-something years."

"I'm glad." He nodded at obviously happy memories. "Burt and I were in school together, you know."

"No, really?" She sounded genuinely interested.

"Yes, really. Little school in Barnett. Couple of rooms, teacher with a face like a lemon."

He gave a devilish laugh clearly enjoying talking about the past. "We used to race our horses from his house to mine. We weren't supposed to, because it meant going over the Kelly place."

I startled at the synchronicity of the reference to their property. "Why not?" I asked, hoping my luck would continue with a mention of the ghost.

"Rumrunners. The lot of them. Store their hooch in the caves in the hills. They wouldn't hesitate to shoot a McCulloch for trespassing. They shot my brother, you know."

I looked at Mrs. McCulloch in alarm. She tsked and said firmly, "Mac, your brother died in Korea. He was shot by the North Koreans, not by John Kelly."

"I know that," said Grandpa Mac, but this time he was clearly humoring her. Leaning forward, he whispered loudly, "Grandpa Kelly . . ." He made a drinking motion. "That rotgut they brewed ate his brain. Never trust a Kelly."

Mrs. McCulloch gave an exasperated sigh, as if this was a frequent topic. "That's the past, Mac. Jim Kelly is a deputy. His son Joe was friends in school with Ben."

Mac brayed a laugh. "No, he wasn't! I may not remember what I had for breakfast this morning, but I remember my grandson's first black eye." He sounded rather proud of it, actually, then looked back and forth between Phin and me, archly. "Which of you is dating him?"

"Amy is," said Phin.

"I am not!"

Grandpa Mac laughed. "I should tell you about the time when Ben was a kid and he wanted to be an astronaut."

"That wasn't Ben, Mac. That was Dan."

"Don't interrupt!" His face flushed with anger, and I

wasn't quite sure what to do. It subsided, but he lost the clear-eyed sharpness of a moment before, seeming . . . fuzzier somehow, as he took back up the thread of the conversation.

"You could do worse," he said, his voice going sort of fuzzy, too, as he leaned over and patted my knee. "I know he's a serious boy, and maybe kind of grumpy. But I remember when he came home from that dance you went to. What was it? The one at your college . . . the pie social . . ."

In confusion, I glanced up at Mrs. McCulloch. She had her hand pressed to her lips, and the tip of her nose was turning red. "The Alpha Delta *Pi* Christmas social," she said.

"That's right." Mac chuckled, lost in the past. "Dan came home and said, 'Dad, I met the girl I'm going to marry.' And I told him he was crazy to marry a college girl. She'd never want to spend her days on a ranch, slopping for ranch hands and washing the manure out of his socks. But he did what he wanted. He always did."

Mrs. McCulloch's eyes were brimming with memories, and bittersweet affection for her father-in-law. She settled her hand on his shoulder and said, "I was very happy with your son, too."

He smiled with paternal fondness that made my own heart ache. Then the past tense seemed to catch up with him, and the moment crumbled into grief, as tangibly fresh and sharp as if I'd only just told him the news of his son's death.

I didn't know what to do, and looked in panic to Phin, who'd handled him so well at the start.

"Grandpa Mac." Her voice was assertive and kind. "Can I call you that?"

He looked at her without recognition, his gray-blue eyes brimming. "Who do you think you are, missy?"

"I'm Phin Goodnight. My sister Amy told me about you, and I brought you a present." She unfastened a macramé hemp bracelet, knotted and beaded in very specific stones, from around her wrist. Our cousin Violet had given it to her for graduation.

Grandpa Mac watched her wrap it around his arm. "And what the hell is this?"

"This is geomancy. Rock magic. For clarity of thought and better memory. I happen to be a genius, so it's wasted on me."

"Hmph." He touched the lapis and hematite beads. "If you're such a genius, you wouldn't believe in magic."

"If you weren't such an old coot, you wouldn't need it."

Mrs. McCulloch gasped. Mrs. Alvarez, who had risen from her chair when Grandpa Mac became upset, made a choked sort of sound.

And then he laughed. "All right, Miss Goodnight." He shook his wrist at her. "See? 'Goodnight' like the song. This piece of string must be working."

Ben's voice cut in from behind me. "Is everything okay, Grandpa?"

Hell. I'd been too intent on the discussion to notice the band had stopped playing. His words were concerned, but his tone was a knot of controlled anger.

As Ben stepped into my line of sight, Grandpa Mac looked up and grinned. "Ben! I've been talking to your girlfriend."

Shock swept the ire from his face, and color, pleased

color, flushed his cheeks. I wondered, my heart twisting in sympathy, how long it had been since Ben's grandfather had recognized him on sight.

Mrs. McCulloch knew a good exit strategy when she saw it. "I think it's time for Grandpa Mac to have some rest. Mrs. Alvarez?"

The old man made a grumbling protest, but as they helped him from the chair, he didn't fight them. Ben recovered himself before they left. "See you in a little while, Grandpa."

Mac grumped something about the prison warden as he went off with the two women.

Ben turned to me and I braced myself for an explosion. I didn't even dredge up an excuse. I knew he hadn't wanted me to talk to his family about ghosts, or the past, and I had. I deserved whatever he threw at me.

Finally he put his anger away, shelving it for later. "I thought you might like to know there's someone looking for you."

I was so surprised that he hadn't yelled at me, that it took Phin's reaction to make me realize what he'd said.

"Here comes the cavalry," she sighed. I followed her gaze to the marquee tent, where Mark was talking to a familiar tall redhead in a short black skirt and combat boots. Cousin Daisy had arrived.

30

the dig crew was vastly amused by my cousin.

Lucas watched with amazement as she downed two ears of corn, a pint of potato salad, and three tofu kabobs. Rather than ask where she put it all, he inquired, "How did you find us . . . your cousins, I mean. And the party?"

"I always know where I'm going." She licked her fingers, and I swear, I saw Phin roll her eyes. "Also, there was a number on the pad by the phone. Some guy named Mark."

She winked at Mark, who grinned back.

Ben had excused himself to do hostly things, but I suspected it was to cool off and make sure I hadn't damaged his grandfather. Daisy's arrival was better timed than she knew. Or maybe she did.

"So," she said, digging into her third bowl of peach cobbler. "Tell me what's been going on."

"You mean you haven't already Seen it all?" Phin capitalized the *S* with sarcasm.

Daisy smiled sweetly back at her. "You mean you haven't already fixed it with your mad-scientist skilz?"

Mark watched with gleeful fascination. "Holidays must be so much fun at your house."

"You have *no* idea." I leaned back in my chair, because this could go on for a bit. "I worry every year someone is going to get strangled with the Tofurky."

Ray's Garage had left, and a DJ had taken their place. As dusk had fallen, the lights strung around the dance floor invited couples to take a spin. I watched them while Phin and the gang filled Daisy in. The scene was so happy and normal, while we sat there discussing skulls and specters.

Finally finished eating, Daisy pushed back her plate(s) and set her elbows on the table, all business. "And you're sure it wasn't the ghost that scattered the bones?"

Phin said, "There's absolutely no evidence to lead to that conclusion. My philosophy is, if it's at all possible for it to have been human action, presume it is."

"Like Amy's tire," said Jennie. "And the notes on the windshields."

Mark unfolded a piece of paper from his jeans and took out a pen from his shirt pocket. "Let's look at what we've got. There's the notes, Amy's tire, the grave robber—those are the things we know are *not* supernatural. Then there's

306

Amy's apparition—that can't be human or natural, so it must be ghostly." He looked at Phin for approval. "How's that?"

"Good so far."

"Let's leave my ghost out of it for now," I said, because the specter *was* different from everything else. Phin and Daisy had both caught on to that when they suggested we had more than one entity at work here. "We've also heard mechanical sounds in the field, and I saw the diesel truck. Nothing supernatural about those. So . . . there's something weird going on in the pasture that's not paranormal at all."

Mark suggested, "Maybe those sounds and the truck were other ghost hunters. Ben said that sort of thing has been going on since the first remains turned up."

Jennie looked over my shoulder and said, "Oh, hey, Ben. We were just talking about you."

I swear, that guy needed a bell like a cat.

"So I heard." I didn't turn around, just let his voice drift over me, so I could filter through the nuances. It was much easier to say what his tone was not: not angry, not accusing, but not apologetic, either. "Can I join you?"

"Please do," said Queen Daisy, and nudged out the chair beside me with her foot.

He sat, and I risked a glance at him. He was risking a glance at me. "We may mention ghosts," I said, giving him fair warning.

"As long as you're not mentioning them to my grand-father, I'll deal with it."

I started to tell him that his grandfather had come to *me* about the ghost, but Daisy interrupted.

"Amy." She called me back to my theory. "You were saying? Something weird but not necessarily paranormal?"

Ben looked at me in surprise, I guess because I was capable of seeing a horse for a horse and not a unicorn. But I gave him credit. "It was something Ben said last night, about how he didn't believe in the Mad Monk business, but there was something hinky going on in his pasture. I figured he knows this place better than anyone."

He gave a modest cough, and I continued. "And Phin pointed out that the Mad Monk stuff is all hearsay or after the fact theorizing. So, say someone *is* up to something. They might use the Mad Monk legend as cover."

Jennie laughed, though not meanly. "That sounds like a movie plot."

With a grimace, I admitted, "I know."

Emery, who'd listened to all this cynically—how else?—gave a snort. "Nancy Drew and the Mystery of the Mad Monk."

Phin cocked her head, analyzing my theory. "I always thought it was a stupid idea to generate a ghost rumor to keep people *away*. Wouldn't they want to come and investigate?"

Mark chuckled. "That's your upbringing, I think. Well, and those ghost hunter shows. They must frustrate the heck out of masked villains with complicated plots."

"Unless whoever is messing around out there is counting on that," I ventured.

Ben finally spoke up. "You mean, count on a bunch of idiots running around looking for ghosts?" The logic of the idea seemed to surprise him. "The trespassers could basically hide in plain sight."

Jennie jumped on that idea. "If they got caught on the land, they could just say they were looking for the ghost."

"It's probably a local," said Mark. "Otherwise they wouldn't know the Mad Monk legend."

Phin drummed her fingers thoughtfully on the table. "Ghost hunting would give them an excuse for being on the property. But how would they hide what they're actually *doing*? Whatever it is."

"Maybe it's out of sight." I glanced at Ben, looking for his input. "In a barn or something?"

He gazed thoughtfully back. "Or underground. In one of the caves."

"Bootleggers used the caverns up at Longhorn State Park," said Daisy. "I remember the park ranger told us."

"Do people still bootleg liquor?" asked Jennie.

"To avoid the taxes, you bet," said Lucas. "They also make incredibly cheap swill—poison, really—then sell it for slightly less cheap."

"There are other things that might be traded and trafficked," I said, and waited for them to catch up. Joe Kelly and his stoner friends had to get their weed from somewhere.

"You mean drugs?" said Emery. The idea definitely brought down the mood.

"This could be serious," said Jennie, chewing her lip. "Maybe we should tell the police."

"Do you think they'd believe us?" I asked. I knew Deputy Kelly wouldn't. Not me and Ben, anyway. "That's probably the reason movie amateur detectives always have to unmask the villains themselves."

Ben didn't quite roll his eyes. "And their plans always go so smoothly."

Mark laughed, then checked his watch. "Okay. It's time for someone to go relieve Dwayne. Who's next?"

"Emery and I," said Caitlin, pushing to her feet. "I drew the short straw."

"So stay," Emery said, getting up, too. "I don't need company to sit around and wait for nothing to happen."

Mark handed her a key on a tag. "Be careful. The van is signed out to me. If anything happens to it, they'll never give me my doctorate."

"I'm flattered by your faith in me." She gave Ben a wave. A friendly, non-datelike wave. "See you, Ben."

Lucas got up, too. "I think I'll have a beer. Anyone else want one?"

"I do," said Daisy.

"Nice try, kid," said Lucas.

After a moment's hesitation, Jennie followed him. Daisy watched them go, then turned back to Mark and Phin, and Ben and me. "This is very cozy. Everyone paired up."

"Not hardly," I said, meaning the dig team. But it sounded like I meant . . . well, Ben and me. Face flaming, I slid down in my chair, avoiding his eye.

"Uh-huh." Daisy gathered her bag from the back of her chair. "I'm going to the house. Swing by and get me before your shift at the dig site. I've never read a mass grave before. It should be a kick."

"Read?" asked Ben, and I really wished he hadn't.

"I'm a clairvoyant," said Daisy, ignoring Phin's snort.

"Among other things, I can read objects and places associated with the dead. I also have had some success as a medium, but that's hit-or-miss." Another snort from my sister. Daisy turned to Mark. "I don't suppose you have any artifacts still here?"

"Everything went up to Austin with Dr. Douglas," he said, looking genuinely disappointed.

"Too bad. The ground insulates things, makes them harder to read. But maybe I'll get lucky." She turned, waving her fingers over her shoulder. *"Ciao!"*

"Don't touch my stuff!" Phin yelled after her.

I wondered if anybody would notice if I just crawled under the table.

"Come on." Ben stood and held out a peremptory hand to me. "Let's dance."

I stared up at him. "Seriously?" He *looked* serious. A lot more serious than one would think, issuing a dance invitation. But then, it *was* more like an order. "After that boatload of crazy, all you've got is 'Let's dance'?"

"It's a party. It's my *mother's* party. You look miserable and she's going to blame it on me."

"Instead of Daisy," said Phin.

"Instead of *all* of you," Ben said.

Across the way, I caught Mrs. McCulloch watching us with a pinch of worry between her brows. I was helpless against maternal disappointment, even when it wasn't *my* mother.

"Fine." I pushed back my chair and stood. Ben waited stoically and Mark grinned, much too broadly. "Maybe you and Phin should hit the floor, too," I suggested sweetly, because our tiny tots tap dance teacher had refunded Phin's tuition and suggested Mom use it to buy an art set.

Unsuspecting, Mark turned to Phin. "Are you game?"

She studied him for a long moment, as if assessing his motive, then shrugged. "It's your funeral."

He helped her over the bench and they were off. Then it was just Ben, waiting on me, and me, unable to avoid the inevitable, though I gave it one last try.

"I'm not much of a dancer." I'd lasted longer than Phin in tiny tots tap class, but only slightly.

"That's all right." He took my hand and pulled me not entirely gently through the crowd. "I don't mind."

"*I* mind." I dug in my heels as we reached the concrete slab serving as a dance floor. The stage now held a DJ playing country music, and colored lights ringed the square, throwing a prism glow on the couples that moved in concentric circles. Mark and Phin were already there, laughing and looking at their feet.

Ben faced me, still holding my right hand in his left. "I should have known you'd be one of those."

"One of what?" I snapped back, then grimaced at the taste of figurative bait going down my gullet.

He kept his expression mildly challenging. "One of those people who never wants to do anything they don't excel at."

"At which they don't excel," I corrected him. "And that's not true."

"Okay." He shifted his weight slightly as we stood there,

looking more like sparring than dance partners. "Name me one thing you do for fun."

"I read novels." I lifted my chin and dared him to say that wasn't fun. "Not literary ones, either. Romance novels, mysteries, science fiction . . ."

"But there's not much chance of falling on your face reading, is there?"

"Ha! I'm not going to fall on my face if I dance with you." At least, not literally, I hoped.

He played me like a deck of cards. "Then prove it."

I wanted to tell him I didn't have to prove anything to him. But of course I didn't. I stepped up close, put my hand on his shoulder, and jerked my chin toward the dance floor. "Let's do this thing."

He surprised me by laughing. Not in victory, but in a warm, that-was-fun way. And I had to admit, it sort of was, even if I'd lost that round.

Then he put his hand on my waist, pulling me closer, and raised our linked fingers. Our bodies brushed lightly, and heat spread across my skin everywhere we touched. It had nothing to do with the hot July night, and everything to do with being in the circle of Ben's arm. His shoulders were broad, and his shirt was open at the neck, so I was eye level with the pulse that beat in his tanned throat.

How was his pulse so steady? Mine was skittering all over the place, and my breath went all ragged, even though we hadn't yet taken one step.

"Ready?" he asked, and I searched his voice for any sign he was as affected as I was. I certainly wasn't going to look up and meet his eye. What if there was nothing reciprocal? Worse, what if he saw, reflected in my face, the thrill that ran through me when my chest brushed against his, when our thighs slid against each other as we danced?

Or tried to. At my nod, he stepped off on the beat and neatly joined the couples circling the floor. After that, the feel of Ben's body became an unwelcome distraction as I tried to concentrate on the steps.

It was a two-step, which should be easy. Two quick steps, one slow. I mean, even Phin was doing it; I saw Mark swinging her by. Shock made me lose the beat, and I got off step–*again*–bounced against Ben's chest, rebounded and almost ran us into one of the other couples. And then I stopped, right in the middle of the floor, and *another* pair had to make a hasty detour around us.

"Wow," said Ben, in bland understatement. "You really aren't very good at this."

"I know the steps." I wanted to howl with frustration, but that would be even more embarrassing. "I just can't seem to keep the beat."

"Come on. Let's stay moving." He suited actions to words, stepping forward with his left foot, prompting me to step back with my right. *Quick, quick, slow . . .* This time I managed to keep the rhythm, but our graceless progress around the floor was more like a wrestling match than a dance.

"Maybe if you would quit trying to lead," he said, the muscle in his jaw tight. "Stop trying to be in control."

I laughed, and not in a good way. "That's funny. *You* telling me to relax."

He scowled, but just for a second, before it lifted with a grudging twitch of a smile. "Okay. That's a fair point."

"Maybe this"–I made a sawing motion with our joined hands, which was a pretty good imitation of our dancing–"isn't all my fault. It takes two to tango, as they say."

"*I* am a good dancer," he said, with a bit of an edge. "If you would just let me steer."

"Maybe *I* should steer," I said, breathless because at some point he'd adjusted his hold on my waist, fingers spread from my ribs to the curve of my hip. He had to feel my heart beating double-time, but maybe he would think it was the exertion of the dance.

"You can't steer," he said equably, as well he might, since he was in control and I wasn't. "You're going backwards."

"Why do I have to go backwards? Because I'm the girl and you're the guy?"

"Because I can see over your head."

My laugh was more of a snort, but it was a concession all the same. "You have an answer for everything, don't you?"

A smile acknowledged that briefly before turning wry. "Except for the fiendish plot of the Mad Monk of McCulloch Ranch."

He'd gone for melodrama, but there was a grim thread beneath the drollery. Meeting Ben's family had explained a lot. Like how every time he said "my" land, it wasn't a greedy or egotistical word. It was a lonely one. He must feel the entire weight of the ranch on his shoulders. It wasn't fair–I wasn't sure it was true–but that never stopped anyone from feeling they had the sole responsibility of keeping things running smoothly. I should know.

"We'll figure it out," I promised. He blinked in surprise, and a tide of flustered embarrassment made me add, "Phin and me, and all the guys from the university. Maybe Daisy. We'll get to the bottom of it."

His gaze shuttered. "You just want to find your ghost."

"No," I started; then I had to revise, "Okay, yes. But that's ancillary to getting to the bottom of things."

"Is it all just a mystery novel plot to you, Amy? Or some kind of experiment?"

I didn't temper my bitter laugh. "Trust me. I'm invested in the discovery of the truth. It's not just academic to me, Ben."

"Personally invested?"

I hesitated, because I was talking about ridding myself of the ghost, and he was asking something else. This accord was new and uncertain. Not to mention intermittent. But someone had to go first. "Maybe," I said.

"Maybe I'm glad to hear that." He smiled, very slightly, and I realized that we'd stopped crashing into things. His grip had lightened until his fingers tickled my ribs, and my hand rested, feather light, in his. Which somehow felt like a stronger connection than the death grip we'd had earlier.

"Your cousin," he began, and I braced myself, "she can really do what she says?"

God, I hated point-blank questions. I hated that he asked one now, in this moment, when I didn't want to lie to him, even by twisting my words.

"She can do what she says. I could show you Phin's pictures of psychic energy, or I could show you how Aunt

Hyacinth's cream healed my scratches. But you won't believe me unless . . . well, unless you believe."

Our steps had slowed, until we stood at the edge of the floor, not really dancing at all. He opened our linked hands, keeping the fingers joined, but showing my palm, which had been raw and red from climbing the rope the night before, but was now, at most, pink. Then he turned me under our arms, twirling me like a ballerina, but slowly. The back of my sundress wasn't low, but it showed that the scratches from my fall were far more healed than twenty-four hours could account for.

"Unbelievable."

I sighed and completed the slow spin. "That's what I thought you'd say."

"You take this completely in stride. How do you do that?"

"I've lived with it my whole life." I shrugged.

Wariness—the first hint of it—crept into his expression. "So what do *you* do?"

I stepped back, knowing the moment was over. "I hold it all together."

31

ben and I started bickering again as soon as he told me he was going on the stakeout with us.

"You don't have to do this." I was still arguing in his truck as he pulled up to the gate at Goodnight Farm, where we were picking up Daisy. "Mark will be there. It's not like Phin, Daisy, and I will be sitting out in the middle of the field waiting for the boogeyman to come and get us."

He turned to face me, bracing a hand on the back of the seat. "I'm not worried about the boogeyman, I'm worried about your damned diesel truck. I'll deal with whatever weird thing anyone says or does. I won't comment or call them crazy or anything. So *you* just deal with the fact that I'm going to be there."

I clamped my jaw on another useless protest. Daisy was waiting inside, ready to go, having exchanged the miniskirt for a pair of camo cargo pants. I ran upstairs and put on my last clean pair of jeans, herded the reluctant dogs out of the house, threw some feed down for the goats and the donkey, then dashed to the truck, where Daisy was sitting in the middle of the bench seat, telling Ben God knows what while they waited on me.

Mark and Phin were already at the dig when we pulled up. They climbed out of the Jeep as Ben parked the truck farther up on the hill overlooking the V-shaped slope of the excavation field. Phin wrestled with the heavy satchel on her shoulder until Mark took it from her. And she let him.

"Well, I'll be dipped," murmured Daisy, leaning against the truck fender to wait for them. "Is the mad scientist human after all?"

I raised a warning finger. "Do *not* tease her, Daisy Temperance Goodnight, or I will make you sorry."

Mark set the satchel on the tailgate of Ben's truck. Phin had changed clothes, too, and if she'd done so in the car, that could account for her ponytail coming loose. Maybe even the color in her cheeks, visible in the light of the battery-powered lantern Ben had set in the bed of the pickup.

I slanted a look of narrow-eyed speculation at Mark, but his attention was on Daisy. "How about you?" he asked. "Do you need any equipment or anything?"

"I leave that to Phin," she said, and Phin shot her a death glare, then started handing out gadgets.

She handed me the EMF meter and plopped the infra-red thermometer into Ben's hands. It looked a little like a sci-fi laser pistol and he asked, "What do I do with this? Shoot aliens?"

"Just be ready to take temperature readings if there's a paranormal event," she said.

"Um. Sure. And I'll know when that happens?" Phin gave *me* a look, like I'd purposely inflicted him on her. I took over, explaining how to work the thermometer. It wasn't brain surgery, and he nodded to show he understood. "So, what do we do now?"

"We go watch Daisy's dog and pony show."

While we'd been talking, Mark and Daisy had gone down the hill. I could see him gesturing to the various holes and explaining the stakes in the ground as Phin went to join them.

I risked a glance at Ben. "How are you holding up?"

He looked lost and a little grumpy. "I feel like I've gone into the Twilight Zone."

"It helps if you don't think about it too hard." Catching his hand, I tugged him away from the truck. "Let's go."

Daisy stood at the farthest point of the partitioned field. She shook out her arms, shrugged her shoulders, closed her eyes with her hands down by her sides, looking a lot like a gymnast preparing for a routine.

She frowned and flexed her hands, as if reaching toward the ground. "I get very old death—violent death—but it's . . ." She shook her head like she was considering and rejecting descriptions. "Old. Finished."

"Is it because the bones have been removed?" asked Mark. Ben, Phin, and I stood beside him, out of Daisy's way.

She shook her head again. "No. I've read empty burial sites before."

Ben glanced at me with a question, and I answered quietly so I wouldn't distract her. "Daisy sometimes consults for the police. They keep it on the down low. 'Police turn to sixteen-year-old psychic' isn't a headline city hall wants to see."

Daisy ignored us. Hands extended to the ground, she walked up the hill, stepping carefully over the stakes and twine. "Okay, there's still something here." She pointed, and Mark made a note of the spot. I hadn't noticed until then that he was carrying his clipboard and grid diagram. He penciled in two more places she indicated as she went.

When she came to the pit the grave robbers had made, she bent and gathered a handful of dirt. "Wow. They managed to tear through this site. I'm just getting greed and self-interest, not malevolence."

"Anything older?" Phin asked. "That's where we found the rosary and the satchel with the gold ore in it. It might help to know what the grave robbers were looking for."

"Let me see." She dropped to her knees and dug both her hands into the ground. "Earth doesn't conduct very well. It's more of an insula– Whoa."

"What?" I took a step closer, hopeful for some clue. I noticed Ben did, too.

Daisy pulled her fist from the dirt and opened it up. Her hand shook slightly in the beam of the flashlight, and lying in her palm was a small chunk of metal.

321

"Is that a musket ball?" I asked.

"Oh yeah," said Daisy, in a strained voice. "Somebody take it, please."

Mark jumped forward and plucked the bullet from her hand. The whoosh of her relieved breath stirred the cloud of dust around her. "That's definitely what killed *that* guy," she said.

"But we found an arrowhead by the A site," said Mark. "We'd been thinking perhaps a party from Mexico was ambushed by Apache or Comanche."

"Native Americans had firearms, too," said Ben. "They were pretty quick to step up the arms race. I mean, wouldn't you?"

Daisy sat back on her heels. "Here's all I can tell you. Definitely violent death, I'm thinking you're right about the ambush. There's a surprised quality to it. That guy"—she pointed to the musket ball in Mark's hand—"was thinking about gold, but not for himself. Spain, the Church maybe. God was on his mind, but . . . well, God usually *is* just then. Or so I've seen."

Tentatively, I held out my hand for the rusted metal ball, and Mark dropped it into my palm. Nothing weird happened, and I let out my breath. The bullet wasn't really round anymore, but misshapen and pitted.

"I saw the apparition around about there," I said, pointing to a spot not far from her. "And the local ghost rumor concerns a monk and a treasure. It seemed too much of a coincidence to find a rosary and a bag with gold ore in it. Even if the Mad Monk is a smoke screen, is it possible the actual apparition has a similar story?"

She shrugged apologetically. "I don't know what to tell you, Am. This whole site is . . . well, it's dead. What's here is old and done, like a closed book."

Mark ventured an interpretation. "So, even though these men died violently, they've moved on."

"Right. So your monk, Amy, either has something unfinished, or maybe fears what happens next. Maybe he died in a state of mortal sin, as my principal, Sister Mikaela, would say, and doesn't want to face judgment." She climbed to her feet and dusted off her hands, the spikes on her bracelet and collar gleaming in the glow of Ben's flashlight. "But he didn't die here."

Disappointment sank heavily onto my heart and I realized I'd pinned a lot of hope on Daisy. I don't know what I'd expected her to find, but it was more than this.

"So, that's it?" said Phin, voicing my feelings. "You drove two hours for a little hand waving?"

Daisy glared at her. "I didn't say I was finished."

"What about a séance?" Phin asked.

"Are you kidding me?" Daisy had to say it, because I was speechless.

"Whatever it takes to figure out Amy's ghost problem. No matter how unscientific." My heart warmed at her sacrifice. Even when she added, "Besides. I want to see what the Kirlianometer shows when you do your thing."

Daisy rolled her eyes, and Ben, who'd been quiet all this time, said, "Okay, you guys. I've gone with the flow so far. But I have to ask. What's a Kirlianometer?"

I laughed at the surreality of Phin explaining paraphysics, or whatever she was calling it now, to Ben

McCulloch. Maybe I was a little hysterical. I was definitely sort of sleep deprived.

So when that sudden, deep *whump* grabbed at my insides, for a moment I thought I'd imagined it. But the others all jumped, too. Ben looked at me, startled, and asked, "Is that the sound that—"

He didn't finish the question. Over the hills came a low groan, an unearthly moan that rose to a squeal of protest, sharp enough to arrow to heaven, soft enough to float there. The hills carried the sound and transformed it to an eerie chorus of sighs and whispers, until they trailed into silence.

Mark grabbed Ben's arm as he turned his head, trying to echolocate. "Which way . . . ?"

"That direction," said Ben. He pointed toward the granite outcropping that had loomed over me the night before. "Let's take the truck."

And with exactly that much discussion, they ran for transportation—Ben, the *same person* who'd yelled at *me* for running through the pasture chasing mysterious noises. But I understood completely that desperation of trying to find *something* concrete to hold on to in a sea of frustration and mystery.

"Guys!" I yelled, and sprinted after them. Like hell they were leaving me behind.

I was so caught up in the moment, I didn't notice the cold until I was already through it. I dismissed the gleam that wasn't moonlight. But I couldn't ignore the command that barked across the night.

"¡Alto! ¡Cuidado! No vayan ustedes."

The only thing more shocking than the order was the

voice. I spun to stare at Daisy, who stood like a marble statue bathed in moonlight, suffused by the unearthly glow and a chill that reached between us into my bones. Her eyes were hollow and unseeing as she lifted a heavy hand toward me.

"Escuchame, niña. Escuchame o tu puedes morir."

Listen to me, little girl. Listen to me or you will die.

32

ben's curse broke the silence in the wake of Daisy's voice. "What is wrong with you? What are you playing at?"

Mark spoke low, a warning. "Dude. It's not a game. *Look* at her."

She wasn't completely still after all. She shivered, her lips blue with the cold, as her breath fogged in the air around her. It was strange seeing it from the outside, but what was happening to Daisy seemed different from what happened to me when the specter appeared.

The ghost wasn't struggling against the barrier between

the plane of the living and the world of the spirit. It had found a door in Daisy.

Phin recovered first. "Ask it what it wants," she told me.

I made a wordless sound of protest—was this the time for Twenty Questions?—but swallowed it. How would I know if I didn't ask?

"¿Que quiere usted?" I asked, forcing my cold lips to move and my brain to find the words.

Daisy's voice said, *"Búscame."*

"Look for you where?" My breath fogged the summer night air, and when I looked at my hands, they were like Daisy, mottled with cold. *"¿Dónde?"*

"Puedes encontrarme. Búscame."

My brain stumbled over that one. Mark, moving closer to me, supplied the translation. "You can find me. Look for me."

"Where?" I repeated.

"La mina. Búscame. La mina."

"The San Sabá mine?" Mark ventured, making the same leap I did, but voicing it before I could.

"Puedes encontrarme, niña. Búscame. Búscame...."

"Amy," said Ben. I could feel his growing horror even through the ice that seemed to encase me. "*Do* something."

"I don't know what!" I said through chattering teeth.

"You do," said Phin. "You've got this. Don't let it be the boss."

I was so cold, moving felt like cracking ice in my joints. But I pushed forward and threw up a hand, just like the ghost addressed me. *"¡Alto!"* I said. *Stop.* "Leave her alone."

"Déjala," whispered Mark.

"¡Déjala!" I shouted, putting everything into the command. All my air, all my strength, all my love for my family and for Daisy and her squabbles with Phin. I reached down through the layer of ice and found something Goodnight in me after all.

The glow snuffed out, and I felt the sting of warmth returning to my fingers. Daisy's arm dropped and she staggered. Ben, of all of us, was the quickest to react, and he jumped forward to catch her. His flashlight dropped to the ground and rolled down the hill.

"Whoa," said Daisy, in her normal voice, as she hung limp from Ben's steadying grip. "That must have been a doozy."

And then she turned away, just in time to avoid throwing up on his shoes.

Mark and Phin took Daisy back to the house after that. She still looked green, and moaned about her head exploding. I personally thought Phin needed to shut up for a while about parapsychology being useless.

Ben and I stayed to watch the dig site, though I suspected both of us considered it a token gesture at that point. We sat on the tailgate, the night so quiet, I could hear the tiny squeals of bats hunting for their dinner, and I shivered.

"Still cold?" Ben asked.

"A little." I rubbed my hands together, even though it was my insides that didn't want to warm up.

He went to the cab of the truck and came back with a

Thermos and a bunch of cookies in a zipper bag. "Mom packed us a lunch."

I laughed, and a lot of the chill left me. Turning to sit cross-legged, I took the Thermos cup of coffee he offered and a chocolate chip cookie.

"So, this is your life," he said.

Mouth full, I shook my head, then swallowed. "This is unusually exciting. Is your life full of skeletons and ghost-hunting trespassers?"

He frowned. "Only since you got here."

"That's not fair! Or true."

"I'm teasing you, Underwear Girl."

He was. His amusement heated my skin, and I sulked to hide my discomposure. "It's hard to tell with you, McCrankypants."

He chuckled, and I smiled, then we munched in silence for a few minutes, sharing the coffee cup, since apparently Mrs. McCulloch hadn't thought of *everything*.

"So, tell me the deal with the Los Almagres mine," he said.

I wiped at a crumb on my lip. "It's a lost Spanish mine. No one knows exactly where it is, but there are records of it . . ." Then what he actually said caught up with me. "Which you must know, since you called it by the proper name."

"What does it have to do with the . . ." He couldn't bring himself to say it, and I didn't make him.

"It's a theory that came up when we found the ore. What if this expedition"–I gestured to the field–"was returning from the mine, taking samples of the gold they'd found back to Mexico? If they were attacked, and never made it, and the location of the mine died with them?"

He refilled the coffee cup slowly, as if organizing his thoughts. "*Los Almagres* means 'the ochre hills.' The color is supposed to show mineral deposits, like gold and silver. So folks have been speculating about the location being everywhere from Enchanted Rock to Sugar Mountain."

"So basically, all over the Hill Country from San Antonio to . . . right around here?"

"Yep. Your Mad Monk"—I started at the name, because he'd never spoken it voluntarily before—"was supposedly on one of the expeditions sent to bring back sample ore to Mexico. That's all I know. Except some people say he was scalped and that's why he's always striking people in the head."

His reaction to the mention of the tale had always been so vehement that I was expecting some kind of scandalous tale, maybe even about his own family. I was more incredulous than angry—almost—when I snapped, "Why couldn't you just *tell* me that?"

"Because I *hate* that story. Joe Kelly and his asshole cousins scared the crap out of me with it when I was a kid. They put on monks' robes and . . . Okay, it's stupid now, but when you're six, and someone in a scary hooded cloak locks you in a feed silo for a couple of hours, it makes a big impression."

My anger faded. That would make a big impression on me *now*. "Why do the Kellys hate your family so much?

Seems like it's more about the land thing than the cattle rustling."

"I don't know." He emptied the coffee cup, then screwed it onto the Thermos. "I don't want to talk about Joe Kelly anymore."

"Okay. Then what?"

"I don't want to talk at all."

"Oh." What did that mean? We'd actually been having a conversation without yelling or much name-calling. We'd broken cookie together. Or maybe he just needed to think about what a nutty world I'd dragged him into. Or just wanted me to shut up. I wrestled with hurt and disappointment, and told myself not to be silly.

"I can go into the cab of the truck. Give you some space."

He gave a laughing sort of sigh. "Seriously, Amy? Do I need to draw you a map?" He grabbed the waistband of my jeans and slid me across the tailgate, closing the space between us. I fell against his chest and he wrapped his arms around me. My squeak of surprise was colored with approval, but it still made him pause, holding me against him, his gaze roaming my face, lingering on my mouth before coming back to meet my eye.

"This would be the time to tell me if you still hate me," he said.

"I don't hate you, you moron."

He didn't even waste time laughing.

All my kisses so far had started tentative, inquiring, diffident. Ben had gotten the inquiry out of the way, and captured my mouth with his in a kiss that took permission as given. Which it was. Totally. Even if I'd called him a moron.

His hand slid up to the back of my head, and he kissed me more deeply. I cupped his face with my hands and answered some questions of my own. He had a rough chin this late at night. He tasted like chocolate and coffee.

When he pulled back, he was gloriously out of breath, and so was I. "You still want to go inside the truck?" he asked.

"Here is good," I said, and kissed him again.

"I haul manure in this truck," he said when I gave him the chance to speak.

That had to be the weirdest way to phrase a proposition ever, but it worked. "Inside is better."

33

It's hard to walk while you're kissing someone. Harder still to work a door handle. And that's not a euphemism for anything dirty. So don't ask me how Ben and I managed to get where we were, tangled up together on the bench seat of the truck, somehow working around the console and the steering wheel and the gearshift, and only once blowing the horn.

That's not a euphemism, either.

I only know that when Ben was kissing me, the whole world retreated. I felt things I'd never felt before, in places I never knew were connected.

But I was pretty sure that whatever was buzzing against my thigh was not normal. For one thing, it was ringing.

Ben dragged his mouth away from mine and mumbled a curse that was a little shocking and kind of hot.

"Ignore it," he said.

That was easy for him to say when his cell phone was rounding third base. If anyone got a home run tonight, I didn't want it to be Verizon Wireless.

"I can't," I said when it buzzed again. "It's in a really distracting place."

He shifted his weight enough to reach into his pocket—I sucked in my breath at how high his hand grazed my thigh—took out the phone, and tossed it toward the dash. It fell to the floorboard and kept ringing.

"Problem solved." And then he kissed me again, and I forgot about the ringing, until there was a chirp of a voice message and oh my *God* how was I even paying attention to that?

I turned my head, asking breathlessly, "Aren't you going to see who it was?"

"No," said Ben, his voice tickling the spot behind my ear. I shivered all the way to my toes, and I wanted to lose myself in that sensation, but a *really* unwelcome worry kept tugging me back to earth.

"What if it's your mother?"

"It probably is. I don't care."

My insides melted at the rough edge in his voice. Mr. Responsible wanted to be with me so badly, he didn't care who was calling. It was, quite possibly, the most flattering thing a guy had ever said to me. Verbally *or* nonverbally, and trust me, he was really eloquent with the nonverbal just then.

"What if something is wrong? It's really late."

He tensed, and it had nothing to do with me, or with the way his weight pressed me into the cushion of the truck seat or the way our shirts had worked up so that the skin of my stomach was so hot against the hard muscle of his.

"I don't care." He touched his forehead to mine, his voice frayed at the edges with a conflict that went beyond us and the cab of his truck. "I've given up my fraternity and my apartment and my band, and I've been wanting for three whole days to see your underwear again, and for just one hour I'm not going to let the ranch interrupt."

That was really presumptuous, that he was going to get to see my underwear again. But considering he was kind of seeing my bra by Braille at the moment, maybe not so much of a stretch.

And God, if anyone understood about wanting to just be there, breathing the warm air that he exhaled, seeing how long we could prolong the moment before my head cleared or his did or we started arguing again . . . that person was me.

Which was why I couldn't let it go. I wouldn't have been there with him like that if he hadn't been the uptight control freak that he was.

"What if it's something with your granddad?"

And that was that. He drew back a fraction and looked at me. I could see him pretty well, thanks to a clear night and a country sky. It's amazing how bright the stars can be, and all of them shone down on us just then, as we were caught between what we wanted to do and what we—both of us—knew had to happen.

"Dammit," he said.

"I know." Boy, did I know.

He pulled his hand out from under my shirt, letting his fingers trail over my stomach. I shivered and wished I could be an enabler.

"Where's the phone?" he asked, tactfully looking for it while I straightened my clothes.

I found it on the floor and handed it over. He thumbed through the menu until he got to voice mail, and listened. In the cool glow of the phone, I could see the animation leech out of his face. The nagging worry that had tugged at the shirttail of my conscience bloomed into an ominous dread that pushed everything else out of my head.

"What is it?" I asked when the message was done and he clicked open the keypad to send a quick text.

"We have to go." He dropped the phone into the console between our knees. "Granddad's missing. Mom doesn't know where he went."

"Where could he have gone?"

He'd turned on the engine and put the truck in gear. "If I knew that, he wouldn't be missing, would he?"

I didn't appreciate the sarcasm, and that was *not* the tone you took with someone you'd been making out with just three minutes ago. The pitch of his brows, the tightness in his jaw—those I got. It was his grandfather. But I didn't understand the walls going up, pushing me back.

Those worries, however, could wait. "He can't drive,

336

right? And none of the cars are missing? So he'd have to go on foot or on horse. How far could he go?"

"That's just it. Mom doesn't know how long he's been gone. She's got Steve looking in the stable to see if Grandpa took one of the horses. They're also checking to make sure none of the guns are gone."

My stomach dropped. It was an abrupt, elevator sensation, and I really thought, for a moment, that it might come back up again. I hadn't thought about that. Aunt Hyacinth had a .22 rifle just because she lived in what was pretty much wilderness, but otherwise the Goodnights were not a gun-toting family.

"The gun cabinet stays locked, and it's in the ranch offices, which are also locked. Granddad doesn't have a key to either. Hasn't for a while."

The reasons for that would be pretty obvious. And I knew that Alzheimer's patients could turn in a moment to depression—and Grandpa Mac definitely had some mood swings. But he wasn't so far along he couldn't almost pass for a forgetful curmudgeon.

"He's probably headed over to Goodnight Farm."

"Because you know him so well?" he snapped.

"Oh, don't be an ass, Francis." The words burst out of me, because what I wanted to say was *Please don't go* back *to being an ass because I like you, and I'm not the kind of girl who likes guys who are asses.* "I'm trying to help. I really like your grandpa, and I can tell Aunt Hyacinth does, too. And he seems to really like to visit her."

"Yeah, to chat about the Mad Monk and my dead grandmother."

"Well, maybe she's the only one who doesn't act like he's crazier than a sack of weasels because he talks to his departed wife."

He was silent for a moment, hands gripping the steering wheel, eyes straight ahead. But I could tell he recognized his own description of my aunt, because I could see the muscle working in his jaw. So square, strong, and stubborn.

"I get your point." The words seemed dragged out of him. And they were far from an apology. "Except that it's not my grandma Em who sends him out searching in the pasture like he's on a freaking snipe hunt. And even if he heads straight for your place, there's miles of terrain to cross. You already know what that's like, even without ghosts or grave robbers and people pretending to be Mad Monks."

"Just drive," I said. That was all he could do at the moment, and no amount of willpower would make the truck faster or the road straighter.

But when we reached the gate, I realized what I *could* do.

"Turn left," I said.

Ben looked at me like I was crazy. "I need to get home to join the search."

Right was the way to the McCulloch house. Left would take us to Goodnight Farm.

"We *need* Phin and Lila."

"*I* need to get home to my mother and the search party."

"Ben," I said, letting my conviction color my voice. I turned in the seat so that I could look him in the eye. "Your mom has called in the cavalry, right? So they're searching already, spreading out from your house. You lose nothing by coming at it from a different direction. Literally and figuratively. And Lila is a search dog. She has a vest and every-thing."

It was an impassioned plea, rooted in logic. I could see him try to dismiss my points, and fail.

He closed his eyes and gripped the wheel. "He's my grandpa, Amy. He's not always himself anymore, but losing him completely . . . And after Dad . . ."

I touched his arm. "I know, Ben. And I know it's a lot, on top of everything else you've seen tonight, but please be-lieve that we can help."

Without saying yea or nay, he put on his left turn sig-nal. I exhaled for the first time in minutes, and reached for my phone to give Phin the heads-up. She answered on the first ring.

34

delphinium Goodnight, when she got her game on, was a force to be reckoned with.

Mark and Lila met us at the door. All the other dogs were confined to the mudroom. Daisy was upstairs in one of the bedrooms, her migraine so bad, she threw up whenever she moved.

"That would be the opposite of helpful," I said after Mark explained. "Where's Phin?"

"In the workroom." Mark glanced at Ben, who had been silent the whole drive, his tension like an electrical field around him. "How are you holding up?"

"Let's just get this done."

I'd pushed Ben way out of his comfort zone, and I wasn't sure *we* would ever be comfortable together again. I met Mark's sympathetic gaze and led the way to the back room.

Phin had covered the center counter with printed-out maps, tiled together into one big plot of the McCulloch Ranch. I was stunned she'd had time to run off all those pages, let alone match them together.

She was crushing something up with a mortar and pestle. When I came in, she handed both to me and said, like I was her lab assistant, "Keep crushing that until it's a smooth paste. Then put it in that copper bowl with about an inch of water."

I did as she said. A curious sniff identified marjoram, ginger, lavender, and pennyroyal, but I couldn't begin to say what they were for.

Phin turned to Ben with the same brusque efficiency. "I don't suppose you have anything on you that belongs to your grandfather? Something he wears or uses every day would be best."

Ben shook his head slowly. "No. I wasn't expecting to need a toe of bat or eye of newt, either."

"Toe of dog," she corrected him automatically. "What about something that he gave you? Or an item that symbolizes something you do together? I need a link between you."

He pulled a guitar pick from his pocket. "How about this? Mac taught my dad to play, and he taught me."

"Hmm. Yeah, okay." She took it from him. "I can make this work. Strong emotional resonance, and three generations. Three is a good number."

"What can I do to help?" asked Mark.

"Light that Bunsen burner for Amy. She's got to heat that potion."

We obeyed like trained minions, while Ben stood back and watched. It didn't take long, and then Phin handed him a silken cord, from which dangled the wrapped guitar pick. It seemed to be weighted, so that it swung like a pendulum.

"Put this in the potion Amy is heating. And don't think such negative thoughts. Think about your grandfather. Hold him in your mind. That's why *you* need to do this, because you're close to him."

I grabbed the bowl with a pot holder and moved it off the flame. I hadn't made a potion in seven or eight years, but it comes back to you, like riding a bike.

"Hold on to the string," I cautioned. "The water is hot, and you don't want to have to dig it out with your fingers. Trust me."

He did as I said, watching me as I held the bowl between us while the potion steeped. "I thought you were the normal one."

I smiled up at him slightly, despite the urgency of the situation. "No, you didn't."

"Well, relatively." He watched me as if he were seeing a stranger, and I wanted to plead that I was still the same girl I was an hour ago in his pickup. But this was more important.

"I'm a Goodnight," I said. "Some things I just can't get away from. But we're going to find your grandfather, Ben."

"You can't promise that."

"No. But I believe this is our best chance." I raised my

342

gaze from the bubbling leaves, a strange purple sort of tea. "Thank you for trusting me."

He looked away first. "How long do we have to hold this in here?" he asked Phin.

"Until you have your granddad pictured in your head," she chided from over by the map. "So stop talking to him, Amy, and let him concentrate."

He closed his eyes, but it had all the sincerity of a kid pretending to take a nap. "This is never going to work."

"Ben, listen to me," I said, tapping into the part I never reached for, because it was too scary, too painful a stretch. "You know your grandfather better than anyone. When you think of him, what does he smell like?"

He shifted awkwardly. "Leather. Sweat. Horse. Tobacco."

I caught Phin nodding at me in approval, and went on. "Tell me something he taught you. Did he teach you any songs on the guitar?"

"Of course."

The purple of the potion was seeping up the white silk cord more quickly the more he immersed himself in memory. Phin checked it and said, "A little more."

"Can you sing a song he taught you?" I asked Ben.

He opened his eyes, and the purple stopped rising. "Seriously?"

"Yes, seriously."

He sighed, but started a hoarse baritone croon, so like his grandfather's my skin prickled.

"As I walked out on the streets of Laredo . . ."

His voice, knit with memories, drew the potion up the

silk, until the length was soaked through. "Keep going," said Phin as she took the weighted cord from Ben's fingers. She lifted the weight from the bowl and it dangled, twisting on its string, dripping sodden leaves into the water.

Ben kept singing, eyelids lowered as Phin moved to the map on the table. *"I spied a young cowboy, all wrapped in white linen . . ."*

Linen like a shroud. What a macabre song to teach a little boy.

I could sense something, like a rising breeze, curling around me, around Ben, and Phin, stirring the curtains, and the papers on the table. The door was still closed, but the silk-wrapped weight began to swing in the invisible wind.

Phin extended her hand over the map, and the pick swung like a mad pendulum, though her hand remained steady.

"All wrapped in white linen as cold as the clay."

"Got it," said Phin.

Ben's eyes snapped open. "You know where he is?"

"I know the area." She circled it in red marker and handed the map to him. "Now Lila does her thing."

Lila barked at her name. She was already wearing her harness and search-dog vest. As we gathered the first-aid kit and supplies, I stole a moment to ask Phin about our next obstacle. "Do you know how to work Lila on a search?"

"I'm not going to do it. You are. She likes you best."

Last fall Aunt Hyacinth showed me how to work with Lila so I could write a paper for school. We practiced together one afternoon—but that was her *normal* search-dog training.

344

"I'm talking about her special training, Phin. I don't *do* magic, remember?"

"You need to quit saying that. Besides, most of the doing is done, you just have to use it." She handed me a familiar tabbed notebook as the guys waited impatiently to leave. "Aunt Hyacinth really did leave instructions for everything."

Ben was wound tighter than a watch. His anxiety seemed almost a physical force, pushing me away. Even Lila felt it, laying her chin on the seat between us and whining very softly. I stroked a reassuring hand over her back. He could push, but we weren't going anywhere until we'd found his grandfather.

Mark wasn't far behind us, following in the Jeep with Phin. A stretch of highway, two gates, and a lot of dirt road later, we reached the coordinates Ben had entered into his GPS from Phin's map. It was a rugged stretch, where years of water runoff had carved ravines and arroyos into the limestone hills. And it was deserted, as far as we could see.

"No search party, and no Grandpa Mac," said Ben. "This is a wild-goose chase."

"This is where he is. Trust me."

"How can you be so sure?" He scrubbed his hands over his face. "I can't believe I got so caught up in this crazy idea."

I let all the pitfalls in that statement lie and concentrated on the important part. "Phin may seem like a nut, but there's no one smarter about this stuff."

He dropped his hands and looked at me, reading the certainty in my face. After a long study, I read the recommitment in his. To the plan, anyway.

"Okay," he said. "What's next?"

I scratched Lila's ears as she panted eagerly on the seat between Ben and me. On the drive over, I'd read Aunt Hyacinth's instructions, and they weren't complicated, especially since I'd done some casual training with the dog already. "Next, Lila narrows the search."

We climbed out and I held the door open for her. She jumped down, circling without taking her eyes off me. As if she knew how important this was.

Ben gazed over the daunting stretch of terrain. "But it's a big spot."

I crouched in front of the collie. "That's why we need the dog."

Mark's headlights swept the truck as he reached us. Phin rode with him, and as Ben and I conducted this part of the search on foot, they would follow.

Clenched tight in my hand, I had the soaked and wrapped guitar pick. It was staining my palm purple as I held it out to Lila to sniff. She snuffled it, inhaling the essence, then licked my face. With a scent item, I'd take it away so it wouldn't distract her from what she was supposed to sniff out. But this wasn't about a physical scent—it was about a supernatural bond.

Lila turned in a circle and looked expectantly from me to Ben.

"Tell her to find your granddad," I said. "Picture him really clearly in your head, and then tell her to go."

As far as he'd come with me—with us—he still hesitated. "This is crazy."

"Ben." I stepped in front of him, took his arms, and

346

willed him to look at me. It was hard to meet his eye. I felt like I was standing there naked, letting him see a part of me, my life, that I kept hidden away from everyone. Even myself.

I was the gatekeeper. And tonight I'd thrown the doors open to the enemy forces. I was *full* of anxiety: that breaking my rules would let something bad happen, that I wouldn't be able to protect myself or my family from a world full of contempt. I had to push worry aside and show Ben that I believed in magic completely and this would work.

"You don't have to trust in magic," I told him. "You don't have to trust Phin or my aunt. But trust *me*. This is the best chance of finding Mac in a hurry. Please. You don't even have to trust me for long. Just long enough."

He gazed back at me, doubt behind his eyes. "You and your magic dog."

"Me, my sister, and my magic dog." I smiled, reassuring. "Yes."

"Okay." He closed his eyes and took a deep breath. I wondered what he was picturing behind them. "I'm ready."

"You have to have Grandpa Mac firm in your mind. Clear. Vivid. His smell, his voice. His essence."

"Got it." Then he looked down at Lila and said, "Find Granddad Mac."

Lila barked and spun on her back legs. She set off in one direction, then the other, then back again, tracking. I heard the change in the tenor of the Jeep's engine as Mark put it in gear, ready to trail us as we followed Lila on foot.

We were able to keep up because, while she ran side to side, narrowing each time as she homed in on the target, we could take a straighter path. But at the top of a hill, the dog raised her head, gave a loud bark, and took off like she'd been shot from a cannon.

"Come on." I broke into a run, with Ben behind me. We skidded down a valley, then climbed up the steep slope on the other side, the dry, loose soil making it hard to get traction. At the top I paused, searching for the glint of Lila's reflective vest in the dark. I spotted her arrowing across a flat space, then up another hill.

This time she stopped, panting, waiting expectantly for me and Ben to catch up. When we reached her, I said, "Where's Mac, Lila?" and she turned in a circle, then lay down.

"What does that mean?" asked Ben.

"She's supposed to lie down when she finds something." I tried to remember exactly. "Maybe she can't follow his trail any farther."

Ben turned in a slow circle. "But he's not here."

I turned, too, scanning the terrain. I could see Mark and Phin headed our way in the Jeep, driving carefully over the rocky hills. The night carried the purr of the engine and the sound of Lila's panting breaths.

Then Ben grabbed my arm, his hand hot on my skin. "Do you hear that?"

When I froze, Lila did, too, and her panting quieted for a second. Just long enough for me to hear what Ben did. A soft voice singing.

The breeze carried it through the hills like a phantom, but as we listened, Ben still holding my arm, the song strengthened, until I could hear words as well as a tune, even over Lila's panting.

"When I walked out on the streets of Laredo . . ."

"Which way?" I asked Ben, who knew the terrain.

"Here." He started along the ridge, and I realized why Lila had stopped where she did. The drop-off was terrifyingly steep.

Ben doubled back on a cutback that took him lower, and as he made the turn, he stopped to get his bearings and sang out, *"As I walked out in Laredo one day."*

The answer came right away. *"I spied a young cowboy all dressed in white linen . . ."*

They finished the stanza together, with Ben picking his way down the steep drop, holding on to the branches of trees as he went.

"All wrapped in white linen and cold as the clay."

Mac lay halfway down the slope, his fall stopped by a dwarf cedar. I could see his outline in the moonlight. He tried to get up as his grandson approached, but Ben ordered him to stay where he was.

"Amy!" he shouted up at me. "Get on the phone and call nine-one-one. Have them connect you with the sheriff. I think Mark and I can get Grandpa up and into the Jeep. Have the ambulance come to gate thirty-two."

I barely had any bars of service, and my fingers shook as I dialed. We'd found Mac, but in what kind of shape? I was surprised how much relief could hurt when it cycled right back into worry.

35

Once I made it down the hill, I handed Ben my flashlight and knelt by Mac's head. "Stay still, Mr. McCulloch. Let me check you over."

He ignored me, of course. "I saw him, Ben," Mac said, trying again to rise. Ben, after a moment of still surprise, gently but firmly pushed his grandfather back down.

"Hold still, Grandpa. We called for an ambulance."

There was a soft hitch in his voice that made my heart hurt. Ben left his hands resting on Mac's shoulders, reassuring both of them, I think.

A wet darkness soaked Mac's gray hair, and I ran my

hands lightly over his skull, feeling for lumps. My fingers came away smeared with blood, but it seemed to be tacky and clotted, and there was a good-sized goose egg on the back of his head. He was certainly showing no lethargy as he batted my hands away.

"I don't need a damn ambulance. I just fell down the gol-durned hill and couldn't get up. So I sat here to wait for someone to come the hell and find me."

"You did the right thing," said Ben.

"Were you singing so Ben could find you?" I asked, meaning to distract him as I checked for other injuries. No problem moving his arms, for sure. But his legs . . .

"I was singing," snapped Granddad Mac, "because my leg hurts like a sonovabitch and it was sing or cry like a gol-durned girl."

He was not saying "gol-durned." And when I ran my hands over his lower extremities and he hollered "mother effer," that wasn't what he really said, either. Ben looked mortified at his grandfather's language. Not to mention the name he called me as I confirmed his hip was broken.

It didn't help that Mark and Phin arrived just then, half sliding down the hill. "Did you find him?" Phin asked. "Is he okay?"

I ignored them all. I ignored the language, and my own tender sympathy for Ben and Mac both. I focused only on the problem I could do something about.

"It's not your leg, Mr. McCulloch," I said, all business, and using his full name since he didn't seem to recognize me. "It's your hip."

"Baloney," he said through his teeth, lying back—finally—

351

with a horrible grimace. "Only old women break their hips."

"And old men who fall down cliffs." It wasn't much of a cliff, but it was enough. "Phin," I said, "hand me the ice pack from the first-aid kit."

She dropped the bag by Mac and found the instant cold pack, crushing and kneading it before handing it to me.

Ben made another call while we worked. "We found him," he said. One of the knots of anxiety in my chest came a little loose at that "we." I heard the tiny sound of distant cheers over the phone. But Ben's expression didn't change as he held my gaze with his unreadable one. And a new knot drew tight around my heart.

"We already called for an ambulance. Come in at the gate at mile marker thirty-two. Mark will meet you out there in his Jeep." He looked at Mark, who nodded his cooperation. The brusqueness of Ben's tone made me think he was talking to the sheriff or deputy, but he softened a fraction when he said, "Tell my mom . . ." He paused uncertainly, then drew up his resolve and finished, "Tell her it's going to be fine."

He said it like he was going to *make* it fine, by his own force of will if necessary, and I shivered, for no reason I could name.

Granddad Mac was as restless as he could be with a broken hip. He kept moving, cursing at the pain. Whenever I came near his head with the ice pack, he shoved it away.

"Come on, Mr. McCulloch. This is going to make you feel better."

"Nothing but a horse tranquilizer is going to make me feel better, missy!"

Phin took the cold pack from me and shifted to where he could see her in the spill of the flashlight. He stopped his restless thrashing. "I remember you. You're the Goodnight witch."

"That's right," she said, and held the cold pack up where he could see it. "And this is a magic ice pack. I put a potion inside that will ease your pain and make you feel calm and relaxed."

"Now wait just a minute," said Ben. I opened my mouth to shush him, but he ran over me. "If you're seriously planning to use some kind of sedative on my head-injured grandfather . . ."

"It's not—" I started, because I knew that was a standard cold pack, nothing at work but natural chemistry. But Phin shot me a look that froze my tongue, then leveled a stare at Ben.

"You're right," she said. "This is *powerful* stuff. But I think we should let Grandpa Mac decide if he wants it."

"Hell yes! Bring it on." Mac practically snatched it from her.

"Grandpa . . . ," said Ben. "You're not exactly—"

"What?" Mac demanded, holding the ice pack to his head. "I'm not what? Sane?"

"That's not what I was going to say." But from the clench of his jaw, that had been what he meant.

"Deep breaths, Grandpa Mac." Phin held his hand, stroking his arm. "The potion won't work if you get yourself in a lather."

Whatever Phin did, the fight seemed to slip from Mac's body on the sigh of his exhale. He retained enough to glare at Ben. "Why do these Goodnight girls treat me more sane than my family does? They actually ask me about things. No one else ever consults me anymore."

"But what were you *doing* out here, Granddad?" asked Ben. "What were you thinking?"

I was only thinking about calming the waters until the ambulance got there. "What happened, Mr. McCulloch? Did you hit your head when you fell down the ravine?"

"I hit my head when that damned ghost rose up from the ground and scared the bejeezus out of me!"

"You saw him?" I asked, startled. "What did he look like?"

"Great hulking shadow, came out of the dark. Hit me on the head with his cross. You know, the long-handled ones." He pantomimed something like a cross that leads the processional line in a church. I'm sure it had a technical name, but I didn't know it. Mac voiced my own thoughts when he said, "Not very monklike of him, was it?"

"No." It didn't sound much like my ghost, either, which had always had a sort of light associated with him. I would describe the shape as tall and lean, not hulking. And he'd never had any kind of staff, crook, or cross when I'd seen him.

I picked up the flashlight and shooed Phin out of the way. "I'm going to look at your head for a second," I told him. Phin did a lot of eye rolling toward the ice pack. I took a guess at her meaning and said, in the same hypnotic voice she'd used, "Don't worry. The magic ice pack is already working. You won't feel anything."

"Oh for crying out loud," Ben burst out. But Mark, who'd been silently standing by, surprised me by shushing him. "It's Dumbo and the lucky flying feather, dude. Let them do their thing."

Ben glared at him, too. But he didn't say anything else, and neither did Mac as I lifted the corner of the ice pack to get a look at the knot on his head.

The lump was good sized, but it went out, which was good, not in, which would be very bad. The blood that caked his white hair came from a cut, and as I examined it more closely, I saw that a bit of what I had thought was dried blood was actually a sliver of something else. "Phin, hand me the tweezers from the kit, will you?"

"What are you doing now?" asked Ben. Then to his granddad, "Are you okay?"

"Oh fine," said Granddad Mac, sounding a little drunk. "This stuff is great. Too bad everyone doesn't know about magic, or we could put this stuff in a bottle."

"Good thing," said Ben, through not-quite-clenched teeth.

I ignored that as I concentrated on pulling a sliver of old wood from the cut in Mac's scalp. I was willing to bet real money that it hadn't been a ghost that knocked Granddad Mac down the hill.

The sky was beginning to lighten by the time the EMTs whisked Grandpa Mac off to the hospital. It seemed everyone had been there: Steve Sparks, Mrs. McCulloch, and Deputy Kelly, and the search party, which included his nephew Joe, along with Dumb and Dumber. The last two were on ATVs, which seemed to be asking for trouble, even if the head-bashing Mad Monk was a complete myth.

Then most of them left again: Mark offered Mrs. McCulloch a ride to the hospital with him and Phin, and Steve Sparks went back to the ranch to keep an eye on things, which left Ben stuck with me and Lila, who couldn't go to the hospital.

We stood a little ways from where the remaining searchers were debriefing. "I'll get someone to take us back to Goodnight Farm," I offered, but hoped he would say no, that he wanted me to come with him.

Which goes to show that you shouldn't ask questions, even unspoken ones, that you don't want the answer to.

"That would probably be best," said Ben, without meeting my eye.

In the grand scheme of things, getting dumped just hours after hooking up didn't rate a blip on the world radar. But all the same, it hurt like hell.

Later, I'd give in to it. Now, I reassured him, "Granddad Mac will be okay."

He raised his brows with a sardonic edge, more cutting than I'd seen in a while. "Did you see that in your crystal ball?"

I flinched at the hit. He hadn't even given me an *en garde*. "Seriously?" I asked. "You want to do this now?"

"I don't know," he parried. "Is there *ever* a good time to

ask what the hell were you thinking doing magic on my grandfather?"

"I–" I wanted to explain that it hadn't been magic so much as psychology and the Phin Effect turned up to the maximum. But the door I'd thrown open to Ben had been slammed in my face, and the instinct to now bar it was too strong for me to ignore.

He leaned close, keeping his voice low, but tight with anger. "I specifically told you not to talk to my family about the ghost. About any of that mess. Even for a trespassing, busybody ghostbuster, that takes a lot of balls."

I could *hear* the fuse sizzle in my head, but I was helpless to stop the inevitable explosion of verbal shrapnel. "Well, maybe if you weren't such a secretive, neurotic control freak, you could have told me what I needed to know."

"*Want* to know."

"*Need.* Ben, you *saw* what happened tonight at the dig." It seemed so long ago, so much had happened since Daisy had channeled the ghost's warning.

He scrubbed his hands over his face, like he was trying to rub off the fatigue and emotion of those intervening hours. "I don't know what I saw anymore."

I should have guessed that without Phin there, his acceptance would unravel. I could see the thread, but I couldn't catch it, and I didn't have the power to knit it back together, except with my words.

"You saw what you saw, Ben McCulloch. If you can't believe me, why can't you at least trust me?"

"Because all I can *see* is my grandfather lying in a ravine telling me that a flipping ghost knocked him down there." He swept a hand toward the drop-off, but encompassed the entire breadth of our relationship. "You talked to Granddad Mac about the ghost, and then he went wandering off to find it!"

I didn't need help feeling guilty for that. "Do you really think he hadn't heard the rumors from anyone else? His memory is shot, not his ears."

"So now you're telling me how to handle my own family?"

"No!" The protest burst out of me, and I wanted to burst, too, the pressure was so strong in my chest. Beside me, Lila whined, and I lowered my voice because I knew people would be straining to hear. "How did you even get that? Could we please stick to my *actual* offenses? Which, as far as I can tell, are simply, A, existing and, B, treading on your hallowed domain."

"It's about you existing in complete *chaos* and bringing that here. When I'm around you," he said, sounding as miserable and frustrated as he did angry, "I get caught up in you and your crazy world. I can't handle that. I just want to go back to a time when I didn't know that people could see ghosts or find people with magic or make me forget my responsibilities in the cab of my pickup truck."

I blushed, certain every one of the search party had heard that last part. "That wasn't magic," I murmured, low and hurt. "That was just you and me."

He sighed. "It was, Amy, because you're *you*. You're the most dangerous one of all, because people can't see you coming. They just think you're this quirky, nosy, annoying, adorable girl who yells at cows in her underwear. Then before they know it, they're relying on spells instead of good sense."

His words cut my heart. They stabbed at the weakest part—the stitched-together edges of my divided life.

"That's a lousy thing to say, Ben McCulloch." I hated the catch in my voice and I hated him for putting it there, and I hated myself for letting him. "You're just as bad for making me think you're a sweet, stand-up guy who takes care of his family, when you're just an uptight jerk trying to control every facet of his life. Well, you can't. Life is too full of crazy things that don't fit in neat boxes."

Before I could waver, I grabbed Lila's harness to go. "But at least you'll have one less crazy thing in yours. Have a nice one."

Then I marched past him to find my own ride home. For the first time ever, I'd managed a great parting line and a grand exit. And it still felt like crap.

36

deputy Kelly drove Lila and me back to Goodnight Farm in tactful silence. I unkindly suspected that he was glad to see a McCulloch get dumped—though only on the technicality of my being the one who walked away. Which I wouldn't have done if I hadn't been pushed.

"Quite an adventure," the deputy finally said. His first name must be Obvious.

I stared out the window, stroking the dog's soft fur. "I'm just glad Lila was able to help find Mr. McCulloch."

"Yeah. I've worked with Ms. Hyacinth a time or two

when someone goes missing in the hills or out on the river. You Goodnights are real good at finding things."

"So I've heard." The sun was coming up. It didn't seem possible how much had happened between dusk and dawn.

"Too bad what you find is usually trouble."

That got my attention.

The deputy pulled in at the Goodnight Farm gate, put the Blazer in park, and regarded me with his beady wolverine eyes. "I'm getting really tired of hearing your name attached to wild rumors and factual reports, Miss Amy."

The old-fashioned address didn't sound strange at all coming from him. He wanted me to think he was an old-fashioned lawman. A law unto himself, and he was laying it down.

"I think that after tonight," he warned, "you'd better keep to the farm for a bit. The university students are headed home, and things'll quiet down at the river. I don't think Mr. Ben is going to much want to see you around his place anymore, either."

He paused. "And really, we're lax about the eighteen-to-twenty crowd at the roadhouse, as long as they don't drink, but technically, I could come down on you. And your sister. I don't think Ms. Hyacinth would like to come back from her slow boat to China and find out her nieces were in jail."

I was *not* in the mood to be threatened by this sawed-off lawman two generations away from cattle thieves and rum-runners. "Deputy Kelly," I said, in a clipped but polite tone, "you can't put us in jail, as long as we didn't drink. And if you came down on us, you'd have to come down on the

Hitchin' Post, and I'm betting their taxes pay a big chunk of your salary. Also, I might have to mention all the pot smoking that goes on outside the back door, that people might wonder why you haven't noticed. So I'm going to get out now and walk down to the house, because I don't want to see *you* anymore, either."

I was just full of great exit lines today, none of which was making me feel any better.

Daisy had gone, and she'd left a note. *Got a call. Wouldn't leave you but it's a kid. God and St. Luke bless Aunt Hyacinth's headache powder. Love and kisses, Daisy.*

The notepaper had skulls on it, and she'd dotted the *i* in her name with an appropriate flower. At least she advertised her weirdness. I supposed Ben would approve of that.

I told myself I didn't care. I just wished I weren't already feeling so adrift and far from my *own* comfort zone.

What would I be if I weren't the normal one? The gatekeeper and the fix-it girl? Phin thought I had some connection with the restless dead. Was I going to be the fix-it girl for the spirit world, too?

Hell, I already was for one surly, ungrateful ghost. And would be forever if I didn't *busca* him. The San Sabá Mission seemed as good a place as any to start looking for *la mina,* and it gave me a reason to get away from McCulloch Ranch for a while. Maybe the drive would clear my head.

I fed the menagerie, threw some stuff in a backpack, left a note for Phin, and headed for the door. But as I passed the coffee table, I saw that Daisy had left the *Haunts of the Hill Country* book on top of the carton from Mom. She'd stuck a skull-paper note in it at the appropriate page, and I could tell from her shaky script that she'd written it this morning, post-migraine.

The name is bunk. He's not a monk. So I don't know how much of this is true. But if it is, be careful.

When Daisy told me to be careful of a ghost, I listened.

What had I tied myself to? Surely Aunt Hyacinth wouldn't have asked me three times to take care of a real baddie. I scanned the entry Daisy had marked, my fingers shaking.

Reading as I went, I walked out to Stella, brushing aside the dogs, who seemed determined to get in my way despite the fact that I'd fed their thankless furry faces. The latch on the gate stuck, but I gave it a hard yank between paragraphs and slipped out, closing it behind me.

It wasn't exactly engrossing literature, and the prose was as purple as you might expect from an author named Dorothea Daggerspoint. But I gulped it down like nasty medicine.

The book said the ghost was a monk but didn't explain why he was accompanying an expedition to locate a mine in Texas. The expedition was, as we'd theorized, attacked on their way home, and massacred. Except the "Mad Monk" wasn't killed with the others. The story went that he turned on them, conspired with the Apache, or a French explorer, or both, to kill the party, and absconded with the gold. Only, his allies then turned on *him* and left him for dead.

I was so immersed in the tale—or rather, in the wild, spiraling extrapolations my mind was making from it—that I only dimly registered the sound of an ATV approaching. I chalked it up to kids out joyriding, or to Aunt Hyacinth's field help, who came twice a week, or to anything other than what it was: something important.

"Hey, Ghost Girl." I whirled, but it wasn't Joe Kelly standing between me and the gate to the yard. It was Dumb, or Dumber, and I wondered if these were the asshole cousins who had helped Joe torment Ben as a kid, or if they were just his random pothead buddies.

"What are you doing here?" I demanded. The dogs were barking so hard, I thought they were going to tear down the fence. Dumb shifted like he had ants in his pants, either because of the dogs or because we were standing just outside Aunt Hyacinth's defenses.

Just *outside* her defenses.

Oh. Hell.

Right about the time I wondered where Dumber was, pain exploded in the back of my head, and blackness blossomed in front of my eyes, and unconsciousness saved me from lecturing myself on what an idiot I was.

37

My first memory, on waking in stuffy, cramped darkness, was of Phin speculating on how much brain damage Nancy Drew must sustain from getting hit on the head all the time.

Which wasn't the only inaccuracy in those books. I couldn't recall the girl detective ever waking up in an attic or stable or basement prison with the acrid taste of vomit in her mouth.

I vaguely remembered puking on one of the guys as they moved me. At least my unconsciousness had been intermittent and not prolonged. And when I touched my head, there was a huge lump. Out was better than in. Yay for first-aid training.

My prison was not an attic, stable, or basement. It was moving. I could hear the crunch of a gravel road, and as I bounced around, unable to uncurl my arms or legs from my fetal position, I realized I was in the trunk of a very small car. Like a Mini Cooper. The ride was ever so slightly lopsided, so I knew it was Stella, with her donut spare tire.

What kind of morons drove a sports car with a donut tire over hilly gravel roads? All I knew was they better not put a scratch on my car, or I'd kill them.

I could just barely hear them talking, one of them yelling at the other. "You dumbass. We were supposed to talk to her about finding the gold mine for us. Not knock her brains out."

"Not steal her car, either, but you did that."

"All I could think about was getting away from there."

"Me too. It was freaky. That whole family is freaky." There was an anxious pause. "We probably shouldn't have messed with them."

"You think?"

I couldn't hear them for a while, and I thought maybe they had lowered their voices, but they must have been thinking, and the effort was too much for them to talk at the same time.

"Let's do this: We'll drive over to where those old abandoned shafts are. We'll park, and we'll offer her a share in whatever gold she helps us find."

"And if she won't help us?"

Whatever they would do was lost, because they hit a hard bump and the loose tire iron tapped the bump on my head, and the sparkles of white across my vision were so pretty, I had to fall into them and go to sleep for a while.

When I woke up again, Stella was stopped at a distressing angle, the engine was off, and the moron pair was—I listened intently—not just silent, but absent. The stillness was too complete.

It was stifling hot, and I'd slid to the side of the trunk, crumpled in a stiff, aching ball. My wits must have been returning, because I had the sense to be terrified at my predicament. Had they decided to just leave me to bake? July in Texas in a closed car. It wouldn't take long. I might have been dead already if it had been the middle of the day.

I finally worked through my panic and remembered the inside handle. It took me a minute to find it, pull it, and lever up the hatch.

The sun had climbed high overhead. Maybe an hour longer and I would have been cooked like a turkey.

Woozily I climbed out of the trunk, holding on to my head when it threatened to wobble off my neck. Dumb and Dumber had managed to throw my backpack in with me, and I drank half the bottle of water, took an aspirin, and looked at my cell phone.

No bars. I glanced around at the granite outcroppings that surrounded me, and didn't wonder why.

I was at the foot of the ochre-colored mountain that ran through the middle of the McCulloch property. I'd been heading toward this bluff the night I'd fallen into the sinkhole. The dig site was far on the other side, but I'd never seen this area in daylight.

My kidnappers were nowhere I could see. The keys were still in the ignition, though it didn't really matter because they'd hit a hole and the spare had blown out like a party balloon. Stella wasn't going anywhere.

And neither was I, except on foot.

Eeny-meeny-miny-mo. I headed for more-open ground. It might be a hike, but the highway was in that direction.

I didn't expect to trip over Dumber's body.

I didn't expect to hear the sound of a diesel truck engine approaching over the hill.

And this time, I didn't need a ghost to tell me I was in trouble.

Scrambling for cover, I threw myself into a dry rain gully just deep enough for me to lie in. The truck came nearer, and I could hear booted footsteps approaching from a second direction. Suddenly the ditch that hid me reminded me too much of the graves we'd excavated by the river. Sweat gathered under my shirt, and I wondered if an anthropologist would find me someday and take my remains back to a lab to determine that my cause of death was a bad case of recklessness.

Too bad I couldn't imagine my way out of this situation as clearly as I could imagine that scene.

The truck stopped, the engine rumbling and gasping into silence. A door opened and closed and someone, I think it was the driver, said to Boots, "What the hell happened here? Why is Bob Dyson lying in the dirt where anyone can run over him? Is he alive?"

"For now." Both voices sounded familiar, though I couldn't quite place them. A gravelly Texas drawl wasn't exactly unique around there. "Had to give him a conk on the head. It's going to start being a joke before long."

"That's what the Mad Monk does," said Truck. "But what was Bob doing out here?"

"I don't know, but I don't think he saw anything. I can set it up so that someone finds him when we're clear."

"That would be better," said Truck.

Better than what? The possibilities took my imagination to ominous places, chilling despite the heat. They talked dispassionately of conking people on the head and something "worse" than leaving poor Dumber–Bob, I mean–lying there to get more brain damaged than the pot had already made him.

Truck's next words dribbled icy fear down my neck. "Where's his ATV? And his buddy? Maybe we'd better have a look around."

Crap!

I had to do something. Fire ants of panic ran through my skin. I could lie there, desperately sending psychic 911 calls to my sister–who could be *anywhere* right now–and let Truck and Boots find me in a convenient, ready-made grave. Or I could make a break for it.

What if they had a more long-distance weapon than the shovel–or whatever they'd hit Bob with, and Mac, and how many other people?

Two sets of boots crunched on the sand. The gully hid me from the approach, but once they were up the hill, they had only to look down to see me.

A cool breeze wafted over my fevered skin. I raised my head, searching along the gully, and saw a hole maybe twenty feet away. A sinkhole, a cave, I didn't care. I low-crawled through the dirt until I reached it, then peered in. It was a steep but climbable slope, shale hardened into something like concrete. I slid down on my butt into the dark recess, and willed my heart to stop pounding so I could hear what the men were doing.

I could see surprisingly well, and my stomach dropped at the sight of a pale glow from the recesses of the cave. But it wasn't the glow of the specter. It was an electric lantern, and it was on, which meant I'd managed to hide in the bad guys' lair.

Frying pan. Fire.

I needed to get out of there before Boots and Truck came back. I scrambled up the slope, my head throbbing so hard that my vision wavered like a mirage.

The men had passed the gully, and they would come across Stella any minute. No way to hide a blue Mini Cooper in sage and sand country. I had to take my chance now, hoping they wouldn't glance back the way they'd come until I was out of sight.

I clambered up and over the hill, running for the diesel truck, praying for all I was worth that the driver had left the keys in it.

Crap!

Not only had he taken the keys, he'd locked the door. I whispered a few more frustrated curses. My head felt like the sprint had split it open. My vision was so blurred, I could barely read the letters on the box in the passenger seat. But my subconscious spoke up and said it was important, so I steadied myself against the truck, shaded my eyes, and squinted as hard as I could.

BLASTING CAPS.

Whoa.

Blasting caps. Mining. Gold mine. Dumb and Dumber weren't so far off at all. Someone else was looking for–had found–the lost gold mine already.

I stumbled back and looked at the truck. I knew it, and not just by sound. It belonged to Steve Sparks, the ranch manager.

When my luck ran out, it ran out big-time. I heard running boots and whirled–oh God, bad idea–to face the two men. With my vision still spinning, it took me a second to recognize the bulldog face under an equally familiar ball cap with "Something Mining and Drilling Company" on the front.

Mike Kelly. Of course he would have known the right rumor to spread to hide their treasure hunt in the pasture. And he knew the land, probably better than anyone.

"Oh, you have got to be kidding me," said Mike Kelly. "Can no one keep this kid out of here?"

I didn't even try for a riposte. I was so nauseated, the wittiest thing I'd be able to manage was barfing. I just turned like a cornered animal and ran the other way.

Steve Sparks caught up to me before I could focus my eyes on escape. Even after I'd recognized his truck, I hadn't believed it was him. Mrs. McCulloch thought he was a nice guy. A loyal guy. No one trusted a Kelly, but the McCullochs trusted Steve Sparks.

And then biting fear took hold of me, because I realized I was probably never going to have a chance to warn them.

"Dammit, kid." Sparks actually looked regretful. "I was hoping this wouldn't have to happen."

I knew "this" was going to be bad. He grabbed me, and the pain in my head gave me an idea. I let myself go limp. His hold loosened in surprise, and I slid from his grasp to land in a boneless heap on the sand.

I lay still and faked unconsciousness. It wasn't much of a stretch; their voices seemed to float from far away.

"Damn, Steve! What did you do?"

"Nothing." I heard him bend close and prayed the tripping of my pulse or my quick, terrified breaths wouldn't give me away.

Steve Sparks gave an incredulous huff, almost a laugh. "You're not going to believe this, Mike. Someone already hit her on the head."

"I doubt it was the Mad Monk." Mike Kelly sounded grim. "I guess hitting her again would look suspicious."

"More suspicious than a ghost hitting her once?" asked Sparks.

"We could put her in her car, run it into the cliff, but the bump's on the back, not the front." Something in Steve's expression must have made Mike add, "Come on. It was only a matter of time before the Mad Monk had a fatality. And everyone knows she can't keep on her own side of the fence. My brother has been griping about it for days."

I stiffened on the ground, unable to stay limp as fear burned through me. How could this be real? Ghosts and magic were nothing compared to these yahoos having a cold-blooded discussion on the best way to kill me.

"It's just . . ." Sparks was wavering. "A big step."

I heard it before they did—the rumble of truck tires over stony ground. My heart gave an almost painful leap of hope.

"Hell," said Mike Kelly. "What now? When did this turn into Main Street?"

Sparks walked away a bit, I supposed to take a look over the hill that hid his truck from view from the road. He wasn't gone long enough for me to think of jumping Mike, and when he came back, his voice was strained. "It's Ben."

Yes, Ben!

And then I heard Mike Kelly inhale. An anxious breath of anticipation and excitement. A fiendish inspiration.

He had something planned for Ben. My heart beat so hard, I couldn't believe they didn't hear it. Ben was driving right into a trap, and I didn't know how to warn him.

"Listen," said Steve, and something in his voice made me think he'd realized the same thing I had. "You hide, with the girl. I can bluff through this."

"What if she called him?" Mike didn't sound worried at all, but as excited as if he'd been handed a birthday present. "We need to get rid of him, too."

"I can handle this, Mike. I've done it before. I've got every reason to be here."

"Don't get squeamish. With him gone, Helen McCulloch will turn to you to run things, and you can suggest she sell this land back to me. Or hell, marry the grieving widow, then *you* sell me the land."

I didn't think I had any room inside me for one more emotion, but indignation managed to squeeze in with the others. I was sure it was Kelly who had hit Mac the night before, and the only thing that surprised me now was that he hadn't killed him. Maybe he'd tried but hadn't been able to get down the ravine.

Steve hesitated long enough for me to know he was thinking about what Mike Kelly had said. And if he could think about it, he could do it. Or at least stand by and watch it be done.

As soon as Ben rounded the hill, he would see Steve's truck and it would be too late for them to hide me. Steve would have to go along with Mike's plan or give up and go to jail. I was not taking bets on that.

With a burst of energy I didn't think I had, I rolled under the diesel truck and out the other side. My head seemed to keep moving after my body stopped, but I couldn't spare the time to be sick. I pushed myself upright, swallowing the bile that rose in the back of my throat.

Surprise had given me a precious head start. I staggered to my feet and ran.

The pounding of my steps was like a hammer to my skull. In the corner of my eye, I saw Ben's truck, and his stunned face through the windshield. My goal wasn't to get to Ben, but alert him to danger by my wounded-gazelle-like flight across the pasture. I wasn't worried about myself. I didn't consider the possibility that either of the men could catch me. I was all-star varsity soccer. I was *Braveheart* in Urban Outfitters. I was Supergirl.

I was seriously delusional.

Steve Sparks did catch me. Didn't even have to hit me on the head. The jarring stop rattled my bruised brain, and I slid into genuine, dark, dismal unconsciousness, seriously wishing I hadn't compared myself to William Wallace, who had met such a very sticky end.

38

this time I woke up cold, not hot, and not moving. At least, I tried to convince my stomach of that. I cracked open one eyelid, then the other, and my vision was filled with Ben McCulloch, lying on his side facing me, and looking like hell.

I'm not sure what alerted him to my waking, but he asked, "Are you okay?"

Swallowing first, I managed to croak, "That's a hell of a question from a guy who looks like he went two rounds in a cage match."

He smiled ruefully, then winced as the motion pulled at his split lip. "Have you ever *been* to a cage match?"

"No," I admitted.

"I don't look that bad."

But he *did* look bad. Awful and wonderful and frustrating. His lip was swollen and split, and so was the bridge of his nose. There was blood all over his face and his cheek was bruised, and he was going to have a black eye soon, too.

"Where are we?" I tried to lift my head to look, but it was so heavy, I left it down for a little while longer.

"A cave." He paused and corrected himself. "A mine, I guess. Twenty-first-century claim jumpers. It really is a plot out of a movie. They've been blasting small sections, trying to follow a vein of ore. That was the sound we kept hearing."

"Gold?" That motivated me to sit up. Or work at it, anyway. My head still pounded, but my stomach seemed willing to behave.

Ben rolled over on to his back with a groan. "Don't be greedy, Amaryllis."

"Ben, this could be Los Almagres. The lost Spanish mine."

He chuckled, then winced. "It would serve that bastard Mike Kelly right. Your Mad Monk's expedition might not have made it back to Mexico with a report, but others did. Los Almagres was abandoned because they never found anything worth the trouble of refining."

A chill eddied through the chamber. "Don't call him that," I whispered.

Pushing himself up onto his elbow, he looked at me closely. " 'Your' ghost?"

"The Mad Monk. He's not a monk."

"But the madness is debatable?"

The nape of my neck prickled under my hair, and I snapped, "Ben!"

He sat up too abruptly but didn't pause to moan about it. "Amy, it's just . . ." He stumbled over saying it aloud. ". . . a spirit. You're a person. You're the one in control."

I stared at him, baffled. "What makes you say that?"

"Because I've *met* you, moron."

Warmth chased away the chill. A blush, and a memory that had no business intruding now.

"What are you doing here?" I asked. "And why didn't you get away while you could? *I* had the sense to run, so who's the moron?"

"Phin called me."

I struggled to process that simple phrase. "Phin called you," I clarified. "And you just . . . came? Without any *proof*?"

He shifted, as if uncomfortable with the reminder of our argument. "The proof was in her voice. She said I would know where you were, because it was dark and underground. I immediately thought of your bat cave. I was on my way there when I saw you sprinting across the pasture."

A horrible thought shuddered through me. "Phin's not coming *here,* is she?"

"No. Well, yes, but she and Mark went to contact the state troopers. She said Grandpa Mac told her never to trust a Kelly."

The shudder broadened to shake my whole, aching body. "Speaking of Kelly . . ."

"And Sparks. God, I can't believe I trusted him. My whole family did."

"Where are they?"

378

Sobering from his ire, Ben avoided my gaze, so I knew it wasn't someplace good. "They're going to park my truck at your house. Then I believe the plan is . . ."

"To flip Stella into a ravine with us in her." I looked around the cavern, which was fairly bare. I couldn't see any sunlight from the cave mouth, and the slope up was hidden in darkness. "Are we trapped?"

"They put something over the opening and then parked a truck on it. They've got their routine down."

"Not to be flippant about it or anything, but I wonder why they didn't just, you know." I mimed hitting myself over the head. "Cosh us before they left."

"How should I know?" he snapped. "Maybe they're worried about time of death. Everyone knows about those things now, thanks to television."

I snorted to hear him echoing Emery, and then shivered as the barrier of unreality crumbled. This was *my* time of death we were talking about. Mine and Ben's.

"Cold?" he asked.

Eyes closed, I nodded, and heard him slide over on the stone floor. A moment later he wrapped me in his arms from behind, pulling me tight against his chest. His body heat seeped into me, and his breath warmed my neck. Even under the circumstances, it was a nice way to hear him murmur, "I'm sorry."

"For what? I mean, for what lately?" I twisted to look at his battered face. "Do *not* say 'for getting us killed.'"

He raised his brows carefully. "I wasn't going to say that."

"Because we're not going to get killed," I asserted.

"Or," he contended, "because that's not my fault." Then he rubbed his hands on my bare arms, chafing away the goose bumps. "And because we're not going to get killed."

"Right." After a moment I melted back against him. "Then what are you sorry for?"

He took his time to answer, but we weren't going anywhere. "From way back at the beginning, I blamed things on your aunt that I shouldn't have. And this morning . . . I was really unfair."

"You were a jerk."

This time he agreed without hesitation. "I was a jerk. But . . ." He paused, and I wondered if this was just another version of the same send-off. "Your life, Amy . . . it's a lot to take in. And very chaotic."

"There *are* rules," I said. "And before now I've always been able to keep things contained. Magic world, non-magic world. You've just met me right at the moment that everything sort of . . . broke loose."

"Then I was doubly a jerk for taking my frustration out on you. And for not understanding when you said you were following up the Mad Monk legend. If I hadn't argued, maybe we *wouldn't* be here."

"Oh my God." I sat up and twisted again to face him. "You're apologizing because you think we're going to die."

He stared at me. "What?"

"You want to die with a clear conscience."

"Amy," he said, "I don't want to die at all."

I looked him right in the eye. "What if Phin and Mark don't get here with the troopers in time? Do you think

Sparks and Kelly are really capable of going through with their plan?"

His hand came up to gingerly touch the bruise on his cheekbone. "Mike Kelly would." He said it with certainty, and I wondered what other bruises he had that didn't show. Someone–a Kelly, I guessed, from his answer–had really worked him over.

"We have to get out of here." I didn't know what made me say it with such force, or why the awful feeling of being trapped and waiting for rescue had turned to the worse feeling of being trapped and waiting to get thrown off a ravine to my death. Other than the rational fear of that, of course. Some *sureness* was coiling tight in my chest, and I didn't question it.

Ben dropped his hands to his knees, ready for any suggestion. "If you've got some spell for lifting a half ton of truck, I won't complain."

I chewed on my lip, thinking hard. "Phin could probably magically MacGyver something, but that's not my thing."

"What is your thing?"

"Ghosts." Saying it aloud seemed to solidify something in my mind. It felt real and tangible. True.

"That's not particularly helpful in this situation," said Ben, harshing my moment of self-actualization. "Unless your *ghost* can lift a half-ton truck."

"Maybe it can." I didn't know. Believing one thing had just left me with more questions. "I do know it's warned me twice about danger," I told him. "I mean, it nearly froze me to death, but it kept Sparks from finding me the other night."

Cuidado. I could almost hear the ghost now. Was that why I was so certain we couldn't wait on Phin to bring the authorities?

"I'm going to call it." The idea was on my lips before it had fully formed in my brain. "Maybe if it could warn me before it can help us now."

Ben raised his hands, as if holding me back. "Whoa. Didn't you just say this thing nearly froze you to death?"

"Yeah, it did, but I think I can control things now. You said it. I'm the human. This is my world, my rules."

"Amy, honey." He rubbed my arm gently, as if telling me bad news. "You shouldn't listen to me. I don't know what the hell I'm talking about."

I ignored him—because he was right—and stood, wobbling only slightly. Ben pushed himself to his feet using a stalactite. Or stalagmite. The stone was all dry, which meant this wasn't a living, growing cave, but stable. Or maybe not, if people were blowing holes in it.

I found the knotted spot in my psyche that had looped tight the night of Aunt Hyacinth's call, feeling the tug of the bond in that place deep inside. The place where you got hunches, where you dug down deep for courage.

My head pounded with the effort I put into my thoughts—*Come to me. Help me. If I don't get out of here, I'll never find you.*

Nothing happened. I opened my eyes, looked around for confirmation that all was still, that the air was cave-cool, not cold.

This was going to suck if I failed in front of Ben. It was

going to suck if I failed and died, but if Ben weren't here, at least no one would know about it.

He must have seen the doubt in my face. "You controlled it before. I saw you."

"Yeah." The stabs of doubt faded to pinpricks.

"Maybe you need to speak Spanish."

I didn't quite groan. "Great. Señora Markowitz would be laughing now."

Shaking myself out, much like Daisy had done, I spread my fingers and toes, the flex of tendon and muscle sending warmth and energy to my extremities.

"Venga aquí. Venga a mí. Ayúdame a encontrarle." I hesitated a moment, then added, *"Por favor."* Because politeness never hurt.

Air currents swirled against my skin, a coolness on my flushed cheeks that stirred my hair and soothed my headache. The air swirled faster as I flexed my fingers again. Controlling the moment, but giving up my stubborn, fearful grip on the mundane world and giving in to the Goodnight one. Falling down the rabbit hole, and not worrying how I would get back out.

The light was electric and white, not luminous and blue.

"Turn off the lantern, Ben."

After the smallest hesitation, he did as I asked. In the utter blackness, the current strengthened. Icy fingers lifted my hair, and steam collected in front of my mouth. I could see it in the faint glow coming from deeper in the cavern.

Búscame . . .

The word breathed through my mind.

I felt for Ben's hand and held tight. "I think we need to go that way."

"I thought you were calling it to you," he said.

"My Spanish is a little rusty." I looked up at him, barely able to see his outline in the spectral light. "But do you want to stay *here*?"

He cast a quick look around the cave, the dead end of our current situation, and squeezed my fingers. "Let's go, then."

The light led to a passageway, became brighter as we followed it through twists and turns. The passage narrowed until Ben had to squeeze through, and I saw him pale with pain as the rock dug into his ribs.

I wanted to let him rest, but an urgency pulled me forward. When I'd connected with the psychic knot inside me, it had drawn inexorably tight.

When the passage got too low I dropped to my knees and crawled. I finally emerged into a small chamber. The ghostly glow suffused the space, illuminating a dead end, and a dead man.

The skeletal remains of the soldier were dry and ancient and lay sprawled on a fall of earth like a rocky bed. The tatters of a uniform still clung to the bones, but the buckles and buttons and insignia had fallen ignominiously from the scraps of cloth.

Ben, muttering pained curses, squeezed through the entrance into the small cave, falling onto the floor with a grunt. "Your ghost," he wheezed, "must hate me."

"Shhh." I knew better, from working on the dig that

week, but I reached out anyway, picking up a brass crest, marveling at how old it was. It was still shiny under a layer of tarnish. "Ben, look. He *was* a soldier."

He did look. He looked at the bones, then looked around the cavern, which was barely tall enough for him to stand up and stretch his arms. "This isn't an escape, Amy. It's a tomb."

39

"Your ghost," accused Ben, "has led us to a trap. Maybe the same trap that killed him."

"Don't jump to conclusions," I said. But he was right about one thing. I couldn't see an exit. The side of the cave where the skeletal figure rested seemed to have collapsed. Maybe that was why he'd died here. Or maybe he'd been killed by someone and never found.

"His head is resting on something," I said, crawling closer to look.

"Amy, are you listening?"

"It's a bundle of black cloth!" With apologies to Dr.

386

Douglas, I eased a finger under the stiff and rotted material, gently bracing the skull with my other hand so I didn't dislodge it. "There's something shiny. I can just see it."

"Amaryllis!" Ben's voice seemed far away. "Come back to earth. We are in trouble here."

He grabbed my arm just as I pulled free a heavy metal object that rasped across the stone. The sound echoed through the cavern and down the passage we'd crawled out of.

In my hand was a solid gold cross, barely tarnished, and inlaid with gems. They didn't gleam in the ghost light, and I couldn't see their color. But this was a precious item.

Ben stared at it, too. "Oh my God. It *is* the Mad Monk."

A faint breeze stirred the dirt on the floor. "I don't think so, Ben. This was hidden. And it's not very . . . monkish."

"Did you read the story?" he demanded. "The one in the book? About how the Mad Monk—or whoever he was—ran off with the expedition's treasure and was killed by his collaborators?"

The wind was getting stronger, and colder. "If you knew that story," I snapped, "why did you follow the light?"

"Because we didn't have a lot of options." He chewed on his next words, and spit them out reluctantly. "And I trust you. But I don't trust this ghost."

I could see his breath, as the temperature kept dropping. "Ben, now is *not* the time to be a jackass."

The glow that suffused the cavern seemed to pull in on itself, to gather near the wall closest to the skeleton. It brightened in the center, until I had to shade my eyes against the blue-white light.

Ben's hand tightened on my arm hard enough that I gasped in pain. Surprise made me drag my eyes from the gathering specter, and I saw that the fog of Ben's breath had gone still and his other hand clutched his side.

I knew that feeling. But if he struggled against the grip of the ghost, tried to force his lungs to work, and he had a cracked or broken rib . . .

"Leave him alone." I didn't bother with Spanish, but took hold of the knot of connection between the specter and me and pushed my demand through it.

Inocente . . .

The word bloomed in my mind. Ben swayed on his feet, and I caught him around the waist, staggering under his weight.

"If you're innocent," I said to the ghost, "let him go."

With the suddenness of a snapping bone, the specter released Ben. He gasped in a breath and clutched my shoulders as his strength returned.

"Now," he panted, "do you believe he's a traitor?"

Ben learned lessons the hard way. He held me against him, as if protecting me from the specter that had appeared, a colorless figure of light and shadow, across the tiny cavern.

The figure raised its hand, but instead of pointing at me, it pointed to a chest next to the skeleton, half hidden by the fall of earth that had trapped him.

Inocente . . .

The voice seemed to be only in my head. Ben looked at me for guidance. I collected my courage and edged to where the ghost pointed. Ben followed me, still watching the figure warily.

We dug it out together, a banded wooden chest the size of a toaster. Finally, exchanging looks and deep breaths of cold air, under the dark stare of the specter, we opened it.

"Empty," said Ben. He looked from the box to the motionless soldier, sorting through legend and evidence and trying to reconcile what was in front of him. "So he didn't steal the expedition's treasure?"

I studied the ghost, who seemed to study me back. I'd never seen his clothes before, but as I took them in now, the pieces began to come together.

"Look at him, Ben. He's got a monk's robe over his uniform. Maybe he was in disguise. He could have been a decoy."

He paused, fitting the idea into a theory. "Let their attackers see a priest with a shiny cross running off with a treasure chest?" He seemed to unbend, admit he could be wrong about the ghost. He nodded at the jewels and gold still in my hands. "I guess if I were a robber, I'd go after that."

Inocente.

The ghost faded out, leaving us in utter darkness.

I held my breath for a moment, waiting to see if he would come back, but the connection between us felt slack and unraveled, like a string with no tension on the other end.

In the silence, another sound reached me. I knew Ben heard it, too, because his shoulder, pressed against mine in the close quarters, tensed.

An engine noise, and a scraping, and the murmur of voices.

"Do you think it's the cavalry?" I barely dared to whisper.

Ben murmured back, so close to my ear his voice didn't even stir the air, "I think we should be very, very still."

40

My heart tapped out a Morse code of tight, trapped panic. I might have fulfilled my duty to the ghost, but I'd still be linked with him forever, because my bones would lie with his for eternity.

And Ben's. I could feel his breath on my neck, stirring my hair. A strand tickled my nose, and my legs began to cramp. I ached to move but any scrape of rock would echo through the cave and give away our position.

The voices became clearer as they rose in frustration and anger. Definitely not Phin and the state troopers, but Sparks and Kelly.

"They're searching for us," Ben whispered against my ear. "We must have left a trail like a wounded buffalo."

I could feel his fight-or-flight tension, but there wasn't room for fight and there wasn't any place to go.

And then I heard a rustle, something I'd never have heard if we weren't crouched like mice in a trap. The sound made me notice something else I'd missed while distracted by bones and ghosts and the certainty of my imminent demise.

"Do you smell that?" I whispered.

I felt him inhale, then sort of cough. "Guano."

"If there are bats, then there's an opening to the outside."

Ben carefully twisted to check all angles, and I felt the change in his tension when he saw something. "Over there."

There was a flat opening hidden behind the soldier's resting place, an infinitesimally lighter darkness against the cavern wall. I'd missed it because I hadn't wanted to disturb the remains. But there was no helping that now.

We had to crawl over the skeleton to get out. I tried to be careful, but in the dark I had to feel my way across. The fabric disintegrated, and bits of remnant flesh fell like scraps of leather. The bones cracked like dry twigs under my hands.

On the other side, Ben boosted me over a row of stalagmites, and we worked around a bend . . . and suddenly I knew where we were.

"I've been here before." I looked up in disbelief at the cave opening, shaded with an overhang covered with bats. I'd been only twenty to thirty yards from the ghost's remains two nights ago. "This is my bat cave."

Ben stumbled on the uneven footing of the layers and layers of bat guano and followed my gaze to the mouth of the cave. It was a long way up. "But we're still trapped."

The rabbit warren of the cave carried Sparks's voice to us, calling that he'd found our trail. How badly did they want to follow us? If they presumed the cave was a dead end, maybe they'd just let us rot, like the soldier without a grave.

But the voices were getting closer, and Mike Kelly was a small guy—he could probably worm his way right through. I backed up a step in spite of myself, edging up against the nearly vertical cave wall. Ben stepped forward, hands clenched into fists.

Then I felt a hard tug on the knot in my stomach, a wrench of warning.

Cuidado, breathed a voice in my head.

On instinct, I reached for Ben and yanked him against the wall. The phantom knot in my psyche gave a jerk and came loose, wrenched free by the force of what came next. There was a bang, and a *whump* that shook me to my bones, and the stone sky crumbled with a mighty crack that sent the bats into the air with squeals that made my teeth ache.

I'd pulled us to the one spot without rock overhead, and Ben swung around, putting his back to the thundering stone rain, pressing me against the wall, tucking my head against his chest as he covered his own with his arms. The shaking of the earth melded with the shaking in my bones and the quake of fear even deeper, in the part of me that wasn't ready to die yet.

The roar went on and on, until I realized we were standing in sunlight, and the noise was in my head. Dust swirled in thick clouds around us, but it wafted up into open air. The roar became a ringing, and Ben raised his head to look around in amazement that must have mirrored my own.

"Are we alive?" I asked, still in the shelter of Ben's arms, squashed between his body and the rock wall that had saved us.

"Seem to be," he said, turning his head stiffly to look down at me, and wincing when he tried to smile. "I hurt too bad to be dead."

The sinkhole was now the size of an Olympic swimming pool, and we stood at the deep end. The roof of the bat cave had collapsed, at least as far as the low cavern where the solider lay. It cut Kelly and Sparks off from us, but judging from the continued rumbles and curls of dust, it might have done worse than that. The cave-in might continue far into the mine, trapping the men . . . or their bodies.

I looked up at Ben. His hair was white with limestone and dust. Pale dirt clung to his face and caked in the places where he was bleeding. He had new cuts, and there were probably more where I couldn't see them. And I didn't even want to think about the bruises.

Very carefully I stretched up and kissed the unswollen side of his mouth. "Thank you."

"For what?" He started to smile and thought better of it. "Not that I'm complaining."

"For making sure that I didn't end up spending the rest of my life with you."

He laughed, then winced, then cursed. Then he said, "The hell with it," and kissed me the best he could. It would be giving him too much credit to say it was as good as the night before, but it was still better than ninety-nine percent of kisses in the world.

"Great Caesar's goat." Phin's voice floated down from the rim of the sinkhole. "The earth caves in, and you two are making out?"

I craned my head to squint up at her. "Tell it to me when *you've* had a near-death experience, Phin Goodnight."

She put her hand over her heart. "I just did. You gave me a coronary. We are going to have to invent an entire new category of the heebie-jeebies for you."

Mark appeared over her shoulder, lacking his usual upbeat luster. "The troopers are yelling at us to stay back until proper rescue workers get here. They're worried the cave-in is still unstable."

Ben let me go, after making sure I could keep my own feet. "Tell them to get a move on. Amy needs to go to the hospital. She's not as hardheaded as I thought."

Mark nodded. "Ambulance is already on the way. We found a guy with a head injury, dehydrated, but mostly coherent, except for talking about a ghost hitting him on the head. When we saw the dust, and felt the quake, we weren't sure . . ."

I waved that off for more pressing concerns. "Warn them there's a whole network of caves under here, Mark. It's a mine. Mike Kelly and Steve Sparks have been blasting underground, following the vein. . . ."

I trailed off, thinking about the ghost's warning. Had he

known the caves were going to collapse? Or had he caused it?

"The blasting must have destabilized the caverns," said Ben. "They're in there, somewhere."

My stomach twisted in guilt, even though they'd been plotting to kill us. I looked at Ben, hoping he would understand. "Was there any way they could have survived?"

He ran a comforting hand down my arm and linked my fingers with his. "If *we* did, maybe they did."

I hoped so. I didn't want to be responsible for anyone's death. Even secondhand, through my connection with the ghost.

The field was full of emergency vehicles: state trooper units, the sheriff's department, the fire department, an ambulance, and the CareFlite helicopter on standby.

I offered to get Lila to look for the missing men, but another rescue-dog team was on the way. The EMTs wouldn't let me do much but sit and watch and wring my hands with guilt. They wanted me to go in for an MRI, and Ben was threatening to haul me off to the hospital by force, but Mark pointed out that he'd probably keel over from his own injuries if he tried.

The state troopers were on hand to confiscate the blasting caps and the dynamite I hadn't seen. They had no trouble chalking up the collapse to an accident by a pair of claim jumpers, though Deputy Kelly insisted that, while he didn't condone what his brother did, since Mike worked for a mining company, he would know how to handle explosives. The state law enforcement didn't necessarily agree, and had some pointed questions for the deputy about why he hadn't noticed someone was blasting underground in his part of the county.

I'd figured that Sparks and Mike Kelly had used the old Mad Monk stories to stir up the ghost hysteria–to keep people speculating about any strange sounds rolling through the hills–but I hadn't really thought about whether they'd included the other Kellys in their plans.

Phin hung up her phone and slid it into her pocket with a decisive motion. "Mom is on her way to the hospital to meet us. Let's go. No arguing."

I looked up at her from my seat in one of the patrol cars. "But I want to see if they find Kelly and Sparks. Steve Sparks just got in over his head, I think."

"Amy, they tried to kill you."

"I know."

"And they collapsed the cave with their own blasting caps and dynamite."

There, I paused. "No. Well, yes. But. It was the ghost's last act. I felt our tie unknot. I found him, and he saved me."

She considered that for a second. "Well, that's a fair trade. I'm sorry I called him ungrateful."

"But that makes me responsible for . . ." I gestured to the massive hole in the ground, and the emergency vehicles all around us.

"How do you figure that?"

"I called the ghost. And it led us to it and then it warned me . . ."

She gave me a long look. "Could you have warned Kelly and Sparks?"

"No."

"Did you make them explode dynamite and hit people on the head and try to kill you?"

"No."

"What a relief. I was worried you'd developed an over-inflated opinion of your powers of mind control and time travel. Because that's what it would take for all this to be your fault."

I just stared at her, wondering if it was my headache that made her sound like she had actually mastered irony. Gingerly I touched the lump under my hair. "I don't know what I think about your developing a sense of humor, Phin."

"Does that imply you don't think I *could* build a time machine or master mind control?"

I wasn't sure how to answer that, so I didn't.

Phin took my arm and pulled me to my feet. I thought she was going to say something else, but for a long moment she scrutinized every bruise and scrape on my face, as if she were cataloging the damage for some experiment. And then she put her arms around me in a too-tight hug.

I held in an "ow" and a little bit of a sniffle.

Then she let me go and pretended it hadn't happened. "Now stop arguing with me. Mark and I are taking you and Ben to the hospital, because it's obvious you two can take care of everyone but yourselves."

41

The August heat was thick and sticky as toffee as I stood in the private cemetery on the corner of McCulloch Ranch. There was quite a crowd, but Phin and I were among the inner circle, away from the photographers and spectators. Mom had come with us, and Aunt Hyacinth was there, wearing a black and gold cheongsam she'd brought back from China. Daisy, too, even though she swore she never went to cemeteries she didn't know, lest there be any unfortunate surprises from below the ground.

The university team attended, of course. Everyone from the first dig, plus a few official types. Mark stood beside

Dr. Douglas, but when he looked across at Phin, he gave her a wink. She wrinkled her nose at this foolishness, but I didn't miss her blush.

Speaking of blushing. Across from me was Ben McCulloch, whom I hadn't seen since Aunt Hyacinth had returned and I'd gone back to Austin. He'd been busy, and I'd been busy, and we emailed every day and occasionally called. But seeing him in the flesh, that was different. He stood between his mother and his grandfather, and his eyes were trained soberly on the officiating priest. Most of the time. I'd caught him cutting his gaze my way now and then.

The priest said, "In the name of the Father, and the Son, and the Holy Spirit," and most of us bowed our heads, except Daisy, who crossed herself, which was *such* a pious gesture with her black nail polish and lipstick. Not to mention her miniskirt and striped socks.

I returned my attention to the priest and tried to be pious, too. "Father," he said, "we ask you to bless the grave of this soul, whose name is known only to you."

The grave marker read *Unknown Spanish Soldier. Corporal. Died for his fellow man. Circa 1750.* The McCullochs had welcomed the idea that he be interred in the cemetery, since he'd been buried on the land for so long already. Only a few—me, Ben, Phin, and Mark—knew that the gesture stemmed from gratitude, not kindness.

Or not *just* kindness—I caught softhearted Mrs. McCulloch dabbing at tears as the priest went on with the litany. The Roman Catholic blessing was in respect for the deceased's faith, but I liked hearing him laid, finally, to rest and sped on his journey with prayers he would recognize.

The only person who'd objected to the service was Granddad Mac, who was still convinced the Lost Soldier, as he was now called, had hit him on the head. I'd tried to explain that the Mad Monk was only a story. Maybe it had its origins in the real fallen corporal, but the legend had gotten warped and twisted over the years, and accidents and mishaps were blamed on him. The soldier might have inadvertently nearly frozen me and Daisy a couple of times, but head bashing was merely unfounded allegation.

When the priest was done, a university bigwig stepped forward and spoke, starting with congratulations to himself and the excavation team, and ending by turning to include the priest. "And I want to especially thank the Diocese of Central Texas for arranging that the university museum should be the home of the beautiful jeweled cross that was found with our unnamed friend. When the team tracked down records and survivor reports, we were able to clear the name of this long-departed soldier who, seeing his comrades besieged and outnumbered, attempted to lead off the attackers by disguising himself as the expedition's priest and carrying an empty chest, filled with no treasure but his honor."

"Oh brother," muttered Phin. Mom hushed her from the other side, so she just whispered more softly. "'No treasure but his honor'? Who writes this stuff?"

From Dr. Douglas's glare, she might have had a hand in it. But I thought Ms. Daggerspoint of the alliterative bent a more likely culprit. I'd heard she'd come to town to interview people for her new edition of the book, which would include a chapter about the bodies—three so far—dug up by the river. They'd now been dubbed "The Lost Legion of Llano County."

After the service, when the press had left and the townsfolk had gone back to Barnett and the major players were making their way to the McCulloch house for a sort of wake-slash-celebration of Dr. Douglas's grant to excavate the riverside site that fall, I finally got a minute alone with the guy who'd given me so much trouble that summer.

"So . . . ," I said, standing beside his headstone. The smooth gloss and laser-cut engraving was modern and jarring. "I suppose I should say thank you for saving me and Ben. And for getting me back in touch with my Goodnight side, though I suspect that's going to be more of a pain in the long run, if any others like you come along."

Then I thought maybe I shouldn't make this all about me. "I'm glad to know you didn't betray your comrades." Once I knew what to look for, and with help from Lucas—history grad student as well as champion beer drinker—it wasn't hard to find reports so we could piece together the whole story. "I'm just sorry you had to get the blame for so long."

"Having a chat?"

I turned to examine the familiar profile—familiar, except for the bump on the bridge of his nose—of the well-dressed cowboy who'd stepped next to me. He'd told me in email, that the rest of his bruises and cuts had faded. I was glad to see that for myself.

"Just saying goodbye," I said.

Ben glanced at me with a ghost of a smile. "He's not talking back, is he?"

"Oh no. He's long gone."

I faced him full on; he looked as handsome as ever. The bump on his nose sort of went with the whole package.

"I heard Dr. Douglas thinks you should go into anthropology," he said, in a making-conversation tone.

We had so much to catch up on, and that was what he picked? "What she actually said was, 'If you don't want to waste your talents on the living, come dig up the dead with me.'" I looked over to where the others were milling, loading up the cars to go to the house. "I told her I'd think about it."

"I guess you heard Steve Sparks is doing pretty well."

"Yeah. And Mike Kelly may be out of the hospital soon." I turned back to him, squinting because the sun was behind him. "Is this really what you want to talk about?"

His smile broadened. "No. I'm just making chitchat while we're in public."

"You're not very good at it. So far you've covered dead bodies and attempted murderers."

He reached out and caught a strand of hair that had blown across my face, tucking it behind my ear. "I'll do better later."

"Um . . ." My brain short-circuited as his fingers brushed my neck, maybe by accident, maybe not. "I'm perfectly willing for you to give it a try."

His laugh was warm as the sunset. "It's a date. You're staying at your aunt's?"

"Yeah. The goats really missed me."

"*I* missed you," he said, taking my hand and linking our fingers.

"How's the bridge?" I asked, for a good reason.

"Started." He seemed to get what I was really asking. "But I talked with Mom. I'm going back to school, whether it's done or not. I've already got it squared with the university, since I only took a hiatus."

"Ben, that's wonderful. I'm so happy for you."

And I was selfishly ecstatic for me. We'd be at the same school in just a few weeks.

He scratched the bump on his nose and said, "I know you don't like football, but I wondered if you might go to the first game of the season with me."

I took his other hand and looked up into his steely blue eyes, very earnest, very serious. "Ben McCulloch. I'd face ghosts, claim jumpers, cave-ins, bat guano, mad cows, and tree-climbing goats for you. But I absolutely *will not* go to a football game."

With a slow, rare, devastating smile, he said, "We can fight about it later, if you want. I just have to hang around until the university people leave."

I pretended to consider it. "Oh, all right. But only if we can park overlooking the bridge."

He kept hold of my hand as we left the graveside and joined the others. We still had too much unresolved to say we were a couple, but I didn't mind thinking we'd have the chance to try. And after all, the human variable makes nothing certain.

In life, or in death.

In magic.

Or in love.

Acknowledgments

This is the first book I ever started. My dad was a font of Texas legends and history, and I plotted out a very different version with him during a family trip to San Antonio. The lessons here are (a) don't ignore your dad's crazy stories and (b) never throw anything away. I still have the first draft of the opening chapters of this book, written on notebook paper (um, during biology class). Nothing is the same except the bones by the river and the title: *Texas Gothic*.

I owe thanks to Dr. Jerry Melbye, who answered my forensic anthropology questions, and to Jayme Lynn Blaschke, who shared his fantastic pictures of a cold-case crime scene investigated by the students at Texas State University in San Marcos. My fellow YA author Marley Gibson might not have realized I was picking her brain for ghost investigation hints, but I was. Likewise, author Vickie Taylor, who trains Search and Rescue dogs, was informative and awesome. And Hope E. Ring, MD, did not bat an eyelash when I asked her things like: "Say I were to throw a seventy-five-year-old man down a ravine and break his hip. . . ."

All mistakes made and liberties taken with the valuable information these people provided are entirely my own.

Thanks to Shawn Scarber for naming Ray's garage.

Here are the things that are real: the San Sabá Mission, and how it was rediscovered; the lost Almagres mine (also called the lost San Sabá mine, or the lost Bowie mine); the beauty of the Hill Country (visit in the spring, when the wildflowers bloom); Semyon Kirlian's research in coronal aura photography; Spanish colonization and the Apache's objection to it (and who could blame them); conflict between ranching neighbors over river easements; rumrunning; and the University of Texas Longhorns. Oh, and the number of women in criminology and forensic sciences has multiplied in the last decade, and people really do credit TV shows and books that show strong females in what used to be male-dominated fields. (Personally, I want to be Abby from *NCIS*.)

Here are the things I tried to make as real as possible: the techniques of anthropology, the theories of paranormal investigation (with obvious liberties), and the feel of a small Texas town and its surrounding ranch community.

Here are the things that I totally made up: the spells, the Goodnights, and the logistics of fitting the body of a slender coed in the cargo space of a MINI Cooper.

As always, thanks to my agent, Lucienne Diver; my editor, Krista Marino (who really did make this a much better book than I could have ever written on college-ruled paper during biology class); and all the folks at Delacorte Press. Love to my family; my husband, Tim; and my support system of awesome: Candace Havens, Shannon Cannard, Cheryl A. Smyth, Jenny Martin, Jamie Harrington, A. Lee Martinez, Sally Hamilton, the IHOP irregulars, and the DFW Writers' Workshop. Rock on!

ROSEMARY CLEMENT-MOORE
lives and writes in Arlington, Texas. *Texas Gothic* is her fifth
book for young readers. Look for her other books: *Prom
Dates from Hell, Hell Week,* and *Highway to Hell*–all books in
the Maggie Quinn: Girl vs. Evil series–and *The Splendor
Falls,* available from Delacorte Press. You can visit Rosemary at readrosemary.com.